ABOUT FACE

ABOUT FACE

A Novel

WILLIAM GIRALDI

Liveright Publishing Corporation

A Division of W. W. Norton & Company
Celebrating a Century of Independent Publishing

About Face is a work of fiction. All incidents and dialogue, and all characters, are products of the author's imagination and are not to be construed as real. To the extent that real-life historical or public figures may appear or be referred to, the situations, incidents, and dialogues concerning those persons are entirely fictional and are not intended to depict actual events or change the entirely fictional nature of the work. In all other respects, any resemblance to persons living or dead is entirely coincidental.

For information about permission to reproduce selections from this book, write to Permissions, Liveright Publishing Corporation, a division of W. W. Norton & Company, Inc., 500 Fifth Avenue, New York, NY 10110

For information about special discounts for bulk purchases, please contact W. W. Norton Special Sales at specialsales@wwnorton.com or 800-233-4830

Manufacturing by Lakeside Book Company
Book design by Ellen Cipriano
Production manager: Lauren Abbate

Library of Congress Cataloging-in-Publication Data

Names: Giraldi, William, author.
Title: About face : a novel / William Giraldi.
Description: First Edition. | New York : Liveright Publishing Corporation, a division of W. W. Norton & Company, [2022]
Identifiers: LCCN 2022030018 | ISBN 9781324091356 (cloth) | ISBN 9781324091363 (epub)
Subjects: LCGFT: Novels.
Classification: LCC PS3607.I469 A26 2022 | DDC 813/.6—dc23/eng/20220624
LC record available at https://lccn.loc.gov/2022030018

ISBN 978-1-324-09412-8 pbk.

Liveright Publishing Corporation
500 Fifth Avenue, New York, N.Y. 10110
www.wwnorton.com

W. W. Norton & Company Ltd.
15 Carlisle Street, London W1D 3BS

1 2 3 4 5 6 7 8 9 0

For Caleb Nathaniel, my little charismatic

There is the name and the thing: the name is a word that denotes and signifies the thing; the name is not a part of the thing and has no substance; it is an extraneous matter added to the thing and outside of it.

—MICHEL DE MONTAIGNE, "OF FAME"

O my soul, perhaps This Is Fame.

—GERARD MANLEY HOPKINS

PROLOGUE

At eighteen years old, in downtown Boston, Valentino Detti had a vision.

He came into Copley Square on a taintless August afternoon and stopped there midway on Dartmouth between St. James and Boylston. Across the squared expanse of barbered grass, between pedestrians and picnickers, he faced, head-on, a fortress of God: the Trinity Church in its stately browns and beige, its castellated towers and turrets, the entryways arched high in hallowed welcome. He knew that inside, kneeling in pews, were citizens searching for a fortune of soul. Then he peered right, there beside the Trinity, at this mighty mirrored slab, this scraper gashing up at the Boston skyline: the Hancock Tower, all sixty-two stories of metallic cerulean, clouds slipping across their reflective sheen. If he could float on air outside those windows, he knew he'd see sixty-two stories of financial firms, strivers hived in cubicles, a seemingly endless tableaux of aisles, of clickers and scrollers counting their companies' dollars.

Valentino Detti then turned around, because directly at his back, there across Dartmouth, squatting in thick slate block, was the eastern wall of the Boston Public Library, the oldest free municipal library on earth. He read this legend left to right at top, just above the thirteen arched windows:

**THE PUBLIC LIBRARY OF THE CITY OF BOSTON
BUILT BY THE PEOPLE AND DEDICATED TO
THE ADVANCEMENT OF LEARNING**

He knew if he stepped inside the BPL he'd see a very different tableaux of aisles, stocked with learners and scholars whose clicking, scrolling, and reading were aimed at another kind of fortune entirely.

He then pivoted slightly to glance right, across Boylston to the corner of Dartmouth, at the Old South Church, a congregation 350 years old, founded by the pious offspring of separatist Pilgrims. There it hulked in its own brown and beige block, its 250-foot tower of native stone just left of its copper cupola and Gothic windows. This ancient-reaching architecture reminded the bookish in the BPL and all the greedy in the Hancock that wealth of mind and wallet counts for zip without a goodly wealth of soul.

Valentino Detti now turned back toward the Trinity, and there in front of him, on the sidewalk in the center of Dartmouth, was a rectangular plaque of bronze atop what looked to be a slanted sarcophagus of rose-hued stone. An East Boston native, he'd passed this monument in Copley numberless times in his eighteen years, but for reasons that eluded him now, he'd never stopped to see who or what this plaque commemorated. Because he was certain he knew his city's long history—senior-year, college-prep research project at East Boston High—he figured this plaque must be in homage to a Bostonian luminary, some minister or abolitionist, poet or politico, whose conviction helped hone a "city upon a hill," or what poet Anne Bradstreet more aptly called "a city above." William Blaxton or John Winthrop or John Cotton, perhaps. Maybe one of the Mathers, Increase or Cotton, possibly Paul Revere, or even Ben Franklin. Or Sam Adams, possibly James Otis or Joseph Warren. Maybe Anne Bradstreet herself, or poet Phillis Wheatley. John Hancock was always a smart guess in Boston. Could be Abigail Adams or her husband, John, or their son, John Quincy. Perhaps Thoreau, or his doomed soulmate, Margaret Fuller. Can't go wrong with Emerson or Hawthorne. Or Louisa May Alcott, for that matter.

But no, it would be none of these predictable worthies. Valentino Detti stepped closer to this conspicuous monument in the very guts of Copley Square and saw its subject. This was no venerable American hero, but someone most Bostonians had no doubt never heard of. It was guru and mystagogue Kahlil Gibran, author of *The Prophet*, one of the most lucrative books in history, and one that Valentino Detti had, by a coincidence much more than coincidence, he was sure, read when he was an inner-looking ten-year-old. It was his first adult book, from his mother's shelf, nestled improbably there between the King James and *Essentials of Classic Italian Cooking*. And he'd read *The Prophet* again just last month, now that he was more inner-looking than ever. He'd developed something close to a crush on Gibran. He knew that since its publication in 1923, *The Prophet* has never been out of print. He knew that it has been translated into more languages than the Red Sox have players. At ten, he'd been stirred by the book; at eighteen now, he was emboldened by it. Odd that he'd never known of this plaque in his hometown.

Gibran's smattering of adrift aphorisms seemed to him helpfully vague enough to mean anything at all, receptive to whatever weather blew through him, whatever personal profundity he hunted. *Your daily life is your temple and your religion*, and *In your longing for your giant self lies your goodness*. The snippets of poetical wisdom, even in their imitation biblical tone, approximated Valentino's own. They were the very notions—abstract and nebulous, okay, but he was half-sure he could improve upon *The Prophet*—the very notions he himself had been formulating for most of his life. How to live? What is my role in my fate? What agency do I have to attain enlightenment?

Brought up in Boston's South End, Gibran, son of a seamstress, was a truly gorgeous youth, had a face imbued with potency of soul. Here was another coincidence much more than coincidence, because Valentino Detti had himself been told, on more occasions than he could recall, what a phenomenal face he had: a truly unprecedented face, almost shocking in its depth and beauty. Gibran's early beauty, aligned to such able charisma, allowed him to snag the benefactors who sustained his gurudom. Valentino Detti knew this because last month, after he'd read *The Prophet* for the second time—the spare yellow hardback had called to him again from his mother's book-shelf like a—how would Gibran have put it?—called to him like *the soul-whistle from a yellow bird*—he did what he always did after reading a book that bore into him. He researched its author; he took copious notes. If most other Bostonians had forgotten about Gibran, Valentino Detti would be committed to bringing Gibran's shtick back into prominence.

Copley Square, then, in our polis of contradiction, epitomizes great Bostonia: the churches, the library, the skyscraper, the guru; the faith, the knowledge, the money, the mountebank; sacred with profane, preachers with peddlers, ethereal with ephemeral, antiquity with modernity, scholar with swindler. So when Valentino Detti ambled into Copley Square that August afternoon, he'd ambled, he knew, into the epic collisions of American character, the antithetical dynamisms that from our start have defined a land this holy and hellward. We Bostonians have always dwelled inside antinomy, wanting wealth of soul with wealth of mind and wallet to match. To us Yankees of the Commonwealth, the literate merchant minister is no incongruity.

When Governor Winthrop, aboard the *Arbella* en route to Massachusetts, told his flock that they would erect a city upon a hill, he believed that "the eyes of all people are upon us." Valentino Detti, now four hundred years later, wanted the eyes of all people upon *him*. The citizens of this Shawmut Peninsula, we dwellers on Mount Whoredom, believe we're special and always have. That's us: attention-getting troublemakers forged in the furnaces of survival and revolt. Those first Yanks were risk-takers and self-teachers, all right, gumptious God-fearers, pilgriming Separatists and revolutionaries who wouldn't be told, by scurvy kings or their operatives, what they should believe or how they should believe it. And their descendants, Valentino Detti knew, were now everywhere in Copley Square, and ready to be persuaded—by *him*.

Because Valentino Detti perceived himself as their descendant too. Preacher Winthrop had sought to "propagate the gospel in America," while Valentino Detti would do nothing less than self-morph into Val Face, becoming yet another of Boston's enormously famous sons. And like Winthrop and the panoply of city preachers he inspired, Val Face would have the Word to deliver—but the Word from a gospel of his own designs, and, with the internet as accelerant, to an audience global in its ovations.

I.

I was thirty the month this happened, culture writer for the biweekly slick *Beantown*, affianced to Estelle and living an inch north of the poverty line outside Central Square in Cambridge. On the morning this started for me, all of New England quivered in the eighteen degrees it calls December, so I trained to our offices on Milk Street instead of biking it, as I normally did, to save the fare. A nickel-stacking schoolteacher, Estelle fretted weekly over our obese college loans and had us on a crimped budget: she was the Boston Strangler of budgeting fiancées. And she was especially bitter over my loans. Not so much my undergrad loan for that degree in American history that sometimes got dusted off and put to use, but definitely my loan for that grad degree in media studies I couldn't rouse the spirit to finish and quit pursuing with just a semester to go. The title of my abandoned thesis was "Debauched Divines: Celebrity Culture from 1970 to 1990." I had a particular, some said peculiar, fondness for my parents' generation, who had ripened in the 1970s and '80s when rock stars were properly Bacchic and movie stars lathered in deific mystique. You just can't get rockers and movie gods like that anymore, not in a century this cyber. Those stars were determined to *live*, boy, even if it killed them.

So what lay waiting for me that December morn when, two-thirds frozen thanks to a too-thin jacket and the walk from Park Street, I huffed into my cubicle? A prank. Or that's what I'd thought at first: a pranking colleague had violated my voicemail with a message pretending to be the assistant to Val Face. My most recent contribution to the magazine had been three thousand sneering words on Val Face's supposed talents as a celebrity charismatic, guru, Svengali. At this time, at the absolute apex of his fame, he was thirty-three years old and sardining concert halls from New York to Milan, Shanghai to San Fran. His powers of charisma—his primings, promptings of the upended and unstrung—were otherworldly and, we were meant to believe, messianic.

Birth name Valentino Detti, from East Boston, he'd christened himself Val Face, and my God what a face: it was a holy alliance of Rasputin and Jim Morrison—Morrison pre-bloat, before he boozed dull his one-off shine. In certain photos Val Face looked not quite *Homo sapien*: preternaturally beautiful in ways that do not easily offer adjectives to tag it. He had that breed of beauty that causes tiny aneurysms to explode in your soul parts, an eerie beauty born, it seemed, not of woman but of weather, of thundercloud, solar wind in the heliosphere. Even I could see that.

My piece didn't deal with his looks, though, since there was no dealing with looks that celestial. It dealt uncharitably with his self-branding as a charismatic. Certain words had been deployed, *charlatan* and *grifter* being just two. I put forth that he wasn't in any way a charismatic in the Evangelical or Catholic sense, a sandaled seer on a curative mission for humankind, the bucking infusion of the Holy Spirit that makes believers go twang and vroom. No, I pointed out that in the Sanskrit, the term *guru* means someone who delivers light from darkness, and that the Greek term for *charisma* means the special gift of grace. In Romans and Corinthians, you can see for yourself what that wily adman Paul thought of charisma: the robust *faith* of the charismatic, faith mobilized against the crushing strictures of authority, the dispensation of faith to the faithless. Val Face's shtick, I said, mistook the therapeutic for the charismatic. The many hells of history are clear on this: the genuine charismatic comes to upend the existing moral order; the therapeutic comes to mollify it.

So Val Face, my prose declared, was little more than a calculated mash-up of the raconteur, the coquet, and the motivational speaker, a boulevardier with a bulletin, a hunkier Tony Robbins who'd groomed himself first into a TV celeb and then into a supporting beau in Marvel fare, Marvel fare being just about the only fare Hollywood does now. He'd also played a Bond villain that year and his screen appeal was so complete, so mesmeric, you caught yourself rooting for his Gucci evil.

As I say, I thought the voicemail was from a colleague with a penchant for pranks, our sportswriter and Celtics expert, Maud, who wasn't entirely content unless she could incite hysterics from one end of the office to the other. She'd even stoop to whoopie cushions and hand buzzers on particularly uninspired afternoons. Here's the voicemail:

"Good morning, this message is for"—pause—"for Seger Jovi.

My name is Valerie Park and I'm the assistant to Val Face. If you could please return this call at"—and then a phone number with a pompous L.A. area code, followed by a "thank you" that sounded too much like a "fuck you."

"Maud," I said at her cubicle, "nice one."

"Nice one what?"

She was all sneeze and cough and phlegm, on her desk a whole alp of snotted tissues.

"The voicemail," I said. "Val Face's assistant. Nice one. Haha."

"*Seger*," she groaned, "do I *look* in a pranking mood today? I'm dying of plague."

"Ah. Fuming with influenza, eh? Okay, sorry, never mind. Feel better then."

And back to my desk I loped to listen again, libel on the brain, litigation, though *Beantown*'s lawyer had thumbed-up my article. I'd no doubt committed a malfeasance of fact somewhere, though the magazine's fact-checkers are a draconian bunch known to take writers through entire inquisitions until the piece is denuded of any detail that even hints at deception. What then could Val Face's assistant want except to befoul me, hurl vitriol my way, *ingrate* and *dolt*? And how did she get my extension at the magazine? And what possible motive would I have for returning her call unless I wanted to hear myself befouled?

Still, I called. Of course I did. We bottom-rung writers don't often get phone calls from the assistants of A-listers.

"Er . . . may I speak with, uhh, Valerie Park please?"

My speech, you're going to notice, rarely has the same spine as my prose: that's the first thing to understand here, especially when

I'm a turbulence of nerves. I might as well just prepare you at the outset for my sputterings and stutterings, my false starts and switchbacks, my *umm*s and *uhh*s. The usually subdued tonsils kept lurching in the way of the tongue's work, tripping up all the eloquence. I can't perfectly replicate many of these sputterings on the page, and anyway it would gall you to deal with them all, so just assume that most times when I'm speaking to Val Face or his retinue, my clauses and phrases get an abrupt inferiority complex.

So that's how my first sentence came out: "Er . . . may I speak with, uhh, Valerie Park please?"

"Speaking," she said.

"Hi, hello? I'm returning your, your call? I'm Seger Jovi? The, the writer? From *Beantown* magazine?"

"Oh. Yes. You."

Oh. Yes. You. I did some bracing of the self.

"Just to be certain," she said, "you're the author of an article called"—pause—"called 'Tacky, Wacky, and Wrong: The Shtick of Val Face'?"

"Okay, let me say just one, one thing about that title. Oftentimes—very often, I'd say—oftentimes the titles here are a *group* effort. And many times, our editor"—and here I popped up from my chair to scan above the hive of cubicles, just to be sure that Jasmine, our editor, wasn't lurking, looming, and when I plunked back down I plunked with softened voice—"many times our editor goes, err, *rogue*, straight-up rogue, on titles, chooses them herself. So. Yeah."

"Are you the author of the article?"

I can't be sure I didn't gulp. "Yes, ma'am."

"Please don't call me *ma'am*. Val Face would like to see you."

Something runic seemed to be at work here.

"Eh?"

"Please don't call me *ma'am*."

"No, yeah, right, after that."

"Val Face would like to see you."

"Did you say . . . *See me* did you say?"

"See you."

"Ah, I thought so. See me. But, uhh, why?"

"Your article."

"Right. With you there. My article. But, I mean, you know, *why*? And how did you get my number?"

"Does today at one p.m. work for your schedule?"

"One o'clock? Today? To *see* me? But see me how? What do you . . . I'm not in Beverly Hills. I'm in Boston. So."

"We're not in Beverly Hills either. We're in Boston."

More pausing. *Drip, drip.* Was there a manual for a dialogue such as this?

"Did you say you're in Boston?"

"We are in Boston," she said. "Face's New England tour begins this week."

I knew that, or should have remembered it, since his New England tour was what had occasioned my article. But you know how it is when you're on the phone with some factotum to an A-lister: your memory gets glitchy.

She asked it again: "Does today at one p.m. work for your schedule?"

If you'd have glimpsed my iPhone's calendar you'd have known what a truly comical query that was.

"One o'clock. Hmm. Let me see. One o'clock, one o'clock . . . I'd have to move around some, some appointments."

"One o'clock then."

She had this *thing* going on in her voice, much more than mere confidence, a won't-be-refused conviction; hers was a voice chockful of foregone conclusions. And by the sound of her she couldn't have been more than twenty-five, twenty-six tops. Of course that's one of the prerequisites in Hollywood: you've got to be two decades away from a wrinkle if you want them to let you in.

"But can you tell me what this is about?"

"Val Face would like to see you."

"Right, got that part. Thanks very much. Wants to see me. My article and all. Got it. But I mean *why*."

"We're at the Taj Boston on the corner of Newbury and Arlington."

"Ah, just across the Common then."

"One o'clock. The front desk will have your name. Please bring identification."

"Wait, but why. I don't get . . ." but she wasn't on the line any longer to hear what I didn't get.

In times such as these, times to try writers' souls, I texted Estelle for support of the spiritual kind.

"Want believe this, love."

"Want believe what?"

"No, not want, won't I mean."

"Won't want what?"

"Val Face's assassination."

"OMG. He's assassinated?!"

"ASSISTANT. His assistant. Called me just now."

"A boot?" Boot emoji.

"What boot?" Same boot emoji.

"No about."

"Are u asking what she called about?"

"Binge."

"On what?"

"BINGO. Why'd she call u?"

Then those smug ellipses intent to con you into thinking that your correspondent has her reply underway when she's really gone away.

Estelle's ellipses stayed there, conningly, for twelve minutes before she typed: "At work. Gotta go. Tell me latte." Latte emoji.

If it had been part of our budget, a latte would have been most welcome in the growling gut. My breakfast that morning had meant a free-sample granola bar caffeinated undergrads were doling out in the cold near Emerson College; it had the consistency of slightly damp sawdust and tasted how chalk looks. Then, in the kitchen at our office, I downed a jumbo mug of Folgers, since the poor learn to consider coffee food. Load enough sugar and cream into the thing and you've got yourself a meal.

In Jasmine's office I relayed the news, and she said, "Huh?"

"Yup. Val Face's assistant just rang me. I've got a meeting with him at one at the Taj. Do you think he wants to sue us?"

From the left wall of her office, a portrait of our Boston ancestor Margaret Fuller glared upon us with what I took to be pitying reproach. From the right wall, a portrait of another Boston ancestor, poet Anne Bradstreet, "Empress Consort of Massachusetts,"

glared upon us with what I knew was holy censure. Get caught in
the crossfire of these dueling glares and the easily intimidated tes-
ticles retreat an inch or two. If I could look through Ms. Bradstreet,
past the Old State House and Faneuil Hall and Quincy Market and
into the North End, I'd be able to see my mother in her kitchen at the
window, at that hour gripping a cup of cocoa spiked with cinnamon.

"When celebrities want to sue, Seger, they sue. They don't request
a meeting with the scoundrel who put them in a suing mood."

"Right. Don't request a meeting with the, uhh, the scoundrel. So
what does he want then? By which I mean, what do I do?"

Jasmine might sometimes have been a misser of meetings and a
misser of deadlines, less frequently a misser of points, but she definitely wasn't a misser of beats.

"Seger," she said, "I will tell you what you do. You will come back
from this meeting with Val Face with these words to tell me: *Jasmine*, you're going to say, *I just secured a feature profile of Val Face.*"

The noises coming from my gullet might best be described as
flummoxed, after which speech was achieved—sort of.

"Feature profile. Hmm. With Val Face. But, uhh, boss? One
thing? Tiny thing? I refer now to the venom my sentences fanged
into him."

"Venom? Nonsense. Article was perfectly aboveboard cultural
criticism. Critics criticize and celebrities deserve it—am I wrong?
They practically beg for it. Which doesn't mean that we don't want
their mugs on the covers of *Beantown*—am I right?"

Behind Jasmine, the windows let me know what the weather was
up to. Not at all comforting, a wind that white. The barometer is the
enemy of every Bostonian. Henry Adams said that our weather—

infernal summers and wasteland winters—forced Bostonians to develop "a double nature." What he should have said is that our weather forces us to develop a grudge against God. If I could look through all the buildings along Milk Street, I'd have seen, just past where Ben Franklin was born, the December-dark waters of Boston Harbor and the Seaport District shivering there beside it.

"Of course," I said, "our covers. I'm with you there. I mean, there's no way he's going to agree to a feature profile after what we said about him. He wants to see me no doubt so that he can chastise and upbraid me, possibly sue us, probably assault me with metal objects."

"Seger," she said from behind a steaming mug with the motto *The Editor Is Out*, which, in Boston, could have been taken more ways than one, "I'm reminded of a lovely conversation I had with your better half at our office gala in the fall. Emily, am I right?"

"Estelle."

"Hmm. *Looks* like an Emily. But then so many of them do. Anyway, a lovely conversation. Ambitious, that one. She's giving herself four years to realize her dream of opening her own Montessori training program."

"Oh. That. Three years, actually. The *pressure*, don't get me started. But go on."

"And one of the things Emily said to me, she said: *Jasmine, that boy's ambition needs more ambition*. Emily meant you. *Jasmine*, she said, *we need to push that boy to achieve larger things*. Apparently she's super pissed about student loans . . . How did she say it . . ."

"*A crater of debt* is her pet phrase."

"A crater of debt, right. Well, Seger, you've now got an appointment with that larger thing at one o'clock. A feature profile of Val Face will definitely convince Chris Squared"—Chris and Chris, a status-whoring pair who couldn't read without moving their lips, owned the magazine—"to get you on the masthead. *Seger Jovi, Contributing Editor.* A-buck-fifty-a-word, maybe a steady column, guaranteed space in twelve of twenty-four issues."

I don't know what sort of warmth she was sipping from that mug but it left a frothy yellowness on an upper lip already busy with its Estée Lauder. The noises coming from my gullet *now* might best be described as dubious, after which speech was *not* achieved because Jasmine's cell began chirping to the tune of Marvin Gaye's "What's Going On"—which happened to be my question exactly—and so she shooed me out with fuchsia fingernails.

■ ■ ■

LATER, WITH HALF AN HOUR TO PASS before my meeting with Val Face, I sallied forth from our offices to collide with a tantrum of snow-stuffed wind slapping off the harbor, slipping in between buildings, and snatching loose scarves, mine included. Away it blew beneath belching trucks. I tripped all along Milk Street, heaving ahead into weather, snow wetting my mismatched socks. Oh, the tapered byways from the waterfront to the Common: we locals call these former cow paths roads. I saw one dropped glove, then another, then, somewhere, damn it, dropped mine, though I didn't forget to pause in salute at the Old South Meeting House, birthplace of revolutionary vigor, a smidgen of which I could have used on my present mission to be confronted by a celebrity I had insulted. If you listened very intently and the pedestrian hubub let you, you could still hear Samuel Adams and James Otis inside the Old South inciting colonial Bostonians to rage, rage against their British overlords. There was, you'll recall, that matter about the tea.

A week past Thanksgiving and all of Downtown Crossing was already and everywhere festooned with Christmas stains, holiday stars strung over Washington Street, elves sleighing in shop windows, and from around a corner "Jingle Bells" playing over an actual bell jingling in the hand of some famished Santa. Shoppers toted green-and-red-glittered bags abulge with items their loved ones would not need or want. A toothless twosome and their bloated backpacks were piled into a quilted blear at the mouth of the Red Line, ignored by both tourists and natives despite one reaching out a vacant coffee cup and the other clutching cardboard that complained *We Wished You a Merry Christmas*—past tense. From a street vender's cart wafted the sweet scent of roasted peanuts; his competition on the other corner hawked hot dogs more rubber than meat. I'd been coming to Downtown Crossing since I was shin-high and the place still successfully roused all my holiday zeal.

A cop stood in the center of Washington Street, unpreparedly cold in the slanting snow, trying to coerce traffic with one gloved hand while with the other ushering people into the Paramount Theater so that they might behold the clamor they'd trudged here for: *The Nutcracker*. His expression said: *Please, Lord, let me win that lotto*. We Bostonians know how to pray—not a surprise in a city whose founders were thumping theocrats.

About Jasmine's scheme for securing a feature profile of Val Face: the Nazarene himself would not forgive sentences such as those I affixed to Face's talent. And so here was my thinking up top uneasily hooked to all my anxiety down low: Val Face planned to berate me. Val Face planned to *show me*, snide and arrogant scribbler that I was. What I couldn't comprehend was why he wanted to, why such a celestial somebody wished to bother with such a microbial nobody. But that's the thing about celebrity, I supposed: it turns onetime comprehendible people into riddles, peculiar fulfillers of their own whims. I once made that point in an article: if it's not mysterious, it's not fame. Fame, let's be honest, is flippant. Fame is ridiculous and doesn't mind.

What irked me most that first afternoon on my walk to Val Face's hotel was my willing dive into what was bound to be a pool of abuse. A celeb comes calling and we non-celebs go trotting. No use in feigning otherwise now, though I was still trying to feign otherwise then: I wanted to meet Val Face. Well of course I wanted to meet Val Face. I'd never before met a cultural icon. And on that marrow-cold meander across the Common that day I was already preparing how I'd apologize for sentences so fiendish. Not that I didn't mean them. Or most of them. I was in a bit of a spot here, since we archers don't ever plan on going to the hotels of our A-list targets.

My wristwatch (Walgreens: $12.99) told me I had twenty minutes to meeting time, and then my self-respect told me that there was no way I was going to be early for it. So I took the longish way through the Common, up toward the State House on Beacon, sharp left at the Robert Gould Shaw Memorial, dodging the Common's resident squirrels. These squirrels are veritable thugs, even in winter, take my word. They've been this way since the Revolution. Pushy, I mean—won't take no for an answer. Just the previous summer I'd had a contest of ideas with one of their infantry, the result of which saw me separated from a much needed slice of pizza.

Scores of chromatic ice skaters scratched across the Frog Pond to Christmas ditties making merriment from suspended speakers. The one o'clock sky was wan and getting wanner, all the afternoon's light tinged with metallic winterness. Summer's gory skies seemed eons off. Three blocks north, the Charles River lay aching in its early ice. I could feel it over there, feel its seasonal pain as it slowed and stopped and settled into its weight.

Hold it—that was *my* pain I felt, my nerves a rumpus. And why was I just then remembering the insuppressible jitters I'd had on my first date with Estelle? Why did I now sense romance inserting itself into my afternoon? It was so cold that the strolling Bostonians I passed had faces that said: "Global warming? *What* global warming?"

Through the Public Garden I went, past the pond in which Swan Boats swim in summer climes, then past General Washington's colossal equine statue, which gazed directly across Arlington Street at the very hotel that was my terminus. See, even General Washington was trying to spot Val Face.

The earmuffed doorman of a hotel this swank—fella looked as if he could use a martini and a smoke—this doorman surely wasn't going to let someone who dressed as I did just waltz into the place. But he did. I passed through the comforting suck of the revolving door, which spun then spat me into the stillness of the lobby. I gave my press ID to the concierge, saying I was there for an appointment with Val Face, and my voice, I noticed, though it needed watering, was chockful of importance when I said it.

Face and his entourage occupied a caboodle of penthouse suites. A bellhop with epaulettes chaperoned me to the gold-plated elevator, swiped a special key card, then pressed the special button. Up and up as I dabbed at my nostrils with a ragged sleeve and looked at my undone shoelace to wonder whether or not I had the time to tie it. I didn't.

When the doors parted, a bodyguarding goon greeted me with his requisite scowl, and this terse demand: "Identification please." His beard then mumbled something into a walkie-talkie. (Eager to sheep along, many earnestly hip men were furred in beards that year, thanks to a razor-shy Red Sox player—or wait, actually, maybe it wasn't a Red Sox player; it might have been a New England Patriot— anyway, *some*body had incited the blasted fad.) Then some species of assistant or intern a year out of college, I thought, soon appeared hugging an iPad to her sweater. Ann Taylor, no doubt.

The sweater, not the intern.

"Seger Jovi?" She asked it with a register similar to the one Val Face's assistant had used with me on the phone that morning: it sounded rather like *Fucking asshole?* But the question was laden with so much aspartame I nearly didn't notice.

"Present. Yes. It is I. Err. It's me, I mean."

"Welcome, hello," she trilled.

"Thank you, thanks. Are you the—who are you?"

"I'm Vera. I work with Valerie Park. I'm her assistant!"

"Valerie Park, right. Wait, who's she?"

"Valerie is Face's assistant! I believe you spoke with her this morning."

"Ah, of course. The assistant. Bad with names, sorry. So you're the—Vera, you said?—you're the assistant. To the, uhh, to the assistant."

"That's right!"

You've seen young assistants like this? Aglitter with mechanical élan. For some reason this one hitched exclamation points to the end of sentences that weren't exclamations. For some other reason she saw nothing wrong with this. In her handbag was no doubt one of two books: *How to Win Friends and Influence People* or *Chicken Soup for the Soul.*

"Aha. Valerie and Vera. Does that ever get . . . confusing?"

"Does what get confusing?"

"Those Vs. Those V names."

"No. It doesn't! Will you walk this way please?"

You can't be a Bostonian and hear the words *walk this way* and not think of Aerosmith, our own mighty mouth Steven Tyler in Dionysian garb and the gypsy scarves flailing from his microphone stand. The asinine lyrics of "Walk This Way" would now be lodged all afternoon in my temporal lobes when I already had enough lodged there and vying for dominance.

So I walked that way, behind her, to a suite whose opulence shouldn't have surprised me. Twelve-foot ceilings and their ornate crown moldings; mahogany chaise lounges; all the wood of the place dripping with scrollwork; big kitchen gleaming with appliances so wise they could do your taxes.

I'm sensitive to kitchens. When you grow up in an apartment in the North End of Boston, eight hundred square feet, your idea of a kitchen aligns with your knowledge of a closet. A walk-in closet, maybe, but a closet. Counter space? What counter space? Two people can't comfortably occupy it, which was why my proudly plump mother was always waving dishcloths at my father and me, whenever we encroached upon her domain. The oven, stove, fridge, and sink were normal size, sure, but they were all crammed into that corner, the one with the lack of counter space. And we spent *our whole lives* in the kitchen, at that sink and fridge and narrow countertop, and at the oval table nearby, one half of which doubled as my mother's desk. We didn't resent this because we didn't have anything to contrast it with: everyone we knew in the North End had the same kind of tight kitchen corner in a similar four-room walk-up. The rich North Enders had bigger kitchens, of course, though I couldn't be sure because we didn't know any of them. Mostly because they didn't want to know any of us.

So how do you think someone such as me looked in Val Face's suite, with a kitchen that excellent? Smudgy, I'd say.

Attending to her iPad, the assistant to the assistant beamed the predictability she was paid for: "Val Face will be with you momentarily, if you'd like to have a seat," and out she went, sans goodbye.

Not much to do then but have a seat, and try to recall that verse in "Walk This Way" with the "hey diddle diddle" and the "kitty in the middle," but first over to the view from windows so clear they looked not there. The Hancock Tower rose there in midtown beside its siblings, the new Dalton building, a silver-blue tube, and the Prudential Building, such a stack of pointed mass, an immense needle. For gridded miles beside them stretched Back Bay and all of central Boston. Matchbox cars crawled; citizens anted along with their cargoes of hope and affliction. The sky was right there by the tips of my disappearing hair.

The wall clock in this suite pointlessly proclaimed the time in London and Tokyo in two smaller clocks within the large one, but at least I could know in two different hemispheres how long Val Face was making me wait. Twenty minutes, as it turned out, which seemed to me some breed of miracle. I've heard some celebrities will keep you waiting twenty days.

Nervous, I sat, I stood. I strolled, I squatted. I hemmed, I hawed. I nearly howled. After ten minutes of this, and still unsure whether or not I was being readied for a prank, I began making mini raids into the kitchen, from which I'd emerge having pocketed a little wrapped globe of Lindt chocolate. Then a banana. Then, as I bravened—perfectly reasonable word, *braven*, and I'm sticking with it—as I bravened, I snatched from the fridge a bottle of sparkling water, some ten-dollar marvel called Aqua Deco. Then an impeccable orange. I was also *this close* to downing a decadent "recovery" drink packed, said the label, with enough vitamins, minerals, and herbs—what's CoQ10? what in God's name does your body do with L-Tyrosine? what are its thoughts about 5-HTP? does it *need* glutamine?—packed with enough of them to have me hopping around like a cartoon character.

Now, in retrospect, this wasn't wise of me, these raids into the kitchen, because any sec an assistant or her assistant could have entered and discovered me in flagrante delicto, as it were, orange-handed. But please bear in mind the surreality of my sitch, and also what I mentioned earlier about that breakfast of mine. Plus it was already one thirty with the day slouching toward early darkness— the day had had enough of the day. I didn't think at the time that it wasn't wise to raid the kitchen because I wasn't planning on having happen all that happened. I wasn't planning on having Val Face say to me what Val Face was about to say to me.

My plan at this point was to let myself be manfully maltreated by Val Face, disgorge my apologies, and then maybe ask for a selfie with him. And maybe, also, an inscribed copy of his memoir, *About Face,* which was just then basking in its fortieth week atop bestseller lists, and which he claimed to have written without help, and which I'd read in prep for my article. The book's prose managed not to make all its paper cringe beneath a glut of bromide and cliché. You get these celebrity memoirs nowadays that take entire confederations to write, though *write* can't be the word we want because *read* is not really what we do with them. In between episodes of palming our foreheads, we attempt to parse, we puzzle through without profit, we gall at the Neolithic-level illiteracy.

These celebs: it seems the only grammar they get right is the grammar of self-love.

Alone in a star's hotel suite for twenty minutes isn't as easy as it sounds when you're in the pickle I was in. I had to think of what praise I'd employ. Well-aimed praise often achieves wonderments. I knew the kind of year Val Face had been having. The muscular Calvin Klein underwear ads. The Dior fragrance, called Dragueuse, which means *flirt,* because career charismatics must have traces of the flirt in them. His triple hit: the covers of *Rolling Stone* and *Time* and *GQ,* simultaneously. The *GQ* spread had him reposing, naked, on a bear rug, nursing a scotch in one hand and a pipe in the other.

Then there were his two flashy commercials: the one for Budweiser in which he rode a horse, of all things—the point being that drunkenness can cause you to hop onto horses?—and then the one in which he charismatically commandeers a Corvette through oddly carless environs. On all the late-night shows, he reversed the paradigm: the man-hosts are supposed to be the maestros with the charm, the undefeated dispensers of charisma, but they couldn't do it with Face. There was simply no competing with charisma that consummate. He effortlessly made each of them look like tiny brothers panting for an alpha's esteem.

In addition to the Bond and Marvel films, he also voiced a winsome cartoon creature for the capitalists at Disney, and then hosted *Saturday Night Live*—twice. And get this: he had a genuine comic's timing to add to his other, harder-to-define abilities. He knew how to exploit the coiled, dynamic tension between his funny pretending and his altogether unfunny appearance. So I had myriad compliments to pick from.

Why then had I penned such a Babylonian takedown of his talents? Because Jasmine asked me to. And when Jasmine comes asking, your pen starts scratching.

■　■　■

VAL FACE SLID INTO THE SUITE and all my blood bounced. He approached. I stood, my stomach one second behind, then two. All the oxygen in the room gained molecules at the sight of him. All sight drinks in such symmetry as this. His in-the-flesh beauty was downright shocking. Here was a face that declared it had no undue awareness of mortality, a face that repelled time, that declared its unkillable health. Here was a Tithonus who in asking Zeus for eternal life did not forget to ask for eternal youth too. This face looked as if it had the ability to reject not only wrinkles and warping but all manner of weather: wind, rain, fire could not mar it. Lips like rose-tinted throw pillows, rectangular enough to be mannish, plump enough to be sensual. His teeth? Two rows of Chiclets faultlessly sized and spaced.

And what to say about such a smile? You've heard of *knowing* smiles? Okay, Val Face smiled knowingly. Not knowingly with wisdom of the ages, but knowingly with a certain knowledge of *me*, as if we'd been pals in our boyhood, and what he saw now was what he'd seen then, and how tickled he was to be beholding me again after so long a spell. I'm talking a twice-in-a-lifetime smile, aimed so fiercely at me and me alone it seemed to insist that he'd never smiled this way at any other organism. A smile that said it computed me in ways I definitely did not want to compute myself. This was his gambit, his opening smile, absolutely easeful and grasping. But then it evaporated from his mug, replaced with the comely censure he had summoned me for. I was pretty glad to see the smile evanesce because having such a face smile at you in such a way can leave you feeling not just exposed, but *solved*. And I don't know about you, but I just don't want to go around being so solvable.

Then Val Face sauntered over to me. I shuffled to him halfway, there on a carpet between sofas. I believe I tried to fix my hair—what remained to fix, if *fix* is even the term we want considering a wreck such as that which lay atop my scalp. His handshake was all costly lotion and hour-long manicures, clasped tight enough to tell me he was ticked but not so tight that I'd whimper away.

And his *eyes*, my God. Writers like to drone on about eyes even more than about smiles: the eyes this, the eyes that, *shining*, *spar-*

kling, piercing when they aren't *windows* or *portals*. When they bulge or widen or do whatever else writers are always saying they do, whatever communication the eyes achieve they achieve in concert with everything else on a face. But Val Face: his eyes did the same uncomfortable comprehending as his smile, except there was no hope of these eyes evaporating. He had Jupiter eyes, event-horizon eyes, tugging you toward them no matter your counter-torque. His eyes had some genre of occult potency you could not blink away from: the eyes of a mesmerist, a metallic color there is no handy name for—some color Nature is still scratching her head over.

And his hair, Jesus. He had Elvis hair—a dark work of art that seemed to have its own inner source of gleam. It looked wet when dry and I wondered how it must look when wet for real. When you're an American male and your hair has begun its irreversible evacuation of your dome, as mine had, you unfailingly notice those other, luckier males with hair that seems a lush gift from Samson himself. How do these garlanded ones get to refuse to go bald?

"Seger Jovi," he said, releasing my hand, though I wished he hadn't. "Interesting name."

Three years older than me, he was also three inches taller than me. For the sake of symmetry, I figured.

I said, "Oh, it's my, uhh, my pen name. An amalgam of Bob Seger and Bon Jovi. In, you know—in homage."

"In homage. To Bob Seger and Bon Jovi. You're an odd one. Why those two?"

"Ah, easy answer. My mom would listen to Bob Seger every weeknight as she cooked. She used to say that it if hadn't been for my dad, she'd have gone off to Detroit and married Bob Seger."

"So now *you're* Seger." Pause. "So you want to marry your mom?"

What was I supposed to say to that?

"Er. Doesn't every son?"

"I don't. And what's the Bon Jovi thing about?"

"Oh. Simple. I was conceived to Bon Jovi. 'Wanted Dead or Alive.' Or else 'Living on a Prayer'—my parents can't recall the exact song since they were, you know, they were distracted."

"You're a child of fame, Seger. No wonder you write what you write. A bit of a ham, though, aren't you?"

That smile!

"I knew you were a ham," he said. "I could tell from your articles."

His voice, naturally lathered in seductive juices, had a way of making a put-down sound like a come-on. A hymnful voice, a controlled pulpit voice, meant for the transcendence of others. Face could speak a line as inconsequential as *Nice to meet you* or *Have a seat* and it would sound as if Increase Mather himself were telling you how singular you are in the see-all eyes of the Lord.

"You talk a lot about the seventies and eighties in your work. I'm not complaining."

"Oh, yeah, I'm a bit of a—ahem—bit of a scholar of seventies and eighties pop culture. Sixties, too, of course, since you can't have the seventies without the sixties. My abandoned doctoral thesis was called 'Debauched Divines: Celebrity Culture from 1970 to 1990.'"

"I get it. I'm into the seventies and eighties too. Guys like us, we were born about forty years too late. We're relics, Seger."

We? Were we a *we* already?

"But I don't know about Bob Seger and Bon Jovi," he said. "I've always been more of a Springsteen guy myself."

Now, how was I supposed to have a tête-à-tête with someone who didn't see the excellence of seventies Bob Seger and eighties Bon Jovi?

"I am too," I said. "A Springsteen guy. Of course. What working-classer doesn't love the Boss? My dad played him all the time at home. His stereo in our living room competed with my mom's radio in the kitchen. There was always a, a kind of duel going on between Springsteen in one room and Seger in the other."

I couldn't exactly tell whether or not this was getting off to a good start. Something at the center of my sternum said nay. We kept standing there on that carpet between the sofas, *sizing up each other*, as the saying has it, though it wasn't a fair fight. His size in every regard was mightier than mine.

The working-classer comment was my way of reminding him, before he began scorching me, that he and I shared a heritage: both Bostonians of working-class Italian stock, Catholic-elementary-school survivors with scars to show for it, severe nuns in certain corridors of our past, grandparents who hummed Puccini and parents who hailed Pacino. I knew this because I'd read his memoir; he knew this because he'd read my essays, the more memoiristic ones about being reared in the North End.

He found his manners and offered to get me water; I declined and didn't admit that my own manners lay in the gutter because I'd already nabbed one from the fridge. Then he sank into one sofa. I sank into the other. Even his smirk was gorgeous. Here sat a guy whose gloss was always on. He gave the distinct impression of being able to *wake up* this way, in a state of deific beauty, whereas the rest of us wake up looking more Godzilla than God. I've got to scrub and pluck and prune for forty minutes each morning before I can even approach what passes for mammalian. At the time, I had a musta-chio of such luxuriance it put you in mind of Tom Selleck circa *Magnum, P.I.* This mustachio helped to make up, I hoped, for my hair's cruel decamping from my dome.

Face sparked up a Marlboro and reclined there with it as billows of the stuff gathered, as if in a halo, about his head. And he did a funny thing with his lighter then: he kept the flame going even after his cig was lit, so that it was in front of his face for him to look through, at *me*. He wanted to see me through a flame, or else he was imagining me on fire. He soon stopped and pocketed the lighter, and now, in addition to smirking at me, he was also smoking at me. His skin lay there on his face like a puddle of pure cream: not the glowing, shining kind, but the immaculate kind that invites you to lick it before you yearn to wade into it. The outer crust of the upper crust is always in enviable shape.

"So," he began. "You're a writer."

"Guilty."

"And they tell me you aren't on social media."

"The *pressure*, right? Who needs it?"

But I *was* on social media, under my real name, of course: I had seventeen followers, friends and family, including my and Estelle's parents, who never commented on my photos and posts because, I think, they didn't know how to.

"Though Estelle—she's my fiancée—Estelle is always telling me it's time to get going on social media, get a following, all that. She's—she has plans for us."

"You know why I asked you here."

Statement, not question. I stifled a gulp. Guess what he grabbed from the magazine rack beside the sofa. The issue of *Beantown* in which I had savaged him.

He said, "You think I play to the cheap seats? All sentimentality and self-help? Isn't that what you wrote? Let me read some of these sentences back to you."

"Oh. Uh. No, no, that's quite all right, I—"

"Shush. Listen to this beauty. You're trying to describe me here: *Think Mark Twain on tour in that signature ivory suit and cumulus of hair, an alloy of politician, professor, poet, priest.* I appreciate the Twain comparison, but other than that I'm sure what it means and I'm not sure you do either."

"Well, I mean—"

"Shush. Listen to these beauties: *Celebrity without achievement is a fallowness, an ecstatic impotence. You really should be required to achieve something before we allow you to be some*one. *You really should be a Washington, a Jefferson, a Franklin, a Douglass, Austen, or Darwin, and not just some dope with a crafty knack for getting your name online and in print.*"

The foremost notes of his Boston brogue must have been eroded by a decade of world travel.

"Ah, right, so, funny story about those sentences. I—"

"Shush. Listen to this: *The celebrity does not have superior talent or virtue, wisdom or nobility. The celebrity is superior in salary, in being known. That's what the celebrity's getting paid for: being known. All celebrity is a soiling: not just of the individual but of the culture. When the most visible are more important than the most viable, when exposure beats expertise, the culture rots from within.* You know what's remarkable about lines like those, Seger?"

My legs kept crossing, uncrossing, and recrossing themselves, which was fitting, crosswise, since that's what I was about to be nailed to by this Roman-faced lovely.

"Well. I mean"—definite gulp now—"I mean there's surely more than one thing remarkable about them. I hope."

"You don't actually believe them. That's what so remarkable about those lines. You don't believe them."

"I don't?"

"You're performing."

"Perform . . . ?"

"Performing. Plus you didn't even attend one of my shows before writing this piece."

"Ah, right, well, about that. Your shows are on the pricier side, plus I would have had to fly to L.A. or some such place to catch a performance, and our budget at the magazine now is being, uhh, *looked at* by our owners. So."

No response. Just his monument of a face, leaking Marlboro from the nose, positioned there as if an uncommon attraction I hadn't paid the entrance fee to appreciate.

"But," I said, "I read your memoir, *About Face*. Tons of info to be had there."

Lots more lacking of response. Lots more Marlboro leaking from the nose. Lots more of that monument of a face and its smirking.

"Oh, and I watched your Netflix special, one of them, what's it called, *Face to Face*? Plus I saw the latest Bond film. The plot went, went pretty wobbly at the halfway mark, but you were great in it. I said so, didn't I?" I paused to point. "In my piece?"

He'd been fanning through my article as I spoke the above,

his face a billboard for the depth of skepticism, so I couldn't tell how much of me he was listening to. His whole face was an arched eyebrow. That was one of the plaudits with which his most besotted reviewers enjoyed soaking him: the expansiveness, the expressiveness, the sheer *presence* of his face. This is mostly what made him such a seductive, effortless movie actor, the same quality you saw in, say, Brando circa *Waterfront,* or in Monty Clift before his face was wrecked against that telephone pole as he drove sleepily away from Elizabeth Taylor. The face alone, in its masculine beauty and range, could whisper or holler whatever inner calm or warp needed vent.

"I noted the places where you're right," Face said. "Listen to this: *All charisma contains a hope: of connection, of partnership, of approval. The charismatic wants something, after all; he has designs. Val Face has found a way to reverse that, to present charisma not as an act of self-service but as an act of giving, of unashamed charity, the improving of paltry egos in an age when our screens have left us desperate for real communion, when tech companies have hoodwinked us with the line that our contentment can be clicked into coming true.* Now we're getting somewhere, Seger. We're simpatico on the internet. That's good."

"We are? Simpatico? On the . . ."

"On the internet. Shows you have discernment and dignity."

"Ah, yes, those. Discernment and, and dignity, right. That's me."

Now wasn't the time for disclosures. Now wasn't the time to admit that I didn't find social media organically wicked. I wasn't online under my pen name because I'd already tried and couldn't lasso any followers, couldn't see a way to make myself look even a little alluring on such attention-deficit venues. Too much competition out there.

But no one's ever accused me of not being able to catch an easy lob and dash with it, and so here's what I said to Face: "Social media is all senseless iniquities and eager forays into sadism, soggy-souled chatterers and smiters of English with their plugged-in anomie."

His was a smile to make all the men, women, children, even pets lean into him.

He said, "You see, *paisan*, now we're getting somewhere."

Besmirching the internet was, and had been from the start, a main event of Val Face's shtick as a charismatic. He saw cyberspace as a goliath for corporate hegemony when it wasn't a soapbox for dingbats and their dazed vaporings. He said it was a *moo*ing, *baa*ing zoo for those defiled on multiple fronts, a hive whose honey is ever lies and bile. He said it was ruin and waste, of time and soul and what was left of mind. Much of his brand depended upon the relaying of that sentiment and his deviation from it. Here was a guru who *understood* how your phone menaced you, even if you didn't fully understand it yourself.

Magazine still in hand, he said, "Listen to this bit now."

"Oh, there's more, eh?"

"Listen to this. Last one. *The power of Val Face's attention to believers is certainly real, and there's no denying the effect he has on these believers. A healer who can establish intimacy immediately, a maestro of human psychology, Val Face doesn't just read people— he pulls out of them their private selves, and in real time he recognizes them, makes them genuine, makes them matter in an electronic culture that has zapped them from citizens into consumers. But Val*

Face's gripe with the internet is, with almost everything else about him, self-interested, because the internet muscles in on his mojo, competes with his own specialness in commodifying attention."

At this point in our strange swap of sentences, still on opposite sofas, my legs still not sure what to do with themselves, Face finished his Marlboro, dropped the filter into an empty can of Diet Coke, and flopped the magazine aside. He sat there aiming those eyes at me, as if it were now my turn for riposte, but no riposte was forthcoming. I felt as Galileo must have felt sitting across from the glower of Cardinal Bellarmine. Having boomeranged my prose back to me, Face seemed to feel a touch better about things, as if he'd used my own ammunition against me in italicizing a point. He looked slightly softer now; his complex expressiveness had relaxed its accusatory edge.

He said, "I *know* you, *paisan.* I know what you're after."

"What I'm . . . You do?"

"The performance prose. The hyperbole. Look at us, a couple of college dropouts living in the wrong century. The only two Bostonians who don't care about beer and baseball. We're versions of each other."

Who told him I didn't care about beer and baseball? I didn't, naturally, but who told him?

"Versions of each other?" I said. *"Us?"*

"I've read your stuff. All of your opposites. You mistrust the tech makers but like the tech. You're the loyal working-classer who wants upper-class things. The resigned schlub versus the ambitious intellect, the hardened cynic versus the sincere apostle. You mistrust the famous but want fame yourself."

"I do?"

"Of course you do. You're an American. I work with writers on every project, and I've never met one who didn't want to be famous while pontificating on the emptiness of fame."

"Pontificate. Well, I mean. I write for the paycheck. I don't have any other skills."

"The paycheck. Right. Because writing articles really pays. Come on. With your skills you could go into advertising and make a fortune."

"My . . . Did you say *my skills*?"

"Your skills. Drop the cynicism. Because inside every cynic is sincerity afraid of itself."

"Sincerity afraid of what?"

"Here's the thing: this cynicism is beneath you, *paisan*. You're too talented for that."

First my *skills* and now my *talent*. What exactly was I being fattened for here? And why didn't I mind being fattened?

The wind still rubbed all over the windows, and my legs still crossed and uncrossed at cross-purposes, but Val Face could sit there with a brand of serenity and sureness that defied you to fluster it. That was the impression: here was someone unflusterable. Here was someone born into virtuosic control. Of his sentences, of his beauty, of his potency with people, his propensity for knowing them immediately and better than they can ever know themselves. He had now turned it on me. And I was, I thought, starting to see what many millions of others saw. Because not only did I want to believe in this bamboozlement he was dishing me—I actually believed in this bamboozlement he was dishing me. Start talking to a writer about his talent and watch all his eyelashes go batty.

"So why are you wasting your talent on this clever sneering?" and he indicated the molested magazine beside him.

Clever I liked, but as for *sneering*: the subject of celebrity *requires* our sneering, doesn't it? Jasmine thought so. I managed to ask him as much with a voice marinated in newfound doubt.

"Fame's an essential part of our culture—come on, Seger. You know it's not meaningless. You write about it because you know how deeply it operates on us. How much it matters. Right? So you can stop pretending now. You're a showman too."

"Well. I mean, you're right, in a way, what you said. I didn't exactly *mean* it all. My article, I'm talking about. A lot of it, sure, I meant. Lots of it. But writing—you might not know this—writing is eight-tenths exaggeration."

"Fiction, yeah."

"No, all writing. Eight-tenths exaggeration. Yup. Pretty sure. I'm sticking to that."

"Apologize," he flirted.

"Eh? Oh, for my article you mean?"

"For your article I mean. For saying that my message is self-serving because it's mercenary."

Not *exactly* what I'd said. I'd said that all charismatics come with a message, yes, a message via their vision, something fresh for our fallen lot. In their conception of imminent Armageddon, all charismatics loathe the present that has brought it on, and in this Face was keeping with history. All charismatics are a spur to revolution. As he saw himself, I argued, and like any genuine charismatic, Face had come to tell of our fall, of the splintered base of our morality. Like our Bostonian forebears who started this city and nation,

Face had a Puritanical, insurrectionist streak, an eschatological itch in him. He'd come to sing of sin and rekindle our awareness of the soul's horror, and to buck against authority with lightning-fed wisdom. I argued that as an agitator of prevailing orthodoxies, Val Face harkened to those Bostonian Congregationalists who, despite their Bible-led conservatism, were reformers and revolutionaries, flocks enflamed toward individualism.

And *then* I said that Face was more in keeping with what we begin to see in the eighteenth century, a certain type of charismatic, a Casanova, Cagliostro *type*, wandering hucksters and exuberant frauds at operas, gaming houses, and salons the whole breadth of Europe. These charismatic adventurers brushed up against varieties of greatness, dukes and bishops and their ilk, by presenting themselves as sapient entertainers, musicians or magicians, painters or pianists, philosophers, sages, healers, diplomats. They were essentially actors, these rogues. And if they were alive today, Casanova and Cagliostro would each be his own Val Face.

So, I'd said, in a certain slant of light, Val Face was merely another American hawker raking in riches off the stricken, and he often did that raking with a dogma and doggerel little better than what you find in Boston transplant Kahlil Gibran. Which helped fuel my confusion over Face's self-branding as a charismatic. He seemed to be a charismatic by virtue of his being a celebrity and not a celebrity by virtue of his being a charismatic.

That's what I'd said.

But, okay, I'd never been readier for an apology.

"I really am sorry," I said. "I didn't think you'd actually read it. I'm amazed that you read it. I didn't know you'd, you know, *care*. We writers are mostly unnoticed nobodies who walk around unread. And you're so—so galactic."

He said, "You wanted my attention."

"Well, uhh, we writers . . . Well, in a manner of, of speaking, I suppose, yes."

"Well, you got it, *paisan*. How's it feel?"

"How's it . . . The attention?"

"The attention."

And I admitted it. "Feels pretty damn great."

"Yeah? Well, get ready to feel greater."

At this point he actually leaned forward, elbows upon knees, and the effect of this leaning was to impel me to lean forward too, elbows upon knees too, though my knees were encased in thrift-shop cords and his were encased in Calvin Klein.

"Greater?" I breathed.

And he nodded. "Greater."

Wait till you hear what he meant by *greater*.

■ ■ ■

I SPENT ANOTHER FORTY MINUTES WITH VAL FACE in his suite as he floated me an offer I couldn't refuse. This happened in between a mystifying quota of counselors, assistants, handlers, and minders sailing in and out to ask questions, seek approvals, get signatures, stimulate his ego. Then he elaborated on what that offer meant for a piddling one such as I was. And after that, I sped home to let Estelle know how our life had just been beautifully upended by Val Face.

We lived in a loft two blocks from Central Square, paying a bar-baric rent for a mere six hundred square feet. Or Mental Square, as the unkind called it, on account of the ever present muster of full-time homeless. There they huddled in shaky concentration, slurring in hobo-ese, in alcoholic, unwashed anti-logic, relating to one another as if incensed first graders. See their hospital wristbands, the ban-daged crooks of their arms, the bruises they've given one another in drug scuffles, territorial disputes, their backpacks bloated with mag-pie belongings. There they hobbled along Mass Ave. at all hours, slack jawed and slumped from opioids. And they had smartphones, these homeless. The homeless might have been bootless and the homeless might have been toothless, but somehow the homeless were not phone-less. Only in America, or perhaps only in Boston, since Bell invented the phone here. The drug dealers in Central Square all looked iden-tical: white dudes in their late thirties wearing tracksuits and white sneakers. A memo must have gone out telling them what to wear.

A particular brace of homeless were my pals whose names and stories I'd learned. Estelle was taxed with reminding me that we were ourselves technically poor and couldn't be donating to the homeless, giving them sandwiches they apparently had no use for, so often did she see these sandwiches dropped in the gutter out-side our place. And when they slept stinkily in the vestibule of our building? She was gracious to them about it, doling out dollars and whatever snack she had in her bag. But if she'd known that I was the one who had let them into the building I would have been sleeping down there with them.

When I returned that day from seeing Val Face, Estelle and I sat cocooned in a wool blanket on our futon, Estelle cracking through the pistachios we'd lifted from her parents' house the week before. You would not *believe* the cost of pistachios. I narrated for her everything that had happened from the time I heard Face's assistant's voicemail that morning to the time Face told me I could prepare to feel greater.

"Greater?" she asked.

"Right, greater. He has an *offer* for me. Ready for this? He said he wants me to join his entourage during his New England tour, to be the tour's *official chronicler*, for a feature piece in *Beantown*. I get full access, go to his shows, everything."

She stopped cracking pistachios and her face informed me she didn't understand.

She said, "I don't understand."

"Right? Jasmine had told me to beg for a profile when I went to see him, but then *he* makes *me* this offer. An offer I can't refuse. Plucking me from obscurity, he said."

"Plucking you from obscurity. I'm so confused. Tell me what else he said."

"Right. So then he said that this profile, this chronicle, could be only the beginning. Face Inc. has big plans, diversifying plans. And as all these plans are being fulfilled, *I* could be his official biographer."

"His what?"

"His official biographer."

"You. His official biographer."

"Right? Me. His official biographer."

When Estelle gets to looking suspicious, her whole aura, her entire air, yelps with it. Our lights were off for two reasons: because we often couldn't afford to pay the electric bill, and because we adored how the streetlamps, just outside our kitchen windows on Magazine Street, splashed their saffron shapes across our place, illuminated ovals and rhombi on our walls and ceiling. By such filched light we could read fine print at the witching hour. Estelle's suspiciousness, excellently lighted by the city, went on.

"But, dear, *why*?" she said.

"To be his chronicler as he goes priesting through New England—"

"As he goes whatting through New England?"

"Priesting."

"Priesting?"

"Priesting."

"You Catholics. But I meant, why *you*?"

"Well, my *talent*, love. I mean, he's *bright*, this guy. He's got *taste*. He's actually *read* my essays. He—"

"Dear, you're sure he's read your essays on celebrity culture?"

"Yup. He's read my essays on celebrity culture. That's what I'm saying."

"Including the one called 'Starve the Stars'? And what's that other one? 'A Basket of Unworthies' or something?"

"Including those, yup. Pretty sure."

"Did he read or just skim? Or maybe have someone else skim for him? You know these celebrities, many of them can't read. They have personal readers."

"Right, I hear you. But this one can read. I mean it, he's *bright*, Estelle. Really knows his way around a sentence. And he has, as I say, he really has literary taste. Get this. He used the word *hopefully* right in a sentence. Who does that?"

"How'd he use it?"

"Something about how we must *goeth forth hopefully into the future*."

"He said that? Like that? *Goeth*?"

"Right? I know."

"What a ham this guy."

"That's what he said about me! A ham."

"Sure. All you boys are hams."

"Well, okay, maybe ham*mish*—some of them. Some of us. But then, listen to this, love. Listen to what he said about my article about him. He said—"

"Hold on, dear. Let's slow down."

She required another few pistachios for thought—she liked to somersault the shells around her tongue—and then she said, "There a catch?"

"I'm a catch, right? That's how *he* sees it! I'm a real catch of a writer and—"

"*The* catch, dear. What's *the* catch?"

"Oh. *The* catch. Right."

It was a good question, I thought.

"It's a good question, I think."

She said, "Serpents still offer apples, you know."

As befits our upbringings, she's usually the one ready with references to the Torah, while references to the Gospels are my purview. We've got almost an entire Bible between us.

She said, "But tell me more about this offer."

"Well, if this chronicle goes well, it could be a big deal for us. That's what he said. I'll be plugged to write the official bio. The advance and the sales could put us on Easier Street. And who knows what else. Maybe Face and I write scripts together eventually. For his movies. Or his TV projects. He didn't exactly *say* that but—"

"Movie scripts. You. You know something about writing movie scripts."

"Really, how hard can it *be*? Have you *seen* most movies? You get the feeling the writers are only sporadically sentient. Maybe we'll move to L.A. and, you know, be among movie people."

"We are not moving to L.A. to be among movie people."

"Oh, wait, I forgot, hold on," and I went to my coat, dropped on the mat near the door, in the right pocket of which was a folded stack of twelve pages.

"I have a contract," I said.

"You have a what?"

"A contract."

She took the pages and held them away from her as you would if they were on fire.

"He had a contract already drawn up and waiting for you, before you even got there?"

For five or six minutes she looked over and through the pages, her head bowed into them. I could see she was hunting for something.

"I can see you're hunting for something."

"Dollar signs, dear. Dollar signs."

"No dollar signs on this one. Conflict of interest and all, right? But this profile will get me more money at the magazine. And then, if all goes well, I'll be the official scribe at Face Inc."

She said, "And we might be able to get out of this neighborhood."

"We definitely might be able to get out of this neighborhood."

"But this is a nondisclosure agreement, you know that, right? Did you read this?"

"No," I said. "I can read only English. That's not English. I looked. I figured you'd read it for us and translate."

"Well, this says in non-English that you may not publish or post or otherwise advertise anything about or even remotely relating to Val Face or Face Inc. without prior approval from Val Face or Face Inc."

"Aha. So. Okay. What's that mean?"

"I think I know. I think I know the catch."

"The catch, right. Do tell."

"Well, think about it," she said. "He's offended by your article, right? So he makes you an offer he knows you can't refuse. I guess so that he can make you look like a hypocrite and sellout. It must be revenge of a kind. And in the meantime, he gets you to write what he wants written."

"Okay. But he's read my work, dear. He talked about my *talent*."

She and her pistachios, the sucked-on shells of which she spat helter-skelter across our carpet, didn't seem to want to register my take. Behind her, the radiator's pinging and banging sounded to me as it always sounded to me: like a prelude to explosion.

"It's pretty crafty," she said, "what he's offering. What chutzpah. And what a pickle for us, hon."

"Chutzpah and a pickle, right."

"Jasmine knows about this offer?"

"Yup. Jasmine knows about this offer. I called her when I was waiting for the train and told her all about it."

"And she wants you to do it?"

"Wants me to do it?" I said. "Hell yes she wants me to do it."

A swath of silence then while we considered the considerations. She said, "What to do, what to do . . ."

"Yup. That's the question, love. What to do."

"I think he wants the challenge of your sarcasm and cynicism, or why not enlist another writer who loves what he does, right? I think he wants to woo you, maybe prove you wrong. Prove your article wrong. That's part of what he does, right, woo?"

I said, "Not all that easy to describe what he does, actually. A pulpiteer, I think. But he definitely woos, yes. He's a wooer. Woosome."

"Maybe we should give him the benefit of the doubt here, hon. Let's not judge too hastily, right?"

"Yes, definitely, good call, dear." Pause. "He's got good taste, right, Estelle? He's read my essays."

"I think we should do it. The profile, the biography. We should sign this contract, right? Your ambition needs more ambition and here's the chance."

I'd thought that Estelle might try to frighten me away from compromising my self-respect and looking like another American pharisee and false-face. But there were our coming nuptials to consider, and our lives just a breath above beggary. There was also my upbringing to haul into the equation, by which I mean I was reared by old-timey guineas who believe it's a capital crime for a man not to provide adequately for his family. And Estelle's blueprint for a family, I should mention, involved not only lighting out of this neighborhood, but having as many offspring as her Jewish parents had sired: five. As a lone child, I saw this as a smidgen extreme, but there you have it. Her folks were already not tickled by me because I'm a sometimes-Catholic and not in any way Jewish except in my reading habits, so to disappoint them in the matter of multiple grandchildren wouldn't be wise of me.

Estelle said, "And now's definitely the time for you to get on social media, hon, right? To get that following for Seger Jovi. You can post something every hour, on multiple platforms, during your time with this guy, accrue a huge following that way. Think about it. There's never been a better time."

"Ah. Right. Never been a better . . . There's just one, one small snag with that, love."

"What small snag?"

"The small snag of Face telling me that I better not get on social media during my time with him. He's calling the shots. I'm the employee here."

More pistachios for her, more fidgeting for me.

"The employee. Okay, I guess that's the way to look at it," she said. "Because I don't want to spend another year in this apartment. I've got plans for us."

■ ■ ■

THAT WAS HOW I GOT VACUUMED UP into the world of Val Face, how I came to do his bidding while trying to do my own, to subvert myself for him and his promotional aims despite my principled misgivings. Ever notice what happens to your principled misgivings when opportunity dings your doorbell? They have a curious tendency to pack up and slip out the back door.

The story I have to tell now, the story of what befell Val Face in the days after I met him, is not the story you think you know, the one you read about all over the web and in every publication that still knows what paper is. No, the story I have to tell now is the other side of what you think you know.

What was next then? Forty-eight hours of anticipating the Boston Opera House. That's where Face's New England tour was set to commence in two nights, and I, the royal scribe, would be there gleaming in the personal access. And never mind that the place is now named the Citizens Bank Opera House. Never mind because I refuse to call it that.

II.

The *mysterium tremendum* that is American celebrity. No matter the ramp up, fame hits its targets with a ferocious suddenness that makes even the targets look around wondering what the hell just whomped them. What were the specifics that had gelled to turn Val Face into a pop culture colossus and Hollywood A-lister, the abracadabra that had transformed Valentino Detti of Jeffries Point, East Boston, into Val Face of the firmament? Had he bartered away his soul to Satan, à la Robert Johnson at the crossroads? Don't dismiss devils and seraphs in the singular story of American celebrity. If fame had a handbook, a how-to, everyone would have it: the handbook, the how-to—the fame. We the lesser ones of the world have a future, but the Val Faces of the world have a fate.

Face's childhood and adolescence, or at least what is known of them, what he writes of them in his memoir, and what I myself could excavate, seem to have been a portrait of Boston normality, working-class humdrummery: his dad a firefighter (Engine 8, Ladder 1), his mom a labor and delivery nurse at Beth Israel Deaconess.

The only things that weren't part of that working-class humdrummery were his burgeoning charisma and his phenomenal face. Twice he'd been approached by astonished modeling scouts—once in the Prudential Center when he was a lad of eight, once on Newbury Street two years later—and both times his father said nah. If you know anything about Boston firefighters from Eastie, you know that the first thing they do not want is their sons being models. In the scrappier section of their Jeffries Point neighborhood, the quickest way to get a boy psychopathically picked on was to get him a modeling contract.

Here's a telling scene that has two sources: the first source is Face's mother, who dishes the story in *Face Rising*, a documentary about her son and his charismatic powers, and the second source is Face himself, who relays the scene in his memoir. It happened in Piers Park, at the foot of Jeffries Point, when Face was ten years old, the blue-mirrored Boston skyline looming like a promise there across the water. His mother had taken him to Piers Park with his sister, Talia, younger by one year, to flee the singe of an unholy August heat. And soon Face went missing from the playground. When he didn't return after ten minutes, his mother took Talia and went to hunt for him.

She found Face near the gates on Marginal Street, at a picnic table beneath an elm with the park's pair of resident philosophers: Jumay Johnson, a vet with bullet dents and jacket patches, and Giovanni Abramo, former groundskeeper at Suffolk Downs. Verbose and didactic and very much retired in their eighties, the men convened at the picnic table whenever the weather let them. Any passerby could hear them sermonizing on whether or not the *Titanic* would have sunk if it had hit the ice head-on instead of scraping it, or whether or not intergalactic travelers could have built Machu Picchu during a rare lull in their riskier endeavors.

On this August afternoon, Jumay Johnson and Giovanni Abramo were hotly following the topic of just how manifest was manifest destiny, which led just as hotly to the topic of whether or not countries or individuals have control over their own fates. Face's mother found him there at the picnic table with the men, both of whom were being rebuffed by the boy for their shared view that the world is too unpredictable, too irregular, for any individual to control fate. Fate, they maintained, was a special, almost cosmic force that worked on people from beyond their own input.

"Some people are lucky," said Jumay Johnson. "And some ain't. Just the way it is."

Precociously ten, the boy was having none of this.

"Sirs," he said, "good luck and bad luck are choices we make. Good choices equal good luck. Bad choices equal bad luck. We make our luck because we make our choices."

The men looked at each other now—Jumay Johnson erected an eyebrow, Giovanni Abramo gave a whistle—as if trying to gauge the substance of the little herald who'd just wandered into their society. What they didn't know was that the boy had just finished reading his first adult book, plucked from his mother's shelf: *The Prophet* by Kahlil Gibran, fellow Bostonian and model for any aspiring sage. He'd scribbled some of Gibran's wisdom into a composition notebook he'd begun keeping in order to catalog his own blooming profundities.

Sitting now in this elm-shaded heat in Piers Park with Jumay Johnson and Giovanni Abramo, the boy could remember the abstractions he copied into his notebook only the day before: *Much of your pain is self-chosen*, and *Your joy is your sorrow unmasked*, and *Work is love made visible*. To impress the men, to reach them and teach them, the boy knew he needed the deliberately cryptic paradoxes that Gibran excelled at, such as *Only when you drink from the river of silence shall you indeed sing*. He knew he needed references to the seasons, and animals, and nature. Dew is always good for a metaphor. Mist, too. Owls and oceans come in handy.

Giovanni Abramo said, "Now, lookit, kid. I worked Suffolk Downs for forty years. Okay? I saw luck. I know luck. Okay? And I know it 'cause I didn't have it. Bet like *crazy* on them horses. My horses never won. See? No luck, kid."

The boy said, "Just as the owl wills its *who* from the trees, the ocean wills its *whoosh* from the waves."

Giovanni Abramo said, "What's that mean kid, *whoosh*? What *whoosh*?"

Jumay Johnson said, "It's them *pelicans* you mean, son. Ain't no owls in the ocean. Tell us more about this will you mean."

The boy said, "Your will is the grass. Your luck is only the dew on the grass."

"Reminds me," said Giovanni Abramo. "Gotta water my lawn. Say something about water, kid."

The boy tried one of his paradoxes. "Only through thirst can you truly drink." And then, "Only the desert knows rain."

Giovanni Abramo said, "Kid's making me thirsty, I'll tell you what. Say something else about luck, kid."

The boy said, "Luck is your love. Love is your luck."

Jumay Johnson had something to add to this. "Now, look here, son. Look at that face on you. See? Can't nobody *plan* for a face like that. Roll of the dice, that's all. Pure luck."

The boy said, "We begin making ourselves before birth."

Giovanni Abramo said, "Now, I happen to know a little something about birth, I do. I'm on my third wife, see, got four sons. I know birth. Now tell us more about how we make ourselves. Never thought of it that way."

"We begin as buoys and end as oceans."

Giovanni Abramo said, "Can't say I see the connection there, kiddo. Must be this heat."

"*I* see it," said Jumay Johnson. "Boy's talking about *wombs*, see? And what's the womb made of? All water. See? Like the ocean. And the baby in the womb—tell me if I'm following you, kid—the baby's like a buoy. I get it, sure. But tell us about the *Titanic*, kid. Ain't no way it'd sunk if only it hit that berg head-on. Fact, I've got my own theory that says—"

"I'm sorry if my child is disturbing you gentlemen."

Enter Mrs. Detti, Talia in hand, behind her newly arrived clouds that darkened Piers Park and pledged to scour all the day's heat.

"Oh no, he's not disturbing us at all," said Jumay Johnson, and he creaked to full height with his cane. "Curious boy you've got here. Can you send him back tomorrow?"

And in the documentary *Face Rising*, Mrs. Detti says, "That's when I knew, that day, in Piers Park, after overhearing him with those men. That's when I knew what he'd be, what he'd become. I mean, I suppose I *always* knew—a mother always knows, and all that—but this is when I *really* knew."

■ ■ ■

BECAUSE I'VE BEEN KNOWN to have reportorial spunk when it's called for, and because I needed to plug some holes in the narrative of Face's boyhood and adolescence, I'd hastily arranged for interviews with two of Face's grade-school and high-school chums. I arranged these sit-downs through a whiz researcher at *Beantown* who'd found them for me—she could find quarks if only the theoretical physicists would think to ask. One interview was with Lucy Genovese, owner of an auto repair shop in Eagle Hill, East Boston; and the other was with Carmine Feludi, adjunct at Harvard Extension School. These interviews happened two mornings after I'd first met Face, on the day of his show at Boston Opera House.

First, Lucy Genovese. At nine that morning, I trained to the Wood Island stop in Eastie, and then hoofed it over to her auto shop. Lucy Genovese was crew-cutted, a cigarette stench coming from her whole upper half, an inexplicable sobriquet stitched over her breast pocket—*Roller*—her every finger a miracle of filth, the backs of her hands graffitied with illegible scrawl that the years had blurred into stains of sickly blue, a melanoma blotch that once must have meant something to her. You know whom she reminded me of? Joan Jett circa 1985.

We sat on folding chairs in the break room, she with a Snickers, half a liter of Coke, and a pack of non-filter Camels, I with a feminized bottle of water and my phone on record, the vending machine in full hum behind us, a too-large clock keeping watch in the lime hue of fluorescent bulbs. Her auto artisans watched us through the glass with the yearning eyes of yarded inmates behind chain-link.

"Thank you for meeting with me, Lucy."

I was looking at the one requisite item for any auto shop: the calendar with the naked blonde, legs impossibly east-west on the hood of a '68 Dodge Charger. She wielded an item of such phallicism it looked more harpoon than screwdriver.

"Loose," she said.

"I'm—eh?"

"Call me loose now."

"Er. As in—not tight?"

"That's right. I don't go by *Lucy* no more. It's Luce. L-U-C-E."

"Aha. Gotcha. *Luce.*"

I was comforted by her working-class singularities of syntax.

Then, about Val Face when he was Valentino Detti, she kept saying, "Yeah, Val was a real pisser."

When I asked how, she said, "You know, just the total package: looks, smarts, funny as hell, all of it. Everyone liked him. Everyone—all through grade school, all through high school. Even my *ma* liked him and my ma didn't like no one, not even me. Val was just a real pisser."

No other place in society smells and sounds like an auto shop: oil and gasoline, concrete and metal, paint and rubber, cigarette smoke and coffee, the clang of wrenches, the metal-on-metal bang of hammers, the quick zipping breath of air tools, and some decades-old, faintly playing ditty by those still-moving undead, the Rolling Stones. As someone who cannot name any piece of any engine, I envied the mechanics' ability to take one apart and assemble it again.

"So he had good grades in school?" I asked.

"Oh yeah. Val was wicked smart. Had the smarts *real* good. He read books. He explained shit to me, when we had English class together, sophomore year, I think. We had gym together too, a few years. Val had the smarts *real good* in gym. Could always get us out of doing gym. We were smokers. I didn't own sneakers, man, I wore mechanic's boots, like these, steel toe. In case I had to stomp anyone messing with me."

Dexterity of the mouth: Lucy Genovese could somehow talk and smoke, chew, sip, and breathe at the same time, which appeared to me just then a marvelous circus trick. And despite the minor speech malfunctions, I thought our interview was going pretty well so far.

"Yeah, Val could con them gym teachers real good, or I guess he'd call it charisma now, or charm, whatever. He'd con these gym teachers, real *smooth*. Yeah, Val was just a real pisser."

I wasn't hearing envy in Lucy Genovese's voice just then. I was hearing admiration. Easy to envy a celebrity with Val Face's powers. But admiration is of a different stripe entirely, rarer and of stouter stuff.

"But did he seem like superstar material back then? That's what I'm trying to get at, Luce. When he was a kid, did he seem special in that way? I'm trying to understand his origins."

"What oranges?"

"No, his—you know, how his past explains his present. His Rosebud. Was he always different, special?"

"Oh yeah, for sure. I *always* knew that fucker would be real famous. You could just tell. He had a real *people* talent. Like I said, everybody liked Val, somehow. Jocks, burnouts, preppy kids, punks. Even the *teachers*. Everybody, man."

"A people talent," I said. "Talented with people."

"Yeah. That's what you can call it, sure."

"So you guys were close then?"

"I guess you could say that. Sure. Problem was, I guess, everybody wanted to be around him. It started in fifth, sixth grade, and then got worse in high school. Everybody wanted to be around him. So it was kinda hard to be close to him since he was kinda close with everybody. I mean, you *thought* you were tight with him but how can a guy be truly tight with so many people, ya know? I guess I was just never sure of myself with him. Wasn't sure how real it was, being his pal."

"All these people in his life. Was he looking for applause?"

"A pause in what?"

I saw the problem now. It was the hum of the vending machine behind us, so up went my volume.

"No, *applause*. Was he trying to—where did his people talent come from, would you say?"

"Shit, I can't say, man. He's just a born performer, I dunno. Or maybe he was trying to escape his family, get his eggs somewhere else."

"Escape his family? What do you mean?"

"Some crazy shit with his sis. She was a real snap cap."

"A what?"

"You know, a wig twist."

"Wig what?"

"Wig twist. Lid flip. Outta her mind, man."

"Oh. His memoir doesn't say much about her. She was . . . not well?"

"I guess you could say that. Her name's Talia. She was a year below us, a fuckin' knockout, this girl, as you'd figure, right, being Val's sis, but she was totally out to lunch, man. Drove the family crazy, I heard. Drugs and hospitals and shit. But what do I know? Just what I heard."

"I never read that about him, about his sister, I mean."

"Probably not something you wanna go around saying. I should just shut my fuckin' yap about it."

She stopped then, sprang up, opened the door to the break room, and shouted out at her toilers, "You fuckers gonna *work* today or just smoke? I want that Ford done by lunch and that Chevy done by two."

When she returned she slid into a silence, a kind of contemplative impasse, in remembrance of more promising days, no doubt, staring at the Camel in her fingers as if it could aid her recall. Out in the bays her auto artisans were no longer looking in at us or standing at the open doors with their smoke. One guy was being swallowed by the mouth of a green Dodge: you could see him only from the waist down.

"Man," she said, "I was just thinking about the best time we had. Night of the Bus, as it became known. Val rented a *bus* for us, for his pals. Senior year, right before graduation. He rented a *bus*. The fuck rents a bus? And from where? There a place called Rent a Bus? But that's Val—he could rent a bus if he wanted to. He took us out all over Boston, all night long, a party bus, man, with a little two-piece band in the back, and even a bartender. It was wild."

After a meditative pause, she said, "Hey, are you guys pals or something? You friends with Val?"

I said, "Sure I am. Yup. He chose me to be his biographer. I'm sort of the royal scribe for Face Inc."

"Damn. *Chose* you." Pause. "You think he'll remember me?"

"I'm sure he remembers you, Luce. Sure."

"Well, shit, man, not everyone remembers me. I saw Cheryl Frangelli last month, a girl from high school, and I said hello to her, you know, real *nice* like, and she said *The fuck are you?* And I *dated* that chick."

"No, I think Val Face will remember you, Luce. I think he remembers people."

"Yeah? Okay. Here's my number then," and she gouged it onto the back of a napkin with a struggling ballpoint. "You tell that pisser to call me. We gotta catch up. Maybe he'll see me at his show tonight. You going to that?"

"Yup, I'll be there. The royal scribe must be in attendance."

"So can you get me backstage? You know, just to say hi."

"Oh. Well. Hmm. I'll have to see. He's pretty busy at his shows, Luce. Lots of security and all."

"Yeah, I get it. No sweat."

"Can I ask you one more question? What's *Roller* mean?" and I indicated the name stitched onto her shirt.

"Ha. As in *hay*, man. I roll the chicks in *the hay*."

As I went away from her auto shop, I heard, behind me, from the belly of the bays, Mick Jagger in full croon about all the satisfaction he cannot get. Which is curious, when you consider it, Jagger not being satisfied. If *he* can't get it how can the rest of us ever hope to?

■ ■ ■

I THEN TRAINED MYSELF TO HARVARD SQUARE to meet
Carmine Feludi, who was much less charitable than Luce in his
remembrance of Val Face as Valentino Detti. An adjunct who tried
to impart human truths to unattentive ungratefuls in Psych 101, he
had bitterness rooted into his face like a cactus. Here was a guy who
went through life puppeteered by pique—a pique gold medalist—one
of those gents who wear their blood pressure on their sleeves. He also
wore a disheveled professorial look that declared he was too preoccupied with heady matters to care about fashion. Then he kept checking
the time on his flip phone—that's not a typo: it was a flip phone—a
relic from 2010 that might as well have been a walkie-talkie.

Not one hundred yards from where we sat, I recalled, in the
sepia of 1837, Mr. Emerson gave his well-trod Phi Beta Kappa speech
on the cultural glories of American individualism. Knowingly or
not, Face cribbed from Emerson in his insistence on self-reliance,
self-betterment, and individualism, in his revolt against cyber
herdthink. For Emerson, as for Face, a return to the inner workings
of the self was our only hope for *knowing* ourselves. Emerson and his
transcendentalists needed to splash some intellectualism and spiritual ardor into a culture of conformity and materialism, which is
what Face saw himself as doing too, and never mind that he conformed to the blueprint for American fame. Because, look at it all
you want, but fame is fame and wealth wealth. They're a nation of
their own, and either you live there or you don't.

My first mistake with Carmine Feludi concerned Mr. Emerson
and his famous speech.

"Is Val Face our new Ralph Waldo Emerson?"

And his response to my stupidity went as follows: "Are you fucking nuts?"

We were seated on chilled metal chairs at an outdoor café in Harvard Square despite the day's twenty-two degrees—his idea. He was a yeti of a man, so held more body heat than I did. Our coffee steam coalesced with our breath as students blurred by in the day's freeze, surprisingly deft at navigating sidewalks, around one another and various poles, with faces aimed down at their devices, headphones vised to their skulls, and fingers tapping madly. If those learned Puritans who founded this place in the 1600s could come back and behold the profane commercialism that has infected their clerical vision, they'd roll up their sleeves, spit into their palms, and ready all the witches for scorching.

"Tell me about Val Face then. What you remember about him when he was a child."

"Tell you about Val. Okay. By the way, I refuse to call him *Face*, I'm sorry. That's ridiculous. *Val Face*. Gimme a break. So, you know what kind of guy Val is? I'll tell you. He'd throw bread crumbs out for the birds in the Common or the Garden, right, when we were teenagers, and then he'd wait for the birds to come eat them, and guess what. When the birds wouldn't come quick enough, he'd get *offended*. Offended by the goddamn *birds* because they didn't come eat the bread he tossed around for them. I'd be sitting there with a cigarette or whatever and he'd be looking around for grateful pigeons. Guy needed attention from *pigeons*."

He waited, looking. I waited, looking back. I think I angled my head, inclined it toward him, in that way that suggests you'd welcome the point, whatever point was being sharpened.

"So . . . uhh . . . pigeons you say?"

"Pigeons I say. Think on that. Pigeons. He's a ruse."

"A ruse. With *pigeons*? Or . . ."

"With everyone. His whole *thing*, he's a ruse. In fact, there was an article, not long ago, I forget where, an article laying out how he's a ruse, a total fraud. You should read it."

"I did read it. I wrote it."

"You wrote what?"

"That article you read. About him being a fraud. It's my piece. The one called 'Tacky, Wacky, and Wrong'? I wrote it."

"So why the hell are you writing about him again?"

"Ah, good question. I've since had a renovation of opinion, Carmine. I figure millions of people can't be wrong."

His beard scoffed, "Is that your criterion? What the millions say?"

Carmine Feludi had a way of talking not *with* you or *to* you but *up against* you, growlingly, with that bass throat of his—a true yeti's bass that fisted down into the deeps of you.

"So, wait a sec," I said. "Weren't you guys—you guys were friends in school, I thought."

"Oh, we were friends, yeah. When the editor or whoever from your magazine emailed me yesterday, I told her: we were friends all right. But that's not saying much. We were friends the same way he was friends with everybody."

"You make that sound—what's wrong with that?"

"Somebody who's friends with everybody is a real friend to nobody."

Carmine Feludi had aphoristic ambitions. One eye, I noticed now, was gray and the other was green, and I wondered if this optical irregularity affected how he saw the world, causing some disruption of self—or Self. David Bowie had mismatched eyes too, and that always seemed to me part of why he was so chameleonic.

"But he was smart?" I asked. "He was special?"

"He was smart, yeah, so? Lots of people are smart. Special? Okay, sure, he was special. I'll admit it. He had magnetism. Real magnetism, something you can't fake. I admit it. Valedictorian, all that. An ace at public speaking. Sure. Even in grade school, even in second grade, man, he could dish you some smart-sounding advice if you needed it. He seemed to know things. And in high school, he could really make you feel seen. Yeah, I remember that. When he was being genuine, especially when it was just the two of us—he could really make me feel seen, make me feel understood." Dolorous pause, and then: "But then the next day, he wouldn't return my calls, ya know? He was on to the next person who needed saving."

"Saving?"

"Guy had a Christ complex, even then. He'd go around our high school making little speeches to clumps of people in the hallways. Thought he was supposed to be saving people."

"Saving people from what?"

"From themselves, I don't know. From their own lack of—what's he call it now?—from their own lack of soul awareness, or whatever the hell he calls it."

"Did he save you?"

"Hell no. He didn't save me. I didn't need saving." Another

dolorous pause. "Would have been nice to have a pal I could count on. But no, I didn't need saving."

"Do you have any other positive memories, Carmine? I met with Lucy Genovese a little while ago and she said—"

"Oh, man, Lucy Genovese. *That's* the company I'm in for this article you're doing? Lucy Genovese?"

"What's wrong with Lucy Genovese?"

"What's wrong with Lucy Genovese? Did you *talk* to her? She's done more dope than Aerosmith."

"Well, she was very nice to me. Working gal. Small business owner."

Carmine Feludi had no wisdom to impart on working gals and small business owners.

I said, "But you really don't have any positive memories of when Val Face—sorry, Val Detti—was your friend? What about the Night of the Bus? Wasn't that fun?"

"Night of the Bus?" He said this through what is typically called "clenched teeth," though his was a clench to take top prize. "I wasn't *invited* to the Night of the Bus."

And then blank-faced silence, as if in underline of his sentence.

"Oh. Er. Wasn't invited. Okay. Never mind. Sorry."

"You want to know what I remember about Val? Okay, here's what I remember. Ready? I lent him a hundred bucks once. We must have been seventeen, eighteen. I forget what he needed it for—I think it was for a part for his motorcycle. He had this Triumph he'd ride around on, always with a different girl on back, you know, real slick, like he was goddamn James Dean. Yeah, I think the money was for his motorcycle. But I damn sure remember that he didn't pay it back. I remember *that*. What's the interest on that hundred bucks, after all these years? Guess."

"The—the interest on it? I wouldn't know, Carmine."

"Guess."

"I really wouldn't know. Math and me—we don't compute."

"Well I know. I calculated it, and every time I see him on a magazine cover, or on TV, or on the web, or wherever, I do the calculation again, with a fair interest rate, the going rate, adjusted for current value, of course. I'm a fair guy. And I figure that right about now he owes me two grand. I added a little for pain and suffering, of course, but that's a fair figure, two grand. You know how much money he's gonna make tonight for his performance at the Opera House? Guess."

"I don't know."

"Per minute. How much do you think he'll make *per minute* tonight?"

"I really wouldn't know, Carmine."

"About two grand. *Per minute*. I did the math. Because math and me *do* compute. So you tell him that for me, whenever you see him, for this article you're doing. Like we need another goddamn article about him. Tell Valentino Detti he owes me a minute."

Becoming someone else means leaving behind the many other someones who can't become someone else.

He said, "Or maybe I'll ask him myself tonight. If he sees me."

"You mean—you're going to his show tonight?"

"Hell yes I'm going to his show tonight. Wouldn't miss it for anything."

■ ■ ■

THE DECISIVE EPISODES in Face's trek to fame did not occur in grade school or high school. The decisive episodes occurred in college, precisely when we begin to comprehend a trusty American formula: who we are is not who we have to be.

Three years and change after his vision in Copley Square, where he gazed upon the plaque to Kahlil Gibran and glimpsed the flashes of his own future, Face began as a busker dispensing his charisma on tourist-rich street corners. He was a senior at Boston University, completing a double major in psych and philosophy, and there he was in Harvard Square or at Faneuil Hall on a Friday night, psychologizing to colorful shoppers and having to compete with Jenny the Juggler and a smattering of itinerant folk strummers. This was the point at which he knew that his notebooks of philosophical self-help, dutifully collected since he was ten, could be turned into a performance. His Gibran-inspired aphorisms and flair for public speaking could be monetized—he was sure. This was also the point at which he began calling himself *Face* full-time, after twenty years of hearing, from strangers and friends and kin, what a galactic face he had.

What's in a name? All renaming has a mythical hue to it, a myth of creation or rebirth: select a new name and you saunter forth with a new fate. In America we pine to *make a name* for ourselves, to see that *name in lights,* wear *brand names*, become a *household name*. In the U.S.A. we do auto-baptism, self-dominion: Louise Ciccone morphed into Madonna just as Norma Mortenson morphed into Marilyn, and you know the results of those enormous morphings. This is the mythology of the American Dream, our national obsession with success, with dull caterpillars bursting into butterflies. Valentino Detti's name changed to Val Face and that change was tectonic. All the plates under the name Valentino Detti shifted and concussed, crumbling the little life on top of that name. This was not mere nomicide. This was the selficide prerequisite to reincarnation.

His early street performances? Onlookers had never seen anything like them. What was this: a come-on, put-on, turn-on? a creep, crook, cretin? Was he . . . panhandling? Was that advice he was giving? It sounded inspirational—no, *motivational*. Was it philosophy then . . . *therapy*? To individuals he'd met just forty seconds earlier? How to describe what he was doing, there in Harvard Square on a summer's Saturday night, or there outside Faneuil Hall the next afternoon, in a soft-fitting white T-shirt with one word, *Face*, greeting you in red letters? Of course he knew our city's history of seditious orating at Faneuil Hall, "the cradle of liberty," our ancestors Paul Revere and John Hancock whipping up the rabble to protest all the blasted overreaching of the Brits. The world's reddest empire was not long a match for Sam Adams and his Sons of Liberty lifting voices and pints at the local meetinghouse. Would our century's mooning conformity and the cyber stripping of our souls long remain a match for Val Face?

Like his revolutionary forebears, Face had insurgent words, but Face's chief tool was, well, Face's face. Face's face was the main event. And before Face's face made him the face of fame in America, he relied on how his face gelled with his supernatural skills of intimate knowing, a facility for telling people details about themselves he could not possibly know. He dealt them facts about themselves that clearly struck them as accurate, facts that weren't the platitudes dealt to them by that palm-reading sham in a head scarf. And he wasn't cheating as do those snaky televangelists when their confederates pipe into their earpieces all the personal info about you—the personal info you yourself penciled onto a questionnaire at the start of the show. Outside Faneuil Hall, at the foot of the steps to Quincy Market, people followed Face's finger reel to come near him, and then he switched it on for them—his charisma. Hunky in that T-shirt and jeans and with the impressive build of an Italian soccer star, he looked at and *saw* these strangers, and those strangers, in turn, could not turn away.

Let's unpack the early-phase performance that made him, what became known in Facelandia as the Jeans Clip, the one that racked up nine million views in fewer than nine days, a six-minute clip that landed Face radio appearances on WBUR and WGBH, and was bandied about and enthused over by a sundry sampling of humanity: dignitaries and senators, landscapers, electricians, chefs, pop stars and sports stars, even the prime minister of New Zealand, of all hilly places.

At the start of this six-minute clip you are confronted by a college-age Face in a horseshoe of people, summer strollers by Faneuil Hall who'd stopped to wonder what this odd beauty was up to, why he had the word *Face* immodestly ironed on his chest, and why he was filming himself, from two different angles, tripods and all, speaking strangeness to strangers. You can't help but notice that the horseshoe of twenty spectators consists mostly of salivating women, with a few middle-aged gay men unafraid to ogle. It must be a showbiz law of some kind: secure the love of women and gay men and soon everyone else will follow.

At first you see him doing his best Sermon-on-the-Mount shtick, which, as you know from other urban street-corner scenes, is usually undertaken by men in alarming outfits whose mental maladies poke out from them like arrows. One sound policy in life says to dodge anyone with an itch to soliloquize, the self-anointed for whom being convivial means getting liturgical. But in this clip, everything about Face's face and Face's stance and Face's voice says that Face is not just sane but sage, says that here is a young man you will need and want to remember. With his edgy blue-collar beauty, in a boulevard of summer sun, he glows. I mean more than a mere halo or nimbus. I mean there's a full-on aureola around him, a luminescence helped by the soft white T-shirt pasted onto his swimmer's torso, by Elvis hair that does not receive but rather bestows the day's light. Face is so crisply in focus that his willing captives look bleared, bedimmed right next to him. At first you think this might be an effect of the camera, a fluorescent editing effect, until you realize it isn't. The fluorescence is Face's own. This is what holiness looked like in the Levant circa 6 BC.

Somewhere off screen, you can dimly hear, an acoustic guitar and a not unlovely alto are sharing what Paul Simon thinks about himself and Julio down by the schoolyard. A gussied-up unicyclist glides by in the background. And Face begins with this: "Tell me what you want and I'll tell you who you are," and then: "Tell me your wishes and I'll tell you your fears."

So far, this doesn't appear to be the thing you leave the house looking for, a hunk at Faneuil Hall asking you to unburden your wants and wishes onto him, a twentysomething eccentric who purports to know you. Who's got time to pause for *that*? Summer strollers at Faneuil Hall and Quincy Market, apparently, because nobody leaves. Nobody even *looks* as if leaving is an option. Rather, each glances at the others as if considering the questions: *What do we want? What are our wishes?* Then Face puts the question directly to a young woman, eighteen, nineteen tops: *What do you want?*

She giggles. "In life you mean?"

And Face says, "In life I mean."

And right away, after glancing at her friend armed with both an iPhone and a digital camera, she says what every American has been groomed from the womb to say, thanks to Mr. Jefferson's well-traveled phrase: "Happiness."

Ah yes, that: happiness. If dollar signs are the great American language, then happiness is the great American religion, and most of us don't have enough of either. I invite you to worry about this.

And so Face tells her, "No. Not happiness."

She glances pleadingly at her friend, then at a fellow spectator, then looks back at Face. She says, "Not happiness?"

"It's not what you want if that's what you want."

You see he's mastered the glib paradoxes Kahlil Gibran trafficked in. The syntax of that sentence perplexes the girl, and judging from the faces around her, she isn't the only one.

Face says, "Unhappiness results from your rush to happiness."

People don't exactly warm to paradox, I've noticed, and never mind that paradox undergirds every truth in life. Never mind that the only way to make sense of things is through antinomy and contradiction. The young woman's face tells Face what she thinks of—or, in today's promiscuous parlance, what she *feels about*—this mystification.

To the young woman and then to all twenty, Face says, "What's your devotion?"

All twenty have looks now with which they look at one another, and these looks declare that this odd term, *devotion*, hits them just as the odd term *sacrifice* would have. They don't appear to know what the odd term means or how it might apply to them.

One of them even asks, "Devotion?"

And Face says, "Devotion."

Someone says, "Oh, you mean to family. Family devotion."

"If family is your devotion, but that's not what I mean. Your *individual* devotion, to your own selfhood. Your absorption. Your *purpose*."

Expressionless faces at the luminous expressions of Val Face.

"Your happiness is the effect of a cause, and the cause is your devotion, so I ask you: What is your devotion?"

And after several seconds of looking in silence at this blinking twenty, Face pops it open, this counsel he'd obviously been practicing in the mirror:

"You say you want happiness, as if it's available in a box, if you can only find the right website, you'll be able to buy it. But your pursuit of happiness is doomed without a guiding devotion. Because your struggles, your *un*happiness in pursuance of your devotion is what makes you, because only through confronting those can you be better, overcome the sources of letdown, by confronting and surviving the struggles, and not only surviving but *evolving*. Only struggle can effect evolution. Evolution is your goal. Only if you are stronger, wiser, can you begin to see what real happiness might mean for you. It's not something you can want. It's a by-product of what you achieve through devotion."

Now that, as you can probably tell, is not the remarkable part. That part can be pulled off by any huckstering self-helper, any mystic babbler with claptrap fit for bumper stickers but not for the radical complexity of human yearning. Self-help today, palmistry tomorrow. But no, the remarkable part happens next.

Into the frame totters some cardboard frat boob with a backward Boston College baseball cap and a sloshing bellyful of Pabst Blue Ribbon. You've no doubt seen males of this sort: inebriated sub-yuppiedom. Splotchy-skinned, pointy-nosed, polo button-up, khaki cargo shorts, sockless in his brown boat loafers and repellently hirsute legs. He's tottered into the frame at the elbowing of his equally inebriated chums, two unnecessary duplicates of himself. They're filming him, egging him on toward the egging of Face's face. But the humiliation about to ensue is not Face's.

This dope says, "Hey, *Face*, Mr. Face, heehee," and sidles up to him, laying his terrible arm across the excellent shoulders of Face, winking, hot-dogging it for his chuckling chums. "Do you have any *advice* for us? Heehee."

Face removes the dope's arm from his shoulders in one smooth gesture, squares to him without threat or perturbance, and says, "What's your name?"

"Heehee. I'm Face too. See?" and he points. "I have a face."

"Are those your friends there? Those two filming you?"

The dope looks; the dope laughs. "Nah, those guys? Nah, they ain't my friends. Never seen them before. Heehee."

"Take a look at them," Face says. "Did you ask yourself why they pushed you in here to act the jackass? Why is it *you* being filmed here and not them?"

"Who, *those* guys? Never met them before! Heehee."

"Take a good look at them filming you right now. What do you think they're going to do with this video?"

The dope mimes outrage. "Yeah! Hey, what are you guys gonna do with this video? Hey!"

"Look at *me* now," and Face takes the dope's shoulders, one boney deltoid in each hand, and he firmly turns the dope toward him. Touch a stranger in this way and the stranger himself gets touchy, prickly, but this stranger, this dope, so physically outranked, doesn't get touchy or prickly, never mind angry. Rather, Face's laying of hands on him has a sedating effect, as if the dope is now caught in one of those tractor beams *Star Trek* always made goofy use of.

They're two feet apart. And this close to Face, with Face's event-horizon eyes hasped onto him, with Face's fit, flexed arms fixing him there, you see something very slowly begin to shift, something scuttle in this dope's own face. This is the first few seconds of the onset of a realization: the realization of embarrassment, of being an unpretty and average male this close to a male of such aberrant handsomeness, a male with hair and skin that inspire entire cosmetics campaigns, a nose and jawline plastic surgeons poster up inside their waiting rooms, teeth your orthodontist dreams about. The dominance Face is about to establish is helped by the vertical three inches and the horizontal four he has over this dope, but the bulk of this dominance comes from—what else?—from his words.

"I know who you are. Did you realize that? I *know* you. And these friends of yours? I know them too. And they *think* they know you. They think you're a jackass they can manipulate into proving to everyone you're a jackass. This video they're filming of you right now, behaving this way? They're going to post it all over social media in an hour, and there it will remain for eternity. Eternal proof that you're a jackass. You don't think about eternity much, do you?"

The dope tries feebly once more to fight the sedation and surrender he feels gathering inevitability within him. He does this with another look at the two other dopes who elbowed him into this, and the look he tries for is one of *mocking* surrender, as if he really doesn't have to be abased in this way, but he's choosing to do it for the sake of the spectacle—for the sake of entertainment. His expression tries to shrug, to say: *What the hell, I'll go along with this.* But the truth disclosed in this failed expression tells a different story. It says: *I am helpless here. I waded into this humbling and now I can't get out of it.*

Face says, "I asked you a question. What's your relationship to eternity?"

The sounds now coming from the dope don't even rise to the level of *err* and *uhh* and *umm.* They're not primate sounds at all— more like marsupial clucking sounds. His splotched complexion has sprawled into one consummate splotch, an ear-to-ear and chin-to-brow blush of chagrin. If he wants to dash loose from Face's hold of his shoulders, he shows no indication of that, either because he doesn't want to dash loose from Face's hold or because he simply can't. The eternity question has clearly stumped him, but then he's clearly someone who spends large chunks of his day in the state of stumpdom.

"You don't seem to realize something," Face says. "The ephemeral is now the eternal. This jackass video will be with you, and with all of us, always. How's that feel? How does *always* feel to you?"

That incipient realization of embarrassment, of being owned, of having stumbled unaided into this punishment, is no longer incipient. The dope's face now registers the full realization of his stumped chumpdom, and for several seconds he actually seems as if he could sob, if only there weren't twenty onlookers aiming their ire at him.

And then Face does something key at this point, a move that showcases his command: he lets go of the dope's shoulders. He lets go of them. He steps back a foot and really looks, really sees the dope. Now, having let go, Face loses this contest if the dope dashes. But if the dope cannot dash, if the dope is compelled to remain fixed there for reasons he will understand only later, then Face wins.

And the dope does not dash. The dope does not move. The dope is held there still, but not by hands.

Face says, "What are you doing with these clowns? These friends of yours. Take a look at them. Do they look like friends?"

But the dope doesn't want to look now. Turn your face from the truth and perhaps the truth will vamoose.

"I have another question for you then. Look at me. What's broken inside you that makes you think you need these clowns? What are you, twenty, twenty-one? We're the same generation. And you're still behaving this way. What's broken in you?"

The dope manages to squeak out a query despite himself. "Broken?"

"Broken. Internally. What are you avoiding?"

More marsupial sounds from the dope.

"You don't know? All right. Let me tell you your story then. I know it start to finish. Your story is written all over your every move. First, you wanted to be an athlete but were too frail. Your bad skin made you a bad pick for the girls. Your parents put you on course for an Ivy League, they didn't care which one, but all you could accomplish was Boston College. You have an older brother who's the athlete and the brain. He's the looker who got all the independence, all the attention—he had all the talents. *He* went to an Ivy League, and you watched this for years, quietly seething. Your older brother never paid you much attention; he sensed you were an also-ran and not worth his time. Your good mother doted on you but your busy dad ignored you. He was busy with work, you knew that, but he was busy also with your brother, who was the winner worth his time, and you knew this too. How am I doing so far? Because you're still a non-athlete with bad skin and a 2.8 GPA, and you'll perform whatever act of desperation might get you not only attention but affection. Isn't that what you want? To show that you're as worthy of esteem as your older brother? Your brother earned that esteem. What have *you* done?"

And the dope utters something revealing then, a line that seems to confirm most of Face's summary. "You don't know my brother," he says.

It's nearly a whisper; you've got to dial up your volume to ten to catch it.

Face says, "Yes I do. I know your brother. I *am* your brother. I have the gifts, all the promise. And I know *you* too. I know *people*. *Don't* I?"

And the dope doesn't say no. The dope doesn't say yes, but not saying no is all the yes we need. The dope blinks at Face, as if attempting to blink away the mushrooming realization that he has always been, in every relationship he's ever had, the unlovable little brother trying for laughs he confuses for love.

"You still haven't told me your name."

"Chad."

"Chad. Yes, you are a Chad. So, you asked if I have any advice for you, Chad? How about this: stop goofing on people who have devotion. You think you're being comical but you're only being cruel. And here's the other thing. Listen to me now. Your older brother? Your father, or these jackass friends? You don't need them. What's your devotion: answer *that*. Because if you answer that then you'll see you don't need to impress all the people in your life you think you need to impress in order to be valued. Find your devotion and you cease being a jackass. Name your devotion and you see your future. Find out what's authentic in you, Chad."

It seems at this juncture, by the way he diverts his look from the dope to consider his twenty other captives, that Face might be ready to dismiss the dope, might be satisfied with the exchange and ready to move on—but no. The complete showman—and it's but a small step from showman to shaman—the complete showman must construct the right finale, or be astute enough to know when the right finale has presented itself to him.

Because incredibly, against every expectation you've ever had of him, the dope says, in another whisper so faint you almost cannot hear it, "Jeans."

And Face says, "What's that?"

"Jeans."

"Jeans?"

"My devotion, I think. What's authentic, like you said. Jeans. I want to design them."

"Jeans," Face says. "You want to design jeans."

"I want to design them. I have this software I use, and I design them. I have a sewing machine, everything. I make them."

"Jeans. You make jeans. Okay. All right, Chad. Now we're getting somewhere."

"Most jeans aren't as comfortable as they could be. Elastane is important, no more than 2 percent—actually I'd say 1.5 percent—but pocket position is also key. Also the inseam: proper inseam width is key too. Also the bottom hem: can't be too narrow, can't be too wide. Jeans have got to *look* fitted without *feeling* fitted."

"Jeans. Chad, I'm beginning to see your future. I can never find the right pair of jeans. Maybe for all the reasons you just said. And you know what? I'd pay for a pair of jeans by you."

"You'd . . ."

"Pay for a pair of jeans by you. I'm thirty-two by thirty-two. Design them, make them. Design them for *me*. How long do you need?"

"How long? I mean, I could make them within, I don't know, maybe two weeks."

"Two weeks from today, right here in this spot, at this same time. You bring me my jeans and I pay you for them. You need someone to invest in you? You want someone to believe in you? I'll do it. Two weeks."

The crowd doesn't exactly gasp but their mouths certainly look as if they *could* gasp. One of the twenty spectators back-pats the former dope, and for the first time since he tottered into the frame, the former dope's whole face breathes into a kind of relief, a full-body exhale.

Face says, "Did you feel that? Just now? Right here between us? What was that feeling, after that deep breath you just took? Your whole posture just changed. Your forehead unwrinkled. Your shoulders dropped. Did you feel that? What's that feeling that just happened with you?"

"I don't know," the former dope says, in another whisper you almost can't hear.

And Face says, "*I* do. I know. You just named your devotion. You just ceased being a jackass."

Cue the applause. One woman swipes at a tear, another gives the former dope a quick embrace. One guy shoots up his arms in a kind of cheer. They are obviously in awe after being present at a genuine revamping. There's one more appreciative nod from the former dope as he walks off screen to the spot where his delinquent pals had just been standing before they left him. The former dope seems to consider their absence for two beats, three beats, and then he pivots and pushes on in the opposite direction. And the video, this viral Jeans Clip that led to radio spots and speaking engagements at companies all over Boston in the following month, ends there.

This clip was my first real glimpse into what I would understand much better as I got sucked up into Val Face's orbit: that Face's face was just his means to get you to hear his take. Because in the U.S.A. we attend only and always to what comes beautifully packaged.

■ ■ ■

ABOUT HIS CONTINUED CALLING in the weeks after the Jeans Clip, his vision to ditch college and unchain himself into the American wilderness to enlighten the hapless multitude: Face would later write of it in semi-Pentecostal terms, as in being baptized by the fire of the Holy Spirit. He didn't employ those terms precisely, but in his memoir he writes of his charisms, those divine faculties passed on to a deserving person by the Holy Spirit itself, so that this deserving person might then wise up the many dullards of the earth, be teacher, healer, chanteur, coherent talker in tongues. This, according to Face, was what Face had been given: charisms.

And before I'd met him, when I was reading his memoir in prep for my fanged article, I thought that here was a guy who runs riot through the glades of megalomania. Here's another American narcissist who wants to rub it all over you. The Jeans Clip emboldened him, and as views of the clip rose and rose, as more radio shows and podcasts summoned him, as more Boston companies sought his wisdom to buck up their personnel, he grew more emboldened still.

But then he got ill—treacherously—for a month during his final year at BU. Doctors of both body and mind couldn't make east or west of it. Total lethargy; no appetite; enigmatic rashes; rapid weight loss; hallucinations; fevers, sweats, shakes. Test after test, each one confirming zilch. He even considered joining the priesthood at this point, so walloping was this unnamed illness and the thoughts it made. Antidepressants were mentioned, then meditation, yoga, herbs. In this illness he conformed to the familiar plotline of gurus: severe distress followed by the slow convalescence, the revelation therein, the enlargement of a vision, a higher calling. You see this with these characters, Ignatius and Zoroaster, Jung and Luther and their guru kin: they mistake the states of their own stomachs for the spirits of everybody else. But the illness and its resultant vision are decisive.

Face's illness, despite the Jeans Clip, was preceded by the "period of doubt" required of every aspiring magus, the "wandering in the wilderness" in order to be shown his holy path. Face's own wilderness was just Commonwealth Avenue between Kenmore Square and Boston University Central, sometimes veering slightly north to ankle along the esplanade on the Charles River, orating at—this is true—orating at uninterested mallards about his devotion, his dilemma: to leave BU, to give up his dual degree in psych and philosophy and become a charismatic, or to remain and become another academic drudge with all the abstruse prose to prove it.

Orating at *ducks*—quacked.

He even had one of those biblical dreams prophets are always going on about, a dream in which he was visited, *spoken to*, by the divine. Yes, his calling came complete, came canned, with a dream, as in Numbers 12: "If there is a prophet among you, I the Lord make myself known to him in a vision; I speak with him in dreams." Gotta be pretty special for that, pretty chosen. (*My* dreams? I'm disoriented in a department store, looking for a shirt without a brand name on its breast.)

After the monthlong decisive illness, after regaining clarity, he dropped out of BU. His firefighting father was enflamed: Val would have been the first family member to finish college. His son dropping out of BU one semester short of graduation in order to enact his gifts of charisma was not what he'd have called an employable choice.

■ ■ ■

HERE'S HOW THE JEANS CLIP and his street-corner capers led to his being booked in Boston clubs. Her name is Matilda Farn.

Matilda Farn was to Val Face what Colonel Tom Parker was to Elvis—well, sort of. Now, twenty-first-century fame doesn't need a Colonel Tom Parker. Twenty-first-century fame needs only an internet connection. But if you've got the internet connection *and* the Colonel Tom Parker, I'd say you're in pretty good stead.

Matilda Farn owned and ran Café Bay, a theater space cum wine bar in downtown Boston, behind Copley Square, a place loosely modeled on Cafe Wha? in Greenwich Village, where Farn had been a barmaid in the late '60s and early '70s. Dylan, Hendrix, Springsteen, the Velvet Underground, Lenny Bruce, Richard Pryor: Farn had framed photos of herself with all of them. Her Café Bay put on folk singers and comedians, singers and poets and violinists, even Fosse-style cabaretists, anyone who could wed razzle to dazzle, who could lure fifty watchers into the joint. She met Val Face one summer eve as he was orating at fifteen Bostonians in Copley Square beside the Kahlil Gibran plaque.

While I was preparing my research, in the midst of being the chosen chronicler of Face's New England romp, I rang up Matilda Farn—Face had passed me her number and instructed me to contact her: he knew she made a good chapter in his story—and she invited me to Café Bay. She still oversaw the place at a robust seventy-plus that looked hardly sixty on her. She'd been dutifully mentioned in just a few profiles of Face, and Face pens a loving tribute to her in his memoir—in a spasm of bombast, he calls Farn his John the Baptist—but he had never before given a profiler permission to interview her.

Our convo happened at the empty café over late-morning java, Matilda Farn so denimized—hat, shirt, skirt—she looked to be a wrinkling billboard for Levi Strauss. Sitting in an empty nightclub in the morning, in lanes of winter sun, felt as I remembered feeling when once, for some reason, I visited my fourth-grade classroom on a Saturday morning: as if I were getting a whole other angle on the scene.

"Tell me about the first time you saw him."

"Well, I'd *heard* him first. He was doing this weekly spot on some show at WBUR, where he'd go around Boston and do his thing with strangers. Then of course I saw the Jeans Clip and just said *Wow*. But when I first saw him, he was in Copley, holding about fifteen people totally rapt. I was on my way here, at my usual time, five or six, and I see this gorgeous kid surrounded by people. I didn't know what he was doing, but I saw him and just went *Wow*. And then I put two and two together: this was the kid from the Jeans Clip."

"Then what happened?"

"Then I watched. I squeezed through people to see what he was doing, what instrument he had, or a Bible, or whatever, but he was just talking. Or *preaching*, maybe, though it didn't sound like preaching. That's what I couldn't explain, how he made preaching sound like the common sense you'd been waiting your whole life to hear. Usually someone preaches at you and you want to run the other way. But with Val, you wanted to get closer. I can't say if I would have stopped and listened if he hadn't had that face on him, and that body, hot damn."

"But what was he saying that first day when you saw him?"

"He was talking about the internet, I remember that. And happiness, too, his whole philosophy. He had lots to say about dedication, about dedicating yourself to your inner realms."

"Self-help stuff then," I said.

"Yes but it didn't sound that way. I can't explain it. It was *smarter* than self-help. Self-help is just corniness that wants your money, you ask me, but Val didn't want anything. That was part of his power, I think. He didn't have a tip jar out on the sidewalk. He'd initiated a kind of conversational circle, I guess you could call it. We had something similar in the late sixties in the Village, spontaneous *happenings* among strangers. We were hippies, sure, and there was always a guitar, a tambourine, a harmonica, whatever. But our conversation was what counted. Strangers became intimates pretty fast in those days. Hell, you had to. But Val had that same quality: with him strangers become intimates."

"How do you explain that?"

"Honey, I can't explain it, as I say. But I think it's these times we live in. These cyber times, the world changing so fast. I think that has something to do with it. People just aren't plugged into each other anymore. Not in any real way, I mean. Not as we used to be. It's scary, I think. So, with Val—I'd say every era gets the healer it needs, the voice of reminder, I guess you can call it. Reminder of what matters."

"Was Face having a conversation when you first saw him, with these strangers, or was it a monologue?"

"A little of both, I'd say. He'd get the fifteen or so people talking to *one another*, not just to him. That's what I remember the most: the balls on this kid. He just strolls into Copley and starts corralling strangers, I don't know how. By sheer *face*. By sheer voice, I guess. You see this kid, he's got the word *Face* on his T-shirt, and he looks like some Roman god, and you just can't ignore him. How many people you know could do something like that?"

"You didn't think he was nuts?" I asked.

"Nuts, no. With a face like that? Those shoulders? Honey, don't be silly. That's the thing about Val: nothing about him says crazy. You've seen these street performers, these guys handing out pamphlets, and you can tell right away: totally bonkers. But Val—I think it's sheer vibe. Something inside him radiates something to you that makes you want to draw close to him, a total stranger. That's the thing I can't describe, that ineffable *thing* he has."

"Some inner power."

"An inner power. I've met dozens of superstars and most of them had it. Jimi had it, big-time. All Jimi had to do was stand there, never mind the guitar, his playing—all he had to do was *stand there* and you went *Wow*. Stevie had it too."

"Stevie Wonder?"

"Oh yeah, Stevie Wonder, for sure, but I'm talking about Stevie Nicks. I was around her a bit in the seventies, when she was in the Village for a time, and she had that ineffable thing, same as Val: the voice, the face, the clothes, yeah, but something *inner* you couldn't name—you just had to be near her."

There on the wall, not five feet from us, was an eight-by-ten black-and-white photo of Stevie Nicks and Matilda Farn.

"That's what grabbed you that first day with Face? That inner power? Why you asked him to perform here at your club?"

"I waited till he was done that day and I just went up to him and told him. I said: *Kid, you gotta get off the street and into my club. Your radio stuff is good but you have to be seen not just heard.* Remember, he was corralling fifteen, twenty strangers without any effort, with sheer charisma, without any prior publicity or any hook, gimmick, anything like that. Think how many people we could get into this place if we actually advertised those talents, that kid's charm, that face, really publicized it all over the city, and on the internet. We could fill this fifty-seat place in a jiffy. So that's what we started doing."

"And it worked."

"It worked. First we'd get maybe a dozen, then maybe thirty, but pretty soon we reached capacity at fifty, and then people would be *lined up* outside. Remember, he was giving speeches to Boston companies too, after the Jeans Clip, and he even did some modeling, some local stuff, at this time, for the money. But I think he's at his intimate best with fifty, sixty people max. See this photo here? That's a hundred people lined up outside here, about a month after he started performing each Friday and Saturday night."

"You gave him his start."

"If you want to put it that way. But I was self-interested too. How many folksingers and stand-up comedians can I have in this place before people start getting bored? I was looking for something different, something unexpected, but I didn't know what. Not until I saw him in person. And when I saw him, I knew that he was what I'd been looking for, even if I couldn't exactly say what he was doing."

"Being charismatic. Giving therapy."

"Honey, therapy's cheap. Therapy's a racket, you ask me. Val doesn't do that. He's not a therapist or guru or anything like that. He really is, as he says, he really is a charismatic, and so that's why I can't fully explain it. Like a magician, right? You love what they're doing but you can't explain it, and if you could explain it, you wouldn't love it anymore. It's like that with Val."

"He has tricks."

"Well, his trick is getting you to release something in yourself, to take back your own understanding of yourself, to identify what's real. You know what was the most gob-smacking thing I saw that first day I met him?"

"Do tell."

"After he was done with those fifteen people, and we were walking over here so I could show him the café—well, the fifteen people he'd been preaching to? They were *still there*, still sitting on the benches and the pavement, actually talking to one another about what Val had been saying to them. He'd been talking about *a soul wound*, he called it—a soul wound. Which was all about how the iPhone and the internet conspire to crowd out our attention to our souls. And that's what those people stayed to talk about among themselves. They were exchanging numbers and emails! Complete strangers. Val did that."

"I've been trying to figure out his Rosebud, you know, what in his past explains his drive, but his memoir makes his upbringing seem pretty ordinary, as if his specialness sprouted from nothing at all. I can't figure it out."

"I don't think greatness will ever let us figure it out. Trust me, I've been around great people and it really is a mystery. You can't explain Val. You just have to experience and accept him."

"But I mean where's the deprivation in his boyhood that makes him eager for a rapt audience and the filmed communion?"

"Beats me. I never met his family and he never told me about any deprivation. But I don't think he's really eager for anything, as you say. He has a gift, and he has a job to do with that gift. The gift demands exercise, so it really doesn't matter what Val wants. But my guess, regarding his fame, my guess is that he came at just the right time, when we needed him most—some relief from the stress of our online lives. He's something genuine in a sea of frauds."

"So how's business here since the days of Face's start? Looks as if you're still going strong."

I indicated the framed photos of Face that bragged from every wall of Café Bay.

"Oh, I don't have to worry about revenue anymore. My nights of worrying about rent have been gone for a while now. Thanks to Val. He pays my rent here every month, and also the salaries of my two bartenders and two cooks. Even got them health insurance. He takes care of his own."

"He's grateful to you."

"I don't know why. He saved *me*."

■　■　■

AFTER HIS TEN MONTHS at Matilda Farn's Café Bay, as views of the Jeans Clip kept climbing, as his radio and speaking appearances multiplied, Face's ascension got a bit harder for me to compute, so rapidly and inscrutably did his star-stars align. That alignment is clutch, because you can have ability and ambition to burn, you can do everything right, but if your star-stars aren't aligned, if your star-stars aren't constellated, you can forget it. Something in the zeitgeist decrees that a certain performer is now needed, now ready for super-stardom, and down swoops the zeitgeist to snatch the performer and propel him upward.

What's clear is that Café Bay led directly to Face's being booked in ever larger theaters and venues in greater Boston, which led to more speaking and modeling gigs, which led to more views of the Jeans Clip and others, and so on, which led to the L.A. talent scout and agent. If Face had been a twentieth-century performer, New York would have been a paradigmatic step in his ascension, just as it was for two of the main faces of twentieth-century American fame, Mr. Dylan and Ms. Madonna. But the twenty-first century rendered New York null in a star's ascension: the Big Apple gave way to a much bigger Apple. Val Face hopped New York entirely, went straight from Boston to L.A.

The L.A. agent, Veronica Klaus, approached Face with exactly what you would expect an L.A. agent to approach Face with: not just modeling gigs with guys whose names you know—Calvin Klein and Ralph Lauren—but with the only L.A. project that made sense for what Val Face did: a reality TV show.

I discover myself saying *of course* a lot in this chronicle. Of course a reality TV show.

For roughly a year Face and Veronica perfected the pitch, the pilot, the episodes, and then began shopping it from studio to studio, to the usual cable players, A&E and Bravo and their kin. During that year, Face became an L.A. fixture, busking on Sunset—from his memoir: "I was always most in my element on the street with a dozen people"—his New England milkiness a welcome novelty among all the feral tans of ersatz persons, all those lacquered dolls.

And along the way Veronica landed him what she'd hoped to land him: TV roles, commercials, modeling gigs. In one *Law & Order* he played an unrepentant poisoner with such magnetism, such alluring witchery, you wouldn't have much minded sipping his cyanide. That same year he was a medium player in one of the *Pirates of the Caribbean* atrocities: he impersonated a gay plunderer and in the process made Johnny Depp look lacking—not easy. Who knew he could act? Be charismatic, sure, but act? Wait a minute: charisma *is* acting, isn't it? His performances were so scene stealing, so nuanced, with such depth of comprehension, such conveyance of complexity, that you began to get what those first viewers were looking at when they saw *East of Eden* in 1955 and James Dean anguished all their hearts with his raw-wound beauty. I do not overstate.

And then the reality show was greenlit, and this reality show was the genesis of how he got to be not just a household face via Messieurs Calvin Klein and Ralph Lauren, but a household name. He and Veronica called the show *American Face*. From a self-marketing standpoint, that turned out to be a crucial, lucrative move. There are lots of great faces on the globe, but a great *American* face—that's something else.

American Face ran for four highly rated seasons, and some weeks, it seemed, you couldn't get away from it, such was the publicity, the online assessments and deconstructions, the social-media puffing and proclaiming. People somehow went gaga for it. The show had him visiting every state in the union to bless everyday Americans with his charisma, proving how adaptable he was, how paradoxically chameleonic and singular. He could show up at spring break in Orlando, Florida, and commune with disrobed coeds sloshed to shreds, kicking sand, and clamoring to pet him before hearing Face's opinion of their futures, the difference between a life well made (devotion) and a life in tatters (spring break). Do you know how hard it is to get sloshed undergrads in Orlando to stand still, quietly listen, and nod with some semblance of comprehension? Very. He could also arrive at a Republican soiree and fund-raiser in Galveston, Texas, and, while proving that authentic charisma defies the categories of herbivore and carnivore, he could seduce a porcine senator into embracing an undocumented worker and actually rethinking his stance on what *illegal* means.

The most popular episode, the one that onliners couldn't stop clicking about for several weeks afterward? The one at that sterile porn château in Burbank, California, and not for the reason you might suspect—haunches, bosoms, deforested genitalia; Richter-scale ejaculations for him, orgasms of the seismic kind for her—but because it was startling to see these sex pros, these seriously insincere moaners, blush and giggle at the charismatic powers of Val Face. Those prodigies of the profane behaved most averagely—most humanly. (They, too, were children once.) These had to be the least subtle, least furtive citizens in America, and so it was truly wowing when they all went limp at Face's shaft of subtlety and furtiveness, his quivering charm, his low-key lauding of attributes nobody ever talked to them about, nobody ever noticed.

There was Misty Middle getting misty-eyed when Face somehow knew about the recent completion of her GED. "As a college dropout," he said, "I honor all those who return to finish their education." And then—genius!—he said: "I hope to follow your example and go back to finish my own degree some day." Some hand just off camera had to pass Misty Middle a Kleenex.

There was big Beau Arrow knocked down to lash-batting innocence at the lauding not of his dick but of his diction: the word *inde-*

fatigable had exited his mouth mostly unmangled (and even Face seemed surprised at this). You should have seen the strong-jawed pride of Beau Arrow when he successfully held up his end of the discourse about *le mot juste* and the similarities between body language and language: "Words and bodies and me have always got along *real* good."

Then there was Ginger Galaxy touched to tears to hear about the importance of the necklace her dead mother had bequeathed her, a silver Cross of Peter. She'd all along thought it meant subversion, badass black magic, but as Face caressed the cross at her jugular and called up the onetime Catholic in himself, he tenderly explained to her that it meant reverence for the tortured Christ. Peter understood that he was unworthy of being crucified in the same manner as the Messiah; the upside of upside down was an assertion of humility.

"I'm in the wrong business for humility," said Ginger Galaxy.

And she sat there on a sofa letting the teardrops dangle from her nose, remembering her mother. If it's possible to see revisionary thoughts on someone's forehead, you could see them on hers. Not long after this episode aired, *Porn News Monthly* reported that she had retired from the biz (she was twenty-two) and, with Face's help (he penned her a letter of recommendation and paid the first year's tuition), entered a divinity program to become—only in America—to become a minister. At the many outraged Evangelicals who criticized her onetime porning, she flung this riposte: "Ain't you squeaky fuckers supposed to be all about forgiveness?"

At the close of that episode, with Ginger Galaxy, Beau Arrow, and Misty Middle gathered on a couch, Face sermonized to them, but not as they were used to being sermonized to. Porn stars bang through life having to endure the censoriousness and scorn of the Normal Class, since everybody assumes that porn stars have monstrosities where their childhoods should be, psyches so agonized they must abase their bodies for our masturbation. But Face pulled a switcheroo and told them, with actual conviction, that they were performing a necessary public service in promoting masturbation—masturbation being the best alternative to pubic disease and teen pregnancy. And then, even more extraordinary, because it was falsity without any hint of fraudulence, Face called them *athletes* and *artists*.

They needed and wanted to hear what Face needed and wanted them to hear, and, more important, they needed to believe it. That was Face's parlor trick: he could make you a believer. As to the quality and applicability of those beliefs: that's a separate question.

■ ■ ■

DURING THE FOUR YEARS OF *AMERICAN FACE*, he compiled much of the team that would remain with him as his celebrity rose into the altitude of A-list. But how does an anti-cyber celeb make it in an ultra-cyber biz? My article suggested that Face, despite his damning of the internet, owed his career to it. His was a twenty-first-century fame in that it burst to life at just about the time cyberspace was becoming necessary not just for celebs, but for everybody under eighty, an indispensable part of every under-eighty's life. Face knew that he needed the internet because he knew that fame cannot be severed from the means of broadcasting it.

So in the midst of *American Face*, scarcely three years after he was effectively the employee of Matilda Farn, Face now had his own employees, namely a regiment of ardent techies, twentysomethings with degrees in advertising and marketing. He had one Video Director, one Artistic Director, two Cyber Czars, and three others under them. These savvy youths created and commanded the web side of his career, hooking millions of followers by posting clips, supposedly charming aphorisms, and lusty photos atop senseless mantras such as *Get Your Face On*. They also live-posted from behind the scenes of *American Face*, from stage performances, from modeling shoots, from commercials, from film sets.

You can see all the clips for yourself. If he attended a film premiere, foxy and tuxedoed on a scarlet runner, his techies loomed nearby, posting said foxiness. Shooting a commercial for GM? His techies were there, showing you what it's like in commercial world, posting pics of a Corvette's steroidal engine. Backstage with the late-night hosts? The techies hoofed along, typing and swiping. Like blinkered horses who never looked left or right, these techies never looked up. Tumbling headlong into public fountains was a not infrequent danger for them.

Despite all the cyber work necessary for the maintenance of his fame, Face frequently went on record to disgorge his view that life was much simpler before Apple got ripe (and never underestimate the aching nostalgia for perceived simplicity). Face's anti-internet shtick was integral to his image, yes, but it was also a barking exhibit of hypocrisy. It was easy, I think, for him to maintain this cognitive dissonance because he didn't handle the cyberspaces of his brand.

If Face could not have avoided this oddly unmentioned hypocrisy, there was something else he couldn't avoid once he became an outsized celebrity: the tabloid romances, dalliances with runway models or musicians who could have shopped for clothes in the kids' section. If Face had unshipped himself from one dalliance on Monday, by Tuesday he had docked himself in another. He had a thing for wispy brown hair and blanched skin, for freckles dappled across intrusive cheekbones, constellated across boney shoulders. The tabloid hacks had followed his erotic esprit with all the gravitas of war correspondents. They ambushed him at airports, museums, movie premieres, concert halls, ski resorts, restaurants, golf clubs, tennis courts; on sidewalks, on bicycles, on scooters, on vacations; beachside, hillside, alpside. Look, there he is in a garish Porsche with garish Porsche, at the Whitney with Whitney—my God, was he cheating on Porsche with Whitney? Had Porsche been blown into the sea by a slight breeze?

He also managed to avoid the familiar celebrity fix of being caught in some form of social insensitivity, caught saying, posting, doing something that grates against current fragilities. These days stars are held hostage by sanctimonious swarms on social media, and if the stars have been found transgressing against those self-appointed commissars of conduct, God help them. They are immediately threatened with banishment, hectored into issuing an apology of rote, sniveling self-abnegation, of forlorn showiness, as if they'd be outed as cannibals: *This video of me in preschool taking a lollipop from another child does not represent the person I truly am. I have spent the last few days listening to the pain my actions have caused, and I am deeply remorseful. My ignorance did damage to friends, colleagues, and fans. I have no one to blame but myself. I set standards for myself, but I have not met them. I am ashamed of how ignorant I was. I am committed to becoming part of the solution and not the problem. Thank you all for giving me this opportunity to grow. To all of those I have offended with my privilege, I am deeply sorry. I can and will do better in the future.*

Face also managed to avoid the snares of hedonism, the drug-and-alcohol woes common to so many celebs. He would not move chemically through his fame; no need to inject himself to sleep, or pill himself awake, or booze himself onto stage. No amphetamine afternoons for him. You get these celebrities, holdouts from 1970s excess, for whom full speed ahead means a head full of speed— splurgers who slurp the sort of narcotics that in half an hour have them speaking in the tongue Gaelic came from, then hopping around after succubae only they can see.

Here's my guess, which I can make now after my time in the presence of an A-lister: superstars, when they are not superstarring in the altitude of the stage, must be bothered by a vampiric fear of worthlessness, the terror that at any moment, they will be found out as frauds. Their arrogance in daylight is really a panicked defense against their self-scathings at midnight. They know how flimsy is the whole edifice of fame. The drugging and boozing are not the effect of boredom in the lulls; the drugging and boozing are a firewall against the scorching self-doubt. But Val Face did not drug or booze because Val Face, I would soon see, was not besieged by fears of worthlessness and fraudulence—not even a little.

After the fourth season of *American Face* his fame was, Oprah-like, gigantically assured. He said see-ya to TV shows and ascended to feature films and huger modeling, to three-thousand-seat theaters, to corporate endorsements and his own merchandise—to one of the outright strangest careers in this nation's whole history of fame.

III.

The marquee of the Boston Opera House exulted his name in bulbs against a leaden sky stacked with the promise of more snow. The flurries were flustered: they didn't know which way to blow. December hadn't received the memo saying that while Bostonians understood a certain chill was expected at the reanimation of winter, we objected in the strongest terms to these twenty degrees. Night had already come down on Boston and it wasn't yet four. In the fulgent buzzings of L.A. and New York, night never comes, no matter the season. But in Boston's mythical winters, night descends with such mass you could be waylaid in some nineteenth-century hamlet just west of the Berkshires. The Boston night is still austerely Calvinist in its aesthetic. Judge Sewall, on a brief respite from noosing witches in Salem, beseeched God to "Tame Thou the Rigour of our Clime." God didn't listen. God never does.

So after a longish day, starting with my interviews of Face's onetime pals Lucy Genovese and Carmine Feludi, it was a popsicled writer who reached the Boston Opera House that night, wearing a coat only

half as padded as it should have been, in boots with fur that left much
to be wished for. My scarf, you'll recall, had been whisked away by
surly wind two days before on my walk to meet Face at his hotel, so I
was frigid through the throat. And my left hand, thanks to an AWOL
glove, was iced enough to unfever someone's forehead. I was twenty
minutes early, since I'd been reared by a man who believed being ten
minutes early meant you were already ten minutes late.

That morning at six a.m. I'd received a text from Face's assistant, or the assistant's assistant, someone with a V name, which had
told me when and how to arrive. In the warm breath of the lobby
of the Opera House I was confronted by a bodybuilt security guard
and her sedentary scowl who escorted me to the rear of the lobby,
through a door guarded by another bodybuilt scowler, and down a
darkish hallway hued red by exit signs. Empty of audience, the lobby
dashed and dinged with Opera House staff and Face operatives preparing for doors-open in another hour.

We came upon greenroom territory, active backstage showbiz
realms. The security guard, having just been walkie-talkied somewhere else, was content to leave me there unattended. Her whole
aspect spoke to my being not her problem. Nothing to do then
but stand there to the side and wait to spot Face or any handler I
could recognize.

How everybody hubbubbed and bustled back there, a whole
choir of Face's minders, entire chorus lines of keepers. I saw crews
with wires, cords, ropes, and others on their devices swiping, scrolling, clicking, into headsets decreeing what must be done and how fast
they must do it. A sound snafu needed fixing; a light issue required
repair; the security checklist demanded checking; bandwidth

begged for band-aiding. The more senior Face operatives gave direc-
tions to interns with the skin of mannequins and T-shirts that said
Face First. Since they were all Hollywoodians, their T-shirts probably should have said *Face Lift*. One had lips so plumply implanted
they looked stuck on. I counted eighteen humans between Opera
House crew and Face's own. That's a lot of humans just so one guy
could pass around some charisma to a houseful of Bostonians.

Three women in their twenties sat at a folding banquet table
with their riot of screens, three apiece, and their latte cups, a snake
pit of cords beneath their sneaks, one grinding a clump of gum so
strenuously I thought it was some kind of new upper-body workout.
These were the trinity of Face's techies, set up like courtside sports-
casters, one of whom was so elaborately inked she looked vandal-
ized, another so pierced she would soon spring a leak. Rather than
stand there conspicuously orphaned, I thought it best to approach
these techies and ask for help. I'm not one of those ass-headed males
who won't ask for help.

"Hi, hello, it's me," and I pointlessly flashed my press lanyard
dangling waist-length. Pointless because it didn't say my name on
it. "I'm the, uhh, the appointed writer? From *Beantown* magazine?
Seger Jovi?"

The first techie looked to the second techie who in turn looked
to the third—looks of slow dawning. The one shrapneled through
the cheeks with shiny objects said, "Right. You wrote that article."

I could see this was going to be a motif with these people. I just
stood there looking guilty.

Said the one with insectoid textures inked into her limbs, "How
can we help you?"

"Oh, I'm looking for Face. Or for—some assistant? Is it—is Veronica her name? Something with a V. She texted me this morning."

"Veronica is not Face's assistant. Veronica is Face's agent."

"Ah ha. So Veronica is Face's agent. Well then, who was the one who greeted me at the hotel two days ago? Was it—wait, I know: Valerie."

"Valerie wouldn't have greeted you. Valerie is Face's assistant. Valerie's own assistant would have greeted you. You mean Vera."

Lord, all these infernal Vs. Face's managerial system was utterly Masonic: wheels within wheels. Why did he travel with a battalion of babysitters? Soon I'd no doubt be meeting the chef, the masseuse, the accountant, the psychiatrist, the nutritionist, the trainer, the pilot. Then the maid, the manicurist, the landscaper. Probably the acupuncturist, then the chiropractor. Face and his wife no doubt had a nanny even though they had no children. Wait—if they needed this much help in life, *they* were the children. To become a celebrity is to commit your own adulticide.

I must have been cogitating on the above in openmouthed silence because the inked one said again, "How can we help you?"

"Can you just point me toward Face please?"

"Vanessa can help you," and she pointed. And when she pointed, this one, she pointed with her whole arm, straight from her neck, as if the harder she pointed, the sooner I'd leave.

I looked yonder. "Ahh," I said, "Vanessa." Pause. "Who's Vanessa?"

"Vanessa is Vip's assistant."

"Is what?"

"Is Vip's assistant."

"Do you say Vip?"

"That's right."

"What is a Vip? Or wait, you know what? Never mind. I'll go ask that one over there."

But by the time I weaved between darting crew and reached where that one over there was, that one over there wasn't there anymore, which put me in precisely the spot I'd been in before—orphaned on the sideline. So I waited until someone became astute enough to notice my waiting, and soon someone did. In her hands was a creature of some sort.

"Will you please hold the dog?" she said to me.

"Hold the dark?"

"Hold the dog."

She appeared to be gesturing at me with an oblong of fur.

"Eh?"

"The dog. Hold him please?"

"Oh. That. Hmm. Well. Actually. Can't do it."

"Can't do it?"

"I was attacked by a dog once."

"Oh, don't worry. Poopsy is as gentle as a kitten."

"I was attacked by a kitten once."

"But my dog's never attacked anyone."

"Looks more squirrel than dog, actually."

"Then why won't you hold him?"

"I was attacked by a squirrel once."

"Well." Pause. "You certainly seem to have led a safari life, my friend. You really must come round sometime to tell me all about what you haven't been attacked by," and she gently passed the thing to a lackey, only to turn back to me two shakes later.

"Who are you, my friend?"

"But I'm Seger Jovi. I'm the chosen writer."

One, two, three seconds for this to land.

"Oh, Mr. *Jovi*, my *apo*logies. The writer. I mistook you for one of ours."

"Oh, perfectly all right. I'm always mistaken. Err—always mistook? Who are you?"

"I am Val Face's wife, Mr. Jovi. I am Nimble. So pleased to meet you."

Five feet two inches tall with a neck like a wrist, London raised, Oxford educated, Nimble was descended from an obscure lineage of Thai royalty. By everyone's account she had an eight-cylinder intelligence and was said to be the mind and spleen behind Face's fame. Her demeanor was both officious and pleasant. She was obviously someone who could step through her days in an autopilot of multitasking pep. When she locked onto you with her own startling eyes she did so with a subtle certainty that said whatever she wanted from you, you will happily make sure she gets it. Armed with a law degree and the metaphysical cross-dressing of Krishnamurti and Kant, she was the founder of her own fashion company, and spoke in an English so refined, with lilts so Victorian, my own Boston patois sounded barely Cro-Magnon right next to it. She spoke like someone who might soon employ *summer* as a verb.

"Ah, hello," I said, "Mrs. Face. Err, or, is it Ms. Nimble? Just Nimble, gotcha. Well, hello, I'm pleased to meet you. Thank you for—for having me."

She wore an ice-blue dress of—was that cashmere?—and indigo boots so suede they were still bleating. They smelled of whatever fawn, kid, cub, or pup had just been butchered to make them. Yes, here we had footwear of unimpeachable animality: they sheathed her feet in barnyard noblesse. She herself smelled of tangerine and let me sully her toy palm, a handshake neither hand nor shake. Her jawline and forehead, her lips and chin and nose: I just wasn't used to such symmetry because such symmetry just wasn't used to me. Most of us will never know skin that sterile. The poreless make me nervous.

"Mr. Jovi," she said, "welcome, welcome. I couldn't be more delighted that you've decided to make amends for your article. Thanks so much."

Again with the article. I felt rather as Dostoevsky must have felt when given that midnight reprieve from the firing squad: grateful, sure, but also a bit peeved at the whole mix-up and wishing others would stop mentioning it to him.

"Well," I said, "you know us unbelieving Catholics, always making amens."

"Not amens. *Amends*."

"Ah, right, those."

"So delighted to meet you. You're no doubt looking for my husband. I can take you to him."

If Face could deafen you with his beauty, Nimble's own beauty might best be labeled nonassertive (an effect helped along by her emancipation from Revlon) because, despite her symmetry and skin, she had a flaw. Her left cornea revealed a white scar across it (scissors accident, second grade), but this blemish, spooky on you and me—it half masked where that eye was really looking—this blemish only added to Nimble's allure, perhaps because everything else on her face was of total harmony.

"Are you hungry, Mr. Jovi? We have food."

We poor ones typically know how to answer that question, but just then, my stomach was a jangling clamp of nerves, so I had to answer in the negative. Then I followed her down a set of metal stairs, along another concrete hallway hued red by exit signs, to a conference cum banquet room showboating an absolutely profligate array of food on long tables, steaming from silver trays. Nimble stopped here to poke her head in, but there was only a chowing coven of crew members done with duties and fortifying themselves for whatever else awaited.

"All this food," I said. "Wow. Face must get really hungry."

I yearned to snap a pic of this manna and text it to Estelle but wasn't sure of the protocol regarding pics of manna. Estelle and I regularly salivated at food magazines the way other poor people went around salivating at large houses. I saw meatballs bathing in marinara, coils of linguine fra diavolo, hunks of chicken parmesan, whole pyramids of cut bread. And those were only the first four trays. Just what lay hotly tempting in the other twelve?

Nimble said, "My husband usually doesn't eat before a show. He supplies this food for our crew."

I'd have remained there in a trance of masochistic gawking, cruelly teasing my gut with the sight of such grub, if Nimble hadn't moved on down the hallway with a gait that said I better do the same. Underlings passed us in the concrete hallway en route to whatever task they were paid to perform, and Nimble knew all of their names. She greeted them, touched them lovingly on their shoulders, told them what stellar jobs they were doing.

"Oh, Ms. Nimble," I said, hurrying to get into pace with her, "my apologies for back there, for not holding your dog. I'm sure it's nice. It? Him? I didn't mean to shun Pooper. Pooper? No, Shitsy. Shitsy?"

"Poopsy."

"That one, right, Poopsy. Sorry—wretched with people's names. I don't know how I'm supposed to keep straight all of Face's Vs."

"Keep straight all of Face's what?"

"All of his Vs. All his people with V names."

We stopped there at the door to the greenroom.

"An interesting coincidence, I know," she said. "Can I ask you something else?"

"Ask away."

"Do you plan to tell the truth about my husband this time? We'd all appreciate the truth this time."

"The truth, of course, I understand, Ms. Nimble. I really am, you know, really am sorry about my article. And I'm so honored to be here."

"And we're so pleased to have you, Mr. Jovi. But one other thing," she said, her hand upon the greenroom's doorknob, "and I hope you won't think me rude. I don't mean to be. But we really must do something about your . . . garments."

"My eh?"

"Please don't be offended. But your attire, Mr. Jovi. It is a mistake."

"Mistake?"

"White socks. Brown boots. Black trousers. Beige belt. Sweater of uncertain shade and provenance. We can do so much better."

Even her criticisms were pleasant.

"Ah, so much better. I see. Fashionly, you mean."

"Well, it's just . . . You make something of a racket in such garments, Mr. Jovi. If you're going to be with us for a spell, why not some fresh apparel? To be more among us."

"More among you?"

"*Among the Just / Be just, among the Filthy filthy too.* Do you fancy Auden? I love him."

"Ah, Auden, you bet. Is that line, though—is it about *clothes*?"

"It's about blending in, I think, in order to observe better. Can my assistant see about supplying you with more fitting apparel? Would you mind?"

Nimble's assistant would see about supplying me with more fitting apparel. Nimble had an assistant. Well, of course she did.

■ ■ ■

You know how it is when you open a door into a room expecting one person or two only to find that it's your surprise birthday bash and the room holds twelve of your closest chums in conical hats who whistle and hoot and shout all sorts of bliss at you? Well, my entrance into the greenroom wasn't anything like that, except that there were twelve people in it, almost all of them on their screens and giving off airs of officiousness. This was Face's central team of handlers and protectors, not one of whom tilted up from a screen to hello and hurrah the anointed writer. Which could have meant that they were responsibly engaged on behalf of Face, or that they abhorred me for my article, or that my duds were such an affront to their L.A. aesthetic that they confused me for a janitor. Which—funny story for later—which wouldn't have been the first time that had happened.

And there, there at the center of what seemed a diorama, there he was—supine on the best sofa, in great jeans (unbelted), great black T-shirt (untucked), and great suede chukkas (untied). His beauty was astonishing, the kind of astonishment that keeps astonishing even after you think you've got used to it. Because you haven't really. There just was no getting used to what you weren't used to seeing, even if you kept seeing it.

"Everyone," Nimble said—and only then did everyone look up—"I'd like to introduce you to the writer for our New England tour. Some of you might have seen him in our suites two days ago. This is Seger Jovi, author of the article you all know."

"Hi, everyone!" and I gave a real windmill wave, just to make sure they all felt waved at.

Unsmiling, they rose. Unexcited, they approached. Unfazed, I met them halfway. Out of sofas and armchairs were coming a body-guard and his bodyguards, a manager and his manager, a publicist and her publicist, and so on with the assistant, the agent, the stylist. Minuscule grins, tiny pleasantries. Coppertone Californians in the fame game, they were primped and nipped, polished and pruned, exfoliated, fitness-trained, name-branded, eyeing me as if I were something the cat had discernment enough not to drag in.

They commenced introducing themselves to me but I couldn't tell one from the other or guess their specific purposes. Nine-tenths of being famous seems to mean encysting yourself with others who have unclear or redundant job descriptions. Aside from buffering the star against juntas of paparazzi and fetching fresh lattes, what did they *do* on tour with him? Was someone going to lay out for me how the manager differed from the agent, the publicist from the assistant? There was an entire lexicon of celebrity I couldn't speak.

Still supine on the best sofa, Face grinned. "Hey, *paisan*, welcome to the Citizens Bank Opera House."

As a Bostonian, he really shouldn't have called it that.

"Thank you, Face!" I said. "Let's do this!"

Everyone turned to my awkward exclamation with miens that said: *Such an awkward exclamation.*

After Nimble watched me get greeted by names I would not remember, she said, "Mr. Jovi, my manners, I apologize. I've forgotten to offer you a beverage. Mario," she said to the bodyguard, "please get Mr. Jovi a beverage? One of the good ones."

This Mario charged to the fridge with a zip that belied such a hard-won pasta gut. A butlerine bodyguard, then. I'd soon come to see that everything Mario did he did with loyal resignation to powers much greater than his own. His head, I noticed, was a hexagon, which didn't seem at all comfortable, and which emphasized the fact that he was barbarically barbered. His haircut looked self-inflicted. You've seen specimens of this sort? Anthropoidal. He had nose hair you could hang ornaments from. And his heft was the kind that didn't look as if it had expanded, blubbily, from some fitter incarnation, but rather as if it had been strapped on, buckled, a meat suit. He looked rather like the ungulate Robert De Niro at the close of *Raging Bull*.

"Seger, come hither," said Face, and after Mario handed me a glass bottle of mineral water, imported and sparkling and so lavish it was corked, I went hither, to the armchair Face had indicated.

"Hi, Face!"

More exclaiming, darn. I couldn't help it. Nerves.

He sat up, stretched legs onto the coffee table, and crossed ankle over ankle while I downed a whole burpful of water so well bred I felt all my organs bloom.

"One of our two cameramen is sick tonight, Seger. We need you."

"Oh, darn, sick? Poor guy. But, err—I'm not a doctor, sorry. Thought about it at one time, actually, but med school is so costly, I just couldn't—"

"We need you to *film*, Seger. You and Marty—Marty's over there in the cap. Say hi, Marty—you and Marty roam through the audience during the show, filming whatever's filmable, the audience reactions, especially when I'm out there with them."

What was the meaning of this? Film the show? *Me*? When there were a dozen people in that room and a dozen more backstage who were privy to what needed doing camera-wise? What other bafflements lay ready to bushwhack me?

"Oh," I said, "I've, uhh, never filmed anything before. I mean, I use my iPhone to shoot funny videos for Estelle. For instance, this morning—"

"Seger. Seger, pay attention. There's nothing to it. You see that camcorder over there by Marty? A caveman can work it. You just turn the thing on and point. It does everything for you. Film what's interesting, all through the show, and later our techies will go through the footage and choose the clips we need."

What could I say?

"I'm your guy, Face. Let's do it!"

I'd planned to use this pre-show block of time in observation and interview mode, getting down every behind-the-scenes detail, speaking footnotes of wisdom into my iPhone. But now Marty the cameraman was passing me a machine, a digital camcorder with a stabilization handle so that even a palpitating rube such as myself couldn't mess it up.

Marty said, "Here's the power. Here's the viewfinder. Here's the record button. Just press this on and point."

And my thought just then, holding the impressive density of the machine? Two days earlier I was a distinct nobody, and tonight I was an integral cog in the charismatic mechanism of Val Face's fame. Here we had what might be dubbed *vicarious importance*, precisely the feeling every star's entourage walks around with. This was the closest I'd ever get to knowing what lotto winners feel when all the numbers on the screen match all the numbers in their hands.

With twelve typing, texting minders in this greenroom and my inability to distinguish one from the other or recall their names, and with Face now consulting with an Opera House operative, I strapped the camera over my shoulder, checked my responsible list of questions, tapped record on my phone, and went to Nimble to get it started.

"Our cameraman for the night," Nimble said as I approached her. She was standing by the greenroom's fridge. "So nice of you to help us tonight, Mr. Jovi. I suspect that being down in the audience will give you insights backstage alone can't provide."

"Insights, right, exactly. Do you mind if, can I ask you some questions?"

She looked at her tiny diamond wristwatch and said, "Of course," and then she uncorked a bottle of imported water to make all her own organs bloom.

"Right, okay," and I aimed my phone at her. "How does Face prepare for a show? You know, what's his *process*?"

"Oh. I'd say my husband doesn't prepare at all. I think he wakes prepared. He's always prepared, or so it seems to me."

"Ah, wakes up—prepared. Always pre— Interesting. But, I mean, he's really a virtuosic raconteur and soloist, so what's his, his process to accomplish that?"

"*A virtuosic raconteur and soloist.* I love that, Mr. Jovi. Can that apt description appear in your profile? I love it. But as I say, I don't think there's much process or prep. My husband improvises. It's all completely genuine and spontaneous. No set list, as it were. I think my husband walks into an audience and *feels*."

"Feels. Gotcha." Pause. "Feels what?"

"The crowd, its aura, its energy. Things like that."

Uh-oh, bad sign, those two words, *aura* and *energy*. They usually precede the word *universe*, and not at all in the way Mr. Kepler meant it. And I noticed then, around Nimble's wrist-neck, a diamond cum crystal pendant, which naturally made me wonder if she was a crystal lady. You know the sort: they believe in the mystical bunk of crystals, take retreats to New Mexico, usually have something reverent to share about UFOs and the Great Pyramid of Giza. Wear a lot of purple. Also beads. Typically smell of aromatic oils. But *don't* typically sport degrees from Oxford, as Nimble did.

"Right," I said, "the crowd's energy. Can you just, maybe just a bit, elaborate?"

"Well, I'd say my husband walks into a crowd and feels. Feels what they need. That's his gift. An intuitive power, I'd call it. It cannot be planned for. Cannot be set up. Each show is different because

each crowd is different. My husband accurately intuits the tempera-
ment of each audience, but each audience of course consists of individuals, right? And so my husband has a direct individual interest
in every person. I'd say my husband must gauge what is needed. My
husband must divine."

Divine, the verb, though she no doubt meant the noun and
adjective too. She'd poured her corked and sparkling mineral water
into a glass and was sipping it now as if it were chardonnay. She held
the glass with her pinky cocked.

I said, "So that's part of his personality then, divination."

"No no, not *personality*. Personalities are for other people. My
husband has a *character*."

She spoke with such magnanimity, with such a welcoming face
and soothing voice—a voice that sounded the way lilac smells—that
it was hard to tell if or when she was ribbing me.

"Character, gotcha. There are lots of people here behind the
scenes. Does it always take this many hands to get Face on stage?
When he started out—you know the Jeans Clip . . . uhh, obviously
you do, sorry . . . but when he started out, it was just him and a digital camera and a street corner."

"That's right. So much has changed since the Jeans Clip. That
was a decade ago, give or take. Our full team is not always with us
on tour, but we're now in the process of launching several merch
lines, work that has to be completed within the next two weeks, and
my husband needs our team with us to facilitate all this. It's a lot, I
know. But my husband does not want video calls, emails, or texts for
such important work. My husband wants our people with us. His
performances are only one aspect of Face Inc. What you see here is

only the beginning. We have plans that go way beyond performative charisma and my husband's persuasive oratory."

"Which merch do you mean?"

"Well, let's see. There's our clothing line, called Facer. A cosmetics line called Facial. A bedding line called, for now, FaceDown. I'm working on a better name than that. The words *face down* remind me of someone dead, I'm not sure why. Drowned in a pool. Oh, and there's a sporting line called FaceOff."

"That's a lot of—lot of lines. When does he have time to prepare his charisma? Oh, wait, shoot, forgot: he doesn't prepare. Err. Another question. His fan base, from what I can tell, is all over the map. Every type appears to love him." Pause. "That wasn't a question, sorry. Does every type love him?"

"Well, I'd say, in the West, definitely. In the East, probably less so, and we've measured it, believe me. But in the West, my husband's fan base is always eclectic." She paused to aim a smile at me. "My husband is the human phenom."

Nimble, I could see, was in command here, and one of the things she commanded was ecstatic approval for her husband. Her presence alone seemed to murmur plaudits for him, even though, if you had asked me, Face's abilities spoke pretty much for themselves.

"The human phenom—gotcha. But the tickets are more expensive than many humans can afford. Have you ever considered, ever thought of lowering them for the—for, you know, the working class? Since Face comes from the working class."

"I know what you mean. And I sympathize. We're working on that. But, on the other hand, transcendence isn't cheap, Mr. Jovi. My husband's fans make an investment in this experience. Right? One gets what one pays for."

"I suppose, yes. Would be nice, is all I mean. For the working-classers."

"Have you been to a show before?"

"I haven't."

"Well, what you're about to see tonight is reciprocal. My husband does most of the work but not all of it, and reciprocity has its price. I think the investment they make is the investment they *must* make. And all get their money's worth, Mr. Jovi. I hope so, anyway."

Someone said, "Fifteen minutes to doors open, everyone."

"Last question," I said. "I've been pondering this. What's the *origin* of Face's, I mean of your husband's, talent and ambition? I mean, where does this drive, this drive to commune so intimately with strangers *come* from?"

Up she pointed, and up I looked.

"The ceiling?"

"You're funny. No, no, the *cosmos*, Mr. Jovi. I think my husband at his best is a conduit to the sublime, as any real poet is. Of course I'm biased, but as far as I'm concerned, he was born of a virgin"— and her half grin told me that she was only half kidding.

We guilty unbelieving Catholics just don't know what to do when immaculate conceptions are introduced into the dialogue. It must have been hard on his mother, this virginal status.

"Let me leave you with this thought, Mr. Jovi, and then I've got to be off. How many individuals in history could have done what you're about to witness my husband do tonight? Holding such an audience rapt by sheer force of charisma? I'd say ten, maybe twelve

individuals in history could pull off what you're about to see. That's
no hyperbole. You'll see. I'm so glad you're with us tonight," and
off she went to consult with somebody who looked lawyerly enough
for consultation.

About the ticket price: a fascinating spout of rationalization, you
have to hand it to her. The tickets are expensive because otherwise
fans wouldn't believe they were getting anything valuable. Pay so
much to see Val Face and you damn well *will* have a religious awak-
ening, if you're not a sucker. What a lucrative way of assuring the
profundity of the experience. Prepaid revelation.

Just as I was eyeing over Face's central handlers and trying to
gauge which one would welcome interruption, Face said from the
other end of the room, "Seger, Marty'll take you out into the house
to show you around, where you should film, the balcony and orchestra, the whole space, just so you get your bearings," and there was
mustachioed Marty already at my elbow.

I mentioned earlier that at this time I sported a talented mustachio to rival that of Tom Selleck circa *Magnum, P.I.*, and while Marty's shrub couldn't match mine or Tom's, it looked sharp on him,
showed he had a mind for style.

"Marty," I said, "I salute the upper lip," a greeting we mustachioed ones often exchange.

"In salute," he said, and we both performed the members-only
gesture: running the right thumb across the left side of the mustachio, then across the right, and out we went into the house.

Marty took my nodding self through the orchestra, the mezza-
nine, the balcony. I appreciated the upper-lipped companionship of
my fellow cameraman, but I already knew the layout of the place,

having seen, about fifteen years earlier, from three different angles, the White Stripes play three memorable nights here, tickets that ate half my teenage savings but worth every nickel of that gorging. So I guessed I understood what Nimble had just told me about the Face fan who didn't mind paying so much to experience him. *Transcendence isn't cheap.* She could have said that again.

Marty's voice: sometimes you had to squint your ears to hear him. He was instructing me to switch my angle if my angle caught him in the frame. Face didn't want footage of either cameraman filming, though sometimes this was not to be dodged.

"Whenever Face comes into the audience—he spends about half the show in the audience—we've got to be on him, but from different angles. That's our job, to get him when he's down in the audience. The two stationary cameras will get him when he's on stage, so our purview is only the audience. Don't film what I'm filming. Keep moving. If you don't, they'll scream at you because the camera blocks their view of Face."

"They'll scream at me?"

"Oh yeah. They'll scream at you all right. Comes with the job. So you gotta keep moving."

Opera House security in maroon blazers, outfitted with walkie-talkies and flashlights, talked on the apron with Mario the bodyguard's two underlings. Like most A-list entertainers, Face had fans who reminded you of what *fan* is short for. The previous year, a garlicky warp in Cleveland, feeling insufficiently tended to, charged the stage with an idea to strangle the star. Nimble went ballistic but Face wouldn't press charges. In an interview, Face said that this flipped-out Clevelander was the natural result not of living in Ohio, as some of us might have suspected, but of "the malaise of the Electronic Generation, the plugged-in madness technology has forced upon them." Battered by anomie, this Clevelander. After that show, Nimble enacted a security apparatus to shame those of sultans and shahs.

My and Marty's filming of the show was necessary because no one else in the crowd would be doing it. It was Face's stipulation—he was the first major performer to push for it—that nobody could enter his shows with a gadget. Your phone got incarcerated into one of those incisor-resistant pouches when you entered, pouches with the electronic lock from which you can't jailbreak your phone unless you step back out into the lobby and use that device, the electronic open-sesame.

There was another stipulation, too, this one Nimble's, so serious was she about Face's safety: if your venue wanted her husband, your venue provided metal detectors. Nimble, you understand, wasn't chiefly worried about phones. Nimble was chiefly worried about guns. Because this is America. Because as a Londoner of Thai descent, she could not fathom how a society permits its citizens to amble round with military-grade firepower.

Guns and Fords: without them, an American is just a Canadian.

Someone appeared from stage right to shout at all of us other someones on the apron and in the aisles.

"It's doors open. Everybody back please"—and back everybody went for another ninety minutes before showtime.

■ ■ ■

YOU WOULDN'T THINK NINETY MINUTES could whir by in what seems half that time. All of this adrenalized prep tends to quicken the clock and blood both. Since it was so close to showtime, none of Face's minders was free to be on the receiving end of my queries, though they all promised me slivers of their time the following day when I'd be back at Face's hotel for our first substantive sit-down. Since I couldn't be in interviewing mode, and since Face himself was being requested from every direction, he suggested I eat, a suggestion he didn't have to make twice.

Amazing what tortellini, ravioli, and fettuccini, when augmented by buttered bread and diversified by bowls of Cobb salad before being capped off by Black Forest gâteau and coffee gourmet enough for all of South America—amazing how such larder automatically gives you a sunnier disposition on the whole human lot. After an hour's euphoric feasting, I felt downright drugged, all my neurotransmitters in a cha-cha, stepping slowly lest my digestion become unmoored.

That was my inner state of things as I made it back to the greenroom just before Face was scheduled to saunter on stage. Nimble, a moon in orbit of her host, wheeled a lint roller across his great shoulders and chest, down his belly and spine. Then appeared a dreadlocked blond dude with spikes and studs through his lips and septum, with hula hoops in his nostrils and brows (from the mouth up he looked like something that might hook a halibut), with nonsense hieroglyphics etched into his throat and nape. This stylist brushed makeup onto him, which was a redundancy since Face's face was already wholly without error. You simply could not edit his face; there were no typos there. With fingers like blades did this stylist stab into Face's do and rummage there, grooming his kempt storm of burnished black.

The three bodyguards were getting into guard formation; two handlers who an hour ago had not donned headsets now donned them; minders who had been sitting and swiping were now standing and watching.

I put my phone near Face's chin and said, "Face, with three thousand people out there waiting for you, can you tell me what you're thinking right now?"

"Seger," he smiled. "You're funny. I'm thinking that you better not screw up the camerawork."

Pause.

"Kidding. You'll do great."

"Yeah, let's do this!"

I couldn't seem to eject anything more interesting when excitement whammed into nerves.

Marty then said to me (he'd clearly forgotten my name, mustachios notwithstanding), "I'm going out there to film some of the audience before Face comes out. You tail him to backstage, and get good footage back there, then, as soon as he comes out, you join me in the audience. Good?"

"Great! Let's do th— Okay great."

Then, at someone's word, out we went, down the hall, up the stairs and into the rear of the house. We could feel the throb of the crowd, its chatter, its energetic anticipation. The very air was charged with exaltation and the arrival of eminence, as if exaltation and eminence had actual mass. I never knew excitement could feel like a measurable force.

Someone in a headset, armed with an iPad, flashed Face an inquisitive thumbs-up and Face returned an affirmative. The atmosphere had pulse to it, break-a-leg ethos, though Face, at the hub of it all, looked serenely detached—a professional showman's Zen. Nimble, I noticed, was massaging his right hand: his microphone hand. The three tatted techies zeroed in on their screens as if they were a Mars crew remotely landing rovers into stubborn onetime riverbeds. I filmed it all.

In another minute, as Face and Nimble were having a lovers' powwow in the wings, the houselights dropped, the three thousand roared in the dark, got to their feet, applauded, chanted, "Face, Face, Face." And then the music rose, Springsteen's "I'm Goin' Down," a get-up-and-dance ditty of lapping sensuality. The crowd stomped and clapped in unison, stomps and claps that said *Let's get it started*.

Face smooched Nimble and then, *bang*, he swaggered into the lights center stage, both arms open as if to embrace them all, these fans undeterred by a surprise December storm. Their blast of appro- bation made the building's joists and plinths vibrate; I could feel all my bones humming with it as I hurried back and down into the crowd to start shooting. The crowd *goes* wild? No—this crowd *came* wild. See their willed raptures in his midst, faces contorted as if in the ecstasy of Eros. The whole place was a swaying of hands, and the flock was head-to-head to see who could out-hoot the other.

And all the swaying, all the raving and praising—it all got wilder when Face went into the crowd. Mario and his two lookalike goons rushed to bracket him, venue security helped, while the houselights roused again, revealing a Crayola sea of caps and shirts plugging the Red Sox and Celtics and Patriots, plus the initials we were all used to seeing in Boston: BC, BU, MIT. As Springsteen did his Garden State growl through the amps—the song was on repeat—Face grasped hands around and beside the human wall Mario was, gave back pats, golden grins for all. And I don't mean only to those in the front row of the orchestra, but to clumps of people in every section. They had all arrived with the tingling need to be personally acknowledged by his Highness.

Roughly half of the straight females and gay males between the ages of twelve and eighteen were in full swoon now. Some sweated; some had come prepared to faint. Their squeals were uncannily akin to what you hear on *Animal Planet* when a vixen is calling to her beau. Some of them seemed as if smelling salts might soon be needed. Their pheromones were sticking out all over the place. I hadn't readied myself for such an electric sight. The only time I'd seen anything like this was in black and white footage of Elvis Presley in '56, or the Beatles in '64. You can find more contemporary examples—Bieber fevers, K-pop convulsions—but the real swooning went down in the center of the last century. The zeitgeist seemed to decree it.

Marty and I trailed the security trailing Face, up and down and around, and, damn it, I kept filming Marty filming him. It wasn't easy to alter my angle, what with three bodyguards and two blazered security dudes, plus the fans deserting their seats for the aisle, hoping to pet him, scent him. Funny: when fans couldn't get to him, they got to *me*, clapping, backslapping *me*, as if magically through me Face would receive their ardor. I wasn't prepared for that stamp of spirited fan who, when he spots a camcorder, must stick his head into it, howling and whooping for posterity.

Face's greeting of fans didn't take an hour, only a bit longer than it takes the president to reach the podium at his State of the Union. He couldn't readily get to anybody in the center of the rows but, not

to worry, he blew kisses, gave waves. I couldn't hear what he was saying to anyone, such was the piping applause.

To say that this was an eclectic crowd won't quite do: I'd never
before seen this much aesthetical concussion under one roof. Tweeds
in eyeglasses, some in bow ties. Adolescent males with titanium
mouths. Frat-looking middle achievers high-fiving each other. Teenage girls giggling into rainbow fingernails. The silver-haired and
slumped, cane-led. Veterans of at least two wars, maybe three. Air
Force guys in buzz cuts. The dark-skinned, the mocha, the peach,
the albino. A muster of hippies. Longhairs head-banging as if at a
Metallica show. Preppies in boat shoes, tomato slacks, polo shirts,
canary sweaters. Buff women in Harley bandannas. *The human phenom*: I supposed Nimble was mostly right about that. Or perhaps
the middle-class phenom, because this was definitely a middle-class
jamboree. There is no celebrity without the middle class to bolster
it. What is our obsession with celebrity if not an expression of our
abundant middle-class leisure?

When Face gave a housewife the hug she'd come for, her knees
went wobbly, and as she fainted, a security goon caught her before
her head hit an armrest.

Face then returned to the stage, his forehead asheen with sweat,
the crowd rhythmically clapping even as the houselights shied again.
With mike in hand, he seemed as if he might be ready to unload a
comedy routine. Stand-up comedians were, I thought, the closest
comparison to Val Face since they have only language to work with.
Or else it seemed he might be prepared to descant something Sina-
tran, since there were elements of the young Sinatra in his easeful
charm, his effortless abilities of voice and face. How a guy could look

so imperial, so robed in sanctity, in only a faded black T-shirt, dark blue jeans, and blue suede chukka boots—"Lay off of my blue suede shoes"—was more than my styleless self could comprehend.

"Boston, it's been too long."

Roar.

"How long has it been, Boston?"

Roar.

"Four years? Never again, Boston. From now on, I come back to you *every year*."

Roar.

"My beautiful Boston," he said. "Thank you, thank you. Always good to be back home. Sit, please."

Cheers, blushes, swooning. Teenage screaming. They wouldn't sit.

"I knew I could count on you to come out on a night like this. Thank you, Boston. Please sit."

Cheers, blushes, more mad swooning, more fainting and screaming. People still jabbing up their hands as if in a classroom with the correct answer.

Then, someone snatching at the elbow of my sleeve. It was Luce.

"Luce!"

"Hey, uhh, *you*. Told ya I'd be here."

She'd forgotten my name, even though I had interviewed her just that morning.

She said, "You're the camera guy, too?"

"I've got a whole constellation of talents, Luce. Gotta go. Gotta film! Enjoy the show."

Mario the bodyguard and his two lugs lurked between the pit and the apron, ready to pounce, lunge should anyone get to feeling froggy.

Face said, "Hey, Boston . . . How about those . . . *New England Patriots*," and we were walloped by an intestinal roar.

It was the final year of Brady's reign in New England, and the Patriots were undefeated so far, on track to take the Super Bowl—again. I was just about the only vertebrate in Massachusetts who didn't care about this, although I had to pretend otherwise or else risk the mob getting fascistic with me. The Red Sox were a larger problem: I didn't care about them either, and that's a capital crime in a city where everyone knows scores and stats, where the uninitiated are not just oddballs but apostates. You'd think that a cradle Catholic, even the admittedly tepid kind such as I was, would have taken to such with-the-blood wham and worship.

"Let's hear it for Tom Brady," Face said, and hear it we did.

Everybody was eager to fall for the Tom Brady bit. Sports: it's what we have when we don't have anything else. Sports and celebrities.

After they had tenderized their palms on the Patriots, the crowd finally sat. Some of the swooning was on pause. The teenage girls who'd looked as if they needed an ambulance now looked averagely euphoric. But when Face said, "How's it feel to be without your phones tonight?" the crowd got up, and so we had to listen to another minute of upright, aimless applauding. Then they sat again, but when Face said, "Who's here tonight for self-inventory?" the crowd got up again. All this yo-yoing, this up and down to liturgy. Church had prepared them well. Because this was Boston, after all: the city *started* as a church.

Face said, "Forget your internet connection. Who needs a *real* connection?"

Roar.

"Who wants communion?"

Roar.

"Which are you going to choose? The spiritual or material?"

"Spiritual!"

"Desecration or consecration?"

"Consecration!"

"So what have you been focused on lately, Boston? Renovating your kitchen?"

"No!"

"Are you shopping online? Getting new patio furniture?"

"No!"

"Have those been your concerns? Because if so, you are totally disconnected from yourself, Boston."

Face was against patio furniture? Where are you supposed to *sit*? And never mind that most Bostonians didn't even *have* patios. I mean, the ones on Commonwealth Ave and Marlborough Street did. Of course *they* had patios. I mean the rest of us didn't.

"How are you going to satisfy the demands of your soul? That's the question I want to consider tonight. How do you become aware of those demands? It's getting harder and harder, Boston."

Evangelistic operations were underway here; he was about to turn this entire place into his own tabernacle. I was up at the apron now, beside the orchestra, because I couldn't see anything otherwise. Everyone kept not sitting. And a woman had hollered at me— I'd forgotten Marty's admonition—hollered at me to move the hell out of her way. My camcorder was obstructing the pricey view she'd paid for. When at last everybody sat again I could tramp through the house again, looking for angles that didn't contain Marty and his—his angles.

"Thank you, Boston. Thank you. It's good to see you. I want to talk with you tonight about our problems. We've got problems, don't we?"

Lots of nods.

"Living is a problem. That's what we think anyway. What are these problems we're hooked on? What's broken in your world?"

Trained, people said, "Our souls."

"Your souls. All these distractions everywhere. This is what we do: we obsess over the symptoms because the real problem, the injury underneath what we think is wrong, is too scary to deal with. We patch up what we can because it's easier than fixing the actual injury. Am I right?"

"Right, right, you're right."

"But we can't locate the actual injury because of all the noise we put on top of it. We're terrified of seeking our silence. Where's our depth? That's the question I want to ask you tonight, Boston. Where's our depth? Because it's not on social media. So where? We're merely skimming the surface of ourselves."

His voice on stage was a combo of baritonal beauty and common-sense calm, conveyed not so much by the words as by the glow behind them. Judging by the rapt and raptured faces of many in the crowd, it could have been doubtful if they heard his actual words at all. His voice, vibrantly solemn, seemed to work on them as an enfolding music. You could actually see, literally feel, how he siphoned strength and spirit from the crowd. It was as if their gimlet attention lent him extra breath. He was an ecclesiastic to his own liturgy.

"Have you seen one another tonight?"

Loads of clapping from about half.

"Don't clap. *Look*. Have you seen one another tonight?"

He shot a stare into the wings. "Bring up the houselights," and up they went.

"Look at each other, the person next to you. Not the person you came with. *Take in* one another. Do you see?"

"We see. We see."

"That's flesh, bone, and blood. The Catholics here will know what to do. Embrace, Boston. Embrace your neighbor. No, don't just shake hands. That's not what I mean. And definitely don't fist-bump. Embrace. That's it. Human beings. Say each other's name. Say it. All five senses are firing. Smell one another. Really sniff. Don't laugh. Sniff."

Face gave everyone a minute to embrace and see and sniff, to hear and feel, which might have been forty seconds longer than what was good for them, but this was his show.

His delivery was bathed in a coolness too natural to be calculated. As Nimble had boasted, this was improvisational, although I was sure some of it couldn't be. I mean, as he prowled from stage left to stage right, from the apron to the curtain and back, he made gestures of voice, hand, and breath to convey his sincerity: the right spots to pause, to accelerate, to slow his sentence and his gait, his pace, the way he looped a finger or lifted one shoulder. This had to have been practiced.

But his entire air conveyed that he was on stage saying these words not necessarily because he wanted to, for ego's sake, but because he *had to*, for our sake. And while conveying this he also conveyed something else: the sense that he genuinely liked these Bostonians, liked being here with them in this way, and in return the audience liked him even more. Face had the true performing artist's bipolarity: contemplative and wounded enough to have acquired these insights, he was audacious and whole enough to get on stage and proclaim them. To demand attention for them—at three hundred bucks a pop.

■　■　■

DURING THE EMBRACE-YOUR-NEIGHBOR MOMENT, Face spotted a teen in the first row who looked insufficiently acknowledged by the stranger next to her. This teen weighed about ninety-eight pounds, with treasonous skin and a pink band dyed into her sallow hair. It was hard to tell exactly what was going on with her. She was a whole anarchic wardrobe of emotion, low-level frantic, almost inconsolate without her cellphone, no doubt here because her parents thought it would be resetting for her, and here it was merely *up*setting. She kept jabbing a hand into her jeans only to come up empty, to remember that her phone was jailed within a pouch in her purse. It's a jolt, isn't it, that empty pocket: the closest thing we have to the oh-shit those ancient mariners must have felt when the sextant splashed overboard. At one point this girl held her hands midtorso, in prayer position, her fingers turning and tapping in a mime of texting, then swiping the air as if it were a screen—the *air*.

Face stepped off stage then, and every time he did this the houselights came up, then Mario and his goons glued themselves to him. Then Marty glued himself to Mario, which didn't leave me anyone to glue myself to. So I went around, aside, betwixt, behind for the unexpected vantage. Face went before this teen with that rested grin, that able-bodied body language that said *I'm here just doing my job*. The girl's expression began showing what it shows when star-struck at this proximity: the moist buggy eyes and quaking lips, the looking left and right and left again for confirmation that this was really happening—to *her*. Was she about to be . . . Could it be that she was . . . Was she being *chosen*? By *Val Face*?

I knew the feeling.

"Hi," he said. "What's your name?" and he held out the mike.

"Ruth."

"What school do you go to, Ruth?"

"I go to . . . Winsor?"

"Winsor. The best all-girls school in New England. I'm not sur-prised. But you're nervous, Ruth."

"I'm a, a big fan."

"No, you're not nervous because of me. You're nervous because of something else."

"I'm doing my, my senior research project on you."

"Your senior research project. That's a big honor for me."

He turned to Mario. "After the show, make sure Ruth gets back-stage so she can get an interview for her project."

Then back to Ruth. "So you're nervous. But not because of me. You don't like the spotlight. You're shy, Ruth."

"I'm shy."

"You'd rather all these people not be looking at you."

She looked at them looking at her. "Yeah. I guess."

"Why?"

"I'm shy, I guess."

"Shyness is fear, Ruth. Shyness is uncertainty. What are you afraid of?"

"I guess I'm—I don't really know. Just shy."

"Big Irish family, right? Lots of brothers and sisters?"

"Umm yes. Six of us."

"And you're right in the middle of the six."

"Yes. Well, sort of. I'm the fourth."

Face looked up into the crowd. "How many middle sibs here tonight? Raise a hand."

Two hundred hands shot up. I filmed them doing it, including one upright lout in an aisle seat who wanted me to whiff all his Right Guard.

"Look around you, Ruth. Look at all the other middle sibs. It's hard to carve out a spot for yourself in this noisy world. Hard to find the silence to know who you are. You're worried about *trends*, Ruth."

To everyone: "Remember when *trendy* was an insult? Remember when it meant groupthink? Now it's news. If it's not trending, it's not worthy. Remember when viruses were to be avoided? Now *viral* is an aspiration."

Back to Ruth. "And if *you're* not trending, not viral, then *you're* not worthy. Isn't that your real fear, Ruth? How to *become* yourself, to become valued in a world this noisy and disregarding?"

"Umm, maybe."

"I can see it in your posture, I can see it in your breathing. It's everywhere on your face. You don't think you're worthy, Ruth. Worthy of the world's notice, worthy of being who you are. You don't think you will ever become yourself. Am I right?"

"Yeah. You're right."

"But here's the thing. Listen to me now, Ruth. Becoming who you are—that's not up to them, to the internet, to the world, to your classmates, or your parents, or your siblings. That's *your* call. You know what I'm going to ask you now, don't you?"

"Yes. I mean no."

"Yes, you know. What's your devotion, Ruth? What will you give your life over to? What will *define* you?"

"I've got to do my senior research project."

"Yup. That's your mission right now. And after that, when your project's done, what then? What's your absorption?"

When she didn't expel the answer, because at seventeen she couldn't possibly know the answer, Face lifted his chin and to everyone said this: "I ask the question because we think we have the answer, but the answer obscures the question, and only the question matters. We think the answer is success, or happiness, or one of its American varieties. Wealth, fame. But that answer's not important. Only the question. Are you hearing me?"

"We hear. We hear."

Lots of earnest nodding. Lots of looking inspired.

"Whatever that devotion is, whatever it becomes, who will choose it, define it? You? Or everybody else? You or the internet, or your family, or your mate, or whoever?"

Back to Ruth. "So keep that question with you. Who will choose, Ruth? Who will hold the reins of your life? And the answer to the question doesn't come in a word or a phrase. The answer to the question is in *your* own agency, in your own *living*."

Here was a superstar telling a nervous teen that she was important, that she could *become* important if she understood that her life's decisions must be her own. Choose devotion, eschew distraction. It was precisely the reminder she'd come for, what wouldn't have worked if it had been dished by her parents or teachers. And it was what others had come tonight to see and hear for themselves. Face's communicative mojo was pretty impressive: he lasered all his attention onto one young woman, with a specificity and personal insight that ipso facto applied to the three thousand others watching. With conversational ease, Face had a capacity to read our malaise, to figure out what we need, in real time, and then to sell it to us in a manner no one else could, with a style no one else had.

At the time, I was too amped up to have critical thoughts, but later, I thought this: How was it that this fairly obvious stuff he was declaring at Ruth had the sheen of rare wisdom? All the fans I filmed had that look of gushing acquiescence. It seemed they were responding to Face's celebrity and not only to Face's abilities. Here was a case of having one's talent judged by one's reputation and not the other way around. His fans go into his performances pre-sold, rapture-ready. They pay for an experience and they damn well are going to have one. If you're invested, convinced he's a special charismatic with knowledge you need, you come out having got your three hundred bucks' worth.

"Remember Ruth from Winsor, everybody," Face said, "because she's going to high places," to which the house hooted and cheered.

And for the rest of the show, Ruth remained altered—I checked—no longer stabbing into her pocket for the missing phone: calmed, quelled, *approved of.* And I saw then that Face's ban on gadgets was no self-interested gimmick but an essential element of his method.

He couldn't exercise his complete power if everyone was too busy trying to document it, inserting the wrong illumination between themselves and him.

After the Ruth bit, Face passed thirty minutes on stage hurling obloquies at the internet, the kind of homiletic harangue Moses knew, chockful of Fate and Work and what wonders the Soul can make. His jeremiad followed the pattern of his early Boston forebears: level blame, point out how damned everybody is, then tell them how to repent and make good. Just as those first hot-blooded Bostonians couldn't accept a world made by sin, Face couldn't accept a world made by cyberspace. And no one in the audience seemed to find him a flatline bore during this harangue. Fans couldn't take their eyes off him. Freddie Mercury could do that: watch him at Live Aid at Wembley in '85. It's astonishing. One man with well-nigh one hundred thousand people in one palm of his hand.

Face and Freddie Mercury: whatever they were doing, you couldn't stop watching them do it. It wasn't just their physical gifts plus talent plus intensity that lassoed us, but something else, something other, some inner instability or wildness that threatened to burst sublimely all over us. And whenever Face went down into the audience like a Dante among the damned, he established immediate, uncommon intimacy with fans. It made a tingling en masse.

Just about anything could happen.

■ ■ ■

AFTER FACE'S ANTI-CYBER SCREED came a surprising segment when he spotted someone near the middle, behind the orchestra.

This was a beauty with the gentlest face in the room, insistently open, staunch in its vulnerability. A face like a whisper, embedded in a wishbone of satin black, with a sunless complexion that gave its own light, an organic glisten. It was a face that would not be looked away from. Early twenties, this beauty went to Face in the aisle, and they considered each other there, Face inching closer. All the house-lights had gone up when Face entered the audience, but when he'd found this beauty, he signaled for lights off, and a second later a pole of spotlight found them, fixed on them, only them, two blanched dots in an ebon hollow. The silence was startling. A few thousand people had collectively decided not to wiggle or rustle, to breathe but barely, as if to preserve all the oxygen for Face and this enigmatic beauty and whatever was about to transpire between them.

How to describe that transpiration, that pair of lighted faces, not moving or speaking, hardly blinking, only staring, staring into each other's eyes? The world hasn't yet concocted sentences for such beatitudes. It was as if they were empathic vampires in a kind of limerence, drawing vital substance from each other. As if they were taking on one another's history of disappointment and sting. This was more than merely looking, merely being seen, more than mere attention or acceptance. This was communion of the sort you just do not have in Mass. What were their elevating thoughts, their swell of emotion, as they intently absorbed each other's face in that way? People stared at Rembrandts with such focus. And soon both of them had tears streaking over their cheekbones, tears born of some mysterious mutuality only they knew.

Ponder now: nearly three thousand citizens stood in dark, dark silence watching two faces stare at each other without moving or speaking. And this lasted for four minutes, their silent gravitational lock. Four minutes is a lot of minutes to stare at someone without speaking. Nothing, I was sure, should be beyond our facility to experience it in language, and yet Face and this beauty had briefly entered a realm where words melted into a pool of inadequacy: a realm for monks and their fire-stamped shadows in caves.

In the last seconds of this sharing, their tear-marked faces slowly unfolded into smiles, and when their smiling started, so did the applause, the whistles and woos, and the houselights came up again. Face then hugged the beauty and the beauty hugged back, each dabbing the other's tears with a thumb. Something oddly spiritual had just happened, I was almost sure. They had read, had somehow *felt*, one another's history of ordeal. Was this osmosis or what?

When Face was back on stage, he said, "Your turn. All of you. Go to the nearest stranger and look. Don't talk. Don't blink. Don't *move*. Look. Be two feet apart, no more, and *look*. Really look. Fall into the eyes of the nearest stranger. You have two minutes. Not a peep. See yourself in the eyes of someone else. Go."

And they did it, this loyal flock, for two uninterrupted minutes, which seemed a hell of a lot longer, I tell you. It's not at all cozy, such looking in such silence. That's why we don't do it, not even with our dearest. It's not that we don't want to look; it's that we don't want to be seen. We can't be revealed. And that's why Face told them to do it, precisely because they didn't want to, because it *wasn't* comfortable. Try it sometime: find a stranger and look into his eyes for two minutes without a word or a blink and hardly a breath. Ain't easy, folks.

I would know because, during that segment, someone vised onto my shoulders and crossed all my thresholds. She was clearly from Charlestown, this lady, grew up beside Mystic River. She was draped in official Bruins swag, more dress than jersey. Intrepid and insistent, she and her biceps yanked me to her.

I was in an aisle near the pit, the camcorder rested on one shoulder, when she'd said, "Come 'ere, you. Let's commune." I stood there pop-eyed and frozen and she locked onto me with a stern pinched face that advertised all its concentration. I kept leaning back from her hold but she kept holding fast. I think I let out sounds: *err . . . uhh . . . ohh . . . hmm . . . well.* Then she kept nodding as if she could recognize something in the ponds of my eyes, though I'm certain that what she saw was my own realization that this exercise was essentially un-American. You can't just grab a Yankee and begin boring into his eyes. All the stars and stripes say nay to that.

And after this communion was over, thank God? Another half hour of Face bashing the internet, which was much better than having your eyes violated by a Bruins fanatic from Charlestown, trust me.

■ ■ ■

THE SHOW THEN HAD A Q&A SESSION during which eager interns went into the audience to pass microphones to those fortunate few chosen to ask Face a question. As is typical with a Q&A, the questions kept veering toward the declarative.

The first fan—early fifties, judging from her cardigan—began with "Thank you for taking my question," as if this were a call-in radio show, and then described her son serving in the Third Infantry Division overseas. The audience obediently applauded as they'd been programmed to do, a slow firm applause with stern, agreeing faces of respect and gratitude, at which point the woman looked around and nodded in return, with that refuse-to-cry countenance that welcomes the very pity it's pretending to eschew. Her son was a big fan, etc., and then she thanked Face for giving him and her hope, with Face nodding his humblest gratitude.

The second question that night wasn't an actual question either, though it was definitely a request, the requester a youngish man with such uncontainable bulk he needed help getting up. He had neither neck nor wrists nor waist, neither ankles nor knees: he was unimprovably spherical. I empathized with the sphere, since I have spherical tendencies too, and I rushed to film the exchange before Marty could beat me there. With self-conscious, sacrificial machismo, a woman in the next seat grabbed hold of him and heave-hoed, tugged, damn near yanked. I thought she was going to have to plant a boot on the armrest for better leverage, or else request a plank for prying before she split her pants and spleen, but the guy squirted free after another few seconds and the waiting intern handed him the mike, into which he huffed hard, trying to find his wind after the tremendous exertion of getting up.

"People on my social media, they call me—call me fat. They call me cow. Fat cow. They say go eat—go eat more hot dogs, fat cow. They say, you know, they say I'm ugly, fat and ugly, that nobody loves me, 'cause I'm—I'm fat. I posted a picture, a picture of me and my mom, we were at the beach, at the beach last year, in Revere, and people called me whale. Other mean things, things like that. Fat Frank, they said. Fatty Frankie."

Each phrase was punctuated by a sniffle but Frank didn't seem to be fishing for pity, nor did he seem theatrically bewitched by his own persecution—that's just the way he spoke. The crowd activated that grave hush, that solemn attentiveness required whenever someone inches near bathos while telling of his personal travesty, another macabre tale of victimization by God or man or—or hot dogs.

"Sometimes they send me pictures, pictures of hot dogs. I didn't even really like hot dogs that much, but they kept sending me pictures of hot dogs and they got to looking, you know, looking so delicious, and now I eat hot dogs all the time. So I'm just wanting, maybe, some advice from you, about what, you know, what I should do. I know I'm—I know I'm not—I'm just so hungry all the time, and I need energy."

From the stage, for about twenty agonizing seconds, Face let the venue fill with more empathetic silence, a sizable quiet that stuck to everything in that immense space. Like any showman worthy of the name, Face knew how to exploit these silences to build the requisite tension.

"Frank, what do you think of me?"

"What do I—what do I think of you?"

"Yes. What do you think of me?"

"I mean, I—I like you. I'm a big fan and everything. I read your books."

"Do you think I know what I'm talking about? Up here? Do you think I know things?"

"Yeah. Sure. I think that."

"Do I sound believable to you?"

"Yes, I—yes."

"Sensible?"

"Yes."

"Okay, good. That's good. Then I want you to believe this, Frank. I want you to listen carefully. You're a beautiful man. I'll say that again. You. Are. A. Beautiful. Man."

Compulsory applause.

"Those fiends on social media? Anyone who shames you? They are not beautiful. Hear what I'm saying, Frank. They are not beautiful. I say so. And I know what I'm talking about, don't I? I know about beauty. I'm up on this stage because I know about beauty. Are you hearing me, Frank?"

"Uhh. Yes? But I'm just so—I'm fat, I know I am."

"Okay, Frank. I hear you. I do. Tell me what you think about Rubens."

"Oh. Well, I mean, they're not my favorite, my favorite sandwich at all, but I'll eat them sometimes, sure. It's just that the sauerkraut gives me bad gas."

"Peter Paul Rubens, Frank. The Flemish painter."

"Oh. I mean, I never met him or anything. I'm from Revere."

"All right, Frank. I hear you. Rubens is my favorite painter, Frank. He's a master of sensuality. And he thinks you're beautiful too. He thinks you're lovely. And so does Titian. He's another painter, Frank. Look him up. *Titian*. T-I-T-I-A-N. I want you to look to *art*, Frank, not to the internet. Seek meaning, seek beauty, in what art allows us to know about ourselves. What do you have to say about that?"

"Say? I mean . . . they sound like nice, real nice people, I guess."

"They were great artists, Frank, and they knew things. Things about people, about beauty, about connection. Social media doesn't know things, Frank. Social media wants us to surrender ourselves, to retreat from ourselves and one another, from the most vital and civil parts of ourselves. Social media wants us to despise one another before despising ourselves. And we're better than that, aren't we, Frank?"

To everyone: "I said, we're better than that, aren't we?"

Compulsory roaring, compulsory applause.

"You know, Frank, people want to call me *guru*, don't they? They want to call me *healer*, *sage*. Isn't that what they say? What they call me?"

Nods to the left, mmms to the right.

"That's fine. They can call me whatever they need to. But I'm not any of those things, am I, Frank? You ask me, I'm just pointing out the obvious. Pointing out what you already know but have been forced to forget. *No one* is better than you, Frank, and the minute you see that is the minute your true life begins."

Polite clapping, a bit firmer than golf claps.

"You know, Boston, a long time ago when this city was an infant, there was a thinker who lived right down the street from here, about a three-minute walk, in the North End. His name was Cotton Mather, a holy man, a preacher, and he's got a line I've never forgotten. He said: *The more the flesh endures, the more the soul receives.* Now, you don't have to be a Christian, or even religious, to see the wisdom of that, Frank. Your flesh has endured shaming at the hands of social media, but your soul will be elevated because of it. Believe that."

Well, okay. Not *exactly* what Mather meant, I thought, but okay. I grew up on the same block as Mather did so I'm pretty sure I know what the guy meant and what he didn't. Then, somehow, Face got mortality on his mind, perhaps because Frank looked as if he were a cardiac catastrophe in the making, or perhaps because thoughts of Cotton Mather do tend to shove one into a morbid mood.

To everyone: "Social media drowns out the only question that should really matter to you. What is your relationship to your own death? What does your death *mean* for you? *What is your relationship to your own death?* Seek that answer, *make* the answer in your living, and you will cease to care what the internet offers because you will no longer need it. Are you hearing me, Boston? Do you understand?"

"We hear you," some nodded. "We understand," some said.

"Folks, it took a lot of guts for Frank to stand up and speak tonight. Let's hear it for Frank, everyone."

During this gout of applause, Face said to a handler in the wings, "Be sure you get Frank all of our merch before he leaves tonight."

Because what's the one trusty balm for any American with a problem? Merchandise.

■ ■ ■

THE LAST ACT OF THE NIGHT was an interplay that would, that week, alter everything for Val Face.

Using whatever inner compass arrowed his way, he found a man three rows back from the front, aisle seat, and I beat Marty there to get first dibs on great angles. This man: I'm going to have a hard time describing him because he was a blank, a cipher. There was nothing to him to describe, nothing you noticed, which I think might be why Face noticed him. He was Generic Man, Common Man, totally without expression or distinction. Midfifties, well laundered in clean powder-blue jeans and a plain navy blue sweatshirt, all-white sneaks, thinning sandy hair, smooth faced, average height, average weight—average air. Oppressively average. The only detail on him that might have been noticeable, after you were forced to notice, was a mullet, and not even a state of full-on mulletdom, only the suggestion of mulletdom. This man's manifest lack of specificity radiated something sinister, I thought, or else something sad. With nothing to distinguish him in his looks, you didn't want to look.

But Face saw him. He wasn't invisible to Face. Face didn't seem to care or notice that everything about this man's determined banality said that he was a vacuum. And if there was an enormous nothing to the way he looked and stood, there was also an enormous nothing to the way he sounded. When Face asked him his name, and he said "Bill"—now, hard to get a blanker name than *Bill*—he said it in a voice that was barely a voice. A voice to match his whole aspect of nothing at all.

Face had a slightly bumpy time with Bill because Bill wouldn't bite.

He said, "You feel like just another walking number."

And Bill said, "No."

He said, "Your path to the holy has been stymied by tech."

And Bill said, "No."

He said, "You have ideas about what it means to be alive but nobody hears."

And Bill said it again: "No."

Minutely flustered now, as I was close enough to detect—of all the words Face wasn't used to hearing, *no* was up there—Face had to turn it interrogatory.

"What are you seeking in the world, Bill?"

And with a spooky, noncommittal composure, in that nothing voice from a deadened face, Bill said, *"You."*

The audience didn't know what to do with this, but Face was quick enough.

"Other people aren't our aims, Bill. No authentic connection happens without a guiding commitment. So, Bill, what is your commitment? You don't have to have the answer but you have to have the question."

"But I do have it," said Bill. "I do have the answer."

"Okay, Bill. Let's hear it. What is your commitment?"

"But don't you see?" Ominous pause. "It's *you.*"

Bill was what you might call a heckler in reverse—a heckler inside out. He stood there in all his averageness, disconcertingly still, arms at his sides, staring at Face and ready for more monosyllables. He didn't look agitated; he didn't look torrid. No, he looked consummately himself, nondescript and exactly at peace with the nothingness he was. Fans were getting impatient, thinking, I thought, that Bill was deliberately not playing along, deliberately monkey-wrenching the works. But Face did not dart—Val Face was no darter—and so I kept the camcorder on him.

"You know me, Bill. Everybody here knows me. And you know I call bunk when I see it. You know I can spot the ingenuine from fifty paces. You're not being honest right now. You came here tonight for honesty, for authenticity, but that's a two-way road, my friend. We need willingness, we need reciprocity or you wasted the price of ticket."

"But I did not waste it," Bill told him. "I have wanted this for a long time."

And Bill did something then that Bill definitely should not have done. There in the aisle, three feet from Face, Bill appeared to reach into his back pocket while at the same time taking a step toward Face, and there was something minutely threatening in the way he did it. Mario and his two goons overestimated this threat, guided no doubt by the bodyguard's credo that says it is better to overestimate and be sure than to underestimate and be sorry.

So they sprang onto Bill, and when these three spring, believe me, they spring. They blasted him back, out of the center of the aisle, away from Face, toward the seat he'd come from. But Bill didn't hit his seat. He collided into the people beside his seat, and with others who had stepped into the aisle to get a clearer view. And these Bostonians with whom he collided? Let's just say they weren't the sort of Bostonians with whom you can collide with impunity. No, they were the sort of Bostonians who would have happily battled the British up to their shins in blood while chewing tobacco. These Bostonians, mainly a male duo wearing steel-toed boots and the kinds of jackets that say biker gangs, say skull tats and switchblades, they blamed Bill for the collision and not Mario and his goons for causing it.

So then this male duo, along with one very pissed lady who had been calling *Me, me, me, choose me* while Face had been back-and-forthing with Bill—this male duo and this lady set upon Bill with shoves and elbows and something else that might have been jujitsu. At which point Mario and his goons got into the fray to keep these three from belting Bill. And when *that* happened, when Mario and his pair stepped away from Face to protect Bill, fans spilled from their seats to surround, beseech, attach themselves to Face. If you've ever been in the bleachers at Fenway Park when up pops a foul ball and inebriated citizens trample one another to catch it, you'll have an idea what I mean.

The microphone was then accidentally swatted out of Face's hand. It was on the floor now—you could hear shoes toeing into it: *pfft, pfft*. And then others hurried to this glut of push-and-pull. The whole place had that vague buzzing in the air, whatever happens when a crowd gets frisky and harm is nigh. The font of the air goes from simple Helvetica to something calligraphic, the unreadable loops and swirls of an illiterate.

Heroes, I hear, are made in the moment. You can't *plan* for them. The Seger Jovis of the world live their lives hoping they will never be called upon to rescue the wounded or defuse a threat, but when the call comes in, the Seger Jovis answer. We know that a crisis is no time for flaccid wills. One cannot dilly, never mind dally. Face didn't look nervous when the mob mobbed him—remember, he'd begun his shtick on the streets and, as he attested in his memoir, felt most at home wreathed by a tight crowd—but I was certainly nervous for him. At which point I, our hero, recalled that I had in hand a battering ram: the camcorder.

So I used the machine to plow an avenue through the mob around Face, saying *Stand back, people* and *Clear the way, people*, and *I'm official here, people*. At which point I scooped up Face, so to speak, and, with the camcorder against my chest like Kevlar, and Face under my protective arm, I guided him back to the stage unhurt. *He* was unhurt, I mean. I, on the other hand, had sustained something of a charley horse after being rammed in the thigh by the boisterous knee of some too-tall buttinsky. This act of heroism induced from Face an unforgettable wink and back pat.

Face's Elvis hair had been upset, but even mussed it looked correct, looked intended. Two venue security guards with flashlights like cudgels pointed fans back to their seats, and so back they gingerly went. Some other melee might happen in the aisle and they didn't want to miss it. So another shaky moment passed, Mario talking to Bill, returning him to his seat, while Mario's goons pacified the booted ones Bill had perturbed. Face was on stage again, trying to finger his hair back into place.

"You passionate people," he said. "You lovely Bostonians. Listen, listen, everyone. Retake your seats. Let's applaud your passion, Boston. Let's hear it."

After a minute, after he kept saying it, they fell for it. This was a falling kind of crowd. So they applauded themselves and everyone starting grinning again. And Bill? He didn't at all seem as if he'd just been manhandled by handlers and two booted dudes. No, he looked—*sated*, in his blank manner. Sated but somehow looking forward to something else, something I couldn't see. I got a good look at this guy, at his nothingness, and he must have been tugged, intestinally, by whole astronomies of want.

Things rushed to a close then, Face dispersing his goodbye compliments, his promises that he'd definitely be back the following year. Then he took about sixteen bows to great squalls of applause— he was debauched by applause—and then Springsteen began growling "I'm Goin' Down" again, the houselights at full blare. Helpless not to, Face hopped down into the crowd again to shake hands with the first-row fortunate, to dispense hugs and high-fives, Mario there like a mama bear.

■ ■ ■

BACK IN THE GREENROOM, after several minutes of practically warring my way through the exiting crowd to where I could get backstage—"Make way, people, make way. I'm official here"—I saw Face downing imported water as if he'd just crossed half the Sahara. The effort it must take to give that many people ninety minutes of constant attention and make it come off as not entirely insincere, hokey, or prefab—I'd felt fatigued with astonishment just watching him do it. Now he looked somehow both exhausted and energized. But then exhaustion has its own kind of energy.

Soon Face was getting photos clicked with Ruth and Frank, both of whom had expressions of weepy gratitude.

Frank said, "I haven't left the house in a year."

"Get offline, Frank."

"I will. I'm glad I came tonight."

"Get outside. Give the world a chance."

"I will. I am. Can I ask a favor?"

"Name it."

"Can I—can I touch your face? Please."

This must have happened before because Face didn't seem at all surprised by the request. He took a step toward Frank and presented his shrine of a cheek. Frank raised a quavering arm and placed a hand on Face's face—very slowly, deliberately, as if testing its heat so it would not sear him. He could have been a pilgrim at the Wailing Wall. He snapped shut his eyes and the teardrops began trickling then, as if some sacral potency were flowing from Face's face directly into Frank's body. His hand rested there for a full minute, and the sheer amplitude of this encounter would, it was clear, alter Frank forever.

Ruth, looking on, leaked tears too, but touching Face was something she'd never dare. Face gave her a fifteen-minute, seated interview during which she obtained all the answers she needed for her research project. And the attention Face gave to her then? It was wholly genuine. I watched; I checked. His eyes never veered from her, never scanned the room with impatience, in expectation of something or someone else. He wasn't checking for a better someone to speak with, nor was he silently beseeching some aide to rescue him from Ruth's neediness. Because he didn't see it as neediness. He saw it as humanness. When Face gave you his attention he also gave you the impression that you were the one individual with whom he cared to commune, the impression that there was no one else alive who was more important than you—the impression that you were necessary not only to yourself but to the rest of the world too. I couldn't figure out how he so convincingly pulled that off, but I knew it couldn't be taught. The eye contact, the body language, yes, but something else, something inner, that couldn't be named.

When Ruth and Frank were escorted from the greenroom, their arms were stacked so high with merch—books, DVDs, T-shirts, hoodies, caps, mugs, shot glasses—they couldn't see where they were walking. But their expressions? Dazzled.

Face's custodians all stood talking importance at one another, showing one another whatever was on their phones. I and my fellow mustachioed cameraman, Marty, high-fived our work well done.

"Nice job, man," he said. "Bennett missed a good show."

"Who's Bennett?"

"Guy you subbed in for tonight. The other cameraman."

"He's sick, right?"

"Not sure. He didn't look it. He was here before you arrived. But he just split, I don't know why."

Off Marty went then, foodward. The other dude just split? Why? What did that mean?

Then came Nimble. "Mr. Jovi, wonderful work out there. Thank you *so much*. You're a natural," and she winked.

"Thanks so much!"

I said that mostly to the back of her hair because she was off to somewhere else. And three seconds later something occurred to me, thinking about that wink of hers—call it the sprouting of a suspicion. Winks are tricky. Alone, they mean nothing; you've got to take them in their whole rigging. And here's the whole rigging I suspected. This other cameraman, Bennett, wasn't sick. Nimble had enlisted me, *recruited* me, into filming the show, into being an integral part of Team Face in order to—what? Why? What indoctrination was underway here?

And I didn't have time to figure it out because now, from another nook of the greenroom, along came someone impeccably upholstered in black, as if he might at any moment be needed to help tote a coffin.

"Oh my," his English accent said to my shoes. "Oh dear," his English accent said to my pants. "My my," his English accent said to my sweater. "Dear God," his English accent said to my I don't know what. "Nimble is right yet again."

He had a voice to loosen all your fillings. Is there a thing viler than the sycophantic snob? I doubt it.

"Right again about what?" I asked.

"These, uhh, *garments*," he said, and when he said it, he used his right index finger to up-and-down me. "Nimble said they wouldn't do, but . . . oh my, I couldn't have guessed at the, the sheer . . . *woe* of it all. Dear me."

"Let me guess. You're Nimble's assistant, carrying out a mission to correct my clothes."

This was Boris. Boris was definitely a Boris. He was the kind of person who believes you when you compliment him. You couldn't fail to notice his superior British skin, bucked up by Anglo emollients. He seemed aghast at the sight of me. I resented this, of course, all this *my-my*ing, but, knowing my duds, as of course I would, I had to assent to the essential rightness of his verdict.

"Yes," he said. "Oh my," he said, and again with the index finger upping-and-downing me.

Deep breath—his, not mine.

"Here is a prepaid card," and he handed it over. "For you Nimble requests attire somewhere between Jack Victor and Hugo Boss."

"Nimble what?"

"For you Nimble requests attire somewhere between Jack Victor and Hugo Boss."

"Attire . . . Victor . . . Hugo . . . huh?"

"Just go to Saks Fifth Avenue at the Prudential Center and ask a well-dressed sales professional to save you." And then, eyeballing me vertically, he said it again: "Oh my. Oh mercy," and he winged back over to where I was not.

Face lay on a sofa with his eyes serenely shut, hands folded across his belly—an aftershow snooze, it seemed, was being called for, since he looked postcoital now. His ninety-minute aria had required real endurance, an intense burning of calories. That's why the performing men and women of the world get paid so much. They need the money to make up for having left pieces of themselves on stage. I can recall how Father Grasso at Sacred Heart Church in North Square, after his Sunday-morning, rock-starring liturgies and homilies, would recline in the sacristy and forbid us altar boys from speaking to him, inching near him, even looking toward him. We needed to scram because he needed to recharge, needed that sepulchral silence to jump-start his will for further interaction with everybody else. Priests, you know, are performers too.

■ ■ ■

SOON IT WAS CLEAR THAT WE WERE GOING, though I didn't know where, and didn't ask if I was included, since surely the chosen writer cum cameraman would be included in the night's proceedings. I wondered if we might be en route to a restaurant to sup and quaff accordingly. Face and I and his tagalongs then tailgated one another down a concrete hall, and I had to pause longingly at the door to the room with all the heaving food.

Then out we went to a white limousine nickering warmly in the alleyway, there beside a Dumpster and its heaping reek of trash you couldn't smell thanks to such cold. Five inches of snow had fallen with the promise of fifteen more before morning, and I just went along with Face's core team, eight of them, into the polished leather womb of the limo. It smelled like birth in there.

A right and two lefts around the Common and we were at the hotel. A gaggle of Face's fans had congealed at the revolving door, beside a put-upon doorman, about twenty fervid people and their breath tremoring in the twenty degrees, under several tons of wind and a crooked sleet still midtantrum.

Nimble said, "Is there no way to enter around back, Mario? Did we not plan for that?"

"Yes, ma'am, we planned for that. Face asked to use this entrance."

Nimble said to Face, "Darling, *must* we?"

"Real quick, one two three, love. We can't let them down."

"*How* do they discover where we are staying?"

"Real quick, love, promise."

Mario said, "Don't worry, ma'am. I've got this."

Mario and his men flopped out of the limo then and buffered Face from his twenty trembling fans and a clattering of paparazzi with their rapid-click cameras. As Nimble shivered there, Face let selfies be taken with abandon, and even posed for paparazzi with those Chiclets teeth of his.

Near the door, snow like icing on our coats, waiting for this impromptu commingling to end, Nimble said, "Mr. Jovi, thanks again, so much, for tonight. Valerie or Vera will be in touch tomorrow with your schedule."

My quickness told me that I was getting the boot for the night, though it was barely ten thirty.

"Of course, tomorrow. With my—did you say my schedule?"

"The day's plans, yes. I understand tomorrow is your first conversation with my husband. Valerie or Vera will text you in the morning."

When Face was finished being Face on the sidewalk, and as Mario's two men, helped by two hotel security chums, balustraded themselves against the fans, Face came to me.

"Seger, nice work tonight. I was watching you, *paisan*. You really got around the place."

"Ah, well, you know me: I get around."

"You coming up with us?"

I looked at Nimble with, I think, Bambian eyes.

She said, "Shouldn't you be finished working for today, darling? It's late. I understand there's a full day tomorrow."

Goodnights all around then, and as Face and his team got whooshed into the revolving hum of the door, I watched them go, no one glancing back to see where I might be and what I might think about it. Behind me, city equipment clanged and banged, those orange behemoths fanning sand from their rears, plowing the half foot that had fallen, potholing the pavement, their yellow lights twirling on top.

So I buttoned my coat's upturned collar, hatted the head, scarfed my lower face (I'd somehow acquired a scarf that was not mine), then jabbed a hand into a pocket to retrieve my one remaining glove. I thought a little Bob Seger might swell my newly deflated mood, so I popped in the earbuds and played "Ramblin' Gamblin' Man," and then "Against the Wind," since I certainly was.

But before I turned to lean into the slanting snow, to find a merciful coffee joint somewhere in the lighted chambers of this city, I saw him there, standing, his whole blank self, his elaborate blankdom, at the window beside the revolving door, staring, staring with a dead expression into the hotel lobby.

Bill.

IV.

If you have ever filmed a stage performance with a camcorder at the behest of an A-list entertainer, you know that it's not easy to clamber down from the opioidal high of having been so central to events. About my opioidal highs: it's Estelle's job to reel me back down from them. That night, as the nor'easter pelted our windows, and as my fingers and toes tapped with irrepressible giddiness, Estelle took solemn sips of licorice tea.

"What do you mean that the camera guy you subbed for wasn't really sick?" she said.

"I don't know for sure. The other camera guy hinted at that. Said the guy showed up but then just split. Maybe he felt ill after he got there. But I suspected that something was afoot."

"Afoot?"

"Definitely afoot. But I was a tangle of nerves and couldn't really tell."

She then told me to give her every detail of what happened from the time I got to the Boston Opera House to the time I left it. This took well-nigh twenty minutes.

"I think I know," she said. "It's your devotion to them."

"Aha. My devotion to them." Pause. "What devotion to them?"

"It could have been their scheme to make you a loyalist, a move to get their writer into their clutches."

"Their clutches, right. But, love? Aren't I already in their clutches?"

"More so. More so in their clutches."

"Right. But, why?"

"Maybe because an objective outsider writes the truth. But a writer who's on the *team* writes what the team wants written. And if that writer is a former Face basher who's seen the light? What's better publicity than that?"

"I'm part of their publicity then."

"Right. You're part of their publicity."

"Okay, one question, Estelle. Who cares? We agreed to this and signed their contract."

"Right. I know. Maybe just watch yourself with them? Maybe don't trust them too much."

"Leave it to me, sweet."

And then I was on the floor performing pushups. I could see small tornadoes of dust whirling beneath the futon we used for a couch. Everything about Face hollered fitnessing, carb-counting, rapid metabolic rates, carrots, rhubarb. His whole syndicate of sitters looked as if they spent twenty hours a week jumping rope and another twenty jamming fingers down their throats. I had to belong. But are push-ups supposed to burn so much?

The next morning at nine saw me en route for new plumage at the Prudential Center in downtown Boston. Nimble's assistant, you'll recall, had told me to get myself to Saks Fifth Avenue, if I'd heard him right, which wasn't easy to do, believe me. Hear him right, I mean. When I made the crossing into the men's section, the doors had just opened and I was the only shopper there. A salesman soon saw me. This was Ronald. Ronald wore a name tag. From five feet away, Ronald took me in, and while taking me in Ronald looked as if he wanted to take me back out. Ronald sighed—at *me*. People in novels are forever sighing, absolutely *love* to sigh; it's all some of them *do*, sigh. You start to wonder how they get anything else done. Ronald was like this. Not nice to be sighed at—it jangles the concentration.

Exquisitely appareled, Ronald said to me what he'd say many more times that day: "May I help you, sir?"

"Ronald, you may. I'm the chosen writer for Val Face's New England tour and I'm here to make improvements upon my person."

"I'm sorry, sir?"

"I'm the chosen writer for Val Face's New England tour and I'm here to make improvements upon my person."

"Val Face. O*kaay*."

Obviously not okay, though, because he was eyeing my attire as if he'd soon be called upon to bludgeon it.

"Improvements to your clothing you mean, sir?"

"Improvements to my clothing I mean, Ron."

"What do you have in mind, sir?"

"Victor Hugo."

"I'm sorry?"

"Val Face's wife's assistant, he gave me this prepaid credit card"—I showed him—"and this assistant said for me to dress like Victor Hugo."

"I'm sorry, sir?"

"French novelist? Nineteenth century? *Hunchback of Notre Dame*?"

"I don't understand, sir. You're looking for . . . clothes for a hunchback?"

"No no, the clothes are for me, Ron. *Totally* support the hunchbacks. But I'm not shopping for them today."

"So the clothes you'd like are . . . Can you tell me again, sir?"

"Victor Hugo, the French novelist. I have to dress like him."

"I still don't . . . Can you show me a picture of what you have in mind, sir?"

I clicked Victor Hugo photos onto my iPhone and showed him.

"This is what you want to dress like, sir?"

"Just following orders, Ron. I think, you know, since I'm the chosen writer, Val Face wants—I mean Nimble wants, and her assistant, this guy, don't get me started—they want me to, I guess, look the part."

"Are you . . . certain, sir? This doesn't seem correct."

"Correct?"

"It's strange, sir."

"Look, Ron, the thing to understand about Val Face is that when you walk into his world, strangeness assaults you from every side. Nothing to be done about it."

"But are you *sure* about this, this guy, Victor—who again?"

"Hugo. And well, Ron, I'm as sure as I can be. I'm sort of the royal scribe. So, as I say, I guess I have to look the part. Not so strange, when you think about it."

"Can you double-check? Call someone?"

"Right, I hear you. But the thing is, Ron, I better not. I don't want it to seem as if I don't understand."

"But *I* don't understand, sir."

"I empathize, I do. We've got to do our best together, Ron. I can't call anyone and plead ignorance. I'm already on too-thin ice with these people. My article? On Val Face? In *Beantown*? Remember that?"

"No, sir, I'm sorry."

"Ah. Okay. Anyway, back to Victor Hugo," and I waved my phone at him.

"I'm really not sure we have anything like this. Is that tweed, this guy's suit?" His expression at my phone was all lemon. "It can't be polyester. Wool maybe? We definitely don't have that style of bow tie, or is that an ascot?" Pause. Sigh. Long blink. "I really didn't expect this so early in the morning, sir."

"Ronald, you and me both, friend. But the thing to understand about being Val Face's royal scribe is that all your expectations are booby-trapped going into the gig. So. There it is."

His expression spoke half a tome about the enigma I was to him.

"Look, can you match these clothes, Ron?" I was waving Victor Hugo at him again. "You must have something that comes close."

"I just don't know if . . . Is there a designer you're looking for?"

"Not really, Ron. Just put yourself in Victor Hugo's shoes for a sec, okay? What would *he* choose if he were here today?"

"I can approximate this white button-up, and also a bow tie, though not one *exactly* like that. As for the vest, jacket, and slacks, I believe that's tweed. Might be wool, though probably tweed. *Could* be polyester but I doubt it."

"Trifles, Ron, trifles. Lead the way to my new rigging."

The long of it was that it took him a long time to find my rigging, and the short of it was that most were too short on me. It was quite a morning Calvary, this process, finding the right shirt, bow tie, vest, jacket, and pants, or *slacks*, as Ronald kept calling them. If we matched fabrics we tormented much over matching colors, and vice versa, although as per Victor Hugo, our colors were limited to black and gray and maybe brown. The intact three-piece suits that were sure to have the same fabric and color were either too modernly tapered, too stylish, or else didn't want to fit me in length. If they fit me in length they didn't want to fit me in width. Into the dressing room Ronald kept gophering me armfuls of clothes.

Here's an example of one of our many mirrored dialogues (the others were racking variations on this):

Ronald: "But it's not . . ."

Me: "Not . . . ?"

"It's just not . . ."

You've spoken to people who speak this way? Elliptical.

"Go on, Ron, you can do it. Just not . . . ?"

"It just has no . . ."

"No harmony? No flash. No . . ."

"Yeah . . . No . . . So."

As you can see, when Ronald sets out on sentences he sometimes shuts off his GPS so that there's no telling where he might end up, and here he ended up nowhere at all.

"Have you considered going to a thrift shop, sir?"

"No, Ronald, I have not. I was told to come *here*."

"Or a costume shop? A Halloween shop maybe."

"No can do, Ron. Here I have landed."

"This shirt. Nix it."

"This is no time to bring Nixon into the picture, Ron. What do you think of this shirt?"

"Nix *it*, sir. Forget it."

"Ah, nix *it*. Yes. That's what I was going to suggest."

"I'm afraid we'll have to . . ."

"To?"

"Well, to get a three-piece that fits, if, as you say, you need it right away and can't get alterations . . ."

Half a minute must have passed in the mirror. Ronald looked grim.

"Ron, I'm waiting on the clause that will make that sentence *really* come alive."

"I was going to say, sir, I'm afraid we'll have to mix fabrics and colors."

"You say that as if it's sacrilege, Ron."

"It is, sir."

"Well, I'm a lapsed Catholic, so it's all good. If I'm going to be sacrilegious, now's the time."

The outcome of my and Ronald's one-hour crucible was something to behold: a linen white button-up shirt, a gray tweed four-button vest, a brown wool three-button jacket, cuffed black cotton slacks, and the most Frenchily nineteenth-century bow tie in the joint, which was silk and navy blue. So then, to recap according to color and fabric: white linen, gray tweed, brown wool, black cotton, and blue silk. I should also let you know that while everything fit, everything fit *sort of.* Ronald, I could tell, felt bad about himself when he couldn't supply me with the pocket watch Victor Hugo advertises in all his photos, the one with the chain that gets tucked into a vest slit (pocket watches weren't Ron's purview).

"Shoes, sir?"

"Shoes?"

"For your . . . ensemble." He lemon-faced my shoes. "I don't handle footwear, but just so you know, you can't wear those."

"Oh. Right. But we have a real problem, Ron."

"Several, I'd say, sir, but what problem do you mean right now?"

"Insurmountable, really, this problem. A shame, really. But we can't see Victor Hugo's shoes in these photos. They're all from the waist up."

"Pretty sure any black derby will work. As long as they aren't— what do you call those shoes you're wearing?"

"Not sure." Mournfully, we both looked footward. It was true, I guessed: they were gruesome shoes. "Got these at the Salvation Army."

"You certainly did. Is that . . . are they *rubber*?"

"Probably. Durable substance, rubber. But I'll slip over to footwear and get those derbies. I've got this prepaid card."

We were at the register by this time, I fully accoutered in my Ron-got garments, Ron himself looking as if his hour with me had been the Alamo. He'd given me a Saks Fifth Ave bag to contain the clothes I walked in with after I told him, no, thanks, he didn't need to bring them down to the furnace room. And you're probably wondering: Did I *feel* much like Victor Hugo in this getup? I had to admit, I somewhat did.

Anyway, it didn't matter, as long as Nimble and her assistant were appeased enough to leave me alone enough to do my watching and writing. And understand: you're seeing here an absurdly costumed schlub who didn't entirely realize he was an absurdly costumed schlub—because he was absolutely convinced that his life, thanks to a cocktail of talent and luck, had taken on enormous new dimensions. Absolutely convinced that he'd never be little again.

"Ron, the time has come for us to part. I want to thank you for your stewardship today. How do I look?"

I can't be sure, but I think I posed.

"You look . . . *int*eresting, sir. One of a kind, I'd say."

If ever there were duds to make me dignified, these duds were those duds. I told Ronald to look out for my cover profile of Val Face in an upcoming issue of *Beantown*.

Walking out, I peeked at the receipt and wowed to a stop. The final number could have covered our rent for December, and rather than feel a stab of vulgarity for so much spent on duds and shoes this gonging, I felt a back pat of gratitude that Face Inc. was willing to invest this in me. Slow learner, I'd need about a month to see this scene for exactly what it was: an instance of my being willfully wooed, of my enlisting a severely confused salesman to help me get deeper under the spell of a celeb.

Face Inc. had decided to test my loyalty, and I'd decided to pass that test.

■　■　■

SAY WHAT YOU WILL about my new Victor Hugo rigging, it was warm all right. All that wool. I hoofed it over to Face's hotel for my noon rendezvous with him. In front of his hotel I passed through a clutch of malingerers, selfie-seekers hoping to spot Face—we are all of us paparazzi now—and then wiggled through two doormen charged with keeping those malingerers obediently out of the lobby.

Up on Face's floor, I was again confronted with security goons. Again with the walkie-talkie as I waited, and, in a minute, again with Face's assistant and her mechanical élan.

"Hi, hello, welcome back!"

More impotent exclamations: I remembered this one. Midtwenties, her youth upon her like a taunt, she wore a permanent popped-eyed, openmouthed astonishment, as if every hour of her life she were learning news of having won the lotto.

"Great bow tie! If you'll come with me!"

She led me to the door of a swank suite and we stood looking in at eleven people as they typed, clicked, scrolled, sipped from mugs in their governance of Face's fame. Here were the hunky-dories and *get-er-done* bunch in their command post.

I thought I recognized most of them from the performance the night before. There sat the makeup dude cum stylist, on a couch with his tattoos and piercings and a mug of something asteam in one hand as he thumb-typed with the other. In the kitchen corner with coffee cups stood two of Face's techies, sipping and smartphoning and saying things to each other without looking.

To the assistant I said, "Who are all those, over there by the window? I don't recognize some of them from last night."

I meant those giving off a sheen of obnoxious good health.

"No, they were all there last night! Those are some of our interns and assistants!"

"Is Face here?"

"I thought so but it looks not. He has a separate suite! Actually, I'm not sure where you'll be speaking with him. Let me check the schedule with Valerie!"

"You mean Vera."

"I'm Vera."

"What!"

"I'm Vera, Valerie's assistant! Valerie is Face's assistant!"

Christ.

"Valerie handles his schedule," she said. "Give me just a sec!"

Watching her go, I had a question: Did all of these handlers yearn to be famous themselves? Was Face the step stool to their own eventual celebrity? Because the big American fantasy says that you too can be famous, and not just George and Ringo famous, but Paul and John famous. Now we all can be players in the theatricality of self, if we can net enough nobodies on social media. No matter how puny or talentless or radioactively boring, you too can be a star. Americans welcome the sacralization of self-interest, the varicose self-love of fame.

Vera the assistant's assistant then rematerialized with Valerie the assistant.

"Hello," she said—Valerie, not Vera—"we're glad you could make it back today. Thanks so much."

I couldn't be sure if she'd just squinted at my new rigging, and if she had, I couldn't be sure if the squint squinted censure or assent.

I said what you say: "No, thank *you*."

"I know you're scheduled to speak with Face now but he's still in a meeting with Vivienne and Violet."

Vera the assistant's assistant gazed upon Valerie the assistant as a desert nomad gazes upon a golden calf, nodding left, nodding right, nodding when there was absolutely nothing to nod about.

"Ah," I said, "still in a meeting with Vivienne and Violet," and I waited for more data. It didn't come. "Who in the world are Vivienne and Violet?"

"Vivienne is Face's lawyer and Violet is Face's publicist."

"Okay, can I ask you something, Valerie? You're Valerie, yes?"

"That's right."

"Right, okay. Can you tell me if Face deliberately, you know, *seeks out* people whose names are crammed with Vs?"

"I don't understand the question."

This Valerie was a moodless wonder with a Mona Lisa look of unobliging bemusement.

"Okay, never mind then. You were saying, about a meeting Face is still in."

"It shouldn't be too much longer. If you'd just wait in his suite he'll be with you soon."

So then, to recap: Valerie the assistant, trailed by a nodding Vera the assistant's assistant, would lead me to Val Face's suite where I'd wait for him to be finished with Vivienne the lawyer and Violet the publicist. I'd been here, exactly here, seventy-two hours earlier: same suite, same time, same winter wallop, same state of waiting. I'd never thought so much could happen to a scribbler's soul in just two days.

But just then I had some other, more important points to bow the brain, chief of which was this: I don't know when you last sat down to orchestrate an interview with a superceleb, someone whose name and face are known to citizens from Cincinnati to Cuba to the Congo, but I was fairly twitchy inside, because the setup, the pas de deux, is glaringly artificial. You're never not aware of the fraudulence. Here's a shameless, mutually beneficial business transaction between a god and an apostle that pretends to be a smart exchange of ideas among equals, while of course still looking and feeling exactly like a shameless, mutually beneficial business transaction between a god and an apostle. Both parties affect a kind of insouciance, and for the profiler not to seem the sycophant he knows he is, he has to affect an attentive apathy, lest he look as adoring as he feels. Because the profiler knows that nothing will make the megastar revere him less than the giddy excitement of a greenhorn the megastar must surely be sick of already.

So the profiler feigns control. The profiler feigns cool. He thinks this cool will earn him the respect of the cool megastar, because cool responds to cool. And that cool is not at all easy to assemble and execute when you're a fever of titillation. A face as photographed as Face's is intimidating to look at when you're looking at the real thing in the flesh. Just think how outmatched Moses was up there on Sinai in his liaison with the Lord. Fella must have had a hard time keeping cool.

■ ■ ■

MY ANXIOUS REVERIE was popped by someone's entrance into the suite, an extra-dapper gent with his own great face straight out of Bollywood and a handshake to die for. This was Vip—as in V.I.P. Vip was Face's manager. Midthirties, degrees from three places on two continents, Vip had lips that were the kissing kind. And if Vip had a flaw, it was this: he was a giver of malicious handshakes, as if he'd been paid to injure your wrist.

"So you're Face's manager," I said. "Real quick: how—I've been wondering about this—how do you differ from the agent and the assistant and the publicist and all the etcetera?"

We were by the windows, each leaning against a red oak dining table, looking out and down at Boston, which had more winter on its mind.

He said, "Must sound confusing, I know, but basically we're all problem solvers. With a career like Face's, all these moving parts, every day has a slew of problems that have to be fixed. I could tell you horror stories."

"Please do. Journalists love those."

"You remember that Budweiser commercial last year."

"Yes, with that horse."

"That horse, yes, and that horse was the whole problem. Face is passionate about animal rights, of course—"

"Of course."

"And so his contract stipulated that he wouldn't work with animals out of concern for their unalienable rights. So we had to—"

"Wait, I'm sorry, but did you just—not sure—did you just say *unalienable rights*?"

"Yes, unalienable rights."

"Of animals? The unalienable rights of—of animals?"

"That's right."

"What about that bear rug?" I asked.

"What bear rug?"

"In *GQ* last year. That bear rug. Face was naked on it."

"Oh that. That was a *faux* bear rug. We made sure. I was in charge of that one, getting the faux bear rug. You probably know, that photo shoot was a tribute to the famous Burt Reynolds *Cosmopolitan* centerfold of 1972. Face's idea. He loves those old Burt Reynolds movies."

Burt Reynolds! Google that centerfold from '72: it's pretty great. And speaking of Burt: he's an untarnished example of fame's capriciousness and cruelty. I write about him lovingly in my abandoned doctoral thesis. In the 1970s he was, with Robert Redford and Clint Eastwood, one of the three most famously male movie actors in the world. And then Redford and Eastwood went on being enormous while Burt definitely did not. Burt shrank. Burt was broke because Burt wasn't Burt anymore. Few sights are sadder than the postcelebrity. Because Hollywood is Homeric: you are at the top and sung of, or you are not and not. And everybody knows there can be only so many Achilleses.

"Anyway," I said, "you were saying. About that poor horse in the Budweiser commercial."

"Right. So our end of the contract stipulated that Face wouldn't work with animals, and they missed that clause on purpose, because they were intent on that horse. And then the whole contract needed to be redone at the last minute. These were up-all-night negotiations. Lasted a week. And they had to pay out a lot more money in order to keep Face on the project because he threatened to walk."

"He has a thing with horses."

"With their unalienable rights. The point was that time is money, and they were wasting Face's time."

He looked at his watch when he said that. I don't think it was a Rolex but it was certainly the first cousin to one.

"But the horse *was* in the commercial," I said.

"No horse was hurt during the filming of that commercial."

"Did you run that by the horse?"

"No horse was hurt," he repeated.

"Well it didn't exactly, you know, *look* happy, that horse. Anyway—you were going to share a horror story."

"I just did."

"That? Please do tell me where I can get in line to have one of those horror stories."

No response to that one, but it didn't matter, because in came Face and Nimble trailing a strenuous bustling of minders.

"Vip," I said, "it was a pleasure I hope to repeat. Thank you," pumping his hand most chummily, and away he went.

In dark Calvin Klein jeans (with a box of top-secret Marlboros peeking from the top of the front left pocket), soft leather belt of brown that rhymed with leather boots, a heartland white T-shirt, and his lustily unkempt swirl of hair and slight overnight stubble, Face looked begentled by rest and whatever nighttime tea he downed to get it. About that strenuous bustling of minders: they were fingering their phones and iPads with such cycloptic gravitas they could have been relaying launch codes for thermonuclear weaponry.

"Seger," Face said, "whoa, *paisan*, what's that?"

"What's what?"

"That gear you're wearing."

"Oh. This. Well."

"Oh this well what?"

"Nimble," I said.

"Nimble?"

"Well, Nimble's assistant. They wanted me to get new duds."

"Nimble told you to dress that way?"

Face wore the face he usually wore with me: humoring approval. We both turned to spot Nimble in the kitchen, aides like moons around her.

"That is correct," I said.

On cue, over came Nimble from the kitchen with an iPad in one hand and a can of Diet Coke in the other. When she saw me she put down her iPad and peeled off her glasses, in the slow dramatic way Don Johnson did in *Miami Vice* when he witnessed a ponytailed scallywag bazooka his Ferrari.

"Mr. Jovi," she said, smiling, "what is *on* you?"

"Oh, these? The new duds you told me to get."

"I did?"

"It's Victor Hugo. Your assistant told me. Last night, at the show? Victor Hugo style. Remember?"

"I believe I said, Mr. Jovi," and her smile was still there, thank heavens, "a cross between Jack Victor and Hugo Boss."

"You what?"

"I said a cross between Jack Victor and Hugo Boss."

"Er. Those the gents who make the duds?"

"They are."

"Aha."

I looked to Face for help in dealing with this fallout from my unsuitable suit, but Face, being Face, leaned there against the table with a sheen of unperturbable cool.

"Well," I said, "it's all a bit confusing if, you know, if you happen to be reading *Les Misérables*."

"Do you happen to be reading *Les Miserables*, Mr. Jovi?"

"Well, not at the moment, but . . . still."

Nimble was now wearing one of her two facial expressions: reluctant tolerance. The other facial expression was unreluctant intolerance.

Then along came Boris, her British assistant, the one who'd given me the prepaid card. He was forced to halt midway between me and the door, in order to eye me with a face that said he'd never seen a sight as unspeakable as my person. Boris was again impeccably upholstered in black, but this time he donned a dog. He was holding Shitsy. As he stepped to where I and Nimble and Face were standing by the windows, he stepped with a tread so dramatically delicate he could have been tiptoeing barefoot over smashed glass. And then he started in again.

"Oh my. Oh no. Oh how. Is it true?" He rubbed one eye.

"How's he look, Boris?" said Face. "Pretty snazzy, right?"

"Oh my," Boris emitted. "Oh how," Boris ejected. "Oh no," Boris exclaimed.

"Seger looks pretty great in this new getup," Face said. "Very distinctive."

"Oh no. Oh my."

And then Nimble stepped in to rescue me from Boris.

"You know what? I love it. Darling," she said to Face, "I think you're right: very distinctive. And it's an improvement over what he had on yesterday, right?"

Boris looked as if blasphemy were being spoken.

"Darling, I'm off for my one o'clock," Nimble said. Peck peck. "Mr. Jovi, a pleasure to see you again. Until later."

Nimble and her own colony of minders swooshed out of the suite, Boris included, taking the lion share of chatter and bustle with them. Then out of the kitchen came Vip; apparently Vip and Valerie—was that Valerie?—planned to hang around for tone, or else to keep Face in their protective custody during my first substantive sit-down with him. I suppose an aide never knows when an interviewer, already guilty of literary fisticuffs, will start pelting the star with queries that have potentially self-injuring answers.

Face was shaking a Poland Spring bottle into which some assistant or other—the *water* assistant, no doubt; the hydration engineer—into which someone had sprinkled a pinkish crystalline elixir. Minerals, vitamins, probiotics perhaps. Echinacea, choline, a litany of unpronounceables. We sat on alternate hillocks of sofa so pillowed they seemed to inhale us. Vip was perched on a stool with a Coke and a phone, Valerie on another with a phone and a Coke, because these people lived on the stuff—phones and Coke. Face Inc. received free Diet Coke for life, Diet Coke by the crate, pallets of the stuff parachuted down from cargo planes, because Face had starred in a Coke commercial the previous year, one in which you could see all the great nipples of summer street dancers soaked by a berserking fire hydrant.

"Seger," he said, "slight change of plans this afternoon. Valerie, tell him," and Face began downing his elixir.

"Violet has arranged for Face to be at Addison Rehabilitation Center," she said.

"Ah," I said. "So Violet has arranged for Face to be at Addison

Rehabilitation Center." One pause. Two, three. There were four or five total pauses by the time I was done pausing. But then I had to ask it. "Who is Violet and why has she arranged for Face to be at Addison Rehabilitation Center?"

"Violet is Face's publicist. Whenever Face is back in Boston he does important promotional work for worthy causes, for the arts or medicine or scientific research. Where did we go last year? Oh, the homeless shelter. This year it's Addison."

The only thing I could think to say to this information was "Can I come?" And I got affirmatives all around.

Then into the suite barged Mario the bodyguard. This guy gave off an assurance that you'd never be on matey terms with him, not even if you were the only two schmucks shipwrecked on that desert island you hear so much about. He was the kind of guy who drinks milk when he's thirsty. He could trek through Death Valley in late June, find a 7-Eleven at the end of it, bypass the cooling case of spring water, and head straight for the milk. And I don't mean that watery 1 percent stuff. I mean a half gallon of whole milk. I wouldn't put it past him to grab on occasion a quart of heavy cream instead.

"The car is ready, sir," Mario said.

■ ■ ■

THE CELEBRITY'S PROMOTIONAL TRIP, his photo-op outing: a see-my-mercy visit to some dust-deviled hellscape that hasn't seen rain since Reagan, or to a God-gone cancer ward where children have been chemoed into dotage. Addison Rehabilitation Center, on the outskirts of Boston, was a pretty bland choice, I thought.

Not counting the Israeli chauffeur (whose build spoke of martial arts if not of Mossad, and who'd splashed on the kind of cologne that could kill all the mosquitoes in Mozambique), the five of us off to Addison were: Face, myself, Mario the bodyguard, Violet the publicist, and Valerie the assistant. I kept mixing up Violet the publicist and Valerie the assistant. *You* try to keep them straight. I suppose I wasn't trying too hard to keep them all straight because I was irked by the affliction of having to keep them all straight. There were so many of them. And it didn't help that they were all so young and smart and beautified into a terrorizing perfection.

Guests in the hotel lobby pointed at Face when we emerged from the elevator and passed through. Some aimed their phones at him, asking incomplete questions: *Is that?* and *Are you?* Once we made it outside, Mario guided Face through a bellowing of selfie-seekers on the sidewalk, or he tried to. Because Face insisted on giving some of these seekers what they'd come for. "Hi, thank you for being here" (phone's faux camera click), and "You're so sweet, thank you" (phone's faux camera click), and variations on those. The whole while Mario was inserting his manifest size between Face and them and looking most gravely at their hands. The doorman, unused to having this much work to do, helped bar fans from getting too close. Nimble, I thought, wouldn't be too tickled that Face was yet again using the front entrance instead of the back.

And then I spotted a familiar someone, or thought I did. There, at the back of this fan clot, trying to wedge his way in and over to Face, was Bill, the perplexing blank from the Opera House the night before. He was wearing the same clothes. It occurred to me for a sec that I should point out Bill to Mario, but I didn't have time to do it because Mario began pawing everyone into the waiting Chevy.

This Chevy Suburban was the kind of thing that dignitaries lumber round in. I couldn't quite figure out what its airy interior smelled of, and then after a minute I knew. It smelled as the limo had smelled the night before—it smelled of money.

I couldn't be sure what route we drove to Addison because the windows were tinted into opacity. The windows were not windows, in other words; the windows were walls. Being inside that tank was like being folded in utero. You lost your conception of time and distance and just hoped that time and distance did not lose their conception of you. Up front, as their potent colognes clashed for unnecessary eminence, Mario on Team Italian and the Israeli on Team Hebrew bickered about whose food was better. Violet the publicist and Valerie the assistant were buckled in the middle row of seats, their heads dispensing citrus aromas of medical-grade shampoo, and from their napes came clouds of perfume vying for first prize. Face and I were strapped into the third and roomiest row. I overheard this: a news crew from Channel 10, Boston's NBC affiliate, was meeting us at Addison.

Of course a news crew from Channel 10, Boston's NBC affiliate, was meeting us at Addison, because what's the good of a celebrity's altruism if TV cameras aren't on hand to film it? And how was I supposed to conduct a cogent interview in a moving vehicle?

"So, Face, I was thinking, for our chronicle, we could have several angles. The personal, the professional, lots of history, your own philosophy of living and art, things like that. A real overview of your existence, I mean, with input from your staff, family, friends. You know, the total picture. That's why I met with Lucy Genovese and Carmine Feludi yesterday: to help get the complete picture."

"You did what, Seger?"

Was it me or did that question come out sprinkled with peeve?

"Uhh. I met with Lucy Genovese and Carmine Feludi yesterday? To help with the, the complete picture?"

I mentioned this earlier, but Face's face was almost always the same with me, that look of humoring approval, as if he authentically liked me but was surprised at authentically liking me. But now Face's face for me had something minorly galled in it.

"We don't do that, Seger."

"We—we don't?"

He wasn't frothing at the lips, true, but there was definitely what you might call an inner froth underway.

"No, we don't," he said. "In high school, we're not who we are. They knew Valentino Detti but they don't know Val Face. So let's keep this profile focused on Val Face, okay? The present is here, the past is not."

Four points appeared to me simultaneously. First, one doesn't have to be over-Freuded to see that the past is always here, in our guts and sweat and breath, working its mischief on our present. Second, referring to his two selves in the third person in that way was a curious exercise in disembodiment. Third, Face didn't want me unearthing too much of his history because the denizens of that history had unexceptional and/or unflattering facts to share. And fourth, I could say none of that.

Most of life, it seems, is not being able to say things.

"Well, shoot," I said, "I really am sorry about that, Face. I was only being, you know, comprehensive."

"Zeal. I get it, Seger. You're good at your job. But how did you find them or even know about them?"

"Oh, a wiz researcher at my magazine, the most competent person I've ever met. She could find all those needles that, for mysterious reasons, frequently go missing inside haystacks." Breath. "Farmers who moonlight as upholsterers, I suppose."

"The present, Seger. Stay in the present."

"The present, gotcha. I was just trying to understand your origins, that's all. Your Rosebud. I've got a narrator's stubborn sense that the present can't be explained without the past. I'm just wondering where your drive comes from. What explains it."

The minor gall in Face's face had dissolved and he was back to looking at me with humoring approval.

"I suppose I was born into this, Seger. Some things can't be explained in Rosebuds. Some things can't be explained at all. I'll trust you to use your own smarts when it comes to explaining me."

"My own smarts, right. So, I have a theory—I wrote this in my—err—I have a theory that you hate the internet because it competes with your own skills of attracting and commodifying attention."

"Maybe you're right. You're the critic here. But you look at these celebrities nowadays, they're online all the time, posting every whim, giving fans complete access to their every mood and meal and thought, and it just isn't smart."

"Not smart how?"

"You're a scholar of seventies and eighties fame, Seger, so you know what role mystique plays in maintaining celebrity. It's not smart to give fans that kind of access because it erases the mystique, and mystique is essential to maintaining celebrity. They're erasing the *mystery* of themselves, and without that, no one's curious. With-out that, no one's a star for long."

"Right," I said, "but you yourself have all that web presence, all that social media."

"Pretty sure my fans know I'm not the one posting that stuff. I've always been upfront about that. Fans won't come to my shows, see my films, or read my books if they think they can get it all on social media, if the mystique is erased through access and exposure."

"Right. So, I'm not disagreeing with you, I'm just saying, or *suggesting*—"

"You can disagree with me, Seger. I've read your stuff. I know your critical rap. I knew what I was getting into when I signed you up. So disagree away."

My critical rap, and my role as his royal scribe: I was starting to see that these were not opposed. I was the egghead with street cred, and he, like me, wanted both, which is why he'd told me during our first meeting that he and I were versions of each other. I didn't believe him when he'd said it then but I was beginning to believe it now. It seemed he needed me as much as I needed him. Question was, why did I doubt how much he needed me when he clearly had no doubts about how much I needed him? Versions of each other? Okay, but as versions, we had no symmetry whatsoever. We were a pretty lopsided pair.

"Don't you think it's pretty pointless," I said, "to loathe the inter-net? It shows a kind of—an inability to accept reality."

"Depends on your definition of reality. Severing the connec-tion to your inner life won't get you any closer to reality. And hating what's worthy of hatred can be a prelude to change, right? If you're okay with the internet zombifying everyone on earth then you'll have to live with yourself."

Now was that any way to end a sentence? I'd have to live with myself anyhow, no matter what. What is life but having to live with yourself?

Face had a perplexing element happening in his tenor as he held forth on these topics: criticism combined with gratitude. On the one hand, he was contemptuous of our tabloidal landscape. On the other, his fame wasn't possible without it. That was no doubt a tough equipoise to maintain: being cerebral enough to keep his smarter fans, but not too cerebral that he lost those fans innocent of intellect. A successful showman hides his superiority from his audience. A successful showman looks *into* his audience. Not into their souls— into their wallets.

"Next question," I said. "How do you think your fans see you?"

"As a symbol, probably. I'm under no delusions regarding my fans. They probably don't see me as a real person. I'm only a metaphor."

"For what?"

"Celebrities aren't real people to their audience, regardless of how real the celebrity tries to be. I represent something for my fans. The charismatic I am in my work, at my shows, is not the guy I am in the world. I mean that on stage I'm an animated extension of who I really am."

"So you're playing a role then?"

"Yes I am, Seger. And so are you."

"So am I?"

"So are you," he said. "And so is everyone."

This was my first point-blank glimpse into a fact I wouldn't fully get until my time with Val Face was finished: all of life, for every one of us, somebodies and nobodies both, is a put-on, a struggle not to be found out, a daily self-skirmish to conceal who we truly are. The people we are in public? They are many furlongs away from the people we are in private, and no one among us—not you, not me, not Val Face—can afford to be caught.

After that, our interview was torpedoed by an insistent phone call from L.A.

■　■　■

ADDISON REHABILITATION CENTER isn't a building. Addison Rehabilitation Center is a campus. Addison wants you to walk a lot while you're there getting reacquainted with your limbs and spine. It's a sprawl of brick outposts, the grounds prettily wooded everywhere, trees old enough to be wise, lawns like fields that must be a come-hither lime green each summer.

When our tank rolled up to a yellow-brick administrative manse, there was the NBC News van waiting for us, the thudding cameraman with his thudding equipment, the reporter with hers, a microphone and her packaged beauty. There were also two Addison staffers under the high portico, holding themselves against the cold and undeniably expectant, absolutely aflutter with expectation. These two staffers were the facility's PR people, its image assemblers and liaisons, midthirties, Face fans, I could tell, judging from what their own faces were doing when he stepped out of the Chevy. The cameraman and reporter wore the same faces as the staffers: awe that was trying to control itself. Awe that wanted to behave. At the sight of a celebrity ordinary people have all of their atoms rearranged.

We knew the names of these two staffers because their official lanyards told us so: Purdi was one, Roger the other. Roger had obviously put some extra prep into his duds that morning, and Purdi had got a bit hyperbolic with the eyeliner and earrings. The cameraman in his sneakers and jeans and flannel coat clearly didn't care about clothes, and the reporter looked as if she woke that way each morning: laminated. She appeared to be the kind of person incapable of walking by a parked car and not looking at her reflection. These four weren't standing there; these four were *tilted* there—satellites tilted toward the star. All of Face's team was beneath the portico now too.

"Welcome, Mr. Face, we're so honored to have you here," said Purdi, and she looked unsure whether or not to extend her hand for shaking. She kept tucking fugitive brown locks behind the tinseled curve of her ear and straightening her woolen skirt with both palms.

"Yes, welcome, Mr. Face," said Roger. "Our patients are so excited to meet you. They're big fans."

"It's kind of you to have us," Face said, and he took the hands of both the staffers and the news duo, not hand*shakes* as much as intense, elongated hand *holds*, Face's eyes unblinking at their own flapping lashes. He was *on* now. He was working. He had to be: there was a camera right there. For those few seconds apiece, as he held each honored hand, his charisma entered their bloodstreams and stroked all their serotonin.

In his bodyguarding default, Mario scanned the grounds, the doors, the windows, the dead shrubs, as if aspiring evildoers lurked there. As Mario rotated this way and that, I spotted a protrusion from his hip, beneath his jacket, the distinct outline of a handgun in a holster.

Violet the publicist said to Purdi and Roger, "Face has forty-three minutes until he has to leave for his next appointment."

Forty-*three*. Not forty-five.

"We thought to get footage of Mr. Face with the patients," the reporter said. "Speaking with them, meeting with them, you know. And then we thought to interview just him, briefly, if he doesn't mind—Mr. Face, if you don't mind—just to have some input from you about your passion for helping people."

Mario said, "Are there two egresses in the room we're going to?"

Purdi said, "Two—two doors you mean?"

"Two doors," he said. "In the meeting room we're meeting in. I require two egresses in any room in case there is a blockage or threat at one of them. I'll perform reconnaissance now on this room. Can one of you lead the way?"

He'll perform reconnaissance now. On the room.

"Uhh, sure," Roger said. "But, I mean, the patients are in there already, waiting."

"Precisely," said Mario. "I'll need to look them over."

"Look them . . ." Roger began, and then glanced at Purdi, whose pinched eyes revealed how earnestly she was trying to understand.

She said, "Look them over?"

"Look them over."

"You mean—I hope you don't mean frisk them? Frisk the patients?" she asked.

"If I deem frisking necessary," said Mario.

"So, our patients," said Purdi, "are recovering from injuries.

Most are athletes. Skiing accidents, football, things like that. Car accidents, too. Can we frisk them?" she asked Roger.

Mario answered for him. "I'll perform reconnaissance and let you know about that."

Was I the only one shivering out there in that temperature? And did this rigmarole have to happen every time Val Face left the house? Who'd want to leave the house if this was always the awaiting migraine?

"Let's go in, it's cold," Purdi said, and before I could plug myself, I said, "*Thank* you," at which point everyone looked at me, taking several seconds to recollect who I was and why I had orchestrated such an odd outfit.

Down a carpeted hallway our caravan went; from the walls grinned sepia shots of admirably mustachioed MDs circa 1920. The cameraman banged his equipment against a doorframe; Roger winced. The cameraman's furred belly showed between his belt and coat; Roger reeled. Our warmth was short-lived because our caravan bumbled through a double door at the rear of the building, which led to a courtyard with ornate benches. Face's handlers were swiping, scrolling, clicking. I was pleased when we reached the building where the patients were waiting for us because when the wind sliced through the boles and around the edges of brick it also sliced straight into my coat.

But then we couldn't enter this building because Mario first had to perform his reconnaissance. Purdi escorted him in, and as the rest of us stood by beneath another portico, Roger couldn't quit looking at Face. And I don't mean covertly looking. This poor guy, giddy-blooded, giving off tiny ripples of gaiety—he couldn't *not* look. I knew how he felt.

"Mr. Face," said the reporter, "maybe this is a good time, if you don't mind, a good time to get some footage of just you, maybe right here—Carl, is this light all right?—maybe right here in front of this column here?"

Carl was the cameraman. He looked like a Carl. His black Velcro sneakers were definitely the sneakers of a Carl. And the reporter's name was no doubt exactly what you'd expect it to be: Mandy.

"Yeah, I can do this light," Carl said.

Face stepped in front of the column she meant. Violet the publicist had cosmetic duties in the absence of Face's deputy of makeup. From one pocket she pulled a compact and spent a needless minute with it on Face's cheekbones. From another pocket she pulled a comb and spent a needless minute with that in Face's hair.

Both Carl and his camera were dilated now, the reporter had her microphone poised and aimed, and her first question was: "Mr. Face, why have you come to Addison Rehabilitation Center today?"

"Just trying to give back a little, Sandra. These people could use some support."

So her name was Sandra then. But she kept on looking like a Mandy.

"It's really great of you to be here for them today," said Sandra.

"No, it's easy for me to be here, and my honor. They're the heroic ones, fighting against their injuries."

The racket of self-emphasized humility: praise a guy for something praiseworthy and he tells you he isn't worthy of the praise, which causes you to praise him all over again, so humble is he. There was a vetted script he was following here.

"Do you plan to speak with the patients today about their inner lives?"

"I'm happy to speak with them about that, Sandra. I'd like to hear about their hardships and what worries them, about their rehab programs and their plans for when they're released."

The way he was looking at Sandra, that understatedly flirtatious advance of his face, and the unavoidable pull of his eyes, aligned to his surety of voice . . . it hit me then that he wasn't *trying* to be seductive—he just *was* seductive. The guy couldn't help it.

Roger kept ogling Face with that uncomfortable intensity, and Sandra, seasoned reporter though she may have been, sprouted a blush which I'd first thought was the weather's handiwork, but no—it was Val Face. Val Face was his own weather.

After a rote litany of questions, including "What's the most special thing about Boston to you?"—answer: "Bostonians themselves"—Mario reappeared with the thumbs-up. His reconnaissance had discovered no great peril to the bodyguarding of Val Face, and so we were now free to enter the building and enchant the waiting patients.

The room's sofas had been reconfigured into a spacious rectangle, a theater in the round, with a spinning stool in the center for the celeb. The youngest of the patients appeared newly nineteen, the oldest rubbing fifty, all of them in athletic garb. Their walkers and crutches were at the ready; one slumped in a wheelchair.

Purdi said, "Welcome, everyone, and many thanks to Val Face for taking time out of his busy schedule to visit with us today."

One of the patients began golf clapping and the others glared at him in quiet until he quit it.

Purdi said, "Mr. Face will be happy to answer your questions today and"—she looked at Face's people—"and take a photo or two? Is that . . . ?"

Violet the publicist flashed a thumbs-up.

"Okay, then," Purdi said. "Mr. Face, this stool is for you, or would you prefer . . ." and she looked everywhere around the room in the hope of seeing something that would let her finish that sentence.

"This is good, thank you, Purdi," Face said, and he moved to the stool in the center as Purdi and Roger shimmied out of his way.

I sat on the heating unit beneath the window and tapped record on my phone.

Face said hello, how good it was to see them all, and he was about to say something else but a redheaded young woman in a tracksuit, not more than twenty years old, raised her hand, and Face called on her.

"Is it true that you're paying our bills?" she said. "Our bills for this place?"

Purdi and Roger began making astonished sounds. Face looked at Carl and his camera to make sure it wasn't rolling yet. That was important, I could tell: his response would depend on whether or not the camera was rolling.

As Violet and Valerie got busy being stumped, Face, smooth old pro, said to the woman, "What's your name?"

"Ruby," she said. "Because I don't have insurance. I used to. I was on my parents' plan. But they kicked me off. Josh told us"—and she looked over at Josh, midtwenties, clutching a cane—"Josh told us you're paying our bills because you're so rich."

Purdi cut in with a voice lathed in oodles of discomfort. "Ruby, uhh, Mr. Face is not here to speak about *bills*, Ruby. Mr. Face, I'm so sorry."

"I didn't tell her that," Josh said. "I didn't say he *would*. I said it would be *nice*."

Josh was the kind of guy who looked as if he might be weighing the pros and cons of cultivating an ironic ponytail. Adding to his grotesqueries of character, he had one of those stuccoed complexions that could use a good grating with a power tool.

"*Would* be nice," someone else said, a thirtyish woman—she wore woven bracelets by the score—and almost everyone else nodded along with her in eager agreement. Seemed they could all use their bills paid. I understood.

Purdi tried to pry in here with a voice lathed in even more oodles of discomfort, but Face gave her a pat-the-air gesture that meant he'd handle this, whatever this was about to become.

"Ruby," he said, "where are you from?"

"Newton," she said. "I crashed my mom's car." Her teeth and tongue were doing something Draculan.

"Some people should just not drive," Josh said.

"Some people should just not *talk*," said Ruby.

There was something crooked, something canted, between Ruby and Josh. More noises and shuffling from Purdi and Roger; murmurings from Face's minders, who were now looking at Mario to see if he was making protective gestures. He wasn't.

"Everyone," said Face, "let's begin again. Let's—"

"I read you're worth eight hundred million," said Josh. "Is that true? What I wouldn't do with eight hundred million."

A guy in a back brace said, "It's not like he has eight hundred million in his *pocket*. Most of those are assets, I'm sure."

Everyone looked at this one and seemed to be thinking very hard about assets and what could be done with them.

"I'm a financial adviser," he explained, and blinked.

"*Was* a financial adviser."

That was Josh again. Was there solitary confinement for Josh? *Should* there have been?

Ruby said, "My parents told me I have to pay them back for this place, which is why I ask. Really loved your book, by the way, and that last movie, I forget what it's called, the one with the plane."

"You told me you'd wish your parents would drop dead."

Josh again.

"*Asshole*."

Ruby again.

"You *did* say it."

Face said, "Everyone, let's—"

"*Asshole*, Josh."

"Everyone," said Valerie or Violet, "can we please behave? We don't want to shut this down," and she looked hard over at Mario, a look both lawyerly and coplike, something with the eyes and lips that must have meant *Be at the ready*.

Face kept wearing his face, that easeful suavity, and he looked at Sandra the reporter and Carl the camera guy and made a slice-the-throat gesture that meant not to begin filming in here just yet. Purdi was beginning to get moist in the eyes and no doubt under the arms. Roger had gone full-on tomato four minutes ago. Here now was a jam they hadn't planned for: place and time, worry and circumstance, and what they come together to smash. Face's face now advertised some central territory between the wryness of the bemused and the resilience of the determined.

"Everyone," Face said, "I'm here to talk with you today about your challenges and how to overcome them. Let's—"

"Biggest challenge is the bill," Ruby said. "I can't pay my parents back for this place. No way."

Josh said, "If you kill them like you said you wanted to you wouldn't have to pay them back."

"*Asshole.*"

Violet said, "We're finished here, everyone. I'm sorry. Mario, please escort Face back to the car."

Valerie and Violet gesticulated doorward. Mario went to Face to barricade him against I knew not what.

"Wait a sec, guys, wait. Face can handle this. This is no sweat for him. Give him a minute. He's got this!"

That, alas, was me. And I knew it was alas because everyone, including the patients, looked over at me, in stomping silence, with expressions that said how alas it was.

"Uh, no?" I asked. "Can't he? I mean can't you, Face? Nothing here you haven't handled before."

"We are done," Valerie or Violet said.

"We are done," Violet or Valerie repeated.

Face said nothing. He looked at his watch, lifted off from the stool, and let Mario escort him out. So this was it, then. Calling it quits after this small-fry ruffle. Where were the effortless smoothing abilities Face had demonstrated in those early viral videos, in the Jeans Clip? Where was his legendary ability to calm a ruckus and commune with commoners? Valerie and Violet had called it quits and Face let them call it. Poor Purdi and Roger: they wore looks of destitution. They quaked with embarrassment while Face's handlers threw umbrage at those who'd wasted their time. Sandra the reporter, too, threw this same look of umbrage, since she would not be getting her prized footage this day, Face in dialogue with grateful patients. And out we all went.

What other pagan puzzlements awaited us?

Once again beneath the portico, under the piling cold, in the last gasps of winter light, Sandra the reporter talked to Purdi about somehow salvaging this gone-wrong get-together. Tear-borne mascara pathed down Purdi's cheeks, while Roger was still full-on crimson from chin to scalp. Sandra talked with them about corralling some reliable patients in order to film them in conversation with Val Face.

Valerie and Violet almost in unison said, "Not happening."

"Mario, get the car," one of them said, and Mario zoomed off.

"Mr. Face," Sandra said, "if we can just, just for a minute, film you talking with a patient here, it would really make the piece work. My boss is expecting . . . If we could just—"

"Not happening."

Valerie or Violet again.

Purdi sniffled. "I could go get someone, find a patient, or a staff member, maybe a doctor . . ."

"No thank you," said Violet or Valerie.

Roger and Purdi then dismissed themselves with promises to return posthaste. By this time, Face had his top-secret Marlboros in hand and he made the universal signal that meant he was popping around the corner for a smoke while everyone else dealt with this minor disaster.

And when Face was out of view, Carl the cameraman piped up.

"You know, if you're game, Sandy, and if Face's people here agree, actually we can have this young fella here be a patient and talk about meeting Face."

It took me several seconds to comprehend that *this young fella* was me. The *be a patient* part of the sentence had me more stumped than a chain-sawed oak. Everyone turned to consider my person and what possible use it could be put to.

"Huh?" I said.

"I mean," said Carl, "we can, you know, set it up."

Was this Urdu he was speaking at me?

"Do what?" I said.

"You can, you know, if it's all right with Face's people, I mean, you can pretend to be a patient and talk with Sandy about meeting him. You know, say something really great about him. No one would know you aren't really a patient here."

By the way Violet, Valerie, and Sandra weren't saying anything I could tell that they were weighing this crackpottery from Carl the cameraman. And then Sandra the reporter stepped to me with eyeballs that said she was sizing me up.

"Can we shoot something with you?" she asked.

I looked to Face's handlers for help but helping me was not something high on their list just then.

"*Shoot something* . . . I can't impersonate a patient," I said. "That's not done. Is that done?"

"*Could* be done," said Sandra. "And it could work."

Face's people weren't nodding at this, true, but they weren't exactly not nodding either, so intent were they on this promotional footage.

"If we can get these lights on under the portico here."

That was Carl, addressing his demons, apparently.

"We can do it right in front of this bronze plaque here that says Addison," he said. "Be good to have the name of the place in this segment."

Carl had directorial desires. Give a guy a camera and he thinks he's Scorsese.

"So you want me to—say again?"

That was me.

"Pretend you're a patient," Carl said. "We'll get footage of Sandy speaking to you about Face. It'll really make the piece."

"What about my *parents*?"

"What about them?" said Carl.

"What if they *watch* your news show? They'll think I snapped my spine and didn't tell them. Or my fiancée. Estelle has very strict rules against my impersonating patients. So."

"We're not going to air it. Right, Sandy?" said Carl. "It's just a test shot. Rehearsal until the others come back."

"Right, that's right. We're not going to air it. And if we do, you can just explain it to your parents," said Sandy. "They'll understand."

And here we come to the most galling part of this scene: not that a cameraman from a local news channel was suggesting fraud, not that the reporter thought the fraud was a pretty good idea, but that Face's minders were standing there in apparent approval of this fraud. Just how many norms are a celebrity's minders willing to skirt in order to help him sustain superstardom?

"This trip is pointless without footage," Violet or Valerie said. "Can you do it, Seger?"

She remembered my name! Well, I guessed this was no time for me to get all gussied up in sentiments and ideals. I could see I was being counted on. Given the givens, and heavens to Betsy, what choice did I have?

"Okay," I said, "let's *do* this."

Showing verve, you see, loyalty too, though it didn't occur to me then that this segment could be used to blackmail me into further loyalty. At this point I tried, in team spirit, to high-five Violet or Valerie, but she didn't notice and so my raised hand was left there as if bidding goodbye to a grandma at the other end of a driveway.

"But can I mention one thing?" I asked. "Tiny thing. I have no acting experience."

"Don't think of it as acting," Sandra said. "Just be your true self."

And my true self would pass for an injured patient in rehab? Did I *look* gimped?

So now Carl, in Scorsese mode, began positioning Sandra and me in front of the Addison plaque.

"Now, remember," said Carl to me, "you're a patient grateful for the advice of the great Val Face. Perhaps your injury is . . ." He looked to Violet and Valerie. "What could his injury be?"

"Vertebrae," one said.

"Brain," said another.

"Okay, you hear that?" Carl said to me. "For the actor in you. That's your injury: you have brain and vertebrae damage."

Carl, you see, wanted me *in character*.

Someone asked whether or not I should be in costume with a walker or a cane, while Sandra said that the clothes I was wearing clearly indicated that I had sustained a traumatic brain injury. So Carl clicked on the camera's high beam, a gift of blindness, and held up his sausage fingers.

"Three, two, one, and . . . *action*."

Sandra put the mike to my mouth and said, "Can you tell us what meeting Val Face has meant to you, Zachary?"

*Zach*ary? Oh, my *stage* name.

Clearing of the throat, minor stretching of the neck. "Well, it was great. Yup. Super great. Meeting him." Pause. "So."

"Cut, cut, cut." Carl again.

"What?" I said. "What I'd do?"

"You have to say something catchy," Carl said. "Something memorable. Okay? Remember, you're a patient here in rehab who has just had his life changed, totally changed, by meeting Val Face. Act the part. Let's go again. And three, and two, and . . . *action*."

Sandra said, "What has Val Face done for you today, Zachary?"

"Well, you know"—and to show I had hurt vertebrae, I began wincing—"what he's done for me, let me see. Hard to tell, actually, because I have all, all this pain. I wish they'd give me more pain pills here. These pills, holy cow, they're like—"

"Cut, cut." Carl again.

"Damn it." This was Sandra, peeved at me for the second time in as many minutes.

"You can't talk about opioids like that," Carl said. "There's an opioid pandemic on."

"Well, Carl," I said, "if ever there's a time and place to introduce opioids into the conversation that time is now and that place is a rehabilitation center for the injured."

"Goddamnit," Sandra said.

"I think we're done here," said Violet, maybe Valerie.

It wouldn't be altogether accurate to say that she was shaking her head at me. It was more of a total vacillation *toward* me.

"Yes, we are done," said Valerie, maybe Violet.

"What?" I said. "What'd I do? You said I'm supposed to—supposed to be a patient."

"You can't talk about pain pills," Sandra said. "It's tone-deaf right now."

"Well, sorry, everyone, but I'm *nervous*. God. I'm not an actor. Let me try one more time."

But nobody was hearing me now. Valerie and Violet heeled away to find Face, and there I was left to ponder the hereabouts and heretofores, the upshots and outcomes. And it was getting colder, the Grimm cold of fairy tale, nightfall coming on to confront me at midday. And Carl—Carl had this *scowl* on now, as if I'd just sabotaged his chances of becoming Scorsese. Sandra the reporter came closer to me then, her coat infused with some scent Chanel makes.

"Look, Zachary," she said, "please just say a simple sentence, okay? One simple sentence. Carl, get Zachary saying this one line. Just say: *I'm really grateful Val Face came to see us today. He really gives me hope.* That's all. Can you say that one sentence, Zach?"

"That's *two* sentences. And the name's Seger."

"Okay, *Seger*, I'm sorry, what*ever*. Can you do it or not? Please tell me. Can you speak those lines? I'm freezing out here."

What could I do? I snapped to order and said those two lines: *I'm really grateful Val Face came to see us today. He really gives me hope.*

■ ■ ■

I WAS ALL READY FOR THIS ADDISON SAGA to conclude, the scene wrapped before I could muck it up any more. I'd entered a world in which physics doesn't function as it does for you and me.

But for now, I had to hunt a bathroom (from humiliation to urination), and when I finished with that—it was a lonesome leakage—I saw that the calvary had arrived, finally. Nimble. From the warmth of the vestibule, through a window, I saw her out there, and seeing her was like seeing a water park after a week in the Gobi. I hoped she had arrived with a whole throat-load of animus to unlade upon these handlers and newspeople for messing up the PR and making me impersonate a patient. Someone—a spy? Mario?—had obviously notified Nimble that the Addison saga had turned most foul, and so she'd shown up to aim anthemic menaces at the guilty players. She'd come, I hoped, to speak a prose of wham and whir. How she'd got here so fast from downtown Boston I could not fathom. There sat another beastly Chevy Suburban as if leashed to a post and grazing greedily on the asphalt. These behemoths, side by side in their boastful ebony gloss, seemed to be taunting sea levels.

Out I went, intending to gloat as Nimble discharged a reprimand in rhapsody. Against the grill of the Chevy, Face was into another Marlboro, but Nimble and everyone else were all standing in what appeared a clubby oval without tension or reproach. There wasn't any upbraiding underway; there were no threats, no vat of brewing animus. Now that I could actually hear what was being said, I heard their topic: the performance in Portland the following night, certain security concerns, etc. What I had hoped was Nimble's grand prix of impetuosities was nothing of the kind.

"Mr. Jovi," she said to me as I approached, and as others branched off into separate discussions, "I understand things didn't go as planned here. I'm sorry about that. We usually run a tighter ship than this."

"Actually I have to apologize to you. I wasn't that helpful here."

"Not your job to help. It's *our* job to be sure things go well. We've got to think through our PR a little better before just jumping into it like this. The problem is that my husband will enter any crowd to win them over. He began that way, right? But he can't do that anymore."

"This was a tough crowd," I said.

"No crowd is too tough for him, or so he thinks. Valerie and Violet know to shut down any interaction that's loaded against him, and to hell with the PR. I'm sorry you didn't get a good scene for your chronicle. But let's stay focused on the Portland show tomorrow."

Then she and everyone else piled into her Chevy and were off. Just Face and Mario and me now, but I was so unsure of myself, I didn't move. Not until Face looked left and found me there.

"Hey, *paisan*," he said, "let's roll."

■ ■ ■

AS WE MOTORED FROM ADDISON TO CAMBRIDGE and approached Boston via the Longfellow Bridge, I thought how soothing it would be to behold my beloved skyline lit up in the coming December dark—I was thankful to be back on home soil after the extraterrestrial oddities of the Addison crusade—but with these windowless windows, you couldn't see anything.

When I turned to Face, I found him—asnooze. He'd fallen asleep. So *this* is what celebrities do when given downtime from celebbing: they nap. How lovely he looked there with his head reclined in the leather, his lips ever so slightly ajar, the measured flow and ebb of his breast. And then what was I doing, after I checked to be sure that Mario and the driver were ensconced enough in their own culinary chitchat not to be bothered with us in the back row? I inched over on the leather, careful not to squeak it, and reached out two fingers to touch his rich hair, a terrific curve of it behind his ear, feel the silken perfection of it, a Roman toddler's hair, unmarred by time. What a depressing contrast to my own arid patches.

And having gone this far, I braved enough to go further, because touch hair this heavenly and the next thing you need to do is smell it too. Slowly, gently by one inch, by two, by three, my nose cut through the space between us to brush against that curve of locks behind his ear. And once there I breathed, breathed in the scent silently, a scent that defied easy description but should have been bottled as aroma therapy for those who need their dopamine stroked, their ragged spirits calmed. The scent was insistently masculine but not musky, a man-scent softened by some mix of vanilla and mint and the merest suggestion of—was that honey? Here was hair luscious enough to lick. Its aromatic wonderments had sedating effects on me too, and if I didn't reverse course I'd soon be out and drooling on his great shoulder. I tell you, I could have stayed there inhaling him for another hour at least.

Face didn't have long to slumber, because in another twelve minutes we were deposited at his hotel.

"Sir," said Mario, "I suggest pulling around to the back entrance. I know you don't approve, but I think it wise."

"Nah, we can go in the front, *paisan*. It's no problem."

"Ms. Nimble prefers we use the back entrance, sir."

"Stop it, Mario."

"Yes, sir."

They hadn't moved, this swarm of adorers, since we'd departed hours earlier, and Face wanted to be among them. Several of these individuals had been swapped for others, but the swarm had remained: steadfast, hopeful—unemployable. What fame hounds really want, I think, is for some of the celebrity's godliness to rub off on them. They want to be touched. In body, yes, but in soul too.

Before Face exited the beastly Chevy, Face told the driver to deliver me wherever I needed to be. This was touching. When you're a hoofer in the city as I've always been, public transport your only wheels and rails and friend, waiting with the flock in a freeze to be sardined on the T, you look upon a free and comfortable ride as occasion to reach for some B words you were taught by Mrs. Gray in tenth-grade English: *boon, blessing, benediction.* We Catholics hustle our way into the grace of God, though all we really need is a celebrity to bestow it. I thanked Face with a sincerity I hoped he saw.

"What time tomorrow?" I asked.

"What time what tomorrow?"

"Portland? The Portland show. I'm going with you."

"Portland, right," he said. "What time? I don't know that. Valerie will be in touch."

He let Mario bear him from the Chevy then, through the congregation of clicking phones, the squeals of adolescents, some of whom were clearly weakened from the stunning sight of him. Before he reached the doors, he let photos be snapped with a fortunate few, which miffed Mario. If you're the bodyguard of a celebrity such as Val Face, you must wake each a.m. with but one recurring, persistent admonition: *Do not let your guy become John Lennon in the archway of the Dakota.* Those Chapmans are everywhere just waiting to be activated.

When Face had disappeared into the hotel's lobby, I heard this query: "Where to, sir?" Not as if I was used to that one, so it took me many seconds to understand that *I* was the intended sir of the sentence. I gave him my address in Cambridge and asked him if I could put the window down. He did it for me. It was good, I saw, to have a personal driver.

Then I had my head thrust out the window in canine concentration, in case someone I knew chanced to be there looking for important persons in limousinelike Chevys. An ex-girlfriend might see me and immediately be rich with regret for breaking up with me due to what one called my "lack of prospects." And before we took the corner onto Newbury Street, I saw him—though I almost didn't, so invisibly ordinary was he—I saw him sitting in somewhat demented condition on an overturned milk crate like a tramp with a jingling cup—I saw Bill. On that strained milk crate he hunched in a defeated heap of himself. He was, it seemed, having a tearful disagreement with a water bottle.

■ ■ ■

THAT NIGHT ON THE SOFA WITH ESTELLE, aggressively exhausted from my trip to Addison and the strenuous shopping jaunt that had begun my day, I heard her sentences coming, I thought, from down the hall. (When I'd walked into our place in my Victor Hugo getup her only comment was: "Good God in heaven.") We had the cheapest cable package available—twenty channels instead of two hundred—and so were trying to land on a TV show not wholly asinine, since some nights the History channel thinks history means Paleolithic citizens soaring inside UFOs, while the Discovery Channel can't be bothered to discover anything it hadn't already discovered the week before.

Then, remote in hand, Estelle found Channel 10 news. To be slightly more exact: she found *me* on Channel 10 news, the lifestyle segment at the end of the broadcast, and this rattled the self upright from coming slumber.

"Um, dear?" she asked.

I'd neglected to remember—translation: I'd intentionally forgotten—to tell her about this minuscule detail from my day. There I was on the screen, at the end of the segment, nodding most moronically at Sandra the reporter, saying *I'm really grateful Val Face came to see us today. He really gives me hope.*

To say that Estelle looked at me then with *a raised brow* doesn't quite do justice to the height to which her brow can bounce. It wasn't merely raised: it seemed to have been catapulted to the center of her forehead. With eyelids like anvils ready to slam on my sight, I began carelessly telling the truth, though I knew there was no way she'd ever approve of my impersonating a patient in the aid of a celebrity's PR and a reporter's careerism.

"It's hard to explain, Estelle. I did it because when you're with him and his people, you somehow find yourself wanting to please them. It's like . . . it's a *spell*."

Estelle called my role in the Addison visit "subterfuge" and said she hoped her parents and coworkers weren't watching Channel 10 this night. Our wedding was nine months away and no bride-to-be wants this class of embarrassment, her beau on local TV aping an injured person.

She said, "I don't mean to be paranoid, but could they be blackmailing you? Now they always have this deception on you, in case you ever have a mind to betray them."

"No, no. It was that reporter and her, her *camera*man, this guy, you should have seen him. Face wasn't even there at this point."

"The reporter could have been in cahoots with Face. They could have arranged this."

"Estelle, I already have my doubts about this assignment so please don't make me more jittery than I already am."

"Don't be their dupe, that's all I'm saying."

"*Estelle*. You pushed for me to take this gig. 'Don't be their dupe'? You don't get it. Dupery rules. These people everywhere around him, they come from *outer space*. I'm doing the best I can here."

"Are you?"

"*Estelle*. Yes, I am. We can't have it both ways. I can't be the biting critic *and* be Val Face's royal scribe. They have *expectations*. We signed a *contract*, remember. So I'm their puppet."

"You're not their puppet. You're working for them. But you can still be you."

And what was so great about being me? What if I needed a hiatus from being me?

"I like this job," I said. "I like being with him."

"Because you think he can make you a celebrity too. A famous writer."

"A famous writer is not a celebrity, Estelle. This is America."

Instead of unloading upon me further with the reproaches I deserved for taking part in such fleecing at Addison, she said, in her best Lady Macbeth, "Okay then, to bed, to bed . . . *Zachary.*"

V.

Face's assistant had a text message tapping its foot at me when I sputtered from sleep at ten the morning after the Addison debacle. This text told me that Face's buses would retrieve us all from the hotel at noon in order to vector everybody the two hours north to Portland. Face's buses were what you'd get if you crossbred a limousine with a submarine. There were two of the things, their brontosaurian bulk taking up the block nearly in toto between Newbury and Commonwealth. And the sidewalk in front of the hotel? It was off limits for the hour the buses grazed there.

"Mario," I said, when everyone was at last getting seated, "what might be your thoughts about these windows?"

"How do you mean?"

"I mean the thoughts. You might be having. In your head. About these windows."

"What's wrong with the windows?"

"Why are the windows so windowless? You can't *see* out of them."

Incapable of saying what he should, he succeeded in saying what he could, which was nothing much but better than nothing at all: "What's to see?"

The second bus was for the lower-grade team members, the movers and haulers, the assistants to the assistants, the interns and their interns. To that bus was tethered an enclosed trailer which hauled, Vip the manager told me, the many electronic furnishings required to make the show go.

On Face's bus were: Face and Nimble, Mario the bodyguard, Vivienne the lawyer, Vip the manager, Veronica the agent, Valerie the assistant, Violet the publicist, Shitsy the squirrel, and at the wheel perched the Israeli martial artist who'd piloted us to Addison the day before.

"*Paisan,*" Face said to me when he and Nimble finally climbed aboard. "You ready for Portland?"

"I'm ready, *paisan*. And I've got a fresh supply of questions for our interview on the way up. Let's do this!"

"I don't do interviews before a show, Seger. Maybe after," he said, and he touched my shoulder in a way that seemed to say *You sad thing you.* Then he moved on to the suite at the back where he looked prepared to remain for the duration.

I had my own preparing underway: preparing to seethe about this. What was I supposed to do on this bus for two hours if I couldn't be with Face? This is part of what makes the celebrity profile such a trial for the writer: I was never more disappointed in Val Face than when he was behaving exactly as you'd expect a celebrity to behave. And it was a minor woe for me not to be able to say anything about it. Such self-muzzling is bad for a writer's morale. Never mind what you hear about some wicked prince's silencing of this or that writer;

the most pernicious, most persistent censure is the writer's own, that constable in his head swinging a stick down his mental boulevards and whispering through tight teeth *Don't say that.*

I couldn't fully get into my seething, couldn't really put all my weight behind it, because when Nimble reached me in the aisle she and Shitsy paused to squint at my Victor Hugo costume, in which I was sheathed for the second day running. I might have *looked* like a wincing ruin inside of it; I just didn't *feel* as if I looked like a wincing ruin inside of it.

"I think Boris has obtained new clothes for you, Mr. Jovi."

"Oh he has, has he?"

"He's pretty serious about fashion."

"Oh he is, is he?"

"We hope you won't mind. Please don't take it personally. It's a carryover from when he was a costume designer for theaters in London. It's important to him that everyone looks the part. He means well."

Have you noticed that people who go round the place meaning well typically leave in their wakes a miasma of havoc and gloom?

Now, the redecoration of my person I could take. The manipulation of me to secure my loyalty I could take. The necessary self-muzzling I could take. And the prohibition from speaking with Face for a two-hour bus ride I could take too. What I could *not* take was the redecoration of my person, the manipulation of me to secure my loyalty, the necessary self-muzzling, and the prohibition from speaking with Face for a two-hour bus ride *at the same time*. I needed this assignment, and I wanted to be on Team Face, yes. But my pride was just then warming me up for a serious bout of petulance.

Just as I was settling into this petulance, really giving it a go, I had to desist. With everyone now seated, and with Face and Nimble disappeared into their suite at the rear, the driver shook hands with a cop outside the bus and turned to be the last aboard. But as he did this, someone darted from the periphery, darted around the cop, around one of Mario's men, and tried to climb inside the bus behind the driver. At this tense point both a cop and a bodyguard tackled him against the bus before he could enter. I couldn't see his face unobstructed from where I sat—and anyway the windowless windows made looking hard—but I saw his plain jacket, sandy hair, powder-blue jeans, and white Velcro sneakers. I saw the pressing anonymity of the ensemble, and I knew who it was: Bill again.

The cop now had Bill cuffed, Mario debussed to check the fracas, confer with the cop, and in another minute he was back inside the bus, apparently unperturbed by this. Sometimes zealous fans tried to get on the bus. All part of it, his air seemed to say. Good that we take precautions. The cop walked Bill to his cruiser and the last thing I saw, as we pulled away from the hotel, in an afternoon ashen with the promise of more snow and cold, was that cruiser's red and blue heartbeat.

■ ■ ■

I WON'T BE DESCRIBING THE VISTAS aside Interstates 93 and 95 for three reasons: 1) December in New England is nothing special to see; 2) the sun was overcome by a fit of slate shyness; and 3) the windows weren't windows.

After I'd sat there seething alone for the first hour, and since it was obvious that Face would remain cossetted in his suite for the

next hour or more, I decided, petulance notwithstanding, to conduct interviews with his handlers instead, getting (I hoped) juicy
quotes for my profile, the revealing stuff that would provide Jasmine, my editor, with an impetus to the backflips she was known to
execute around the office.

But then Face and Nimble emerged from their suite, as cuddly as
newlyweds. Nimble had a spoon and gaveled us all into silence—why
was she holding a *spoon*?—but the gaveling wasn't done explosively.

"Everybody," she said. "Everybody, we have a bulletin."

All detached themselves from earbuds and headphones; all
pivoted toward the royal couple.

"Val, would you like to make the announcement, darling?"

"You go ahead, love," he said, and put a hand on her belly.

"We're expecting," she said. "A girl," and she let fly a little
screech, a smiley *eek* I wouldn't have thought her capable of.

Yipping and hurraying. Loads of whistling. Eyes oozing tears of
merriment. The children had decided to have children and everyone
was agape with the bulletin. Whole batches of clapping all through
the bus. Mario's version of applause was to deploy a single meaty
palm in a mad attack against the leather seat.

Their girl's huge future was already clear to me. Raised by a regiment of nannies, tutors, maids. Lots of cello, piano, fencing, maybe
one of which she'd excel at. Lithe and leotarded, she'd be abrim with
balletic ambition. Then a model by thirteen. Veteran of the fashion industry by sixteen. First commercial by seventeen. Graduation
(but barely) from one of those obnoxious L.A. high schools that spe-
cialize in spinning third-rate thespians out of the kids of second-
rate thespians. Admittance to the University of Southern California

after a jumbo donation from her father and transcript-tinkering by her mother. Tattooed on ankles and wrists and lower back (flowers, no doubt; hummingbirds, probably; Chinese characters she won't know the true meaning of or how to pronounce properly). A boyfriend who's also the child of a superstar, someone called Cassidy or Gavin, with brooding hair and clichés inked into his arms. A fortune accrued from a mascara line. A social media feed featuring slogans for the slow-minded and bursts of staggering banalities. Et cetera.

Face said to us, "We wanted you all to be the first to know, after Nimble's mom and sister and my parents."

I had to glance about the bus to see if I was the only one having trouble with the mathematics of that statement: how were we the first to know if four other people already knew? Face wanted his people to feel special, I got it. But they were already special just by being there.

Vip slid champagne from the wine cooler and sent the cork sailing and foam spewing to great gusts of cheer. He did this as he no doubt did everything: handsomely, and dressed to perfection. Vip didn't have *taste* in clothes; he had a *philosophy* of dress—a worldview. He was the Kant of clothes. Some of us wake up and don whatever tarp or carpet in view, whatever bag or rag at hand. But Vip had a code. You should have seen the way his gray wool suit sat lovingly atop his violet button-up, or how the caramel leather belt was in cahoots with the caramel leather wingtips.

So, glasses all around then, glasses stretched high, and then Vip's toast to glasses dinging.

"To Nimble and Face," he said, and Mario jingled in with "Hear, hear!" as if we were in the House of Commons circa 1701. It was, the sap in me supposed, a lovely moment, and how courtly of Vip to put Nimble ahead of Face in that toast. Vip was, however, guilty of an embryonic omission, one I was feeling gallant enough to correct.

"And may their little girl be healthy, happy, and wholesome!" I blurted.

Moderately proud of myself for the self-assurance, I was able to notice the few taut seconds during which everyone turned to me with faces that nearly declared my unwelcome intrusion, my enormous unworthiness, until Mario, bless the goon, rescued me with "Hear, hear!" He really was starting to seem less simian to me.

In another few minutes, the bubbly downed, and before I could ask Face if he'd please spare me half an hour for the profile, he and Nimble entombed themselves in their suite again.

So then, on to a handler for juicy tidbits: Veronica the agent. (The only way I knew she was Veronica the agent was by overhearing her phone call earlier in which she told her fellow communicant that she was Veronica the agent.) Just imagine any thirtysomething Los Angelan who gets to the gym thrice a week, jogs on the other days, prefers couscous to rice, halibut to cow.

"Hi, I'm—I don't think we've met. I'm Seger from the—"

"From the magazine, I know."

She spoke without looking at me because something held her eyes just outside her square of window, which somehow wasn't as opaque as the rest.

"Hey," I said, sitting, "how is your window a window? You can *see* out of yours."

"There's a dimmer here underneath. You can pick how tinted you want it."

Windows with dimmers. Wow.

"What's so interesting out there?" I asked.

"Just this—look at this car. You see that? That thing there two lanes over?"

"That's a—a car? That thing?"

I don't know much about the makes and models of cars but this was clearly a 1990s sedan of some kind, brushed a vomitous non-color by decades of weather, an anti-color—the *negation* of color—corroded through the quarter panels, hubcapless, one tire the spare, bumper-stickered into complete comedy, the trunk sutured shut with twine, the driver's-side mirror fastened with a flurry of duct tape.

"It's been following us for the last hour," Veronica said. "Getting close, taking pictures, backing off, then getting close again."

"Who is it?"

"You see him taking pictures of us now? He must know who we are. He's gonna cause a wreck driving like that."

Veronica the agent was multifunctional and hyperalert: she could do her own job of agenting while also doing Mario's job of bodyguarding, surveillance, intel.

"Watch, look," she said. "He's changing lanes now to get closer. You see?"

I saw all right, and what I saw was what I saw when the buses were grazing in front of the hotel in Boston. I saw Bill, and I explained to Veronica what I'd been noticing these last few days, since Face had singled him out at the Boston Opera House. His almost weepful invigilations outside the hotel, then trying to propel himself onto the bus, etc. I'd thought the Boston cops had cuffed him, carted him off after his attempted raid of the bus, but they must have set him loose with only a warning.

"We have to tell Face," I said.

She looked at me for the first time.

"We will *not* tell Face," she said, and the tone of that sentence added an inaudible "you ass" to the end of it. "Face has a show to perform tonight. This is not Face's problem. This is Mario's problem. Get him, please."

Veronica then apprised Mario of the possible threat. Mario in turn consulted his handgun and did something to it, though not knowing anything about guns and not wanting to, I can't say what that something was. Prepared it, I suppose, which made me jittery through my tender parts. Veronica was obviously stouter than me: she appeared unbothered by having a firearm for a seatmate. This had obviously happened before.

Then Mario was on the horn with the second bus, conferring with his two men and exchanging intel. His whole air said *spunk* and *pluck*. Then he was whispering earward to our driver; perhaps his Israeli martial arts would soon be called for. Then he was checking the GPS screen on the dashboard, swiping up the highway, clicking in coordinates. Then he was in the bus's vestibule, on the bottom step of it, clicking pics of Bill's car, which was adjacent to us now.

Veronica's mask of stern worry had disappeared as she returned to her own tasks, and everybody else, save Mario and the driver upfront, sat in unknowing calm, soothed by their screens. In another few miles, Bill now somewhere behind the second bus, we veered from the center lane to the right, and up ahead was the exit for a rest stop, which seemed to be our aim now. If we were worried about Bill in his struggling, rumbling mobile then I couldn't understand why we were stopping, so as to provide him with a stationary target, as it were. I went to Mario up front and managed to say as much in the direction of his sweat-flecked brow and ears that could have detected signals from Alpha Centuri.

"I'm stopping this now," he said to me.

Mario went round with enough *sturm und drang* to rewrite Goethe.

"You're—huh? Stopping what?"

"This stalker. I'll deal with him. Even if he's a good shot he's not a better shot than me."

"*A good shot*? So, okay, Mario, I don't think this fella is a, you know, a gun guy. He's more of a yo-yo guy, I'd say."

"And you know that how? Rule number one: Assume everyone has a gun."

"But I don't have a gun, Mario."

"Not *you*. Everyone *else*."

"Mario, I'm sure the guy's just a harmless blunderer who was breast-fed too much."

"Breast-fed? Hey, fucko, are you the security czar or the *writer*?"

Is there some hidden link between the short-necked and the short-fused? I wasn't as taken by his calling me *fucko* as I was by his calling himself *czar*. All his boyhood ambitions came clear to me then.

"Did you get the plate?" he asked. "You saw the car for longer than I did, fucko. If we have the plate I could get in touch with my pal Jacki, a detective on the BPD. We could find out who he is."

"Sorry," I said, "no plate. But, Mario? Aren't you overreacting a tad?"

"That's my job, fucko. Now go back to your seat, and I'll call if I need you."

"Aye, your czarship," I said.

His eyebrows didn't like that; his eyebrows had an attitude.

"I mean yes, sir," I said.

Off the highway now, the two buses pulled into a bucolic New England rest stop, and still Face's handlers were unaware of what was up, or if they were, they weren't agitated enough to yank the earbuds from their skulls. No, their earbuds were attached to them like signs that said No Trespassing. Or else No Vacancy. Earbuds are the new veils. *I can't hear you* now means *You can't see me*. Hawthorne would have written a story about earbuds in New England that connected them to Puritan dysfunction: "The Minister's Earbuds," he would have called it.

As the driver piloted our bus to a stop, Mario plodded down and up the aisle, ducking to see through the windows where Bill had gone. He wasn't beside or behind us anymore. Mario was on the horn with his men again, saying, "Do you see him? Is he behind you? Get the plate." And still no one roused or powered down as a hand-gunned Mario parted the doors and bounded out into the afternoon to deliberate with his deputies.

He and his men stood in puffs of their breath at the rear of the second bus waiting, it seemed, for Bill's lemon to ache round the bend. The one positive about this disruption with Bill was that it made me less preoccupied with the petulance I felt for Face's neglect of me. Then I too bounded out into the afternoon to see if that gelid air could buck up my lungs.

Then I heard: "Writer." It sounded rather like *Jerkoff*. This was

Mario summoning me. Mario had something on his mind, such as it was.

"Writer," he said, "what else do you know about your stalker?"

"*My* stalker?"

"*The* stalker, this stalker, fucko. Describe him," he said.

"*You* saw him. He was that bland guy you tackled the other night at the Opera House after he reached into his back pocket."

"As if I can remember every wacko at every performance. Hey, I have a hectic job, fucko. And I don't remember faces too good, so *you* describe him."

"We have video of the guy, Mario."

"Well, we don't have video of the guy *right now*, do we? So describe him, fucko."

"Well. Okay. He's a blank. Total blank."

If Mario were a cartoon just then—and he was already more than halfway there—above his head would have appeared that bubble with marks meant to convey cellular-level confusion: (# ! * ?). Also, he was the kind of guy who spat between sentences. I don't mean he spat tobacco or sunflower shells between sentences, either of which you find it in yourself to understand and forgive. I mean he spat *saliva* between sentences. Pointlessly spat it.

"The fuck's that mean? *Blank*. I said describe him."

"Imagine a nothing of a man. A transparency."

Mario looked at his guys and then back at me. Could he wear a cap with a sagittal crest such as that?

"The fuck does that mean, *a nothing*? Talk English. *Describe* him."

"I can't, Mario. There's nothing to describe. Total vanilla."

"You fuckin' writers," he said. "I can't stand when you guys are around. I ask for information and you give me nothing. Fuck off back to the bus or I'm leaving you here."

What could I say to that? Off I fucked back to the bus.

Bill never showed up at the rest stop. For the remaining hour to Portland, because I'd been the closest to Bill at the performance, and had seen him several times afterward, Mario made me park beside him so I could narrate an assiduous physical description of Bill's blankdom and so that he—get this—so that Mario himself could *draw* Bill's face. He then intended to pass this sketch to his men and to all of Face's minders so that they could be vigilant against Bill.

Now, when Mario removes the plastic cap from a ballpoint he doesn't do it as you and I would. He gnashes it off with his premolars in such a mangling that he can't get it back on the pen even if he wants to. And then his fusillade of questions began so that he could draw Bill, questions pertaining to the shape of face, of nose and ears and eyes, to hair length and texture, to lip density, to toothal anomaly, if toothal anomalies there were.

"Anything at all stand out?" he asked.

"There's the suggestion, the tiniest suggestion, of a mullet."

"Mullet, okay, now we're getting somewhere."

And after an anguished half hour of crucifying me with questions and, worse, afflicting me with statements, do you know what Mario produced? Do you know what the face he drew looked like? Did you ever see the 1978 John Carpenter horror movie called *Halloween*? That blanched expressionless mask the wacko wears while rippering teens round town? Google it. That's what Mario drew. The mask from *Halloween*—with a mullet.

Mario, showing me his sketch, said, "Is this our guy?"

"Aha," I said. "Yup. Leonardo's got nothing on you, Mario. That's our guy."

Though of course it wasn't.

■ ■ ■

WELCOME TO THE CITY OF PORTLAND'S Shiny Insurance Arena, a six-thousand-seat cavern that's usually home to rock bands and hockey games. This night it would be home to the charisma of Val Face, and already, several hours before showtime, there were platoons of fans milling about the grounds, the parking lots, the sidewalks, the entrance gates, clutching chain-link out back, trying to catch Val Face as he toddled off his bus. We saw them all as we parked, and Mario, being Mario, wasn't happy about it. He was on the horn with his men in the other bus, making sure they knew just how unhappy about it he was.

"We have a Code 12," he said. "Possibly a Code 11. I doubt a Code 13, but maybe. Definitely Code 12, though. Stand by for sketch of our stalker. Over."

He then clicked a pic of his sketch and messaged it to everyone in Face's retinue. You could hear half a dozen cellphones simultaneously go ding on the bus. Now his duo of goons was, I believe it's called, *sweeping the grounds*, in consequence of Mario issuing a Code 12, which no doubt meant *sweep the grounds, you goons*.

Everyone debussed, and I tapped record on my phone and got in stride with Face, in the event that he'd quit ignoring me and say something printable. The clusters of fans clutching chain-link all hooted his name, the females shrieking with expected rapture, with all the appropriate awe, showing what elation means to their fanatical kind. The arena's security troop stood yonder by the back entrance, holding a gate ajar for the coming celebrity and his two busloads of babysitters. Mario, you could tell, was anxious to take a beeline for this gate.

But Face had just been struck by an alternate inclination. As his people continued into the arena to flee the pummeling cold, Face broke from Mario's beeline. Face was making for the fence.

"Sir? Sir, I recommend we enter the premises directly."

"What's the issue, *paisan*?"

"No issue, sir. Just that—Ms. Nimble's orders, sir."

And up came Nimble behind us in those bleating knee-high boots.

"Darling, it's much too cold for hobnobbing with fans."

"Real quick hello, love. Give me just a minute."

"Sir," said Mario, "if I may say so, I'd prefer we enter the premises directly."

"Is there a threat, Mario?"

Mario looked at *me*.

"No, sir," he said, "no threat."

"Just give me a sec then, okay? They've been waiting out here in this cold. Now let's go, Mario."

And on they strutted to the fence. How much can you commune if there's a fence between you and those you're supposed to be communing with? Mario, walking beside Face, began barking "Code 33!" into a walkie-talkie, at which urging his two goons sprinted from where they were, over there at the back entrance of the arena with everyone else, to where Face and he were now headed, to the fans and their phones fingering chain-link through cumulus breath.

And there were Nimble and me, side by side, near the center of the parking lot. She had her arms crossed in mild disquiet and I crossed mine disquietly too, in kinship.

"Well," I said, being helpful. "This *is* what he does."

"What is, Mr. Jovi?"

"This hobnobbing with his public."

"Yes. But of course you remember Ohio last year."

"Ohio, right. The attempted strangler. I see your point. I think you're right to worry. But still. I don't think he can help it, is what I'm saying. He *needs* to be over there with those fans. It's an intimacy he can't get in a six-thousand-seat theater."

"He doesn't seem to want to understand that people can be crazy."

"People can be crazy, true. Some of them. A lot of them. But not all of them, right? I think he needs them more than they need him."

"Well, he can have his needs, but his wife and child have their needs too, I'd say. Chief of which is his safety."

Over to us humped Mario.

"Ma'am, I'm sorry to intrude, but may I borrow the writer?"

"Borrow away," she said, and she went to the back entrance where the others waited, her handbag flung over her shoulder like an axe about to come down.

"Fucko," he said, "lookit. You saw our guy for longer than we did. You filmed him. So I need you at the fence scanning that crowd, got it?"

"Are you going to shoot someone, Mario? Please don't."

"I'm gonna shoot *you* if you don't help us."

At that portion of fence at the edge of the lot, Mario's men were

maniacally looking at everybody's hands, which meant maniacally looking at everybody's phone, since of course everybody had
a phone in hand. They also tripped right into their default of saying
Stand back, people despite the fence that naturally made it impossi-
ble for them *not* to stand back. There must have been thirty wool-
coated Mainers there, teens and a smattering of adults who wished
they still were. It was a generally well-behaved bunch, as bunches go.
Through the chain-link Face would take a phone from a fan, then
pivot to click an arm's-length selfie with her and her bewitched asso-
ciates, their elated faces obscured by fence, the whole while saying
Beautiful and *Lovely* and *Thanks so much for coming*. He did this up
and down that length of fence and didn't at all seem badgered by the
cold. Face had inner resources of summer.

Mario, though, still being Mario, was irritated enough for everyone and couldn't stop saying *Stand back* and scanning this assembly
for Bill. But Bill wasn't there. There was no telling that Bill was in
Portland, or even in Maine for that matter. Perhaps he didn't have
a ticket and prowled back to Boston when we shook him at that rest
stop. Maybe he went back to the dependable depravity of his base-
ment and his no doubt ailing mass of mother upstairs. I tried in
whispers to inform Mario that Bill was definitely not at this fence
but his eyes wouldn't listen. His heft wouldn't free itself from threat
mode until these selfies were finished imposing upon our afternoon,
at which time we hustled to the back entrance to rejoin the others,
behind us at the fence the fans still wailing for more of Face and
around us the day already sprouting December's early dark.

Here was my post-fence reverie. The superstar must maintain
a delicate paradox: seeming at once godlike and just-like-you, fos-

tering the illusion of intimacy while erecting an electrified fence to keep out the crazies. That's part of the reason we pay tabloids to show us our celebrity crushes in their early-morning unpreparedness, spied unawares in sweat pants and splotched apron. Apostles must be able to identify while also being able to idolize. But if it had been up to Face, there would have been no fence at all between his flock and him. The fence was Nimble's. And the fence *was* Nimble, though she didn't assert her fenceship in Portland that day. Because the trick to power—I'm surmising here—the trick is knowing when to flex it and when to fold.

■ ■ ■

INSIDE, THE VENUE'S REPS began sycophanting at Face— "Wonderful to have you here, sir" and "So honored you're with us this evening, Mr. Face"—as they passed round our security passes in lanyards. Then they led us down tiled hallways, through mazes to the elevator, then one floor up we crossed carpeted hallways to our headquarters, the greenroom behind the stage. Everyone unbagged, woke up laptops, plugged in tablets, looked in mirrors, poured mineral water into waiting glasses. The crew and techies were already whizzing around with wires snaking here and there and here. Bustle was already busy, ordered rumpus underway.

And along came Boris, Nimble's assistant, to heebie-jeebie me with a bagful of garments.

"If you'd please put the contents of the clothes you're wearing into the vacancy of the clothes I'm holding, we'd all feel much better."

"Do huh?"

"If you'd please put the contents of the clothes you're wearing into the vacancy of the clothes I'm holding, we'd all feel much better."

Something traumatically linguistic must have happened to him in childhood. His eyes were closed, by the way, when he spoke that, as if the sight of me would have caused him certain spiritual contusions. He handed me the duds.

"Get dressed in these, you mean? Oh right, Nimble mentioned it. Okay then. Thank you, Boris."

"Oh my," he said at me, eyes now open. "The changing room is there," and he knew where this changing room was located without having to look; he just jabbed a thumb left. The sartorial sort has a radar, a kind of sixth sense, when it comes to changing rooms.

"Can you do this without mishap?"

"Boris," I said, "I will be all hap and no mis. You can trust me."

"No I can't."

Insolent Brit.

"Hey, we Bostonians haven't forgotten about Bunker Hill, pal. So watch it."

And off I hoofed opposite.

The clothes were various shades of black, chosen to deemphasize my figure, I was sure, if *figure* is the word we want here. I preferred my Victor Hugo garb but was feeling dejected enough to know it didn't matter.

When I rejoined the group in the greenroom, Face was about to do what Face always did pre-show. He ankled out onto the stage to behold the cavernous majesty of it? No, that was me beholding the cavernous majesty of it. I followed him out there, and felt much the way those dogged pilgrims must have felt upon entering St. Peter's

Basilica for the first time. One feels oneself a simultaneously minuscule and monumental reveler in such a setting. Naturally I'd never
before stood on such a tremendous stage in such a prodigious space,
and I was most taken now by the huge empty hush of it, knowing that
it would soon be supplanted by a brimming roar of color and acclaim.

It was just Face and me there at the lip of the stage, behind and
beside us in the wings the flitting of his people as they prepped
and roped, wheeled and hauled, lifted and lugged. I asked him
what he felt looking out at this, knowing it'd be full before long.

"I'm not feeling. I'm looking. I'm gauging."

"Gauging what?"

"What my angle will be. My trajectory. How the space looks
from this angle, or from this other angle. I imagine it full, imagine
my approach."

"So you're planning then?"

"I never plan. I *measure*. Planning wrecks spontaneity. The
crowd always knows when something's spontaneous and when
it's not. Anyone can plan and execute the plan. Not many can be
improvisational. So I've got to be improvisational but have it *appear*
inevitable."

"Do you ever get nervous before shows?"

"Never."

"Is there a trick to that? Beta blockers or something?"

"I don't do tricks, Seger. Or beta blockers."

But of course he did tricks: fame is one big bamboozlement.

"You okay with filming again tonight?" he asked.

"Oh. Sure, Face. Okay. I was hoping to get a, a somewhat different angle on the whole affair, but if you need me to film again . . ."

"Talk to Marty if you don't want to. We can get someone else."

"It's fine. I want to. Happy to do it."

Face didn't want to be talking to me—still. Our feckless chat on the stage unfolded without his looking at me. *I* was looking at *him* but he was glaring out into the arena, and not in some orphic pose or with any symbolical attitude, some phony *feel-the-aura* way, but, I thought, rather like the foreman of a road crew sizing up the blueprint.

Just below us there, between the first row and the stage, Mario and his guys earnestly conferred with two of the arena's security personnel. The five of them were a gesticulant bunch. Mario, I could see, still had Bill on the brain. His face, no snapshot of serenity even on a good day, was now much sterner than the circumstances warranted, I thought. The topic of their discussion was the movable metal barriers, those five-foot gates, that could be unpacked from beneath the stage and erected, aligned along the first row to prevent disobedient audience members from getting too close. Mario wanted to use them. Face, being Face, did not.

"Mario, I would *love* to know what's got into you today. Why do we need the gates now?"

"Precautionary, sir."

"Against what, Mario? How am I supposed to move among my people if there are gates in the way?"

My people. Every now and then he got to speaking like Jim Jones.

"I'd like to advise not going into the audience tonight, sir."

"*Mario.* What the hell?"

"Precautionary, sir."

"*Against what*, Mario? Maine?"

Here's what I was thinking just then: Why couldn't we just tell Face about Bill, the possible threat, the borderline stalking, trailing our buses, the forensic sketch Mario made, etc.? Was Face so easily frazzled that he couldn't be told about a possible threat without having that info jeopardize his performance? It just didn't seem a very efficient way to proceed, keeping the superstar in the dark.

"The food has arrived, darling. You missed lunch."

That was Nimble, clicking up from behind.

"Thank you, love. Let the crew eat first. I'm good. Seger, you hungry? Go eat."

Didn't have to tell *me* twice.

■ ■ ■

BACKSTAGE, BETWIXT THE MANY TECHIES and lackeys and interns, I spotted someone to whose face I could finally fasten a name.

"Veronica, hello," I said, "can I ask you a question?"

"I'm not Veronica."

"What!"

"I'm Vanessa."

"Who!"

"Vanessa. Vip's assistant."

"You're not Veronica the assistant?"

"Veronica is not the assistant. Veronica is the agent. Valerie is the assistant."

"What!"

"Yup."

"But you *look like* Valerie. I mean Veronica. Wait. What did I call you? Veronica or Valerie?"

"You called me Veronica. But I'm Vip's assistant. I'm Vanessa."

Christ.

"Can I ask *you* something?" she said.

"Shoot," I said.

"Who the heck are *you*?"

More tonal abuse for the royal scribe, just out doing his job.

"I'm the writer, the chosen one. From *Beantown* magazine. Seger Jovi."

"Oh. You. What did you want to ask me?"

"Food? Location?"

"Up one floor, take a right at the kitchen."

"Ah, thank you very much, Veron—I mean Valer—no, no, wait, it's *Vanessa*. Wait, no, sorry," but off she went, her gait uttering aspersions at me.

What I saw before me in that banquet room promised to rearrange our common conception of what *spread* means. One had to start thinking of a Nero's nutrition, get a Caligula's stance on calories. Here was a sight to help me shelve my petulance over being shunned by Face.

The table spanned one whole side of the room; on it silver warming trays steamed with their goods, with olfactory thrill. Face Inc. proceeded single file round the table heaping upon their plates one delicacy after another. From kabobs of pork to kabobs of beef; from lobster claws to potato slaw; cheese ravioli, cheese tortellini; polenta and bruschetta; here risotto, there panino; first capellini, then fettuccini. Stuffed shells, baked ziti. Balls of bread still breathing heat. Minestrone galore. Ensalada with color enough for Matisse.

Problem was, I couldn't fit every craving onto one plate, so I had to take four plates and pile one upon the other, executing quite a perilous balancing act I hoped would not collapse into a juggling act. This tested every shred of the composure in my possession.

For forty minutes I fed and fed again, and the yum was such that I nearly hallucinated with euphoria. Here was the state mystics and druggies are after. Because when I eat, I eat. You understand that a biological process is underway.

On my way out I stopped a lackey.

"Hey, what's gonna happen to all this food?"

"What's gonna happen?"

"Yeah, you know: the leftover food. It's *a lot* of food. What do you do with the leftovers?"

"Gar-*bage*."

He pronounced it that way, with the emphasis on the second syllable. He also said *bage* to rhyme with the last syllable in *camouflage*. Why someone would find this necessary was more than I could guess.

"You don't give it to the, the custodial staff?"

"The who?"

"The janitors."

"The what?"

"The human beings who work here to keep it clean for you and me."

"Oh. Them. No. So they could sue Face for a food allergy? Are you nuts?"

Food allergy, followed by *nuts.*

"Well, why not drop it off at the local homeless shelter?" I asked. "Or else we can divvy it up among the homeless ourselves. They're everywhere in Portland."

"How would we know who's homeless?"

"Just look for the human beings sitting on the sidewalk looking hollow, hunted, and haunted."

"Sorry, not my purview. Sorry, gotta go, tootles," and he gave me an antiflirtatious finger-dance in parting.

By the time I stepped from that banquet room, cautiously as though tranquilized—I must have been plus six pounds with that meal sighing in my gut—the day had gone black. Doors opened at six, showtime at eight. I appeared to be the only one on that floor now; everyone else was one floor down, backstage getting ready.

I was then abruptly bashed by a soporific fist. The food, yes, but also because I hadn't slept all that well the night before, my dreams dogged by the Addison visit. So guess what I found two rooms past the kitchen: a onetime office that now sported only a couch, a long one Larry Bird could have napped on. And what was that folded over the couch? A blanket; not a very woolen blanket, but a blanket. The rounded arm of the couch was padded enough to be pillowesque, so I sagged down into the cushions of this gift like a strawberry into whip cream, and didn't even have time to belch or think *aah* before I was out.

■ ■ ■

FOR NEARLY AN HOUR I slept that breed of sleep you find in morgues. Then, rebooted by repose, though at first baffled as to my whereabouts,

I descended a floor, found the greenroom, and, still swiping sleep from my eyes and yawning breath back into me, I collided with a crisis. Face and Nimble and everyone else were in a state of anxious concentration. Since Vip and Mario were the only handlers whose names I could be sure of connecting to their faces, and since I wasn't about to speak to Mario, I asked Vip what was up and he said: "Bum."

It wasn't the first time I'd been tagged a bum, so it didn't startle me as much as you'd expect. But Vip had been such a sweet fellow to me so far, I just couldn't figure out why he found me bumish. But then he added a word that really did help clarify the circumstances: "Bomb threat."

A minute earlier I had slipped a breath mint into my maw. I now spat that out.

"What!"

"Yeah. Bomb threat. Somebody called it in."

This was a gloomy development. It appeared any vulgarity at all could happen in this century. Another saga, I saw, was about to mug me.

"Uh. What now?"

"Police are on their way," he said. "Let's stay calm."

A drove of arena security and personnel were conferring with Mario, Face, and Nimble while the handlers and assistants and their assistants scrolled down and up and down again, no doubt having Googled *What to do in a bomb threat*. Good question. What *does* one do in a bomb threat? No one seemed to know.

Nimble began pacing to get her thoughts warmed up. To a security person or venue rep Nimble said, "My husband can't perform in these circumstances."

Mario agreed and said it loud enough for everyone to know it.

"There's no bomb here," Face said. "Everyone relax," and he looked at his Rolex. "Showtime's in fifty minutes. I'm going on. Love, let's all calm down. There's no bomb here."

Alarmed though I was, I thought: *That's it, Face, stand firm, paisan. You're in charge here. Your charisma's got this.*

"How can you go on?" Nimble asked. "We don't know if there is or is not a bomb, and we're not taking chances. We're not."

"There's no time to sweep this place before the show," said a security guard. "Everyone has to get out."

"The police are on their way," said someone else.

"The police," Nimble reminded us, "can be on their way all they want, but my husband is not performing."

Mario, attempting communication, said something about how we were now in a Code 26. How many codes did the guy have?

"Love," Face said, "let's wait for the police and see what they advise, all right? There are several thousand people on their way in and I'm not disappointing them."

That's it, Face, hold firm. Don't capitulate.

"You'll have to disappoint them, darling, I'm sorry. We're talking about your safety right now. This is nonnegotiable, really. Need I remind everyone that we're expecting?" and she pointed at her belly.

I asked Vip if there could really be a bomb and he said, "Could be, yes. This is Maine."

Now what was *that* supposed to mean? I offer my apologies to all Mainers.

Everyone was looking toward Face with lots of impatience and anxiety. And so Face relented. Face caved to his sentinels and curators. I knew he had caved to his sentinels and curators because his calm was rather like a full-body shrug, a whispered *Oh well* or silent *Shit happens*, and in another ten seconds he was content in a chair with an obviously succulent Marlboro, smoking beneath a No Smoking sign, resigned to let everyone else cope with this breach to his evening. He drew on that top-secret cigarette as a Romeo looks upon his paramour.

He'd disappointed me at Addison the day before when he let his minders shove him from circumstances that the old Face, the street Face, could have handled without creasing his brow, and he was about to disappoint me again by doing the same. When some miscreant wishes to blow up a theater full of Face fans, he blows up a theater full of Face fans. He doesn't call it in ahead of time. Face surely knew this. And he was in charge here, wasn't he?

Earlier I'd pointed out that most of life, for most of us, is not being able to say things, and Face fit into that reality too, no matter how galactic his celebrity. He couldn't say: *My charisma will defuse this, smooth this.* Or rather, he could have said it if he'd wanted to, but it wouldn't have mattered. He was no longer in charge of his own charisma.

The SWAT team then burst in upon us with their walkie-talkies and helmets and assault rifles, with their air of stern officiality.

"We're evacuating now," a cop said. "Bomb squad and fire department are en route. Everyone out please."

And when someone asked if "everyone out" meant the audience too, the cop said: "Affirmative."

"But what do I say?" this someone said. "If I say there's a bomb threat everyone will panic, right, and there'll be chaos getting out. No?"

"Are we canceling the show completely?" asked a Face functionary. "Or just postponing it until the threat is cleared?"

Nimble said she wanted her husband back on the bus immediately and Mario sprang.

But someone was still saying, "Wait, wait, what should I tell the audience?"

And someone else suggested she tell them that Face had a cold and couldn't perform. Tell them the truth, this someone said, and they'll stampede.

"They'll definitely stampede," said someone else. "This is Maine."

Okay: *what* was with these L.A. denunciations of Maine? It's Vacationland, for God's sake. Says so right there on the license plates.

"Excuse me," said Nimble, "but please do *not* tell them my husband has a *cold*. So that they can get on their social media and malign him for canceling because of *a cold*? Val Face does not get colds."

If you're wondering about that sentence, *Val Face does not get colds*, you have plenty of company.

I heard: "Remind me why we came to Maine."

And I could keep quiet no longer.

"Now look," I said.

But no one looked.

I heard: "Only in Maine."

"Now listen," I said.

But no one listened.

Face was still sitting there smoking through this. Only a celebrity of Face's standing could sit there and smoke, beneath a No Smoking sign, in the armored presence of a *SWAT team*.

When someone asked why this place didn't have a protocol for a bomb threat, the arena and security personnel began glancing at one another in a kind of collective shrug, with looks of *Don't-blame-me* and *That-ain't-MY-job*.

"Only in Maine," someone said again, and I could take it no more.

"Okay, this defaming of sacred states has got to stop."

But by the way everyone in the greenroom stopped and turned and considered me, you'd have thought I was an E.T. in a diaper and scuba tank. Their looks said *Who are you again?* and *Who let this clown among us?* It wasn't pleasant, and, what's more, nobody answered my question. I wouldn't learn why Maine was the target of their castigation. What did they have against vacations?

Then, as if on queue to ratchet up the tension, a boom sounded from the stage area. We could feel this boom in our shoes and shins. Face's face and the faces of his crew said: *Oh shit*. Later we'd learn that the largest speaker backstage had smashed over flat, but that was later. In the present moment, everybody understandably thought that the bomb had bombed.

Here, now, within, we had a meeting of the mammalian and reptilian. Which would win? And everyone did exactly what I'd predicted everyone would do: fretted and bolted, jackets in hands and bags over shoulders, no time to wonder or inquire, to text loved ones a sobbing goodbye. The cops billowed in the direction of the boom while the rest of us did not. The rest of us went the other way, guided by blesséd red Exit signs. The rest of us rushed down the stairs and down the hallways toward, we hoped, a rear emergency door that would push out onto bomblessness. Between my ears I had on repeat the opening two minutes of the "Carmina Burana."

No time to wonder how the utmost deals with the foremost, lowermost with topmost, or how so-and-so will fair with such-and-such. My intestines were a clenched debacle, but my legs were lubed enough to amble with the others. A scene such as this really does shove a fella right back to the Pleistocene. Once adrenaline starts striding through the blood the brain gets left dustily behind, its creaking cogs, and you are *all* legs, all hoof and dash—but to where? Wherever you think the bomb is not. Just follow the fleeing multitude and pray their internal GPS is not fritzing, getting all the avenues wrong.

Then we found it, the emergency exit, despite the mazelike byways of this first level. Some architectural loon was guilty of this maze and should be caned. There were about twelve of us there at this exit, the kind that blares an alarm when you press the handlebar and swing it free. But this door had never before been used, never before been needed, and so it simply would not unstick no matter with what initiative some intern or assistant shoved.

But Mario, who always seemed as if he would soon kick open a door, kicked open the door. And out into the chilling dark everybody went, Face and Nimble girded by security goons.

I remained there inside, in the histrionics of that alarm, despite the inner tussle that signals a coming threat. And my thought just then? The food. The food two floors up.

It became half clear to me, what with the lack of fire and rubble, smoke and stampede, that what had boomed upstairs by the stage was most likely not a bomb, and that everyone would live to see another week. This realization got my digestive tract on track again, and I thought: *Save the food.*

But then something else got in the way. Vip would later tell me that a SWAT officer and not one of the arena personnel was the one who instructed the audience to evacuate, and this had precisely the effect the security person had feared it would. Nothing says panic like SWAT regalia. He didn't dispel fret but fueled it, and the audience, being an audience, beset all the exits and made massive clots as they did so, which increased the panic, which increased the clots, which increased the panic, which . . .

I thought I could hear them all midtrample from where I was at the exit one floor down. Horde panic stirs up a pretty specific din that sounds as nothing else does. Even when you can't exactly hear it, you can feel it. Panic has energy. Harness all the panic in America and you could light up the grid for months. But that's when I thought that perhaps the bomb threat was legit after all, and so I knew what I had to do before all was unfixably lost: *Get back upstairs. Save the food.* One must pounce, leap like Balanchine into action.

I had in mind a mission of mercy: take the food to my houseless chums back home in Central Square. Because something overtakes me when I see such plentitude and know it's going to get trashed. Such plentitude is vulgar to begin with, but trash a third of it and the vulgarity becomes absurdity. Looked at another way: what Face did with his fans, I was deciding to do with my houseless chums—see them, feed them. Looked at yet another way: my unconscious was trying to get me fired from this assignment because I resented the manipulations and machinations, the unending strata of abettors, and Mario calling me *fucko.* And never mind what I had decided

the day before: that I did *not* resent their manipulations and machinations, that I'd blithely do whatever bidding they had in mind.
Because I needed to be on Team Face. I needed to be somebody. And
usually when you hang up your principles on a hook in the barn in
order to be somebody, it's no good pretending that those principles
can still ride again when they want to. But at this tense point, I could
feel those principles strapping on their spurs.

■ ■ ■

MY BRAIN WASN'T SO DUSTILY LEFT BEHIND by adrenaline
that I couldn't make quarter-smart choices. I knew, for instance, not
to take the elevator two flights up but to use the stairs, and so up
those stairs I bounded. The third floor was just how I'd left it post-
nap: personless. And silent too: I couldn't hear the alarm up there,
or the din of the horde.

But I had an issue now. How was I to rescue the food if I didn't
have suitable containers into which I could scoop it? And then I
knew: the kitchen! Ransack the kitchen for Tupperware, for Chinese
takeout containers, buckets, barrels, anything would do. And there
they were in a kitchen cabinet waiting for me, practically whispering my name: plastic food containers. Large ones too, and a bunch
of them, shoe box size, accumulated from years of feting celebs and
their toadies. I chose five of the sturdiest containers, and then it took
me two minutes to match the right lids to these containers. What a
bewildering harvest of lids was here.

Once I accomplished the maddening match of lids to their confederates, I sped back into the banquet room and proceeded to save

a sampling of food, a goodly selection, as much variety as I could carry. I recalled Christ with the loaves and fishes, feeding five thousand. And if I alone was going through this epic ordeal of saving the food, in gallant risk to my own skin, then I thought it only properly Christian that ownership of the food should revert to me. Anyway, at this point, I was probably the only one who had his intestines where his cerebellum should have been.

Out of the room I rushed, down a hallway to the stairs, and down several flights, to the lower level, in my arms piled and balanced five food containers. And when I made it through the still-blaring emergency exit and out into the frigid dark of the parking lot, what did I see? Not only an armada of emergency vehicles washing a black night red, but Face's bus, pulling away—without me. I knew it was Face's bus because the other bus had that equipment trailer hitched to it. So I started sprinting—with five food containers, in twenty degrees, in ruby-hued flashes from firetrucks, which was a tripping hazard in the stylish but not exercise-related shoes Boris had procured for me.

The bus, though clearly departing, was at a crawl, turning itself in order to access the exit, which was kept by the parking lot's guardian, a sentry in her outhouse. Neither this sentry nor the bus's driver could see me in the dark, and anyway, the driver was preoccupied with navigating that mammoth. So I sped up my sprint, which was quite the torment, I tell you, what with my quarry of food, my unathletic figure, my shoes, and the feast still gaily breathing in my gut. But I made it panting to the bus and, somehow balancing the food in one arm, began clobbering the door with the other. That's right: clobbering with my *arm*.

"Hey," I yelled, clobbering. "Stop, for the love of—for God's sake."

And he did, the driver; he stopped for me. The sound of the bus's breaks hissing to a halt was such sweetness to the ear. And feet.

So I panted up into it, my thighs burning to match my lungs. In the forgiving warmth of the bus, everyone fixed on me. What an awful sight I must have been. Their expressions confirmed this.

Mario said what you'd expect Mario to say: "*This* jackass."

I was still standing there beside the driver, facing a silent everyone, as if about to conduct a speech, food containers stacked against my gut and chest. The doors sucked shut again and the bus inched for the exit.

The breathy sounds that came from me then were these: "Uh. So. Err. Well. The thing is, you see . . ."

"The fuck *down* and the fuck *up*," Mario said, eloquence successfully stifled.

Yes, that litter was his language; his version of our alphabet was frequently susceptible to such heresy as that. By some scant miracle, though, I got his meaning: *Sit the fuck down and shut the fuck up*, which I thought it prudent to do without further comment.

VI.

Nobody said anything to me during the ride back from Portland, and only Face and, I think, Veronica the agent said anything to me when we pulled up to his hotel in Boston. "Hungry, Seger?" Face said, looking at the food in my lap. I didn't answer. Everyone debussed into the teenage temperature. I wanted to wait until they were all inside the hotel so I wouldn't have to have my unworthiness confronted again. Veronica was the last one off the bus.

"That's a lot of food there," she said. "How are you going to carry it all without dropping it?"

"Well I've done a pretty good job thus far. But, yeah, I see your point."

"I'll get you a box. Hold on."

My reverie: There hadn't been a bomb in Portland. It had taken the police an hour to figure that out, and while they were trying to trace the call that delivered the threat, they'd be led only to a phone booth. Like some public retro-art installation, Portland still had a phone booth. Say what you will about Bill, but when he makes a bomb threat he knows not to do it from his own cellphone. Bent fans are as I'm told children are: roving founts of want. If Bill couldn't have Face as he wanted to have him, then nobody was going to have him. The bomb threat was Bill's way of saying: *Behold my barbed heart.*

All of Face's Portland fans who'd been evacuated from the arena thanks to Bill? As they quaked in the cold for an hour, as the cops and their dogs sniffed for a bomb, they did so phonelessly because they'd all surrendered the things to those impenetrable pouches with the electronic locks. So they had their phones *on* them; they just couldn't *get to* their phones on them. Six thousand people in a parking lot without their dopamine hits. Just imagine how that foiled them; picture their inner scuffle. And then picture the elongated chaos of this crowd getting back into the arena's lobby to access the unlocking devices for the pouches. Out there in Maine's refrigeration, without their phones to mother them, they were pilgrims without a path, without a god.

Veronica, this sudden paragon of mercy, came out of the hotel two minutes later with a large cardboard box that had once been used to transport paper towels.

I said, "Thanks so much for this. I really—I appreciate it. So hard to, you know . . ."

"To be alive?"

"Mmm. I was going to say *so hard to carry five food containers,* but yeah, *so hard to be alive* applies too."

"Tonight was an oddity. That hasn't happened before."

"Can I ask you something? Totally off the record. Mums the word, promise," and when she nodded ascent, I asked it. "Is Face a diva? A flaky diva?"

"Why do you ask that?" she said, but her little grin showed me that the question wasn't as befuddling as her own question made it seem.

"He flaked on me today. Total flakery."

"Well, he had a show to perform, right? I think we can't really imagine the pressure he's under. I know he might seem like a moody or controlling diva sometimes but remember how fame is itself so controlling. Stardom must seem pretty strange even to the star, right? These were normal people once. I just think the pressure on him is immense. *I* wouldn't want his schedule, all these demands every day, would you?"

"God no. The salary I will take. The schedule no thank you."

"I agent some other celebrities, and trust me when I tell you that Face is no diva when compared to what I see. You would not *believe* what I see. Maybe I'm biased because he's good to me. He's good to us all. But you're the one writing this piece so I guess you'll have to call it as you see it."

"I can call it as I see it but I think Nimble will probably edit whatever I see that she does not like being seen. That's the vibe I'm getting."

"I can't help you there. But I will say, thank God for Nimble. Without her guidance, her structure, his career wouldn't work. No way. Not his career as it is today. She covers all his bases because he's no good at it."

I thanked her, fist-bumped her goodnight, then cabbed it back to Central Square. (We still have a cab or two in Boston, though not, I'm sure, for long.) All of my houseless pals were there in Central, heaped outside the Quik Mart, clustered beside Dunkin', overcoated and quilted on the asphalt, a tarped togetherness their only warmth, and I bearing a box of shock for them. My pals were: Bobby, midforties, always in a puffy orange coat, frequently conversing with stop signs. Sixty-year-old Sam had hair to her belt and in her reflection of the Quik Mart window combed it with protracted care and practiced honor. Felix at fifty walked with one foot booted, the other sneakered. Eleanor's age you could not ascertain because hunger and weather morph Barbies into Medusas, but I guessed fifty-five. Mackenzie looked like my father's mother if I took my glasses off. Skylar, formerly male, made a comely woman but I couldn't tell her age either, though it fell somewhere between forty and sixty, I was almost sure.

"Bobby, hey buddy, sit up. Mackenzie, hi there, sweetheart, look here. Felix, hey friend. Sam, Eleanor, come hither. Felix, I know you're going to like this. You too, Skylar. And you too, guy, you there, I'll get your name in a sec. Your friend too, come round, see what Santa's brought. All this is still warm. Not hot but warm. Well, not *frozen*, let's put it that way. Beef kabobs, some potato slaw. Also, let's see here, cheese ravioli, yup, and cheese tortellini too, with just a suspicion of oregano. Got some yummy risotto here. A pasta too: capellini, I think. Dig in, everyone. Did I mention the ravioli?"

"You got forks?" Felix said.

"And plates?" said Bobby.

"There's dignity to be considered," Felix said.

I hurried into the twenty-four-hour CVS, only to remember that I didn't have any cash left after the cab ride. My credit card wouldn't work, I knew, because I'd maxed it out last month. Ditto my ATM card. But guess what I did have. I had the prepaid card that Boris had given me to buy my Victor Hugo clothes with. So I emerged from there with a bagful of utensils, plates, napkins, and bottles of spring water. Food, like birth, fights the fear of death, and watching my houseless dine let me feel less harassed by the hell-on-nerves I'd endured this night. Estelle, I knew, was bound to be pestered by my parting with eighteen bucks for a cab home, and so I hoped that the two containers of food I walked in with would help balm the inevitable wound.

After I explained to her why I was wearing what I was wearing, all the dark clothes Boris had dressed me in, I told her the bad news and good news. Bad news: I had to take a cab and so my week's lunch money was lost. Good news: I had lobster, shrimp, and a medley of Italian savories to help along the inhibition of our serotonin reuptake.

"Did you *steal* this?" She gaped.

"I wouldn't say *steal*. I rescued it."

"From?" and at our tiny table I told her the night's tale front to back as we slurped, chowed.

Ballooned once more, leaned back couchward to aid this rare digestion, Estelle's socked feet in my lap, the radiator hissing its assurances, I had things to say.

"I'm not right for this assignment, love."

"Sure you are."

"I just don't think I'm *right* for the whole thing."

"Course you are."

"Really, sweet, I'm pretty out of place with everyone. As you said yesterday, I can't be me."

"I've had second thoughts about that. What's so great about being you? Be someone else for a change. Say it with me now: *starvation*. We need the money, love."

"I sense I'm being monitored and manipulated. I'm under the bootheel of invigilation."

"Your metaphors, dear, please. And if you quit, we're going to have a bad, bad winter. We're broke, remember?"

"I was almost blown up tonight."

"You were not almost blown up tonight."

"I could have been almost blown up tonight. First my feelings are assaulted through sheer neglect and then I get bombs thrown at me."

"Okay," she said, sitting up. "What's really going on here?"

"What's that mean, *really*?"

"I mean, what are your feelings for Val Face?"

"My what?"

"Your feelings for Val Face. You want him to befriend you. That's what's going on here. You want a bromance with Val Face. And he's not doing that. So you're hurt. Dear, is he your man-crush? You can tell me."

"*Estelle*. I do *not* have a man-crush on a celebrity. I nearly have a doctorate in media studies."

"Non sequitur, hon."

"Are you going to help me out here or not? I'm doing this *for you*."

"Us, you mean. And you Catholics are so dramatic. Must be all those crucifixes as a kid. You walked into this assignment just as excited as I was, so don't point fingers, buddy."

"I'm not pointing fingers. I'm trying to finger pointers."

"Well finger this pointer then. Remove your feelings from the equation and replace them with our stomachs. Don't quit, okay? Stick it out. You can do this."

"Remind me why he's so famous," I said. "Tell me again what he *does*."

"You don't need a reason to be famous in America. All you need is America."

She kissed away my agitation, and then all that gout-giving food knocked her flat only a minute after we wrapped ourselves into bed. Dejected right down to my platelets, I soon followed her. I smashed into sleep while listening to Bob Seger's "Turn the Page"—live from Detroit in '75—and *turn the page* was my concluding thought before slumber: *I need to turn the page on this assignment, regardless of Estelle's fear of destitution.*

I recalled Felix's remark from earlier in the night: *There's dignity to be considered.*

■　■　■

THE PREVIOUS DAY'S EVENTS had caused my dreams that night to be a mix of Bronze Age burblings and Picasso portraits. One is liable to wake some morns with a thought waiting there on the hunted heart as if in ambush: *Ah, another day of God knows what ghastly misfortunes lie ahead.* Some days you get up, you get going, and before you know it, you get lost, all your meanings muddled.

That thought alone is enough to force one back into sleep's protective custody, but what rattled me more awake at ten a.m.? The ring-a-ling of an L.A. area code. What fresh evil was about to fang me now? Surely one of Face's handlers with guidelines for another day's debasements of me. My *hello*, I heard, sounded rather like *What now?*

"Fucko." I then heard, "It's Mario."

The second part of that greeting really wasn't called for after the first.

"We need you here," he said.

"Need me huh?"

"Here. The hotel. How much time for you to get here?"

"How much time? Err. Time, time. Maybe an hour?"

"*Nothing* takes an hour. I'll send a car in thirty minutes. Be ready. Text me your address."

Nothing takes an hour. What kind of cryptogram was that? Had he never watched *60 Minutes*?

"Mario," I said, "what's this about?"

"Thirty minutes. Be outside."

Twenty-nine minutes later, the Israeli driver was at the curb, and although my neighbors couldn't hear him call me "sir," I did hope they saw his black-suited self open the door to the polished Suburban for me. Sixteen minutes after that, we were at the hotel.

In Face's main suite all of his majordomos sat on sofas and at the red oak dining table with their laptops propped open. Face wasn't there. Face, I'd been told, was visiting his old high school in Eastie, escorted by Mario's two lookalikes. But the pack of his handlers were there. Nimble, Boris, Shitsy too. A tattooed techie was squatting by the smart TV, connecting a laptop to it. As for me: I was back inside my Victor Hugo getup. Boris, I could see when I'd entered, was discontented by this. Nimble, though, had larger things to be discontented by.

Someone new was standing next to Mario. A woman, late forties, I guessed, a working-class stylishness to her, a white cotton button-up beneath a chestnut leather jacket, Levis tapered over brown-heeled boots of suede, her makeup-less face serenely in control, her cropped white-blonde hair swept left. And around her neck? A badge. This was Jacki Jaworski. Jacki Jaworski was Mario's detective friend with the BPD. That bulge on Jacki Jaworski's hip beneath her leather jacket was the Glock she'd use against enterprising sadists. She and Mario had the floor as the rest of us sat and stared at them.

Mario began: "Thanks for convening on such short notice, everyone. This is my pal Jacki. We did two tours together in Iraq. We were in the shit in Fallujah back in '04. Right, Jack?"

"What we were in was definitely the shit, Bunny."

Wait. *Bunny*?

"She saved my ass. And I've asked her here to help us with the possible threat to Face that some of you know about."

Wait, wait. *Bunny*?

Now Nimble's own face was a mask of stern focus; on the sofa she leaned forward with one elbow on a knee and her chin in her hand. The others looked either anxious or baffled or both.

"Good morning, all," said Jacki, and gave us the chummiest wave. Her whole air was of an optimistic college professor who adores her students and not of a warrior who had saved asses in Fallujah in '04 while machine-gunning unlucky insurgents. Just goes to show that you can be a warrior who had saved asses in Fallujah in '04 while machine-gunning unlucky insurgents *and* be a congenial citizen who smiles and nicknames big guys "Bunny." Her accent gave her away: I guessed either Quincy or Weymouth. Possibly Hingham, but I doubted it. Like many Marines current or ex, her posture was impeccable. And her welcoming demeanor declared that if you forced her to shoot you, she'd aim at your knee and not at your chest.

"Now," said Mario, "the writer is with us. He's seen our guy better than anyone else, and more than once. Writer, tell Jacki what you know."

After the requisite throat clearing, I stood and launched into what I knew and when I knew it: Bill's description, his presence outside the hotel, his trying to force his way onto the bus, his trailing us to Portland, the bomb threat, all of it. Jacki nodded encouragingly, as if I were dishing the teacher all the right answers. The others looked dismayed that a former Face basher could be so essential to the dealings. And how did I feel being so essential to the dealings? I felt as if I wanted to be this essential to the dealings always.

"Thank you for that intel, writer," said Jacki. And then to everyone, she said, "First, let's not assume his name is Bill. My bet is that he gave a false name at the performance that night. Second, Bunny has told me about the bomb threat yesterday in Portland, and that remains the most concerning aspect of this threat. I'll be in touch with the Portland PD this afternoon to see where they stand on this. Did anyone happen to get the plate number of his car yesterday? Bunny? No? Just the description of the car? Okay. I understand we have video of our guy?"

"Hazel," Mario said to the techie, "how're we doing with that hookup?"

"We'd be doing a lot better if this TV weren't a year old, but I've got it now. One more sec."

Mario told Jacki Jaworksi that I had shot this footage at the Boston Opera House, and Jacki in turn shot me a thumbs-up. It was the most boosting thumbs-up I'd ever been shot. And in another minute we all watched my camerawork. Jacki Jaworski, I could see, was pretty impressed by it. And my new ambition just then was to impress Jacki Jaworski every chance I got.

"A real creeper this guy, eh, Jack?"

"A definite creeper, Bunny. Okay, everyone, here's what I want to do. I want a roster of everyone who bought a ticket for the Boston show that night. Is a roster possible?"

Valerie the assistant, I think, said she'd have her assistant fetch the roster posthaste.

"If we get names," Jacki told us, "we can get faces, and once we get faces, we can try to match one to our guy and get a name."

"But, detective," I said, my hand half raised, "one thing? Tiny thing. What if Bill scalped his ticket? I saw three scalpers at least outside the venue that night."

"You have detective chops, writer. Good question. But there's nothing to be done about that. We'll have to start by trying to match the roster to his face and see where that lands us."

I have detective chops. But now it was Nimble's turn. And when Nimble takes a turn, the whole room gets slammed to one side. She stood to do it.

"Detective, are you telling us that this person poses a serious threat to my husband? Because if that's what you are telling us, then there's no need to match names because I'll be canceling this tour and taking my husband back to Los Angeles."

"I understand your concern, ma'am. If Bunny has detected a threat, I'd say there's a threat. In Fallujah in '04, Bunny—"

"Please never mind about Bunny in Fallujah in '04, detective.

In your *experience*, does this person seem to be someone who will harm my husband?"

Nimble had scratched all the nail polish from her right fingers.

"I'd say he's concerning, ma'am. Following the bus, the bomb threat: this shows me we're dealing with someone willing to take risks. I've worked stalker cases before and they tend not to give up until they make their contact."

"What's that mean, detective, *make their contact*?"

Nimble was now scratching all the nail polish from her *left* fingers.

"Contact with their targets, ma'am. In whatever way they intend."

"Wonderful. A target. My husband a target. In his hometown. Okay, all, I think we can plan on packing it up and canceling this tour."

She then resat herself with such tearful, arm-crossing finality there almost seemed nothing more to say.

But Vivienne the lawyer—I was half sure she was Vivienne the lawyer—found something. "Nim, if I can remind everyone, we're about to launch these new merch lines. I really don't think the timing is right on this. To cancel the tour, I mean."

"Can we rethink this, Nim?" That, I knew, was Violet the publicist.

Then Veronica the agent said, "We should definitely rethink this, Nim. These merch contracts are loaded in favor of the manufacturers and vendors. They've given themselves *a lot* of exits. They wouldn't like a canceled tour."

Nimble looked as if she were about to raise both her voice and her blood pressure at them. But she didn't. She calmly said, "And, ladies, thank you, but I wouldn't like a hurt husband." Her eyes, I saw, were getting dewier.

I'm not sure how long I'd had my arm raised to be called on, but I'd almost forgotten I'd raised it until Nimble said, "*What* is it, Mr. Jovi?"

"Oh. Right. So. I was just going to say. Why don't we ask *Face* what he wants to do about this?"

Someone started going *No no no* and in another second they were *all* going *No no no*. Jacki Jaworski and I were the only ones not going *No no no*. The only ones perplexed as to why they weren't going *Yes yes yes*.

"Ma'am," said Jacki to Nimble, "may I ask why not? I've talked with Bunny about extra security measures and we're going to need your husband's cooperation."

"Because, detective, you don't understand. My husband has asked not to be apprised of problems. He has his art to focus on. We pay this *entire room* to handle problems so that my husband does not have to."

"It's his safety, ma'am."

"If my husband's safety is the issue I will just cancel the tour, detective."

Now all the *no-no-no*-ing was aimed at a flustered Nimble.

"Ma'am, if I may ask. How am I supposed to help Bunny in the security of your husband if we can't tell your husband there's a threat I'm here to help him with?"

"Everyone, everyone, leave this to me!"

That, on cue, was Boris. Remember earlier when Nimble told me that Boris had been costume designer for London theaters? Well, he was about to enact his theatrical ingenuity. And to do this he slid to where Mario and Jacki were standing on the area rug in the center of the suite and began gesticulating. And when Boris gesticulates, it looks like interpretive dance of some sort. The effect was helped along by Shitsy in one arm.

"Okay, everyone, picture this! Here we have not Detective Jacki Jaworski of the Boston police force but, ta-da, Florence Dupont!"

Excited face.

"Florence Dupont, you see, is Mario's cousin! And she's recently lost a baby in the second trimester. Very sad."

Sad face.

"After all the IVF, at her age, very disappointing."

Disappointed face.

"And she must spend time now with her loving, devoted cousin in order to lift her spirits! She and her cousin were best mates in childhood, you see. They did everything together. She needs her cousin's support now! Because there's something else. Something terrible."

Terrible face.

"Cancer. Liver. Only stage one, but still, very concerning. She'll live, of course! But very concerning. She needs her cousin right now. Say it with me, everyone: *Florence Dupont*."

And for some reason we all said it: "Florence Dupont."

Boris: "Mario's *cousin*."

Us: "Mario's cousin."

Boris: "Lost baby."

Us: "Lost baby."

Boris: "Cancer."

Us: "Cancer."

"Nim," he said, "what do you think, sweetie? Doable?"

Nimble removed a hand from an exacerbated brow. She couldn't speak for half a minute. And then she could.

"Well, detective?" she asked. "Is this doable? I'm at a total loss here."

Jacki Jaworski looked to Mario; half her mien was considering this; half was asking *What have you roped me into?*

"We'll proceed as you see fit, ma'am," Mario said.

Boris hip-hipped; Boris hurrayed.

"Now, for the costume," he said.

He put his chin into his right hand and walked around Jacki Jaworski with a stern, inspecting stare. This lasted twenty-three seconds. I counted.

"No, no, won't do," he said. "Florence Dupont would not wear this. *Could* not wear this. No, you see, Florence Dupont's recent troubles have forced her into a *chaos* of style. Florence Dupont wears— no one gasp—wears *tennies* and a—forgive me, all—but she wears a baseball cap. Often *backward*. Slacks are simple khakis *slightly* fitted, *slightly* tapered at the ankle, and, as for up top, I'm sorry to say . . . a hoodie. Now, no one panic, please. I'm not speaking of an *obnoxious* hoodie, mind you, nothing so vulgar as a pullover with *strings* and a *sporting* logo, but rather a simple zippered hoodie of, I'd say, lavender. Yes, jersey knit lavender. Lavender, you see, *soothes* Florence Dupont after her recent losses."

"Gotta be the Red Sox," Jacki said.

"I beg your pardon? Red socks," said Boris, "as everybody knows, should be outlawed. There're simply no circumstances *ever* in which red socks could be countenanced."

"The baseball cap, I mean. Gotta be the Red Sox. I won't wear an enemy team's cap, I'm sorry. My captain would consider it grounds for firing. And I'd never be able to show my face again at the precinct."

"But Florence," said Boris gravely, "once we go so far as committing the crime of actually *wearing* a baseball cap in public, it then does not matter what *kind* of cap it is. The affront is so enormous as to dwarf the details of it. Now, if I may tape you, Florence," and out he pulled his cloth measuring tape.

"Detective," Nimble said, standing, "please answer me one thing? Are you going to keep my husband safe?"

"I'm fairly certain we will, ma'am."

Nimble considered this. "I do hope your certainty will soon become something more than fair," and she retreated down the hallway for the blessing of a bathroom. In a minute everyone could hear her retching into the toilet. It was the most graceful retching I'd ever heard, almost classiness itself.

Minders dispersed, I went to Jacki Jaworski to introduce myself. She was a whole hand taller than me.

"Thank you for your help," she said. "I appreciate the intel you've given us."

"Think nothing of it. It's what Paul Revere would have done."

"So you've seen our guy up close. Bunny said you're a writer. What's your writer's intuition tell you about our guy?"

"Hard to say, detective. You see, I don't have the right disposition for this. I tend to think that average people are basically wholesome."

"Hellsome?"

"Wholesome."

"Oh, wholesome. In my line of work, if you don't assume they're hellsome, you get shot."

"Hey, where're you from? Quincy?"

"Weymouth."

"I knew it!"

"You a North Ender?"

"Yes! How'd you know?"

"Only a North Ender would reference Paul Revere."

"We *are* the city's oldest neighborhood, detective."

"I think Back Bay is."

"Total misconception. False fact. Ours is the Neighborhood of Revolution. But we shouldn't quarrel. You have a gun."

Jacki Jaworski gave me her card—I understand detectives are always doing this—and spoke the line they must teach them at the academy: "If you remember anything at all, however seemingly small, don't hesitate to call or text," she added.

And then she asked if she could ask another question and I told her to ask away.

"Since you're a writer," she said, "I could use some advice. I've got this book I'm working on. A novel story. Detective thriller. It's good, I think. *Totally* true to life. I'm having a lot of fun writing it. And I was wondering if you might, if maybe you'd take a look at it for me? Maybe tell me what I can do with it? How to get a publisher, I mean."

"Oh. A novel. You're writing a, a novel. How unique. I mean, err, for a cop. You say it's a—a what?"

"Detective thriller. Takes place in Boston. It's about this female detective, right, *real* good at her job, middle-aged, a Marine vet, all that. Her name's Jacki Falcon. Her fellow detectives call her simply *the Falcon*. And that's the title! *The Falcon*. Well, she gets wind that there's a domestic terrorist plot to blow up the Hancock Tower and, get this: someone *inside* her department is part of the plot. A terrorist cop! So it's a race against time for her to expose the crooked cop and stop his terrorist pals before they can blow up the Hancock. A suspense fiction story." Lip-biting pause. "What do you think?"

"What do I, uhh, think? Well, I mean, it definitely—definitely sounds like a, a detective thriller. As you say. Race against time and all that. Terrorists and such. So you want me to—what do you want me to do?"

"Maybe just read it, tell me if it's good? I mean I *know* it is, and I'm having *so* much fun writing it. Really expressing myself, ya know? Really getting it all out. But I need to know how to get a publisher. I figured since you're a writer . . ."

"Right. I see. But, darn, I'm not a novelist. Not a scribbler of thrillers. I do critical stuff, memoir stuff. Nonfiction. So."

"Oh my book has *lots* of nonfiction. It's a *realistic* novel story."

"Aha. A realistic novel story. One with lots of, of nonfiction." Pause, a wee bit awkward. "Well, you know what: *of course* I'll look at it for you, detective. Of course. It would be my pleasure. Here's my email, I'll text you. Send it to me."

"Florence! Oh Florence!" we then heard Boris sing, and that was my signal to split.

In a separate suite I stuck around awhile with the hope that Face would return from his old high school in Eastie and give me some attention. I stayed long enough to partake of the spread that was wheeled up and laid out on tables, and this eased the old wound a bit. Turkey wraps! BLTs! Kettle chips! Prepared salads! Cans of Diet Coke! No one said I couldn't eat them and so I ate them.

After two hours of my digesting and delaying, Face still hadn't returned, so here was another missed chance for an interview session. Interview sessions with me were not, clearly, high on Face's list of things to get done. He'd ignored me on the bus to and from Portland the day before, and now he was doing it again. At two o'clock I left, went home, and nothing else happened that day even though I kept waiting for something else to happen that day. But nothing.

So I began reading Jacki Jaworski's novel, and right away, from the first chapter—the opening line was: "Jacki Falcon was pissed off"—I could see that she was a luminous alloy of Dorothy Sayers and Patricia Highsmith. It was so gorgeously gritty, so beautifully *Boston*, done in a whomping, whirring prose, that I soon became convinced she was headed for a million-dollar advance and then an Edgar Award. If my gig as Face's scribe didn't pan out, which I wasn't at all sure it would, maybe Jacki Jaworski would let me be her literary agent. Or, better yet, her co-author.

Near midnight, after reading the whole of Jacki's novel, with the snow slanting down again, with the temperature at eighteen degrees, and with the intrepid character Jacki Falcon strutting through my thoughts, I smashed into the sweet reprieve of sleep.

VII.

In the morning, at ten thirty, a phone call. Another ominous L.A. area code.

"Seger, it's Face."

It was Face. Val Face. On my phone. Calling me himself. From his own phone. My thought just then: *I have Val Face's cell number!* Why was I fixing my hair, covering my bald patch? Should I pout? Play wounded? Sound bruised? Funny, I didn't feel those lashes any longer. Could he smell my a.m. breath through the phone?

"Oh, hello, Face. Good morning."

"Come out and play, Seger."

"Come out and eh?"

"I'm out front."

"You're—did you say . . ." and I stumbled twice getting to my windows, first foot-crashing into a stack of books, then knee-banging into the shelf they would not fit into.

There, through season-sheared maples and the white exhaust of brownstones, two stories down, in the winter gray-white morn, I saw a scarlet machine. It looked like a bloodletting in a blizzard, at total imbalance with everything around it, the B-minus Fords and Subarus in their dulled blues and browns, some of them still frosted to the wheels in recent snowfall.

"Uh, that's you, there, in that—what's that?"

"Corvette ZR1 with 755 horsepower at 6500 rpms with 715 pounds of torque and a 2.65 liter blower intercooled atop a 6.2 liter supercharged V8 with double fuel systems. Seven-speed manual. You in?"

Why was he speaking these mathematics at me?

"Why are you speaking these mathematics at me?"

"Come on, are you in?"

"In what?"

"Are you coming *with me*, Seger?"

"With you? Where?"

"My parents' place in western Mass. I got you a coffee. Let's roll."

Okay. Certain terms need to be reached for here. *Euphoric. Elated. Excited. Erection.* And those are only the Es. Just consider what I could do with the Rs, let alone the Js.

See me flashing through our flat, toothbrush in one hand, deodorant in the other. See my various underthings yanked from drawers and strewn like confetti about the bed and floor. Waffled long johns, oh waffled long johns, where art thou? Ah, already on mine frame: I'd slept in them. Now one wool sock green, the other beige, but who'd know? See me then hopscotching into corduroys, discoing into cardigan, then fluffing the mustachio, scratching sand from the sleep-puffed eyes, doing the comb-over to camouflage the scalp's tundra. Boots? I'd lace them in the car. Jacket, hat, gloves, scarf: got 'em. Phone, where'd I'd put my phone? Aha, there on the bathroom vanity. Keys, keys, where are my keys . . . Right there in the pants I'd worn last night. Breakfast? *What* breakfast? No granola bar to grab. But my pal Face got me coffee.

The sidewalk traffic, though thinner at this hour, had to stop and gawk at the scarlet rocket ship, snap their pics, hear its sexy, throaty idle. They couldn't see who sat behind the wheel because, as with Face's bus and his flotilla of Chevy Suburbans, this Corvette's windows were tinted into opacity.

I could smell the unblemished machine from five feet away— it doesn't seem fitting to call it a car; this was like no car I'd ever seen or sat in—smell its new rubber and steel and chrome, its exhaust somehow pleasant, not assaultive. Into this flabbergasting contraption I went, the robust leather scent wafting up and into my sinuses.

And there in the driver's bucket seat? Someone with yellow hair to his clavicle, lightly tinted specs, and a mustard mustachio. Face incognito. But the largest surprise? No helicoptering handlers. No menacing Mario.

"How are you *alone*?" I said. "How'd you jailbreak?"

"Sometimes a guy's gotta jailbreak. Bad morning. Had to get the hell out."

Did Nimble know about this jailbreak? I was sure she'd be a ruckus of nerves after Portland's bomb threat. I expected Face to be in quarantine.

"And I can't bring everyone along to see my folks," he said. "My mother would flip her lid. How's my disguise?"

"Oh, that? It looks like—like a disguise."

Ah, the coffee he'd got me. I just wasn't wholly anthropoid without that first cup.

"Is this thing yours?" I said, indicating the rocket ship as I tried to buckle myself into it.

Why was the seat belt a full-on harness? There wasn't one buckle to snap into but three, an X across my chest. Were we going into orbit? He told me he had a silver one in L.A. but that his "Chevy people" dropped off this red one at the hotel this morning.

"It's fast is it?"

"*Seger.* This is a Corvette ZR1. A Springsteen fan doesn't know anything about American cars? Oh, Bruce would be disappointed in you, Seger. But of course you North Enders wouldn't know anything about cars: there's no damn place to *have* a car there. You North End guineas like living on top of one another."

"*Is* a bit snug, I suppose. But the restaurants."

"*There* you are correct, my friend."

Face was that class of driver who considers yellow lights an invitation to speed up.

"There are two kinds of people in the world, Seger. Those who slow down at yellow lights and those who speed up at yellow lights. Which will you be?"

"I just don't want to be the guy in the crosswalk when the speeders come through."

We meandered through Cambridgeport to Memorial Drive. When did traffic in Boston get so evacuative? After twenty minutes we made it over the Charles and caught 90 West. We'd barrel down it for nearly three hours till we reached his parents' place in Pittsfield, kissing the New York border. *He was taking me home to meet his parents.* My plasma hadn't been this pleased since Estelle said yes to the question. Here was a sitch to hop up all the hemoglobin. He was obviously brimming with remorse for how he'd ignored me in Portland. The guy had obviously been insomniac for two nights wondering how he could make it up to me.

When we curved out of the city and onto 90, Face floored his machine, unshackled the scarlet muscle of it: thirty to sixty to one twenty with a velocity that was against the grain and law both. Each time he touched the pedal of that toy its torque slapped, pinned me back into the heated seat. The vibrations of its lascivious motor came up through the frame, into all my lumbar, past my sacrum, and caressed, I thought, my prostate. I then saw the logic of the harness.

But how to credit this salvo of chumminess when for the past few days Face had appeared to find me leprous? From whence came this luck of having him now to myself, without the helicoptering handlers? How could coffee taste this good? Three hours is a lot of hours in a car that crammed. Think of the intimacy possible. I dared not fish the phone from my pocket to record for fear that it would yank him from his newfound charity, remind him that I was not really his pal but the balding essayist aiming to crowbar into his private realms.

Face then subjected me to exuberant car talk for the first *hour* of that ride, all the mathematics, the fractions and decimals, momentum, acceleration, the unswayable facts of swiftness. I made *mmm* sounds, *hmm* noises in my feigning of interest. If you want to get someone interested in you, you first have to get yourself interested in him. Guys who love themselves love when other guys love what they love: this is a law of some sort. My contribution to this car talk was: "Do we have enough gas?"

In most of fossil-fueled America, a man without a car is a man without a chance. In America, your car is your soul, which is why we're so fanatical about them—our cars, not our souls. It's all this space we have.

To swerve us from this exorbitant car chat, I asked Face when he first knew he wanted to be famous. But I had, he said, the question all wrong. He couldn't remember ever wanting to be famous, only *important*, to do something with his *special gift*, because when someone has that much *to offer*, if he doesn't offer it, it bursts within, turns him into a marauder of other people's dreams, an artist of delinquency, all snarl and sneer. Face appeared to believe that if he hadn't mobilized his talent for charisma, hadn't actuated his people power, he'd have graduated from Boston University with that dual degree in psychology and philosophy and become just another academic writing waterloos of prose, one more anonymous middle-class drone straining for relevance and slouching through the motions of marriage, mortgage, and mediocre children.

"But hey," he said, "let's quit the fame talk, *paisan*. I don't want to think anymore about it today. So, these speakers? Wait till you hear 'em. Get Bruce on the stereo. Go to the Bruce station."

The multiple beauties of an online stereo: just punch in what you wish to hear and there it is. Despite the wretched morning he had mentioned to me, Face was in too blithe a mood now to notice the hypocrisy of an anti-internet agitator asking me to find the Springsteen station on his car's cyber stereo.

"How do you work this thing?"

"*You're* the internet lover," he said. "Figure it out."

Twenty minutes: that's how long it took me to do this figuring. The stereo hadn't been set up, not programmed even a little. By the time I was able to summon Bruce on it—after a brief Diet Coke pit stop at one of those melancholy highway complexes that offer fast food and gas, in that order—by the time I got Bruce on the stereo, we were nearly two hours into our three, well away from Boston and its burbs. At this time, on this gray weekday, we were the only color on our side of the highway. Soon we were into the undulating ambers and blonds, fields and hills of winter russet, the vast spaces of western Mass that give a guy the urge to write a poem, a welcome remedy after so much city getting, city having.

"Okay," I said, "which Bruce do we want on this stereo? Are we talking early Bruce, circa *Asbury Park*? Middle Bruce circa *Born in the U.S.A.*? How about *The River*? Or how about stripped-down Bruce, circa *Nebraska* and *Thom Joad*? *Devils and Dust* is always a promising choice. Just please don't tell me you want that nineties Bruce of *Lucky Town*. And please don't say the more recent Bruce of *High Hopes*. Anything but that."

Notice anything about my speech? It was miraculously missing its U-turns, speed bumps, switchbacks, its tripping, stuttering, pausing, second-guessing. It appeared that having Face to myself in this way, snipped loose from his babysitters and bodyguards, meant a renewed confidence for the prose I spoke.

"What's wrong with recent Bruce?"

"Lord," I said, "that tight-jawed grunting of his recent singing style. It disappoints me *so* much, because his younger-days singing was so raw, the raw depth of it, but a depth with its own expansiveness. Especially live, especially in the seventies and eighties: some divine singing."

"You have the seventies and eighties so packed inside your head you're missing a hell of a lot about *this* decade."

"That's okay. It was my parents' time and it's always seemed to me better than my own—our own. My abandoned graduate thesis— did I tell you this?—my abandoned thesis was about celebrity culture in the seventies and eighties."

"There's nothing wrong with recent Bruce, you know."

"No, I can't listen to him live from, say, the turn of the millennium till now. All the grunting is as if he doesn't want his *throat* involved in the matter, just his teeth. By the way, I could use a bathroom in a minute or two, if you see a rest stop. All that coffee."

"Let's just listen to his best album then. One of the best of *all time*. Go ahead, find it, it should be there."

"Ah, his best album, gotcha. Let me see." Scroll, type, tap, scroll. "By the way, Face, we must be the only two Americans under forty who know this stuff." Scroll, type, tap, scroll. "Ah, okay, here it is. Got it. *Darkness on the Edge of Town*, baby."

"No, no. I said his *best* album, Seger. Get his *best* album on there."

"Yeah. I know. I heard you. Got it right here. Found it. *Darkness on the Edge of Town*. Done."

"No no. Come on. *Born to Run*, man."

"You said his best album."

"Right. I said his best album. *Born to Run*. His best album."

For about twenty stunned seconds, silence supervened as silence tends to do on such occasions. And don't scoff at twenty seconds—

they can take half a year when the circumstances are as dire, with as many grave implications, as those that now confronted Face and me.

"Face, be serious, *paisan*. You cannot possibly rate *Born to Run* over *Darkness of the Edge of Town*. My parents played Bruce every day in the house for years when I was growing up. Every *day*. For *years*. I think I know what I'm talking about. To prefer *Born to Run* over *Darkness on the Edge of Town*—that's just . . . it's unpatriotic, Face."

"I can't believe what I'm hearing from you right now. I really cannot."

"Well, believe it. Because if you really think that *Born to Run* is—"

"I'm pulling into this rest stop, and not because you have to piss, pal. We cannot go another mile until this is hashed out. I'm scandalized."

"You're what?"

"Scandalized."

"Oh, scandalized. Well, how do you think *I* feel when I hear someone with your insight proclaim something so false?"

I was still stupidly smiling at this point, still stupidly unaware of what was in the process of happening. How was *I* to know? He kept saying I'd committed an "outrage." And I suppose it was the way he kept saying it that clued me in to the gravity of the situation I had caused. Prior to that I'd thought he might be japing. Whatever had riled him that morning before he retrieved me must have still been storming inside him, and here I was, a shaft for his ventilation.

To say that this rest stop in western Mass was devoid of other people would be only beginning to describe it. Not only was it devoid of other people—it was devoid of *life*. No birds in hover; no bears intent to rummage; no deer hoofing twigs asunder. The trees weren't just winter-dead: they were anti-life. The only color in sight was the supernatural scarlet of the car.

We'd both, with considerable agitation and lumps of righteousness, exited the car, though this exiting took me twice as long as it had taken Face because I'd forgotten that I was not belted but *harnessed* into the seat. Some of us aren't used to being harnessed. I couldn't find the buckles' buttons. But then I did.

Do you know what twenty degrees does to your urination urge? We were now standing on either side of the Vette's hood, hands planted on its heat, as if we were consulting a war map. It was, I knew, a fairly ridiculous sight but too late now to alter or reverse. *Turn* of events? No, this was a woozy whiplashing of events, and when I fully realized that we were actually about to wrangle regarding Bruce—at a vacant rest stop in western Mass, in twenty degrees, with one of America's top celebrities donned in wig, specs, and mustachio—when the silliness of this landed on me, I did what you do: I fished out my phone and tapped record.

If we'd just then seen the Road Runner beep-beeping by with Wile E. Coyote roller-skating after him in a rocket pack, it would not have seemed at all out of place. Neither of us, it was clear, could put the brakes on this brawl. Testosterone is Nature's avenue of self-destruction: be led down it and nothing but ruin awaits you.

"Apologize," he snarled.

"For *what*?"

"For the provocation of saying that *Darkness on the Edge of*

Town is superior to *Born to Run*. You were deliberately provoking me. You know the morning I've had. And you provoked me."

"No I didn't. Why would—"

"You *know* how I feel about *Born to Run*, what that album meant to me as a teen. When other kids were listening to Justin *Timberlake*, for the love of God, I was holed up with Bruce."

"And how would I know that, Face?"

"I've said it in a hundred interviews!"

"I haven't read a hundred of your interviews. And I'm sorry to point it out, Face, but there's no *tension* between the instruments on *Born to Run*. There just isn't. The sounds are all laid out and inevitable. No tension. No exposed nerves. Now, the raw sparsity of *Darkness*, the relentless storytelling *vision* of the complete thing—"

"As if *Born to Run* doesn't have storytelling vision, as if—"

"It *does*, I know, I'm not saying—"

"As if it doesn't have a vision just as narrative and complete as *Darkness* but grander, much—"

"Yes, *that's* the problem, Face—or not problem, I don't mean problem, but that's the *difference* in conception, I mean: *Born to Run* is trying to do too much, it's much too *busy*—"

He fist-thumped the hood.

"No way. Bullshit. Right from the opening track of *Born to Run*, you hear the same tension throughout, the same novelistic tenor you're talking about on *Darkness*, except—"

I did some fist-thumping of my own.

"It's *not* the same, Face. It's pop, it's—"

"Except it's an *urban* tenor, with all of Clarence's sax work. Where's the sax work on *Darkness*, man? Where's—"

"It's there! The sax is there. Are you kidding? Clarence's work is even *stronger* on *Darkness*. But the sax on the album is sparer, that's what I'm saying, Face—"

"No way—"

"And that sparsity makes it stronger, gives it a *rural* strength—"

More fist-thumping on his part.

"No fuckin' way, Seger, you're deliberately—"

More fist-thumping on my part.

"Let me finish. Because when the sax comes on *Darkness*, Face, it really hits you, it's been lurking beneath the guitars and bass, it's there, waiting, you can *feel* it waiting to blow, and that tension—"

"*Born to Run* has the same damn tension, but even tighter."

"No it doesn't. It does not. You can't tell me, Face, you just cannot tell me that there's a track on *Born to Run* that matches the lyrical potency of the title track of *Darkness*. Or 'Racing in the Street.' There's just no possible way—"

"Oh yeah? I've got two words for you, pal: 'Thunder Road.' "

He thought he had me there, and he thought he knew it, the way he named the song with such finality, and the way he threw *pal* at me—not nice—and his face now, unrelievedly stern and knowing, even in that ludicrous disguise: the face of Face's one-upmanship. My bladder was throbbing there in my groin like a dented heart.

"Uhh, okay, agreed," I said. " 'Thunder Road' *is* an unequivocal masterpiece of songwriting, only I'm trying to consider the albums in toto, as novels, as complete sound pictures, as Bruce *wants us to do*. And by the way, know-it-all, the version of 'Thunder Road' that really grips the spine is the live version from '75, with only vocals and piano, the one that's on the album *Live/1975–85*. Now, if Bruce had put *that* version on the album, we'd have the beginning of an argument. But as things stand—"

"Crazy talk. This is stupid talk."

"And what about 'Night'? What kind of song is that, Face? The noisiness of it, that third track on *Born to Run*—forget about the laziness of the title—who's he? Elie Wiesel?—the *noisiness* of the whole song is too much, it's—"

"Okay, okay," he said, "tell me about 'Backstreets.' Show me a more beautiful beginning of a song, one better than 'Backstreets.' Show me, you cad. Show me a lovelier opening. And the lyrics, they're brilliance."

No way his Chevy people were going to be pleased with the way we kept punching the hood like that.

"Half of them are inaudible, Face. *Half* of them. And don't call me cad. Now, I move to the point of production. *Born to Run* is *so* overproduced and is simply—"

"Bruce produces the shit out of all his—"

"Let me finish—"

"Out of all his records. Produced just means worked at, perfected—"

"No it doesn't. It does not. It means *garish*. You simply cannot say that *Born to Run* is *mixed* as well as *Darkness*."

I was aware again that aside from us there was still no life or color at or around this rest stop, no cars swooshing along on the highway beyond the hill. Had the world ended? I kept waiting for a giraffe or a Sasquatch to smash from the woods and give us something to run from or else something else to argue about.

"Never mind about that, the production value," he said. "You didn't respond to my point about Clarence's sax work on *Born to Run*, the spiritual, and I mean *spiritual* sax playing on 'Jungleland'—how could you not appreciate that?"

"I didn't say I couldn't appre—"

"You of all people. I've read your essays, you guilty unbelieving Catholic you. For you not to appreciate—"

"I *do*. Christ. That's not what I'm *saying*, Face. And while we're on the subject of your having read my essays, I think you *mis*read some of them, pal."

"Never mind about that. You know how long it took Clarence to record that sax solo on 'Jungleland'? Sixteen hours, man. Sixteen straight hours of striving, striving to get it spiritually perfect. Bruce took him over every note for sixteen straight hours."

"Okay, okay then," I said. "Talk to me about the pointlessness of 'She's the One,' the sixth track on *Born to Run*. What's it about? What's it *mean*?"

"That's ignorant. That's pure ignorance, Seger. I'm beginning to question—"

"And do you care to explain 'Meeting Across the River'? Explain that one to me. *What* is that song doing on *Born to Run*? What is that song doing *anywhere* in the world? Is it even a song?"

"You're admitting you have no heart. That's what you're saying here. Your heart's a dime. No, your heart's a nickel if you aren't touched by that song. Your heart's no bigger than a minute, Seger."

My much maligned heart. What did my heart ever do to him? I thought to bring our bickering back to "Thunder Road."

"*It's a town full of losers and I'm pulling out of here to win*. I love 'Thunder Road' but that's escapism, Face, pure and simple."

"Right, right, because he should *want* to stay in a town full of losers. Right. Makes sense. Are you *kidding* me? He's taking initiative to enlarge his life, man, and if that means fleeing his town, his family, his community, whatever, then good for him. It's a peasant's mentality to say that he should stay and suffer in a dead-end town rather than enlarge his life, to fulfill his ambitions for a larger life."

"You're missing the point on purpose, Face. *Darkness* is an effort at understanding how we suffer, a man near the start of his manhood coming to terms with that suffering. I mean, there are rightly no *love* songs on *Darkness*. The adolescent angst on *Born to Run* is on *Darkness* tempered by an adult accountability, so—"

"No love songs is part of the problem—"

"So, I was saying, Face. Parents, community, compromise, *sin*: how to live with it, how to carry it. Those are his concerns at the time, and the gravitas of that—"

"*Born to Run* has gravitas—are you *kidding*?"

If I didn't urinate soon my bladder would surely mutiny. In addition to being misunderstood and maligned I was about to be wet from the pants down.

"The aural *tension* on *Darkness* is extraordinary, Face, the tension between the voice and the instruments. Austerity, man. Blue-collar concerns. Look at the opposites that *Darkness* holds in the hands of its music. Despair and resilience. Illusion and possibility. It's overwhelmingly *intimate*."

"You're missing the point of *Born to Run*. You're intentionally missing—"

"No I'm not. *Born to Run* is escapist: let's just run away. But *Darkness* is all about accountability, about—"

"No, Seger, no, *Darkness* is claustrophobic," he said, though he was spitting now—hood-thumping and spitting through his faux mustachio. "*Born to Run* is the *start* of *Darkness*, you dip. You simply cannot have *Darkness* without *Born to Run* first. The tracks are so immensely full and—"

"Too full, Face, much too full, that's my point, much too—"

"Wrong, wrong. The songs all begin with those introductions or invitations, the opening notes welcome you into the songs, songs that are, let's be honest here, songs that are epic in their sound. You just don't get that epic quality on *Darkness*, I'm sorry."

"Lies, these are lies, Face. Of course the tracks on *Darkness* are epic. Christ, how can you *say* that? Your definition of *epic* is broken."

"And something else you're missing about *Born to Run*," he said. "The *friendship* on the album. Which doesn't surprise me, actually, seeing as how you're probably friendless. You don't get that, the camaraderie of the album, the loyalty to friends."

Probably friendless? Okay, it was true, but still. And then he had more malevolence to hurl at me.

"You know what bothers people like you about *Born to Run*, Seger? Do you really want to know? I'll tell you. The intelligent innocence of it, its unapologetic youth and Romanticism, capital R. Cynics like you kill innocence whenever they can."

"Face—"

"*Plus*," he continued, "there's a theatricality on *Born to Run* that you simply don't hear on *Darkness*. There's a universality there, an expansiveness *Darkness* cannot accommodate. A *density* of sound, Seger."

"Yup. Density is the problem," I said, pretty quick in apprehending densities. "And don't call me friendless. A cynic, okay, sure, sometimes, but—"

"You fucking friendless cynic you, you're missing the *energy* of *Born to Run*, the optimism of it. *Darkness* is all darkness, it's—"

"No, no. It's Bruce getting back to his *roots,* Face—*that's* the point. His roots. A history, a Jersey upbringing that *sustains* him. He's—"

"That's crap, roots, give me a break. He was a multimillionaire by twenty-six, so don't tell me—and I love Bruce, don't get me wrong: I had *dinner* with the fucking guy in Paris last month, are you kidding?—but I'm saying, this roots argument is crap. He owed nothing to his roots. *Born to Run* made him the biggest musician on the *planet*, and what does he give us after it? *Darkness.* So don't tell me—"

Wait: whom were we really talking about here? And then, before I could clamp it, I said it.

"Ohhh, *I* see what's going on here now. I see. Yup. I see what this is really about, Face. You feel *guilty.*"

Blankness from his neck up, a blankness that made me say it again:

"You feel guilty."

"The fuck are you talking about?"

"Your roots," I said. "You turned your back on your roots and now you're venting that guilt by defaming *Darkness on the Edge of Town* because it remains loyal to roots. You can't stomach a superstar staying loyal to his own tradition because you didn't do it."

"You know something, Seger—"

"Because you didn't *want* to do it. Your lifestyle, your Beverly

Hills *estate*. Your needling entourage and diva behavior. You left Eastie and never looked back, not literally and not in your work, not anywhere that *I* can see, though, to tell you the truth, I'm still trying to figure out what exactly that work *is*, what the hell you actually *do* to be so goddamn famous, but I'll tell you one thing—"

"You know something, Seger? You wanna know some—"

"And I'll tell you one thing: whatever that work is, whatever it is *you do*, it's not loyal to your Eastie roots. Oh, you *pretend*, sure, pretend to care about roots, you actor you, going back to your old high school, what a sham. And you fool 'em by the millions. But it's nowhere in your 'work,' and I'm putting work in quote marks, pal. Nowhere in its conceptions, its executions, it's—"

"Get over your fucking self, you food pincher."

"Food pincher? Hey, *jerk*, I fed five hungry people with what you were gonna throw *into the fucking trash*, so don't—"

Half of his faux mustachio had become unglued and was flapping there beneath his symmetrical nose. *My* mustachio stayed firm.

"Bush league, you're bush league," he said. "You wanna help hungry people, start a foundation, think big. Don't pinch five cartons of pasta."

"And wait, you said get over *my*self? You weren't interested *in the least* when I told you I interviewed Lucy Genovese and Carmine Feludi for this chronicle we're doing, that you manipulated me into doing. They were your *friends*, man, and you didn't have a molecule of curiosity, of concern for them. They didn't deserve that. I can't believe—"

"Are you *serious*? You want to chastise me for not keeping in touch with people I knew in *high school*? What planet are you from?

Do I look like I have the fucking time to pal around with people from *high school*?"

"No, that's an example of a larger point, Face, a larger trend in your career—"

"You don't know the first damn thing—"

"A trend of denial and forsaking roots—"

"You're nuts. I'm sorry I ever—"

"You even moved your *parents* out of Eastie, man, as if to erase all memory of the Detti clan."

"Get my parents out of this conversation, you churl."

"You certainly got them out of Eastie. And, by the way, *that's* why you were so rankled when I told you I interviewed Lucy and Carmine for this profile, because *you know* they view you as a traitor, because they have you pegged as a class traitor. And don't call me churl."

"You *churl*, you don't have the slightest—"

"And while we're on the subject, Kahlil Gibran is a saccharine fraud."

"How is that *on the subject*? That's not on the subject."

"Yes it is. And something else. You know what I admire about your wife? She is who she is and isn't pretending to be otherwise. She's not trying to have anything both ways. What you see is what you get. Whereas you—you want both to *criticize* culture and *profit* from culture. You don't see the, the *dissonance* there?"

"Never mind my wife. But, actually, I'll tell you what: you should thank your fucking lucky stars for her because it certainly wasn't *my* idea to enlist your sorry ass as our writer. After that bullshit you wrote about me. And we *manipulated* you? We didn't manipulate anyone. Be an adult, be responsible for your own choices."

"I didn't say I wasn't respon—"

"And by the way, weirdo, speaking of dissonance: who loves Bon Jovi *and* Bruce Springsteen? Who does that? They're aesthetically incompatible. Just because they're both from Jersey doesn't mean they belong together. Bon Jovi is so goddamn corny."

"What! Blasphemer! I was *conceived* to Bon Jovi!"

About my bladder: you know whom I thought of just then? Tycho Brahe, the sixteenth-century Danish astronomer. Let me explain. Tycho Brahe attended a Prague banquet one night with the king, and he did what you do at a Prague banquet with the king: imbibed most prodigiously. Well, imbibe most prodigiously and soon your bladder is bloody murder. But if the king relaxes into one of his overlong-winded stories about his boyhood or some such, guess what you cannot do. You cannot get up in the middle of this overlong-winded boyhood tale and scurry off to the latrine. The king would be connipted. The king would have your head. So Brahe held it. And held it. Really kinked down on it. And finally, after the king's loquaciousness, Brahe staggered home with an exploded bladder and died of uremia.

"And," I said, "Bon Jovi and Bruce Springsteen are incompatible only if you're tiny minded. If you have no *variety* to your palate, if you—"

"Fuckin' weirdo."

"You're calling *me* the fuckin' weirdo? Look at *your* life, pal. *I'm* the normal one here. I'm the one with all the, with, you know, all the *normality.*"

"And what's with your Bob Seger thing? Explain that oddness."

"Oh, oh now you've done it. You've gone and done it now. My mother *sang* to Bob Seger in the kitchen as she cooked every night! Show me, go ahead, show me a song more American than 'Night Moves.' Go ahead. It makes 'Jack and Diane' look positively Soviet."

"Pathetic."

"And you're no charismatic either, pal. Charisma, give me a break. You're just another American whoring after fame any way you can. Another capitalist greed machine. In the past few days you had two big chances to prove your charisma, to defuse those situations, at Addison and in Portland, and you let your handlers handle it. And you're calling me pathetic? You're a corporation, not a charismatic."

"The gall of you to write that article about me. The sheer snarky gall of you, you fuckin' nobody."

"Oh yeah? That article was the *nice* draft, pal. You should see the nasty one."

My sight was impaired by anger, true, but I could have sworn that the cloud behind Face was shaped like Estelle's head when her hair is knobbed up in a bun.

"I'm done," he said. "I'm finished with you. See ya, Seger. See ya around and fuck you."

I needed several seconds to take in that last part.

"See me—what do you mean, *see me around*? You can't—you're *leaving me here*?"

In me now a panic where a minute prior such fury reigned, because he hurried into his Vette and locked me out of it. I knew it was locked because I frantically, fruitlessly yanked at the door handle, yelling desperations such as *Let me in* and *You can't do this to me* and *This isn't Christian*.

But he didn't care. He didn't let me in. He gassed that beast and tore away, nearly gimping me in the ankle area.

■ ■ ■

As if on queue, down came a coat of snow to tamper with the roads and further frost my feelings. I stood there in the center of that vacant parking lot, watching the Vette roar away, flakes amassing on me. Would those few non-extinct cabbies come this far to retrieve me? Would Uber drivers? Did Uber even function in this stripped pastoralia? But it didn't matter: I couldn't pay them. Wait: Would my phone function out here beyond the reliable resources of civilization? Could I contact Estelle for help? And how would she help? She didn't drive. She didn't drive the car we didn't have. I'd have to hitchhike. And I'd probably be picked up by some lunatic erroneously loosed on parole by a muddled prison staffer.

I galumphed into the skeletal boles to relieve my ailing bladder and watch the steam as the honey-hued remains of my coffee slapped the cracked earth. Perhaps a different fella would have used the restroom behind the vending machines, but I object to the scent. Of the restroom, not the vending machines.

Next thought on deck, midstream: John Rambo. I'll explain. There's that part in the film *First Blood*—1982: *great* year for pop culture—that part, remember, when Stallone is fleeing, huffing from the cops, in winter, in the wilderness, in only a *tank top*. When I say *only* I mean the torso: his pants and boots are still with him, naturally, since he's just fled the precinct on a stolen dirt bike. Even John Rambo would have a hard time on a dirt bike without his pants and boots. Anyway, Stallone's in the wilderness with no jacket, positively iced through. You can't watch this sequence without feeling the freeze of it.

Now, Rambo is a Green Beret, has all manner of survival clout. He invents a fire, then a coat in an abandoned mine shaft. He's got that hunting knife with the hollow handle, remember, inside it some items an outlaw needs while coatless in the winter woods: matches, fishing line, needle and thread, and I don't know what other lifesaving goodies. Here's what I'm getting at: a) when you see me, John Rambo isn't exactly the first image that bubbles up in your mind; and b) even if I had been blessed with Rambo-ing industry, I didn't have on me my phallic hunting knife with the hollow handle and its lifesaving goodies. I had my jacket and everything else, gloves and scarf and hat and all, true, plus thermal underthings and the rest, but I was sure that in every other aspect the circumstances now upon me were perfectly analogous to Sylvester Stallone's in *First Blood*.

I'd finished rescuing my bladder by this point and was zipping up, wondering how I'd hunt down my food, some depressed doe or hare having a day sluggish enough for me to snare it. Could I aim rocks at it?—skin it with shards of flint?—mate two twigs for flame? Just as I'd settled on this method, I thought to check my phone and found that my plans weren't necessary: I had full service. Thank God for those poobahs at Verizon and their 5G. I thought then to text Estelle so I could clue her in to my present hardship and the saga of how it had hardened.

"Stalloned in wilderness. Fought with Face re: Springsteen.

Thinks Born to Run superior to Darkness on Edge of Town. Miles from civilization. Might perish."

I'd finally turned off my autocorrect, you see.

She typed: "Did u just use Stallone as verb? And what in god's name r u talking about?"

Ah right, I hadn't told her that Face had picked me up that morning to accompany him to western Mass, so I rectified that.

She typed: "U fought about what?"

"He thinks Born to Run better than Darkness on Edge of Town."

A smattering of question marks, all in a row.

"Springsteen albums, love."

"U know what I think?"

"Do tell."

"Who gives a shit: that's what." Shit emoji, a happy chocolate chip capped by a swirl. Then: "Call him to apologize."

I didn't own that breed of gloves that allows you to text or otherwise touch your phone, so my right hand was icing fast.

"Will do no such thing. Will perish in this Land of Nod first."

"No time to get biblical." Bible emoji. "U will apologize."

"Won't."

"Will."

"There's, uhh, something else."

"Did u just type uhh?"

"Did."

"Don't like sound of uhh."

"Something I might have said."

"Dear god. What did u say?"

"Might have called him class traitor."

"Face?"

"Yes."

"U called him class traitor?"

"Might have."

"Dear god."

"I know."

"U didn't."

"Pretty sure. Class traitor disloyal to roots."

"Dear god."

"Also might have said he's weirdo, fraud, pony." Pony emoji.

"U called him pony?"

"Phony I mean."

"U didn't."

"Pretty sure. Memory's fuzzy on it."

"Now we're in poor house." House emoji, though it wasn't a poor one.

"I'm sorry, love."

"Apologize to HIM please."

"Can't."

"Must."

"Can't."

"CAN. Or else."

But as I was trying to stir up the old nerve and stamp down the old pride, to think of the quickest way of reconnecting *hunky* to *dory*, to come up with an apology for Face that wouldn't insult all my androgens but that would also get me ransomed from this rest stop and not fired from this assignment, I saw an SUV come into the lot and crawl toward me.

I say *SUV* but these things are, as you know, rather like yachts, the kind of thing Face had a fleet of, that Chevy Suburban or whatever planet-snuffing thing it is. This black behemoth looked keen on iniquity, though I realized that I probably looked that too, solo at the center of an abandoned rest stop, my presence inexplicable without the wheels that had borne me here.

Still, in a contest of which looked keener on iniquity, I'd say the SUV was winning it. What front-page malefaction was about to mangle me now? I briefly considered bolting into the woods for cover, à la John Rambo. Closer toward me this yacht tacked, I motionless there like a writer in the headlights. Who, you're wondering, could be at the wheel of this dark yacht? Good question. Down the window went. And I saw.

It was that Attila of Italian stock, Mario, no doubt come to dump on me a bucketful of the baleful. Turned out he'd been not far behind us the whole time, the whole way from Boston, surveying our progress, forfending disaster, making sure no molestation befell Face. Malignantly complected in the gray slant of winter's light, he was looking at me now through the window with an expression that spoke tomes about the reprobate he thought I was. I knew I wasn't going to be able to count on his empathy, which he couldn't do very well, or on his sympathy, which he couldn't do at all.

"Get in, fucko."

"Get in?"

"Get *in*."

"Ah, *get in*, right."

So I got in, and who was there in the back, set up at a kind of desk with two laptops where the middle row of seats should have been? Jacki Jaworski.

"Oh, hey, Detective Jaworski. Very nice to see you again."

"Florence."

"Eh?"

"It's Florence Dupont. Bunny's cousin. Boris says I have to stay in character."

"That would explain the costume," I said. "Boris dressed you in that? In that hoodie and baseball cap?"

"Boris dressed me in this. Let's not talk about it."

"Don't disturb her, fucko. She's going through names and faces and trying to match one to Bill. She's also on the lookout for his car, which she thought might try to follow Face today."

Which would explain the binoculars round her neck.

Face had known that Mario was behind us somewhere, watching—of course he'd known—and he'd called Mario to instruct him to backtrack and retrieve my sorry self, Face being too pissed with me to endure my travel companionship, but not so pissed that he was willing to have me snacked on by a Sasquatch in western Mass. Whether or not Face had given him the reason for our breach, or where Mario and Florence themselves stood on the question of *Born to Run* versus *Darkness on the Edge of Town*, I cannot say because I did not ask.

On the seat beside him, a bag of sunflower seeds, the shells of which he spat hurry-scurry: he looked snowed on by them. On the stereo, an oldies station, it seemed, Barry Manilow's opinion of what love does to our amino acids. And in the air between us, a tension you'd have needed a chain saw to chop up properly.

I was about to ask if we could change Barry Manilow to a singer less suicide-inducing, but, before I said, it, thank God, I spotted something in that storage area beneath the stereo: *half a dozen* Barry Manilow CDs. Half a dozen Barry Manilow CDs is a lot of Barry Manilow CDs, any way you cut it. It seemed Mario was the deputy or some such of Manilow's fan club. It also seemed he still listened to CDs, as if no one had ever told him that there was an easier way to hear music. When I thought of how close I'd just come to disparaging Barry, to getting thrust out onto the highway, abandoned anew, I blunted the tongue, instructed it to behave, which in this case meant to lie.

"Can we turn up this song, Mario? Mr. Manilow gives me faith in our damaged clan."

And he pivoted to me then, practically from the waist—or from that section where his waist should have been, which isn't simple for a fella that big to do in a belted seat—and considered me over his many eaves, bestowing upon me a look that gooed *Simpatico! Fellow Manilovian! Smart man!* It was definitely the smartest thing I'd done in weeks. He even passed me the bag of sunflower seeds so I could partake.

But then of course he turned up the song.

■   ■   ■

RETURN TO YOUR FAMILY OF ORIGIN and no matter who you are, no matter how high you've scratched, how far you've fled, you return to find your folks and kin essentially unaltered, and to find yourself not as altered as you'd conned yourself into thinking. In a whoosh you get whisked back to a disgruntled adolescence when you were massively oppressed by the gloom of domestic ho-hummery, sibling strife, and the sureness that everyone else was too dim to understand you and your magnificent uniqueness.

Face's parents' home and ten acres included the ten-thousand-square-foot ranch-style abode; the detached three-car garage stuffed with Cadillacs; the hayless, horseless barn; the guesthouse beside it; the swimming pool, the bathhouse, the tennis court. The nearest neighbor was a mile distant. All this for two non-tennis-playing, non-swimming, non-barn-needing sexagenarians who could have done with some neighbors. The driveway was its own road; you needed a golf cart to get from the front porch to the mailbox. And there they were, twin golf carts in one of the garage bays, with His and Hers license plates.

It was even colder out here than it had been in Boston. You'd have thought that with such high property taxes in these parts, they could have done something about the temperature, since what's the point of living in a regal zip code if it doesn't get you certain perks. But no. Nineteen degrees.

We'd followed Face from the main road and parked in the circular drive. I exited the yacht, he exited the Vette, and though I looked at him he didn't look at me. I wanted my look to convey a shrugging apology, an *Oh well, no bad feelings* or *Let's move on*, but he didn't see it. He didn't see it because he was obviously still irked, and because he was looking at his parents, both of whom had come out of the house to greet him. He'd removed his ridiculous disguise so as not to startle his mother.

Mr. Detti liked flannel and disliked haircuts: I saw where Face got his stellar locks. He called up memories of Mike Wallace, if Mike Wallace had disliked haircuts too. He had a senior masculine beauty. Mrs. Detti was in her apron and looked as though she nightly slept in it. The beauty she'd been in her youth was still detectable beneath the face's knife-thin grooves and despite her little rooster's wattle. Whom did she call up memories of? Think Sophia Loren circa *Ready to Wear*. A handsome pair who hadn't let the pasta go to their guts, they looked exactly like two people who'd spawned someone who looked like Val Face.

The first thing Mrs. Detti said to her son was the first thing you'd expect Mrs. Detti to say to her son: "Where's your *jacket*, dear?"

"It's in the car, Ma."

"You're looking for the flu? It's *flu* season, Val."

"Look at this thing," Mr. Detti said. "This a Corvette? Pretty sharp."

Hugs, kisses, greetings all around, even for Mario.

"Mr. and Mrs. Detti," said Mario, "this is my cousin, Florence Dupont."

"Florence Dupont," Mr. Detti said. "That Irish?"

"French, I believe, sir."

"Oh, French," he said. "Never met a Frencher. Didn't have many of those in Eastie. Well, welcome, welcome."

"Come inside and eat, everyone," Mrs. Detti said. "I've got meatballs cooking. Mario, come eat. Florence, do the French each meatballs or just—is it frog legs you're known for?"

"I think so, ma'am. Frog legs and, I think, French fries."

"Well, I don't have any frogs for you, but plenty of meatballs. They'll be ready in a minute."

"This thing a turbo?" Mr. Detti asked. "Eight cylinder, right?"

Face told him to take it for spin and Mrs. Detti said no, he'd kill himself in it.

Then Face waved me over, laid an arm across my shoulders, and introduced me to his parents. I seemed to be, thank God, forgiven. His mother seemed that sort of homemaker who keeps the plastic covers on lampshades.

"A pleasure, ma'am," I said to his mom. "A pleasure, sir," I said to his dad. "Thank you for having me to your home."

"It's *Jovi* you say?" asked Mr. Detti. "That Sicilian?"

"No, sir. New Jerseyan, I believe."

"Huh. And it was *Seger*, your name? Your parents were hippies you say?"

"No, sir, it's my"—and I made the universal hand gesture that means writing, the invisible implement pinched between thumb and index—"my writer's name."

"Huh. Your writer's name. What's wrong with your right name?"

"Lou, it's *freezing*," Mrs. Detti said.

"Mario," said Mr. Detti, "how've you been? How's Barry?"

"I'm very good, sir. And Barry's great. There're rumors online he has a new album coming out soon."

"Hot damn. A new album by Barry. Well, good luck with it, son."

"Thank you, sir."

"Always been more of a Neil Diamond man myself."

"I can understand, sir."

"Nothing against Barry."

"No, sir."

"They're both great."

"I think of it as a difference in the depth of feeling, sir."

"Everyone, I have *meatballs* almost ready. Please," Mrs. Detti said.

But Face was now showing his father the Vette. He was clearly more interested in impressing him than he was in chowing the meal his doting mother had confected for him. No matter who we are or where we come from, raised by royalty or raised by wolves, we boys are helpless not to seek affirmation from our fathers.

There inside the house, at the storm door fogging the glass, peering out at us in the driveway was a shorter, slenderer Val Face—Val Face in a wig. His sister, Talia, younger by a year.

Face, seeing her, said, "Ma, you didn't tell me Tal would be here."

"Tell you? Tell you why?"

"Just a heads-up, Ma."

"Heads-up for your sister? Why on earth? She's your *sister*."

"Okay, Ma. How's she seem?"

"Seem? She's fine, Val. Come in. See for yourself. And *eat*."

■ ■ ■

WE WERE ALL AT LAST in the Christmas-stained vestibule, beneath a promiscuous dangling of mistletoe, as if Mrs. Detti were trying to promote mononucleosis. From the ceiling speakers Bing Crosby hawked his philosophy of silver bells. Face greeted Talia with a smooching "Hey, sis," and her smiling reply was: "Where's Stalina? Overseeing a pogrom somewhere?"

So there you have Face's sister's view of Face's wife: the female Joseph Stalin. Face asked her to play nice.

"*Kid*ding," she said, and she moved in and up to kiss half his mouth, then gently bit upon his lower lip.

"And who do we have here?" Talia said.

"Oh, I'm Seger Jovi, so pleased to meet you. I'm the, the official writer."

"Oh the *writer*, yes. Official, wow, sounds serious. I should have said *Whom do we have here*, right, since you're a writer. Let's start over. *Whom* do we have here?"

"Seger Jovi," I said, "so pleased to meet you. I'm the official writer. Face has told me—"

"*Face* has told you what?" she grinned. "What has *Face* told you?"

I really loved the way her own face advertised a cultivated resistance to taking her brother too seriously. She had a comedian's way with intonation and air, as if she were continually on the lookout for fitting tomfoolery, madcaps to bring the lauded low. But then I recalled what Lucy Genovese had said to me about her: *Outta her mind, man.* Okay, she might have been out of her mind; she just didn't *seem* as if she were out of her mind. And I was beginning to wonder if Lucy Genovese was the proper person to go around saying that other people had been disjoined from their minds.

Mr. Detti was trying to get us all to spend the night, due to the case of wine he'd bought, and the guesthouse that had yet to see any guests.

"We got a good TV in there, Mario," he said. "You can watch some Barry concerts."

"Thank you, sir. We will," Mario said.

"Very grateful, sir," said Jacki.

"What about you?" he asked me, already, I saw, having misplaced my name somewhere in the driveway. "You wanna stay the night?"

"Certainly, Mr. Detti. Whatever Face has planned."

"Lou, take his *coat*, the writer's coat. And Florence's too. Come *on*, Lou."

"How about I take the writer's coat," he said. "And Florence's too."

"Mario, you hunk," said Talia, "where's my hug?"

"Hello, Ms. Talia, very nice to see you again. How are you?"

"How am I? It's a bit soon to tell, Mario. Ask me after I've had four more of these," and she held up the glass of burgundy in her hand. "And you're Mario's cousin?" she said to Jacki.

"Yes, miss. Florence Dupont. Very nice to meet you."

"Florence Dupont. Sounds like a name out of a novel."

"I suppose it does, miss. My parents were . . . novelists."

"Names are like family members, right?" Talia said. "Not a goddamn thing you can do about them. I mean, aside from changing your name and killing your family."

"Talia, *please*," said Mrs. Detti.

"*Kid*ding, mother. Jesus."

"Why are we standing here at the *door*?" Mrs. Detti asked. "There's a *chill*. And I've got meatballs in a minute. Your favorite, Val."

"Yeah," Talia said, "your favorite, Val. And I promise I didn't lace them with cyanide. Hemlock *maybe*, but cyanide, no," and she winked—at *me*. It felt wonderful to get it.

"Talia helped me *cook* them, Val. We don't even have hemlock in the *house*. Don't *start*, Tal."

Val and Tal. But the sibs didn't appear to rhyme in any other way. She was a fizzy one all right; I adored her already. She held that glass of burgundy like a pro, and her blush told me that she'd held four others before that one. The blush said: *I try not to care.* Said: *The world is nuts and we best cackle at it.*

Mrs. Detti instructed all shoes to be removed, which meant that everybody would see that one of my socks was beige and the other green, but I had to be brave enough to bear that. Out of the vestibule and into the kitchen we all moved, a kitchen so bedecked with tinsel, candles, wreathes, candy canes, clay Nativities, Yuletide cutlery, more mistletoe, and overall seasonal cheer that it recalled the section at Macy's, if Macy's still exists, where Santa gets sat on by sinister brats. These decorations promised mandatory merriment, promised to coax festiveness from you, like it or not.

And now, before me, around me, I had something with which to contrast my boyhood kitchen. The Dettis' kitchen can't accurately be described as a room—a room has a perimeter. The Dettis' kitchen had that too, but you had to walk a while to reach it. I'm saying their kitchen was a palatial *space*, an open-plan space with twelve-foot ceilings that without seam turned into the living room on one end—which also wasn't a room but another space all the way down there, where the TV and sofas were—and a dining area on the opposite end, a monarch's table beside regal windows that gaped against a saw-toothed view of hills.

Life, I couldn't help but see, was better in a kitchen such as this. Why were my feet so toasty? Radiant heat, coming up through the tiles! There were two sinks, two fridges, two ovens. A quartz dining island with six stools on one side of it. A walk-in pantry you needed maps not to go astray in. Dishwasher, microwave, toaster oven, blender, all invented by some Japanese genius of convection and chrome. On the stove boiled macaroni in the largest pot I'd ever seen. Like any rank-and-file Italian, Mrs. Detti knew that if you're eating meatballs with marinara gravy you'll soon be craving some species of macaroni to go with it. The aroma in that kitchen? Ambrosial. I would never have another writing assignment that fed me so well.

There ensued a strenuous back-and-forth on who should slice the bread: Mr. Detti won—or lost. And at the quartz island, Talia sat on a barstool flaunting her half-grinned silence, embalming herself with more burgundy. You might have thought there was some secret purpose, some provocation, to her sitting there like that, with that furtive grin that said she'd figured out something you didn't know needed figuring. But no—she was just sitting there like that. Jacki stood at the enormous windows, gazing out past the blanketed swimming pool and lonely tennis courts, taking in the view of jagged hills beyond patches of forest.

Christmas was still about three weeks away and yet the Dettis—not Talia—had costumed themselves in holiday sweaters as if Santa were already reindeering en route. These were frightful wool concoctions in red and green, Mr. Detti's showing Frosty the Snowman, Mrs. Detti's showing, I think, the star of Bethlehem. Mario, too, had costumed himself in a cream-colored sweater with an embroidered Christmas tree on it, worn, I was sure, solely for the delight of Mrs. Detti, since it was clear that these sweaters were her doing.

From the ceiling speakers Bing Crosby's tinseled calm shifted into the brackish Christmas bliss of Mariah Carey. Everywhere you looked your eye collided with Lenox décor, little sledding figurines, rocking horses, snowmen, snowflakes. The fat tree beside the sofa had been decorated with surgical care, with an algebraic precision. From almost every wall grinned ten-by-twelve black-and-white framed photos of Tal and Val in various strata of childhood, then adolescence, then early adulthood, and you couldn't help but see that there were slightly more photos of Val than Tal.

"Let me guess," said Talia, "there's nothing in the way of a salad, correct, Mother? Only all that starch and fat to give me a premature grave."

"Make a *salad* then, Tal. There's salad stuff, dear."

"I'm happy to make it, Ms. Talia," Mario said.

"Oh, Mario, make me your *wife*."

Talia, this tongue-in-cheek compeller of clouds, brought up memories of Liza Minnelli circa *Cabaret*.

"Very flattered, Miss Talia. I'm spoken for, though."

"Tal, don't *tease* Mario," her mother said. "It's not *nice*."

Really can't have been easy for Talia. If you think big celebs make us small non-celebs feel rotten about our own selves, imagine for a sec what those big celebs do to their small sibs.

The bread now sliced into a beckoning mound, Face's father began clinking the wineglasses and making them full. Not a frequent drinker, I nevertheless saw that I was going to have to get well oiled to endure the ordeal of this dining. I'd need some irrigation for the arid soul to go with the meatballs for the empty gut. I still wasn't wholly over my and Face's Springsteen throwdown and wondered if I'd ever be, so unstringing was it. So I took the glass passed to me by Mr. Detti and waited until Face had one too, at which point I sidled up to him and offered to touch mine to his.

"*Salud, paisan*," I said, and he winked at me in return.

I might have still been tumbled by our flap but Face clearly was not. I really did marvel at his capacity to move on from a quarrel in which he'd been insulted as a phony of the first degree. But when I chewed it over later that evening, in the fumes from my wine, I saw that it wasn't a marvel after all, not for him, since he'd reached his altitude in part because he wasn't affected by rejection and insult, didn't care to *credit* your rejection of him. His indifference to insult was itself an insult against the insulter. You just weren't important enough, potent enough a person to rattle him, confound his composure, his whopping belief in his own starlit abilities.

Mariah Carey's schmaltz now at an end, George Michael began bellyaching about the previous Christmas when his hasty heart got squeezed in the grip of some undeserving imp. Meanwhile, Talia's idea of setting a table was to clank and bang as much silverware as possible. She had considerable difficulty telling the difference between help and hindrance, and kept saying *Oopsie doopsie* and *Oops, butterfingers* and *Oops, I hope we have spare one of this set.*

Jacki then slipped out back for, she said, an airing and a stretch, but not before she whispered something into Mario's earhole.

My wine was already gone because when I drink, I drink. I go in for pailfuls of the stuff, a total pollution of the tissues. I aim to really blight the marrow, making up, I suppose, for an assembly line of sober nights. Perched there at the island, I thought it only right to offer culinary help to Mrs. Detti.

"Mrs. Detti, would you like me to slice some butter?"

Her look uttered all the confusion I was.

"Did you say slice some *butter*, dear?"

She was transferring the meatballs from the pot to their plates and ladling them with pools of marinara.

"Yes, ma'am. You know, little squares of butter, for the bread."

"Did you grow *up* eating sliced butter, dear?"

"In a manner of speaking, ma'am. My mother didn't like the sight of an abused stick of butter. She found it vulgar. The lumpy, melty asymmetry of it, I think."

"My. The North End *is* a colorful place. Such odd customs you have there. Butter's in the fridge, dear. And, Talia, when you're done with the setting, the macaroni should be ready."

"Oh, the *macaroni's* ready. I better tend to it then, Mother. Wouldn't want Val to break a nail helping out."

"He's talking to your *father*, dear. *Please*. He doesn't get here very often, let's be under*standing*."

"Mother, I am the very *picture* of understanding," and here she framed her face with both thumbs and pointers, her lashes flapping in faux vogue.

Val and Mr. Detti had walked their wine to the sofas, where father was enlisting son in some much needed help with a wall-mounted TV preposterously large, the kind of excess intent to injure all your vision. You had to turn your head to see from one side of this thing to the other; you couldn't use just your eyeballs in the affair.

"So, Mrs. Detti," I said, slicing squares of butter into saucers, "can I, do you mind if I quote you in my profile of Val?"

"Quote me on what, dear? You haven't asked me any questions."

"Right, okay. So, when he was a child, when Face was growing up, did you know he was something special?"

"Yes, Mother," Talia said, "when did you first realize that your son was the messiah?"

I cherished her grinned winks at me, I did. Each one brought me closer into the womb of her confidence, which was exactly where I yearned to be. She grabbed the vat of macaroni and poured it into a colander in the sink, the steam rising to engulf her from the chest up, which seemed somehow a metaphor for something related to her.

"So yes," Mrs. Detti told me, "I've always known. In those talent shows, in grade school, you know those? When kids get up there and do a little dance or song or something talenty? Well, Val would get up there and just *charm* everyone. Just like he does now. Just charm the whole auditorium. He was maybe ten, eleven years old, just charming the heck out of hundreds of people, going down among them, in the audience, asking questions about their lives, having all this insight into them, into the parents of his classmates—the *parents*. He spoke philosophy, that's what it was. A little philosopher. And there was that time at Piers Park, when he was about ten, preaching to those two old men, those two wise men who'd sit there all day philosophizing. They loved him."

"He read Kahlil Gibran at ten years old."

"Who, dear?"

"The book *The Prophet*, by our fellow Bostonian, Kahlil Gibran. Face read that and was influenced by it."

"Oh. I suppose I'd forgotten that. I suppose that's right. It was my book. I couldn't make up or down of it, but Val really liked it, you're right."

As she stood ladling sauce onto the macaroni, Talia was growing ruddier by the minute—the vino's alcohol percentage tasted twice as high as what's copacetic for your cells—and I approved of her ruddiness because the ruddier she was, the looser her tongue became. By this time George Michael was done bellyaching and, thank God, Chuck Berry came on to rock Rudolph's praises.

"And he's always looked like that?" I asked. "With that face?"

"Oh definitely. He's always been so satisfying to look at. I mean, Talia was beautiful too, of course."

"Got that, Seger?" Talia said. "I was beautiful too, of course. *Was.*"

She jabbed out her tongue and crossed her eyes in an effort to uglify her face, but such a face simply would not be uglified, no matter what tricks she tried to pull on it.

"But you just couldn't believe these, these *motivational* things coming from Val at such a young age," said Mrs. Detti. "A real showman's *presence*. He seemed to *know about* people, even as a kid. I'm his *mother*, of course, so I'm biased. All mothers probably think their children are special, but they can't all be right, right? Not everyone's special. But Val, he was so *smart* so young, and, well, you just wanted to look and listen."

From behind her mother, Talia snagged my eye and mimed puking into the sink, her pointer finger inside her perfect mouth. Then she took that same pointer finger and made loops beside her temple: the universal gesture for cuckoo.

■ ■ ■

WITH A NEWLY RESTORED HANDFUL OF VINO and all the butter sliced, I left the kitchen-island prep and traipsed down to where Face and his father were on the sofas beside the glistering Yuletide fir, on the TV a college football contest that announcers were dissertating upon with the seriousness of churchgoing cancer researchers. Everything about these two TV voices said: *We would die without football to dissertate upon.*

Face corrected his father's television woes by thumbing some buttons on the remote, then drifted back to the island to assist his mother and blister his sister simply by being. Then Chuck Berry's homage to Rudolph slid into Springsteen's version of "Santa Claus Is Comin' to Town," which, on any other December day, would have been ample reason to rejoice, but today, so soon after my rest-stop flap with Face, I feared mightily that the song would remind him of said flap, and thus remind him that I was a scamp and wretch undeserving of his attentions. To my hearty relief, however, I heard that Talia had begun making jokes again at Nimble's expense—I thought I'd heard the terms *harridan* and *hellcat*, then *gorgon* and *gestapo*— and so Face was sufficiently diverted by that.

"So, Mr. Detti," I said, sitting, "do you like your son's performances?"

"Which one's that now?"

"You know, the—the live shows he does. His performances."

"Right, those. Never been to one myself. His mother went a few times. I saw that DVD of his, though. Well, some of it. Forget its name. His mother had it on the TV one night. The one where he's on stage? Talking, I think. Saying things to an audience. That one."

Pause. Then: "Can't understand it all myself."

"Did you like his memoir?" I asked.

"His what now?"

"You know, his—*About Face*, his memoir. His book."

"Yup. His mother read that one. Good book, she said. We're in it. But I like TV. Look at this TV, will you? Great, right? I got about a thousand channels. The gal who put this in—you know they've got gals who install these things now?—well, she wanted to put the internet inside it, said I could have *two* thousand channels, if I wanted. I said I didn't want that internet inside my TV. I heard it can spy on you. And who needs two thousand channels? One thousand is a bunch. I got a dish on my roof—gives me all these channels. Gal said I wasn't taking full advantage of what this TV could do if I didn't put the internet in it. I told her I don't take advantage of nobody, the dish is fine. Look at the *picture* on this thing, will you?"

So we looked.

"I need it out here in the sticks, believe me," he said. "There's no people to talk to. He moves us out here to this wilderness. No neighbors. Who are the neighbors? We don't know. Something wrong with Eastie? With Jeffries Point? Tell me."

"You didn't want to move?"

"Hell no I didn't want to move. Not here. In Eastie we lived next to Rosso's Bakery. The smell! What can I smell out here? Trees. Who wants to smell trees? Every morning I'd walk over to Rosso's, get pastries. Here? I gotta drive fifteen minutes to the bakery, and you call that a bakery? That's no bakery."

Right above the TV? A crucifix, Christ hanging out in the living room. And good news about the lampshades: they didn't wear the plastic covers they came with.

I heard more terms coming from Talia over by the island area. *Smote*, I believe, was one of them, followed by *impaled*, their mother saying, "*Talia*, *please*, Nimble's a nice *person*," and Face saying, "It's all right, Ma, it's fine," and Talia saying, "*Kid*ding, Mother. Did you know that the humorless die an average of ten years earlier than the rest of us?"

Parked there at the island, scalping strawberries and decapitating apples, she really couldn't have intended to go on kidding like this for much longer. But oh yes she could. And oh yes she did.

As I was trying to come up with a possible subject that would tug Mr. Detti away from his TV, something that might inject depth or width into my profile, Talia and her burgundy swanked over to me. Her delicious scent reached me before she did, as if a cloud of it floated in front of her, pushed ahead by a stride that confident.

"It's Seger, right? Okay, *Seger.* I don't mind the name, actually. I thought I did at first, but now I see I don't. So, Seger, my mother told me to give you the Val Room."

"Oh, ah. Very nice of her, really, but I don't take Valium. This wine is enough. But I know what you mean, about Valium. Sometimes you just gotta zonk out."

"I said the Val Room, precious."

"The huh?"

"The Val Room. What till you feast your eyes."

"On a room?"

"A whole goddamn room, Seger, my boy."

"A room, of, uhh, *Val*?"

"Come with, child. And ready yourself for fastidious indulgence."

I bounced up from that couch without spilling my wine.

We had to traverse a few hallways and keep walking a while— keep walking, turn left, a little more, keep walking, bear right— before we arrived at the Val Room at the rear of the house. It smelled of a warm carpeted home. Not a cleaner, not a candle, just that normal carpet *lived-in* smell. The smell said: *Here's a home*. Said: *Have a holiday here*. Whereas my and Estelle's place smelled of rickety urban rent. Smelled of chilly hardwood floors and struggling radiator warmth. It also *sounded* that way, what with the hissing and ticking of the radiators, the drip-dropping of the kitchen faucet, the bathroom faucet, the showerhead.

So, then, the Val Room. Talia entered it with a dramatically curtsied "Ta-da." *Room*? No, it was a *museum*, sans furniture, Mrs. Detti's painstaking shrine to her son, an altar of her adoration it must have been hard for Talia's stomach to stand around in. But I was wowed. On the walls framed posters from films and performances and theater productions—I didn't know he'd once played Oedipus at the Geffen Playhouse in L.A.—framed magazine covers and head shots, various publicity material from a dozen countries at least. On a shelf orderly rows of every newspaper and periodical that had ever made mention of her boy, each one sheathed in protective plastic, newspapers from Brooklyn to Bombay to Bahrain. On another shelf a goulash of doodads and knickknacks emblazoned with Face slogans: shot glasses, for example; also a yo-yo. Key chains, a water bottle.

I hadn't realized there was a Val Face action figure. A pair of them, actually, and Mrs. Detti had them displayed in a kind of tango or salsa that must have made sense to her. On that hook there? Tote bags blaring Face's face. On another shelf folded with Bloomingdale's care? T-shirts with Face's face. In that corner there? Bookshelves that contained Face's memoir, multiple copies, in ten languages, and beneath those were many copies of his DVD concert and every one of his films. Also the box set, boxes of the box set, of every season of *American Face*.

Then photo albums aplenty, Face the only star of them. Every letter and postcard, from every nook of the globe, that he had ever scribbled to his ma, filed—in *chronological order*. Also a portfolio with Face's artwork from preschool up, charcoal drawings and incomprehensible paintings that, Talia said, their mother believed contained tantalizing foreshadows of the colossus her son was to become.

"They don't," she said. "They're just a kid's prepubescent junk. Now, you should see *my* drawings from childhood. Works of wonder, I tell you. I could have been a Michelangelo, buster. But you know the rule: there's room for only one Michelangelo per family."

"Wow," I said. "So this is the Val Room."

"Grotesque, right?"

Away from her parents and brother and the enforced Christmas cheer of the kitchen, Talia's whole disposition softened and reposed a notch. This summoner of storms was momentarily self-quelled, if only by an inch.

"But it gives my bored mother something to do with her life, and that's important. Otherwise, God knows what sort of mischief she'd get into. Once when she was bored she went online and sent me photos of guys from dating sites."

"Well, I can see your point about the room, sure. But for a journalist? Wow. A gold mine. Can I touch this stuff? Take pics?"

While one hand held her wine, the other swept the room as if to say: *It's all yours. It means not a damn thing to me.*

And so for twenty minutes or more, I wowed my way through

lots of it, reading and snapping pics, touching what could be touched, as Talia sat cross-legged on the carpet draining wine, peeling nail polish from her tasty toes. The ceiling speakers reached all the way back here: The Drifters had their 1954 "White Christmas" hymn underway, which, for my money, though I didn't have any, had Bing beat by many candy canes.

"Are you two close?" I asked.

"Who two?"

"You two. Your brother and you."

"Are we *close*? Aren't you a *writer*, Seger? Aren't writers sup-posed to be perceptive, my dear?"

"True, yes, but I just got here and I'm not sure yet what I'm perceiving."

"Let me guess. An only child, right? Such peculiar creatures, you only children."

"Guilty." Pause. "But *were* you close?"

"Were we close when?"

"Growing up. When you were kids."

"The only person Val has ever been truly close to is himself. Himself and millions of strangers. He has tons of attention to give everyone except the people who should matter most."

She snapped her head back and splashed down her half glass. Not to be outdone, though when it came to alcohol she seemed schooled in outdoing, I did the same. Through the curtainless windows, out there to the left, on the many-acred land, two deer, thinking their deer thoughts, hooved on stale snow between patches of pine. To the right, just past the tennis court, Jacki Jaworski stood at the edge of the woods, probing them with binoculars.

"But his memoir makes your family life seem totally normal," I said, "totally loving."

"His memoir is a fucking lie then."

"You haven't read it?"

"I flipped through the pages looking for my name. Couldn't find it."

"Oh. Ouch. Maybe you'll be in, in the sequel?"

"I doubt it."

"But maybe you can help me, Talia. I've been trying to find his Rosebud, what in his upbringing helps explain his drive and abilities. Is there anything you can tell me about that? Is it all right I'm recording this? Sorry, should have asked."

"Record away, what do I care? And you're looking for what? Rosebud?"

"You know, the thing or event or object that explains him."

"Oh, his *ego*, you mean. That's the thing that explains him. Look for his ego. You can't miss it."

"Why don't you like him?"

"Why doesn't he like me? Don't I seem a likable sort, precious?"

"He doesn't like you?"

"My guess is that he and his bride don't like anyone who rejects them."

"You rejected them?"

I was cross-legged on the carpet, directly in front of her, our kneecaps almost knocking, my phone between us hearing it all.

"Rejected his offer, yeah."

And which offer was that?

"To be his and Nimble's personal trainer and nutritionist," she said. "Did you know I'm a personal trainer and nutritionist?" Pause. "Between jobs."

"No, I didn't know anything about you, Tal. There's nothing about you in his—as you say—in his memoir."

"Yeah, he wrote that after I rejected him. I find I like saying that: *I rejected him.*"

"But you didn't *want* to be his trainer and nutritionist?"

"Not the way they wanted me to be it, no."

And how did they want her to be it?

"Submissively," she said, "that's how. Do I seem the submissive type, babe?"

Submissive, I told her, was not the first term that flew into the mind, no.

"But wait," I said, "what was it like growing up with him?"

"How would I know? He never showed any interest in me growing up. Was never brotherly in that way you'd expect. If there were rumors about me, or if I was picked on, he didn't seem to care about helping me. You know high school, it's a torture chamber. Other girls spread rumors about me being crazy, drug addicted, a slut, whatever, and my brother pretended not to notice that. I guess I didn't care that much then, I had my own group of friends, people who stuck up for me. But looking back on it, it would have been nice to have an older brother sticking up for me. I mean, he didn't make matters worse—he just didn't do anything at all. He was a shitty brother, is what I'm saying. But not shitty with abuse, shitty with indifference. He just didn't care, had his own ambitions and emotions that were so important."

"But he wanted you to be his trainer and nutritionist. Doesn't that show he values you?"

"I'm getting to that. So, about a month after he marries Nim-ble, he's suddenly very interested in me, right? They show up with an offer for me to be their personal trainer and nutritionist, huge salary, health insurance, a bungalow on their estate, the works. But they wanted to force me to sign a contract that would prevent me from ever disclosing *anything* about my brother to *anyone*. A non-disclosure contract, can you believe it? Me, his sister. I could see all these tiny manipulations going on, this duplicity, right, how they were trying to buy my loyalty. Buy my silence."

Silence about what, you're wondering. I was too.

"The hell if I know," she said. "About how he's not special? Not a real charismatic? A shitty brother? I don't know. It's the *keep-your-enemies-close* mentality, I guess."

Keep your enemies close. I had an awful thought then. Was that the real reason Face and Nimble had recruited me to be their royal scribe? Not because I was the incisive critic they admired, the writer who could lend his enterprise the combo of egghead and street cred, but because I was the rogue foe who needed to be dazzled into obedience?

"You ask me," she said, "Nimble and my brother are paranoid about having Val found out as normal or fraudulent. Or indifferent to his own sister. And I wouldn't sign the contract. I'm telling you, it was a nondisclosure agreement. I said I'd be happy to be their trainer and nutritionist but I wasn't signing anything, and I wouldn't be told what to do or what to say or who I could and could not talk to. And they just couldn't believe it—*could not* believe I turned them down. And they hate me for it, I guess. He changed big-time after meeting her. But that's fine. They can hate me. Our relationship couldn't be ruined because we didn't have one to ruin."

What could I say? I patted her jeaned knee with avuncular affection.

"It's fine, really," she said. "But now these family get-togethers are—well, you see what they are. Awkward as hell. So, there you have it, that's the story. I wouldn't let them buy me in that way, or silence me, not that I was ever interested in blabbing."

"But you're blabbing all this to me, right now. Why?"

"Because it doesn't matter. Because I sincerely do not care. And because you asked, sugar. You should know, I'm pretty sharp about people—I share that with Val, I guess—and I saw right away what a patsy you are. No offense, precious. I like the patsies and their mismatched socks. They're all so innocent and trusting. Patsies are good people, I mean. But I'm not one of them. Let me guess: they gave you a contract and you signed it."

"Guilty."

"You know the contract probably says you can't publish anything they don't approve of. What's that like? For a writer, I mean. Censorship."

I told her I made a choice. I told her I really didn't have another one, I was getting married in nine months, Estelle wants things, I love her and want to help give them to her.

"See, you're a good soul," she said, "I told you. But it means you're a patsy too, my friend, sorry."

"Ever regret it? Not doing it? Being their trainer. The money, health insurance, bungalow? You could have been famous. Val Face's trainer and nutritionist."

"No, I couldn't have been. The siblings of the famous aren't famous just by virtue of being siblings. And even if I did become famous, I'd always be the Tito Jackson and not the Michael. As I said, there's room for only one Michael in a family. Did you see that recent documentary about the Jacksons? A house of horrors, that family."

We simultaneously raised our glasses only to see that they were both empty.

"I'm saying you're gonna be disappointed, sugar. You became his writer hoping it would make you famous too. I can tell because I almost did the same thing. But that's a losing bet."

She stood then, performed a little stretch, cracked her neck.

"I need four more inches of wine if I'm going to be braced enough to sit across from my brother," she said. "You coming?"

"In a minute. I'd like to go out back with Ja . . . with Florence. Is there a door back here? Somewhere?"

She told me how to find it and I said, "Hey, Talia, thank you, really, for talking with me. I really appreciate it. I think you're great."

"You know what, sugar? I *am*."

■ ■ ■

BEYOND THE BACKYARD began a copse of firs, then a goodly forest of them, and beyond that the hills humped brown against a sky with more snow on its mind. Jacki Jaworski didn't lower her binoculars when I sidled up to her, sans coat, and said, "Hello, detective. I finished your novel and I think—"

"Shush. You see that opening there, beside the footpath? To the right there? You see that knoll?"

What, I had to ask, is a knoll?

"You know, a knoll," she said. "A little round hill."

"We don't have those in the North End."

"You see there? Here, take these. Look at that knoll. Just to the right of it."

I looked. Then I looked some more, fiddling with the focus. Looking and fiddling.

"What am I supposed to be seeing, detective?"

She pointed to where the footpath on the left met the footpath on the right, a knoll at the junction, and just beside it crouched a man. I asked what you ask: what man? A neighbor out for a winter's day stroll?

"A neighbor out for a winter's day stroll doesn't crouch and hide when he sees someone with binoculars looking his way."

"Actually, detective, there's literary precedent for this. When Hawthorne lived out here in these parts, he'd stroll these woods, and when he saw someone else strolling too, he'd duck behind a bush so as not to have his reverie disturbed. Maybe it's Hawthorne."

She told me to stay focused; she told me it could be Bill.

"But weren't you watching the whole time?" I asked. "In the SUV with Mario? You'd have seen him follow us."

"Depends on how stealthy he is."

"*Stealthy* is not exactly how I'd describe this fella, detective. In fact, I'd say he's—"

"Look! There he goes!"

She drew her pistol as she said that, which made all my tubing tighten, and when I looked toward the knoll, I saw someone dashing through and around oaks and pines.

"Go, go, that way," she said, "that way, cut him off," and she ran

onto the footpath to the left without waiting for me to tell her my
outlook on unathletic writers chasing stalkers through the forests of
western Mass. Cut him off? As in *collide* with him? And then what?

I heard myself say, "I didn't bring my coat," as if that would pardon me from this pursuit. But Jacki didn't hear me because she was
already dashing down the footpath. What could I do? I dashed too,
on the footpath to the right, trying to keep two people in my field of
vision: Jacki over to the left of me, running along the footpath, and
this person in front of me, stomping through the brush, kangaroo-
ing over felled trees. He was too far away for me to say who he was or
what he was wearing, but I hared after him just the same, conscious
of the nineteen degrees and my missing coat but unable to do anything about either of them.

From about forty yards away, Jacki hollered with an echo, "Cut
to the right, he's going right," and I stopped then to see what in
God's name she wanted me to cut *on*, since there was no path to the
right. She vanished then behind the knoll and I, panting as I had not
panted before, began leaping over bushes and logs—*leap* might be
an exaggeration—over rotted boles and around stout birch, which I
wasn't at all dressed to do. Prickly things stuck to my sweater; twigs
pierced my pants.

I'd lost sight of the fleer but then I found him again; I could see
him bobbing between hickory and chestnut. Jacki had been right:
our fleer was no neighbor out for a wooded stroll. No, our fleer was
fleeing all right. If Jacki was to the left of me, and our fleer was up
there between us, then we'd pinch him in the middle, if we could
catch him. But if we could catch him, pinch him between us, and
Jacki shot at him—would she do that?—I'd probably be the one hit if

she missed. Getting shot is an exceedingly American thing to do, I know. But still—I didn't want to do it. Hunting accidents happen all the time. Some camouflaged stooge wants to slaughter a doe and he punctures his pal instead. A definite boon for the doe; not so much for the pal.

But then, embarrassment: I fell. Or *crashed* is probably more apt. Exposed roots like arteries atop dirt brought me hard to the floor of the forest, where I lay ascertaining my injuries, which seemed to be centered in the right knee region. At that point, I heard Jacki, but barely, calling my name from somewhere behind the knoll. And then I heard her no more. I lay there face down in the cold damp leaves, wounded and panting, wondering how many minutes I had until hypothermia hit me.

With more difficulty than I would have thought possible, I rolled my body over to lie on my back, to brush the dirt and leaves from my lips, and when I did, I stared straight up into the blank face of Bill. He was standing directly over me, peering down at me, and when I say that he'd startled me as a ghost startles, I mean I had the abrupt need of a bathroom. There's something about lying coatlessly wounded in the woods of western Mass with a determined crank standing over you that really makes you question the decisions you make in life.

He wouldn't say anything; he didn't look agitated; he didn't looked rushed. Newly conscious of clothes, I saw that he was dressed the same way he always dressed: anonymously. His vanilla face sat there on his skull stupidly serene, utterly devoid of expression. The fear oozing through my abdomen and up into my throat felt like a cloggage of some kind. And then I heard myself ask it, though it wasn't easy to speak through such a lump: "What do you want?" It seemed the pertinent query.

And he did something then that I could not decode. He struck a match. A wooden match. He was holding the little box of them in his left hand. He struck this match, held it before him as if to ponder the physics of flame, and then, seconds later, looking at me through deadened eyes, he blew it out. And what did he do with the spent match? He dropped it onto my chest, and stood there staring as if I were a curiosity—as if, through me, he could figure out how to get at Face. Then he turned, almost reluctantly, and was gone.

Half a minute later, I could hear Jacki calling me, but before I could holler in return, I had to teach myself to breathe. It took her and her handgun a while to find me, hidden as I was among felled boles.

"He's here, Jacki. Bill is here. He was just standing over me."

She scanned the woods one way; she scanned them the other.

"Well he's gone now," she said. "You're hurt?"

"My knee would probably say so," and she helped lift me.

"Let's get you back to the house and then I'll get Bunny. Which way did Bill go?"

On my feet, on Jacki's arm, I pointed through the elms.

"What should we tell Face about my battle wound?"

"You're a writer. Make something up."

"But *you're* the novelist. And by the way, detective. Brilliant. Your novel. Jacki Falcon. *Love* it."

"Tell me later. Let's get you back."

"Meatballs, here I come."

■ ■ ■

BUT MEATBALLS, while they might have been foremost in my stomach's mind, weren't foremost in my head's mind. Despite the adventure and fear I had just endured, and the suspicion that my life was just then the most surreal it would ever be, the thought throbbing foremost in my head's mind was what I had decided after my recent tête-à-tête with Talia. *I am nobody's patsy and I'm quitting this gig.* The thought was so freeing that my guts—despite a busted knee and having been stared down at by Bill—my guts immediately lost the low-level nervousness they'd been living in. My and Face's Springsteen fracas no longer seemed so unstringing, and the apprehension I had at having to inform Estelle of this decision was offset by the realization that I no longer had to endure the complexities of Face Inc., or sweat so hard to gratify him and not screw up.

"The writer's *hurt* now? When I have meatballs ready?"

That was Mrs. Detti, seeing my sorry self as Jacki lugged me into the house.

"Yes, ma'am," Jacki said. "He tripped."

"Tripped?" said Mr. Detti. "Tripped over what?"

"Logs, I think, sir," I said.

"Writers shouldn't leave their desks," Talia said.

Face asked if I was okay—sweet of him—and Mrs. Detti asked if tripping was something I did frequently. I was seated at the table by this point, defrosting.

"Well, I was startled, ma'am," I said.

"Startled by what, precious?" Talia asked. "Nature?"

"Uhh, a Sasquatch, I believe."

Mr. Detti asked what most would ask: "A *what*?"

"Sasquatch, sir. You know, Bigfoot."

"Don't know that we have many of those around here, son."

"Did you hit your *head*, dear?" Mrs. Detti asked.

"He's fine, Ma," Face told her. "Have another glass of wine, Seger, you'll feel better."

And then Jacki said, "Darn, I think I dropped my keys out there. Bunny, will you help me look for them?"

They shared a look they must have shared dozens of times while in the shit in Fallujah, and Mrs. Detti wondered why the day was falling apart. First Bigfeet attack the writer and now Florence has dropped her keys. Did Mrs. Detti need to remind everyone that her meatballs were ready?

"Seger and I will eat, Ma. Pop, come eat with us. Tal, you too. Mother's about to be unbalanced."

"*About* to be?" Talia asked.

All my intestines were pleased to see the food posed there on the dining table and ready for use. Since everyone was speaking at once over the scrape and clang of silverware, mostly sentences that began with *pass*—the bread, the wine, the ice—I cocked an ear upward to hear Elvis hunking his way through "Here Comes Santa Claus."

Really makes you wonder, the King, when you consider his terminus, his twilight as a drugged glutton, a grade-A gorger and perspiring self-parodist. Makes you wonder if his fate is not the fate of every star of such enormity. Follow such fame to its natural outcome, lather fully in all fame offers, and you get Elvis self-celled in a Memphis compound, a revolver tucked into his flab, fried chicken sliding down his face, his only company bionic flatterers programmed for nothing else, except of course for the daily retrieval at KFC. You get Elvis fat and dead on a golden toilet bowl. Doesn't seem to end well, such fame. Do you know which book Elvis was reading on the toilet when his polluted heart conked out? *A Scientific Search for the Face of Jesus.* You can't make up stuff like this.

Mrs. Detti, no surprise, had been touched by the demigods of cuisine. I'd have put her meatballs against my own ma's in a contest of succulence. The texture had just the right firmness, because the trick with meatballs is to have them firm enough not to collapse on your plate but loose enough, moist enough, to give a melting sensation in the mouth, and Mrs. Detti's Olympian skills understood this. Plus, the gravy, the basil, the garlic, the onion, the overall sweetness and light of it, not too salty, just a smidgen spiced. What consistency to this sauce, not the pasty, sticky fare of aproned amateurs. Such meatballs render you uncommunicative for many minutes at a time.

When Mr. Detti ate, he ate with some assistance from sound effects, though he somehow managed to make these sounds sound not piggish but pretty appetizing: sounds that made you want to make sounds of your own. So I wasn't engaged in a lot of talking; more like muted grunting, moaning, *mmm*ing—creature noises. All the while, Mrs. Detti tried to get me to eat more meatballs. But after half an hour, I couldn't eat more meatballs. I was positively anchored by meatballs. I'm not saying I didn't *want* to eat more meatballs; I'm saying I *couldn't* eat more meatballs. The trusty seams of my gut were already groaning from the bloat. I felt how dead Elvis looked.

"Here they come," Face said, and in came Mario and Jacki, blushed from the cold.

"Any luck?" Talia said.

"We found Florence's keys, Ms. Talia, yes, thank you."

"Dropped them by the tennis court," Jacki said.

Why was I starting to wobble in my seat? Because Mr. Detti kept refilling my glass. After three of them—amazing how quickly three glasses go—I was already bone-drunk and knew I shouldn't get bone-drunker. My protestations against more wine wouldn't have mattered anyway because Mr. Detti already had a bottle titled toward me—not toward my glass, toward my person. This wine appeared to be doing twice the work on half the volume, causing tiny bonfires to go off in my esophagus. I examined the bottle and saw that it was 16.5 percent alcohol, aged in *bourbon barrels*, for the love of Jove. Here was wine with a real whip hand, the kind of authority you just can't get with those 12.5 percent pushovers.

Italian American hosts at suppertime: it's as if they're trying to *kill* you with drink and food, as if your explosion there at the table would be a compliment. You could imagine Mrs. Detti on the horn with a friend: "We had a *wonderful* meal, Betsy, made my *meat-balls*, and the writer *burst* right there in his seat, kaboom, all over the place. It was a big mess to clean but I *really* got the gravy right this time."

Remember when Estelle accused me of having a man-crush on Face? Well, if you know anything about 16.5 percent wine and the holidays, you know that they can combine to make you warmly romantic. There's a danger of your getting affectionate, profusely grateful for whatever blessings have floated your way. Face sat directly to my right, and I discovered that my corduroyed knee—the uninjured one—kept brushing against his denimed one beneath the table. My knee would wander, brush his, I'd quickly swing it away, and then, a minute later, it would drift back over. And the quickness with which I swung it back in place got slower and slower, so that, at one point, my knee was contentedly snuggled against his. And the more I saw that this didn't bother him, the more my knee stayed there snuggled.

I also discovered that I had, sometime in the previous few minutes, put my woolen arm across the back of his chair. Since I'd decided to quit my post as his royal scribe, I was getting pretty darn chummy, plucky in my self-got liberation, uncaring now if Face thought me gayish. Maybe 16.5 percent wine makes you macho. It makes me gay.

While Mrs. Detti and Talia wrangled over who was going to fetch the coffee, apple pie, and ice cream, and while Mr. Detti and Mario loudly compared the ins and outs of Barry Manilow to the whys and wherefores of Neil Diamond, and as Jacki kept watch on the darkening backyard, I had an awareness ripening within. I'd tipped the glass with too much brio.

So then I had two minds in my head, the brash one that goes groping with an arm draped over Face's chair, and the guarded one that attempts to chasten whatever movements and sentences were about to make my tomorrow a storm of self-recrimination. One mind can't walk a straight line; the other mind is a cop watching it wobble. Those two minds were warring, and funny how the brash one always makes a slaughter of the guarded one. Even as my palm patted Face's shoulder and back, even as my language dribbled out in spates of post-food doggerel, even as my knee kept touching his, that cop in my head was giving advice I couldn't take: *Stop touching him. Cease this blubbering, you boob.*

As Talia discharged a laughing tantrum against her mother (something about when she was six years old and didn't have as many Christmas gifts as her brother), and as Mr. Detti was trying to convince Mario that Neil Diamond's "Sweet Caroline" was superior to Barry Manilow's "I Write the Songs ("No, I'm sorry, sir, I have to respectfully disagree, sir; it's a matter, as I say, of depth of feeling"), what did Face do? Face rose from the table and made for the back door and the spot of freedom it led to. Marlboro had beckoned.

But Mario didn't like this. Mario asked where Face was going and why, and then said he'd have to accompany him outside. But Face held firm and got out onto the back deck without him. And what did Mario and Jacki do without a word? They sprang up and bolted out the front door. Even in my compromised condition I knew what they were about to do: they'd dash around the house, one to the left, one to the right, and look after Face from opposite sides of the deck, each crouched behind a bush. And if we heard a gunshot, I'd know that Bill had tried to pounce and now lay bleeding from Jacki's or Mario's bullet.

I'd definitely forgotten to hydrate, but there was my aqua, eyeing me and ready for use, a lemon suspended beneath cubes of ice as if in fetal sleep. My ailments of head started the long path to healing after that first glass. The coming dawn, I already knew, was going to be an agony of Gothic headaching.

Here's what I heard Mrs. Detti say through the alcohol fumes: "Lou, try to get Val to tell us about his Christmas and New Year's plans. I must know how much to *cook*, he can't tell me last *min-ute* like last year, and Nimble, that girl, I tell you, she has all those *restrictions*, for God's sake, is it *cabbage* she wants?—I can *make* stuffed cabbage but she wouldn't eat what it's stuffed *with*—I wonder how does she *live* on that little bird's diet, and now that she's expect-ing, she needs *calories*."

"The little Führer runs on evil, Mother," Talia said.

"The little Führer does *not* run on evil, Tal, stop it, your brother will *hear*."

And then I heard this, or thought I did: "Son, is it a bed you need?"

Yes, seems I'd heard right. That was Mr. Detti, and the person to whom he was speaking was *moi*, because all the overfeeding and unwise irrigating had gone straight to my eyes. They were, I could feel, swollen into slits. I might have even nodded off for several sec-onds, judging by the blot of drool I felt in one nook of my mouth. I made embarrassed sounds of *err* and *uhh*. Mr. Detti then launched into another speech about their guesthouse and the conspicuous lack of guests to which it bears witness. And then, if I was following cor-rectly, the talk shifted into what I'd wear as I slept in the guesthouse.

"Talia, dear," I heard, "go fetch the writer some of your brother's old clothes, in the Val Room. In the blue bin, the one labeled Val's Sleepwear. Your brother's old pajamas might fit him. Though he's . . . stouter than Val."

Stouter. Okay. It seemed that soon I'd be asleep in the guest-house, which was timed just right, because what was that coming from Mrs. Detti's playlist now? Some truly horrid warbling we heard. The Beach Boys doing "Little Saint Nick."

■ ■ ■

OUT I LIMPED into the sobering crack of cold, in my arms Face's ex-pajamas, a flannel affair that smelled of airless storage. I was on the back deck, looking for the stairs, my eyes straining to adjust to the moonless, starless dark, when the star himself spoke my name. He leaned there on the deck's railing, into his second cigarette, in the block of half light that spilled from the kitchen window. He didn't know that Mario surveilled him from the left, Jacki from the right, and Bill no doubt from the black thickness beyond.

"You done eating, *paisan*? How's the knee?"

"That Sasquatch really had its way with me."

"Mmm. Where're you headed?"

"Your dad ordered me to the guesthouse for sleep. All the wine. These are your old pajamas."

The cold was so still and dry now it hardly felt cold at all, and yet it accomplished all the bracing I needed, a fanning away of the wine fumes.

"Face, I want to apologize for what I said at the rest stop today. I didn't mean it. I don't think you're a phony."

He smoked some more; he squinted some more; he appeared to be processing my apology.

"Yes you do," he finally said. "And it's okay. All stars are phonies. That's the definition of fame. Inauthenticity."

"But I don't think you're inauthentic."

"The more authentic the star claims to be, the more inauthentic he actually is. So, I get it. Anyway, I should apologize to you. I called you names. It wasn't nice. I was bothered by other stuff."

"You're just glum, Face. I think being back with their families makes people categorically glum. You're not inauthentic."

I saw why smoking was helpful. It makes the pauses in a dialogue less worrisome.

"Face, you wanna talk about what's got you down?"

"What's to say? Things run away with you, *paisan*. They get bigger than you are, more complex than you wanted, the whole thing just keeps accelerating." He gestured up with his Marlboro. "It's like the cosmos, expanding, accelerating, and soon you're breathless just trying to keep up with your own Big Bang. Things take on worlds of their own. And then . . . what you thought you wanted, what you worked for, turns out to be not the thing you wanted. Or not exactly."

"How about a break? Take a breather, man. Show yourself a little mercy."

But he was on the rails of his own internal locomotive and couldn't hear about breaks or breathers, or the little mercies we must offer ourselves in lieu of ruin.

"You get stuck," he said. "People relying on you. The pressure of not disappointing them. It never goes away. And through it all, you're a phony doing what you have to do and not what you want to do."

I was at a loss here; my sole reply was about breaks and breathers. But then I realized what he needed: a hug. And so like a boxer gauging, angling for the uppercut, I began gauging, angling for the embrace. The thing about embraces is that one has to time them right. Too soon, and they interfere; too late, and they're useless.

"The more eyes you have on you," he said, "the more you have to become what those eyes want to see, not what you want to be. Since the TV show, since all the merchandising, this is not what I wanted."

The hug wasn't there yet. Too soon. And I thought I understood what he was telling me—abstractly, I mean. The ruse of celebrity, to conceal instead of reveal, to erect a façade that hides the star's true self, until the façade is all there is, all that's left. If only we knew the truth about our celebrities—finish that thought. If only we knew the truth about each other—finish that thought too. The ruse of image: for the famous, more than for the rest of us, image is all. The celebrity's image is famous, not the celebrity himself. And if the image ain't you? Then there *is* no you.

"You'll be a father soon," I said. "Nothing phony about that. She'll stabilize you. Set your priorities."

"I'll have to quit these," he said, more to Marlboro than to me. "The guru in the improvement racket is a self-killer with cigarettes. See? Phony."

"Fella needs a smoke once in a while, Face. Don't be so brutal on yourself. Have a smoke."

"There'll be a lot of things I'll have to quit, actually, after she arrives, though I have no idea how. As I say: stuck. But I don't want to be one of those dads who isn't a dad. I've seen what that's like. No good."

He's seen that in Hollywood, with A-listers who employ a corps of surrogates to bring up their kids? Or he's seen that firsthand, growing up under his own father? I wasn't about to ask. But, just then, with the timing still not right for our big hug, I thought I knew why his phoniness was rankling him. Because being with Talia, he was forced to admit her own bold authenticity, the authenticity she showed in rejecting him, a rejection I myself hadn't been authentic enough to make. Familiar with showbiz frauds, Face must have beheld his sister as the most authentic person he knew, a woman who took heed from her own inner beacons and no one else's. She turned down the life Face and Nimble had offered her in order to remain loyal to her own inner coherence, her own dignified sense of self. She herself made a decision *for* herself, and that was a benediction Face no longer had.

That was precisely what he'd shown at the Addison Rehab Center and in Portland: the relinquishing of his own powers to decide. After his career went supernova, his genuine nexus to people became corporatized. He made that happen, I know, and he fostered it after he'd made it happen, and began paying people to keep it happening, but that didn't mean he was always gratified with what he'd created or didn't pine for rescue from it. The man as brand and not as artist: his minders now made the calls, and he saw no choice but to cede to the dictates of a ravenous fame. There was no way back to that young genuine in a street-corner crowd. In her protection of him, Nimble would grant him his minor victories, hobnobbing with fans at a fence, but when it came to *who* he would be, as artist and guru and star, the brand and not the man would reign.

And I was mostly certain I understood Nimble's choices, overseeing a fame as tangled as Face's. He was the father of her daughter and that meant she had special claims on his safety. I'd meant what I said to Face at the rest stop: I admired Nimble because Nimble was Nimble and nobody else—Nimble did what she had to do in a relationship that complicated.

If only we minor ones had such problems? But at that moment, on the back deck of his parents' house, in a winter night that polar, watching him inspect a Marlboro as if it might hold an answer to an inner enigma, with protectors secretly watching us from the wings and a wacko probably watching us from the woods, I wasn't altogether certain I'd have switched places with him. Stereotypes abound when you're talking about fame, but I'm not trying to bolster the one that says poor people are simple and happy while rich people are complex and not. What I mean has more to do with the serenity of isolation, with a chosen lonesomeness silent enough to know yourself in.

In his shtick, Face relayed the benefits of the inner life, but how could he know the benefits of the inner life when those benefits take solitude to recognize and cultivate? The cliché that says celebrity is a lonely life? No it's not. Everything about Face Inc. and its proceedings yelped the inverse of loneliness. It was all bop and jolt, and you got the sense that it wasn't like that only when he was on tour. You got the sense that it was like that *all the time*. An artist can't have that. And if the artist does have that, the artist isn't an artist anymore.

That hug I'd been angling for? Still wasn't there.

"You ever want to vanish, Seger? Just throw up your hands and vanish?"

"Maybe ask me that after I have complications enough to vanish from, Face. I've been pretty content with my little life so far."

"You like Talia, don't you?"

"Very much."

"What'd she tell you when you two disappeared for half an hour?"

"I think you know what she told me, Face. I asked about your relationship and she told me."

He nodded at his cigarette. "I figured. She's right, ya know. What she told you. She's not making that up."

"I know."

"That change how you see me?"

"No. I'd say it confirms how I see you. I'm not judging you, Face. I can't know what it's like to live your life or to make the choices for that life."

"You want to quit this assignment, don't you? You're done with all this."

"Yes, I think so. I still think you're special. And I think you deserve your success. But your world . . . It's not for me, not even as a hanger-on."

A final drag, he flipped the filter into the dark, and exhaling said, "Let's sleep on it, *paisan*. Everything looks different in sunlight."

All my angling for an embrace? It wasn't necessary because Face, being Face, spotted the proper moment. "Come 'ere," he said, and he sheathed me in his arms, a firm sheathing that showed a tenderness for others he could not muster for himself. Unconcerned that we were being surveilled by an audience of three, I squeezed him back, nose pressed into the cushion of his clothing, and we two swayed there ever so slightly, as if in step to a ballad only we could hear.

■ ■ ■

WHEN I THINK *GUESTHOUSE* I think cottagelike, I think temporary, but this guesthouse was *a house*, another house next to their house. Four bedrooms, three bathrooms, full-on kitchen, skylights, fireplace: *a house*. There was a preponderance of kitsch and wall clocks depicting New England felicities: Cape Cod, Nantucket, Martha's Vineyard, whaling ships, lighthouses, luring lobsters, picturesque fishes, mesmeric moose, tiny houses on silver-sheened ponds in a riot of autumn. If you dropped this place anywhere in Boston it would sell for five million easy, and yet here it was, a mere unused adjunct to the main spread. It smelled, I sniffed, of purring lilac.

I'd always wanted a bedroom with a settee, and a queen to myself with such a quilt. I brought that wrapped sensation with me down into the sweet cavity of sleep, feeling, for several seconds before ultimate blackout, the welcome pressure of the warming quilt. The mattress gravity fixed me there as if in utero, the window giving view onto silhouetted hills. The food-and-drink exhaustion throbbed me into the haywire plots of dreams, though there was one plot I could follow easily enough: the one in which I was attempting to tell Estelle that I'd quit this assignment.

Then, at some indeterminable time later, I had a spot of trouble figuring out why my dream was no longer stocked with Estelle but with Jacki, Mario, and Manilow. For a dream-reason I could not discern, Jacki, Mario, and Manilow were summoning me from my dark and out into a lighted hallway where Jacki's height and Mario's bulk stood waiting, and where Manilow was bragging about having made it. But then Mario reached into the room and clicked on the light, revealing reality. Not a dream—an actual Jacki and Mario actually beckoning me, an actual Manilow actually bragging about having made it.

"Get up," he said. Mario, not Manilow. "We have work to do."

"Er? What time is it?"

"You've been sleeping two hours," Jacki said.

"Hmm. But it sounded as if you said we have work to do."

"We do," she said. "We need your help."

Now it sounded as if she said they needed my help.

"Now it sounded as if you said you need my help."

"Get *up*, Seger," said Mario.

I wasn't drunk anymore, true, thanks to a quilted two hours, but I wasn't sober either. Rather, I lay in that turbid purgatory of 51 percent comprehension, still smudged with wine and salt and red-meat fat. You could still smell the fumes from me, and from across the room you could probably smell my mulch breath, a tongue like compost. And why, having decided to quit this assignment, didn't I just tell Jacki and Mario to go away and get help elsewhere? Well, even though he now comprehended me as a fellow Manilovian, Mario was not that species of fella who responds with peace and light to being told to go away.

"Meet us in the dining room," Jacki said. "We've got faces and we need your help putting a name to one of them."

I could see I was going to have to sit up for this. So I sat up for this.

"You've got Face's what?"

"No, we have photos of faces of everyone named Bill or William who was at the Boston show that night."

"Listen," Mario told me, "I put on a Barry mix to help us work."

"How about some Neil Diamond for a change, Mario?"

"How about I smack you?"

These insurgent views of Neil were not becoming. And anyway, how was Mario not as equally drugged from that assailment of meatballs and wine? I know. Because he was a 250-pound Gigantopithecus with all the bodily tolerance of a 250-pound Gigantopithecus. If you were hunting him with a tranquilizer gun through snake-knotted glades, you'd need *two* darts to take him down.

On the glass table in the dining room Mario and Jacki had

arranged dozens of five-by-seven head shots, all of them spat out from a color printer that hadn't fully learned the difference between greens and blues. Manilow was in midcroon about something or other being a miracle. His success, no doubt.

Jacki said, "Let's examine these, Seger. You know our guy's face better than any of us by now. So which one is him?"

I had post-nap yawning to get out of the way. And then:

"Right, okay, guys. But, as I asked the other day, what if our Bill didn't buy his ticket online through a ticket service? What if he scalped it or got it as a gift? Then we wouldn't have his name."

"Nothing we can do about that," Jacki said. "We've got to start here."

When did so many Bostonians get named William?

"So," Jacki said, "these here on the right are the ones that most closely match what we think he looks like, what we could discern from the video of the performance and from your descriptions, Seger. These on the left don't match at all."

"And for extra reference," Mario said, "if you need it, to freshen up your memory, here's the sketch we made on the bus to Portland."

"Oh, right, this sketch. Well, since we're friends now, Mario. Since Manilow devotees *always* stick together and *never* do harm upon one another's person. I have to tell you: your sketch doesn't look anything like our guy."

His look wasn't a look I wanted looking at me.

"Now, Mario, before you get mad, just let me explain. It's not my fault. I was having one of those days. You know those days when you're on a celebrity's bus and are asked to provide descriptions for a forensic sketch of a possibly psycho stalker, and meanwhile you're being mistreated, ignored by the celebrity and his handlers and called *fucko* by his bodyguard? So, yeah, I was having one of those days."

More of that look.

"But, I mean, the *spirit* of the sketch is correct, Mario. I didn't mislead you. Or not really. I mean overall this looks like the blank that is our guy. *Overall.* Kind of. So hard to say with blanks. But I should break it to you, Mario. It's about your artistic ability. Your drawing talent, Mario. Mario: you don't have any. Talent."

He took back the sketch and balled it up before bashing it down.

"It doesn't matter. Focus on these photos. Listen, Barry is singing to help with the focus. Let his genius really *move* through you, inspiring you to concentrate."

Barry was singing all right, all about how he couldn't smile without me. That's what he kept saying: *I can't smile without you.*

"Okay," I said. "So, these on the left here, as you say, detective, these aren't him at all. You can ditch all these."

She gathered them up, flopped them aside. "Ditched," she said.

"Now, these on the right. Let me see. We have to make allowances, of course. Allowances, allowances . . . For time and weight and circumstance. Could be a title, that: *Time and Weight and Circumstance.* Since we don't know how long ago these photos were taken. Hmm, let's see now. Not him, not him, not him, nope, nope, not him, nope, definitely not him . . . Aha. This. This one. And, maybe, sort of, this one here too. These two. Yup. One of these is our Bill."

"You're sure?" Jacki said.

"Am I sure? Detective, just *four* hours ago I was staring up into this face as it looked down upon my injured sack of self. So yes, I'm sure."

"Bill More," Jacki said.

"Eh?"

"This one's name is Bill More, of Dorchester."

"More? As in *gimme*?"

"Affirmative," she said.

Only in America could a potentially sociopathic stalker be named More. Unless Bill More gets more of what Bill More wants, Bill More will be evermore—fill in the blank.

"How on earth," I asked, "did Bill find us out here in the boonies?"

"He's a stalker," Mario said, "that's what they do. Stalk."

"Detective, is this guy, you know, *wanted*? Or *known to law enforcement*, I think the saying goes."

"Negative," she told me. "I've already checked the records of every William here and nothing."

Then I asked what needed asking: "What now?"

"Now we tail him," Mario said. "We've got his address. One of my guys tails him, right, for the next few days while Face is in Boston, sending us intel the whole time. That way we know when he creeps close to the hotel or to one of our vehicles."

"You're going to stalk the stalker then."

"Exactly. And then," he said, "when he gets too close, we grab him."

"Grab him? And then what, Mario?"

"And then what what?"

"Once you grab him," I said. "What then? He hasn't broken any laws. Well, aside from calling in that bomb threat in Portland, which we can't prove, and aside from trespassing on private property today, which we also can't prove. Detective, am I right? We need *proof*."

"Bunny can talk to him without proof."

"Bunny wants to do more than talk to him, I have a feeling."

"Leave it to me," he said. "I've got ways of persuading guys like this to back off."

What does he do for torture? Duct-tape them to a chair and force them to hear Barry Manilow's ideas of Eros?

"Easy peasy," he said.

And Jacki said, "Lemon squeezy."

Then, for five minutes or more, I had to listen to Jacki and Mario reminisce about that time in Iraq when they had to hunt down and *liquidate*—Mario's word—a particularly iniquitous foe planting IEDs on byways used by Marines.

"Seger," he said, "Face wants to get back to Boston first thing in the morning, so be ready at dawn."

Be ready at dawn. Not words to warm to, and definitely not in December.

"Well then, I'm going back to bed," I told them. "What're you two going to do now?"

"Bunny will keep watch over the house all night. I'm going back into the woods."

"Into the woods? Detective, it's fifteen degrees out there, and the woods are darker than the devil's heart."

"Not with these they aren't."

And what were "these" she'd just pulled from a handbag? Night vision goggles.

"You're going to *wear* those?"

"Yup. If our guy is lying in wait out there, I'll find him."

"Okay, so, detective? This reminds me of that scene in your novel when Jacki Falcon dons night vision goggles in order to catch the terrorist hiding in the Public Garden."

"That's right. And she gets her guy."

"Right, she gets her guy. By the way, *awesome* ending to your book. Can't wait to talk with you about it. That chase through the Common, the shootout on the steps of the State House, and when Jacki Falcon takes cover behind the statue of Anne Hutchinson, as if to siphon power and protection from the *original* Boston rebel. Brilliant."

Thanks and smiles but they didn't seem to be registering the point.

"But I mean, friends, that that is a novel and this is not. This is life. Isn't it dangerous what you're doing, detective? I mean, unnecessarily?"

And what did Mario say to that? Mario said, "Jacki Jaworski eats danger for breakfast."

VIII.

I've spoken here of rapture. It is time now to speak of rupture.

First, I woke that dawn with a self-begot reminder waiting there on the brain: I'd decided to abandon this gig, snip the tether. Close on the heels of this reminder was a reality almost as terrible as the reality that quitting Face meant no bumps to our bank account. I refer to the Augean task of telling Estelle.

Face and I prepared to Corvette back to Boston just as December's sun was striving to stand up. I was in sweet possession of meatballs and macaroni Mrs. Detti had gifted me. Mario and Jacki would follow, keeping watch, looking out for Bill. It was too early for goodbyes to Mr. Detti and Talia, but not too early for Mrs. Detti, who was a four-thirty riser each morn, which I guess isn't all that hard when you're an eight-thirty sinker each eve. She was out there with us in the freeze as the Vette grumbled into warmth, standing in the driveway with her bathrobe tied taut, snow-booted and hatted and gloved. It was twelve degrees. She pushed upon us bullet-domed containers of caffeine, elixir enough to get all the blood slaphappy.

"Oh, your *blank*et," Mrs. Detti said, turning to go back into the house. "Wait here, I've forgotten your blanket."

"What blanket? Ma, we've got to get going."

"Just you *wait* there, Val."

This blanket she came out with: you won't believe it. Or maybe you will, considering everything else I've asked you to believe in this chronicle.

"I made this for you, dear," she said.

It was a thick six-by-eight cotton blanket on which Mrs. Detti had embroidered . . .wait for it . . . the face of Val Face. A six-by-eight embroidery of Face's face is a lot of feet of Face's face. This must have taken half a year. And it looked precisely like her son only if—and you had to stand back a bit to view the thing—only if you squinted, in the half dark, fully drunk. If she had shown it to me last night, I'd have said, *That's him!* But now, in the silvered, sober light of the winter morn, I said (to myself), *That's not.*

"Ma, you shouldn't have. *Really* shouldn't have."

"Of course I should have. You're my *son.* I can make my son a blanket. What, you too famous for a blanket?"

"No, Ma, I love it, thank you."

"It's winter. You need a blanket."

As we left, she was an octopus of embraces and a squall of tears and pleas for return. Face waited till after we snaked through town and hit the highway before he said, "Seger, we should talk."

Where was the glum chum from the deck scene the night before?

"Talk, right. Is this the part in the story when you tell me how you know I'm not a quitter, that the Seger Jovis of the world don't quit challenges, they adapt and overcome like the true Bostonians they are, in the spirit of 1776, and not only for the money but for the sake of their own dignity? Do you have a winners-never-quit speech waiting to douse me with, Face?"

Mrs. Detti's coffee must have had high-octane caffeine in it; the stuff really spunked me up.

"Sounds as if you've already doused yourself with that speech, *paisan*."

"I did have a purgatorial hour last night before I dropped off, true. Fork in the road, as it were. To mix my metaphors. Unless, I suppose, the fork in the road is *in* purgatory, though I don't know the highway systems down there."

"So you're back on board then?"

I filled the car with half a minute's silence, really ramped up the drama.

"I'm back, baby!"

You see, I just couldn't find a way of telling Estelle that I'd quit this gig. And I couldn't find a way of telling Estelle that I'd quit this gig because there *was* no way of telling Estelle that I'd quit this gig.

"*Nice*," he said. "Our ancestors would be proud, Seger."

"Our Bostonian ancestors?"

"The Romans."

"Oh. Romans. Right."

During most of the nearly three-hour drive back to Boston, Face was on phone call after phone call with his various early-rising minders, preparing for his next night's show in Providence. He was on speaker most of the time, forcing me to hear both sides of such maddening minutiae, all the industry talk, the industry details, specs of data from contracts, crimps at the venue that required uncrimping, all the assistants and their assistants deluging Face with issues he needed to yay or nay. Vip had things to relay about a contract. Valerie or Violet had things to relay about a commercial. Someone else relayed something about a movie. Loads of numerals were spoken, followed by loads of more numerals.

Most of his phone conferencing in the car concerned the bogus bomb threat in Portland. It had given Face's team a new anxiety disorder—some *Angst vor etwas*, a Viennese might say—which meant that Nimble was instigating stricter security measures. She had her people relaying grave threats to the Providence theater. Unless this stricter security was met, Face would not perform. I couldn't follow all that this stricter security entailed, though more metal detectors and a doubling of security staff were two of Nimble's demands. Bomb-sniffing canines were also part of the conversation. The venue didn't think that it could double the security staff with such abrupt notice, nor was it certain how to hire bomb dogs, and Nimble's terse reply was: "Then my husband will not be there." So now there was a badminton match between Boston and Providence, people trying to figure out who should pony up for this bolstered security. Loads of more numerals were spoken. You had to be at ease with arithmetic in Face's world.

And then someone put a huge action star on the line. I won't say his name for the sake of confidentiality, so let's just call him . . . Tommy Cruiser.

"Cruiser, how are ya, babe?"

"Facey, babe, how're things? I heard about the bomb threat."

"I'm the bomb, baby."

"That's Mainers, right?"

"That's Mainers."

"Listen, about our upcoming shoot in Montreal. The stunts. That big scene with the space shuttle. Are you game for your own stunts, Facey? I'm really going for verisim . . . verisum . . . uhh . . . veri—"

"Verisimilitude."

"Yeah, that. I'm going for that. Are you game, Facey?"

"Cruiser. Cruiser, look, you know I love ya, babe, but I'm not holding on to the outside of the space shuttle as it takes off. All that rocket fuel, ya know."

"Really, it's a cinch, Facey. Remember, the shuttle doesn't go fully into space, just up a bit and flies around. Remember, the villains have hijacked the shuttle, and some are at the window shooting at us, so we really have to make this scene pop, baby!"

"Does the space shuttle have a window that *opens*?"

"This one does, yeah. It's, uhh, a custom space shuttle."

"Right, okay, but I'm wondering if the bad guys would really be shooting at us, because, remember, there's all that uranium they stole. Won't the shooting make the uranium go boom?"

"That's the tension, baby, yeah! We gotta have them shooting at us. We can't have a movie without them shooting at us."

"I hear ya. Remember what Godard said about all you need to make a movie: a gun and a girl."

"And a space shuttle, babe! Yeah! So about those stunts: the audience knows when you use CGI or stunt doubles. Let's not CGI it, Facey. And we don't need our doubles for this one, *trust* me. Let's hang on to that shuttle as it takes off, yeah! The *rush*!"

"Cruiser. Cruiser, look, let me consult with Nimble and Vinny"— Vinny Deus, his stuntman—"and let's see what we can come up with.

I'm not sure my insurance policies let me hang on to space shuttles. But we'll make it work. Don't worry. You know Facey loves ya."

"Facey, babe, I know you won't disappoint on this. We really need that veri . . . that verisum . . . that stuff you said."

"I hear ya. The Face does *not* disappoint. I'll have my people arrange it with yours."

"It's my people's people who're handling this one, so have your people or people's people reach out to my people's people."

"Ten-four, babe. Say hello to your mother for me."

When Face hung up, I said, "I'm agog."

"You're what?"

"Agog."

"Oh, agog. Yeah, the Cruiser is a real character. Annoying, though."

And I had about five minutes of peace before Face was back on the phone speaking what sounded like the numerology embedded in some contract or other. And then, as Boston began to finger up from the horizon—the Pru, the Hancock, the Dalton—he got on the phone with Mario. You could hear Barry babbling platitudes in the background.

"Sir, I've just spoken to Luigi and Mattia"—his two goons: so *those* were their names—"and they report a larger than usual crowd in front of our hotel. I suggest ditching the Vette and using the service entrance at the rear. I've made arrangements for this already with the hotel."

"*Paisan*, it would be a treat for my fans if I pull up in front with the Vette."

"Yes, sir, a treat, I understand. But not advisable, sir. We're already in Code 41 after Portland, and I might have to upgrade that to Code 62."

"How about we relax the codes for today, *paisan*? Portlandians are already disappointed thanks to the canceled show. Let's not disappoint the Bostonians waiting for me at the hotel."

"I can understand, sir. I'd like to stress, if I may, that your safety trumps the fans' disappointment. Pulling up in front of the hotel in the Vette might cause an unnecessary scene, sir."

"Nah, they'll love it. Stop your worrying."

"But, sir—"

"Mario, stop. It'll be fine."

"Understood, sir. I'll relay this intel to Luigi and Mattia and have them prepared at the door. And, sir? Perhaps you can be the one to tell Ms. Nimble that you're changing the plan? She gave me my orders."

"I'll tell her, Mario, relax. You don't have to be afraid of her, you know."

"No, sir."

"No, sir, what?"

"No, sir, I don't know that."

When Nimble called again a few miles later Face unhitched her from speakerphone. Then a minute later, *my* phone rang, an L.A. area code. I was beginning to shudder at L.A. area codes.

"Seger, it's Mario. Listen, see if you can get Face to forget this plan about pulling up in front of the hotel in the Vette."

"You want *me* to do that?"

"You're *with* him right now, aren't you? You have a connection to him, don't you?"

"What connection?"

"Your connection. With Face. I don't know. What the hell else are you doing with us on this tour? And didn't I see you two hugging on the deck last night?"

"Oh, uhh, you saw that, eh? Well. Brotherly, that's all. Brotherly hug."

"Try to convince him, Seger. If you need to, listen to Barry for incentive."

"Let me guess: the depth of feeling."

Mario used that phrase with every meaning except the right one.

"The depth of feeling, exactly. So, see what you can do with Face. You know why. Until I get this stalker situation under control, I don't want to take any unnecessary chances."

When I told him, in code, that I still didn't understand why we couldn't just level with Face about Bill More—"Can't we just tell him what's going on?"—Mario unloaded on me a barrage of *no*s.

"Strict orders from Ms. Nimble," he said. "Face is on tour and when Face is on tour Face must focus on Face being on tour. Got it?"

"I guess so. Do I have a choice?"

"No you do not."

I can't be sure where such frisk emerged from just then but as soon as Face ended the call with Nimble, I let out this train of clauses without any regard for civil punctuation:

"So there's this guy called Bill, the one you singled out at the Boston Opera House that night, and he's stalking you, he's the one who called in the bomb threat in Portland, he followed our bus up there, which is why we made that detour into the rest stop, Mario wanted to shoot him, he's been lingering around your hotel, and

Florence Dupont, Mario's cousin, isn't Florence Dupont Mario's cousin, she is Detective Jacki Jaworski of the BPD, Mario's buddy from the Marines, he summoned her for help with this, she and I chased Bill through the woods yesterday, he followed you to your parents' house, and so that's why Mario doesn't want you to pull up to the hotel in this ludicrous car, just in case Bill is there, and Mario's goon will begin tailing Bill today, stalking the stalker to have a chat with him, and all your babysitters, err, all your people have been keeping this information from you the whole time, I'm not supposed to tell you, Mario will shoot me, but I operate under the assumption that it is always better to know than not to know. So there it is."

Face's sage grin really was its own work of art.

"I know all this," he said.

"You what?"

"I know all this."

"You *do*?"

"Of course I do."

"How long have you known all this?"

"Since the guy showed up at the hotel after the show that night."

"You saw him there?"

"Yes, Seger, I saw him there. I see everybody."

"You don't care? Not worried about it? The bomb threat, following you to your parents' house, all that?"

"No, I'm not worried about it. Do I look worried about it?"

"I *knew* you wouldn't be. All this *baby*ing your people do. Don't tell Mario I told you. And how'd you know that Florence Dupont isn't Florence Dupont?"

"Mario might be a good bodyguard, and the detective might be a good detective, but neither is a good actor."

"So then we're pulling up to the front of the hotel in this thing?"

"That we are, Seger. That we are."

■ ■ ■

AT ABOUT TEN A.M., after getting entangled in thirty minutes of end-times traffic, we were at the front curb of the hotel in the Vette, a coagulation of fans on the sidewalk who rightly guessed it was Face in such a car. These fans then ecstatically teemed at the Vette's anatomy, against its sides, its front, its back, on the hood, on the windshield, phones flashing, the Vette lightly rocking. It was like being rolled through a car wash when the barrel-size brushes descend to do their rotating cleanse, giving that buffeted sense of being momentarily, soothingly apart from the world. They were squealing, some screeching, some with the smiles of the narcotized.

After half a minute of this, Mario, his two men, Jacki Jaworski, and the doorman succeeded in plucking people from the Vette, repelling the spate of them, enough so that Face and I could uncouple ourselves from it. At which point Face did what Face was adept at doing: salutations and selfies. Jacki, Mario, and his men got mostly between Face and the fans, though not enough to bar all communion, since that would have wrecked what Face wanted.

Let's talk a sec about what Face wanted. Earlier he'd told me that he wanted to gift his fans this treat, but what became clear to me, as I watched this scene, was that the real gift was to Face himself. This treat was his, not theirs. He lusted for this contact, this proximity to those who exalted him. Like any charmer, he was the literal meaning of *philanthropist*: a lover of human beings. And when those lovable human beings returned his love with worship, well, that must give a guy a jounce of bliss. It must get hard to do without, even though he had told me the night before that he wished he could do without it.

Hopping like rabbits onto the hood of the Vette notwithstanding, this was a relatively calm coagulation, as coagulations go: no shouting overmuch, no shoving underway. Which made the single, elongated shriek, when it came, all the more horribly audible. Yes, there came a single, elongated shriek from the rear of the crowd. I don't know the physics of this, but there's something about twenty degrees with zero humidity that makes such a shriek sound lots more shriekful.

In its ungodly pitch, this shriek hit us as if an unlucky coyote was getting its comeuppance from some avenging prey it had harassed, a pair of house cats, say, who'd got together and belted it to a rack. But no, the shriek was not from a coyote being brutalized by avenging house cats. In the few seconds it took for the glut of fans to part—the shriek was such that it had the power to part gluts—I believed I knew the source of this shriek before I saw it. My only question in these few seconds, insofar as I was conscious of having a question, was whether or not, when we saw him, Bill More would be holding a handgun. Or, worse, one of those machine guns you can pick up, along with your milk, at the corner store in any American town.

There he was, the shrieker: Bill. The fans had parted in such a symmetrical way as to put Bill in full view of Face. And what a sight he was, fresh from weeping, his blankdom slightly altered by the large look of anguish on him. He was, thank the gods, not holding a gun.

But Jacki, Mario, and both of his goons were. All four of them stepped in front of Face and pointed their pistols at Bill, which caused the fans to yelp and move, yelp and disperse, as pistols tend to do. Bill shrieked again, this time a name: *Face*. It was appalling to hear, an animal noise born of spiritual devastation, of the kind of despair known to thirteenth-century suicides. At this point both Jacki and Mario were hollering at Bill to get on the ground, gesturing with their weapons. But Bill, who quivered there about twelve feet from us, seemed to be in a state past the grasp of sentences or the persuasive properties of pistols. I won't soon forget his writhing expression, the awful gnarl of it. It was the least blank he'd ever look.

Both Face and I now stood behind Jacki and Mario. I'd moved there, certain that the best place to be was opposite of where the guns were pointed. And since the glut of fans was no longer on the sidewalk, we had an unobstructed view of what Bill pulled from the pocket of his cargo pants. It was a bottle of spring water, the taller kind, one that held not water but, I saw, urine. I was sure it was urine because you see this more often than you'd like to, bottles of spring water that have doubled as toilets, usually dropped on roadsides by male midnight strollers-home, inebriated pissers with no regard for litter laws.

What I didn't get was why Bill was now pouring this urine over his own head and down the front of his unremarkable garb. And then the scent hit us. Not urine. Gasoline. I hadn't seen the lighter in his right hand but I certainly saw it when he flicked the thing to life in order to end his own. It's hard to know what to do when you're holding a bag of meatballs and macaroni and standing behind four people pointing handguns at someone who has just set himself ablaze with gasoline. It's hard to know what to think about this. Wailing, of course, was about what you'd expect from someone on fire, but Bill didn't wail at all. He stood intently silent and still, almost monkish, as if he'd been practicing.

What I didn't expect was what Jacki, Mario, his goons, and all the bystanders did, which was nothing much. I don't mean literally nothing, since most of the bystanders were either filming or screeching or running, but nothing in terms of helping to put out the fire Bill had just put on. I sympathize with not wanting to get too close to a human torch, but still. And, true, it wasn't as if *I* were rushing in there to snuff the flames, but as I've said, I'm no John Rambo. And snuff with what? When you consider our city's lavish history with fires, once taught to every Bostonian schoolchild—from the Great Fire of 1760 to the Greater One of 1872, from the Chelsea disaster of 1908 to the Cocoanut Grove nightclub conflagration of 1942—we really should have been semiprepared for this. Any second, I was sure, someone would show up with a fire extinguisher, before things got too terrible.

Problem was, things were getting too terrible pretty fast. Fire doesn't wait around. Bill had dropped to his knees by this time, his arms out in a pose of why-hast-thou-forsaken-me, his whole front in flames, the blaze lapping up to his neck as he fell frontward onto the concrete. Those someones with a fire extinguisher were taking their time, I couldn't help but notice.

Behold Bill More: from smitten to smote.

And then, dashing into the frame from the right of us, from

the street just behind the Vette, was—cue the music—was Val Face. Val Face with the blanket of Val Face's face, his mother's present to him. Fire tends to transfix you, as long as the thing burning is not your own torso. So while I, Jacki, Mario, and the two goons were understandably distracted, agape at the bonfire Bill had made of himself, Face had dashed into the Vette to get the blanket. Then he tackled Bill with it, as if the blanket were a net, in a move that suggested knowledge of how linebackers go through life. He was now on top of Bill with this blanket, covering him, embracing him, rolling over him.

"Sir, your *face*!" Mario screamed, meaning, I thought, *For God's sake, don't burn your face!* Then Jacki and Mario rushed in to help— to help Face.

It didn't last long. Face succeeded in ending the fire in just seconds—Mrs. Detti knits a mean blanket—and Jacki succeeded in detaching Face from Bill. Face was face down, and Bill, face up, was a sight and scent hideous to behold, facts from slasher flicks you hope never come between you and your afternoon. He was unconscious and, I thought, mostly dead. In my guts was the dread of the damned.

By this time we could hear the sirens from somewhere up on Boylston Street or Commonwealth Avenue: police, fire, ambulance all—each has its own specific rotating whine. (Trivia: Boston had the first fire department in the nation.) There were so many cellphones filming Face face down next to burnt Bill face up that it would have taken one of the decenter citizens half an hour to persuade them all to stop, and still they wouldn't have seen the vileness of their filming.

And then this citizen materialized, a robust fellow, and it didn't take him half an hour. "How dare you," he yelled. "Have you no respect? The gall of you," he said, swatting at their cellphones, attempting to snatch them, then chasing away their holders. He caught one reprobate and shook him silly—for a big guy he had impressive pluck—and then he yanked the reprobate's phone from him and chucked it over the fence into the Public Garden. Boston could use more of such citizens.

How familiar he looked. And then I knew. I was positively stunned to see that it was Frank from the show at the Boston Opera House a few nights earlier, the one who was called Fatty Frankie by online hellhounds. He was the one invited backstage after the show, the one who touched Face's face as if it were the Wailing Wall. I couldn't help but see that Frank, in just a few days, had shucked some pounds. His posture had changed about an inch in the right direction. Even his duds, faded jeans and suede boots and a leather biker's jacket: if they weren't entirely stylish, they definitely weren't the tent he'd been wearing at the performance. With surprising will and resolve did Frank dash in and upbraid the numerous cellphones on the street that were filming Face and Bill. I wanted to cheer "You go, Frank!" but my throat was so arid with fright I couldn't get the cheer out.

Jacki and Mario were kneeling by Face now, attempting to roll him over, and I rushed there to help, thinking that the flames and smoke had smacked him unconscious. But when Mario succeeded in getting him to his back, we saw it. I saw it, Jacki saw it, Mario saw it, his goons saw it, the doorman saw it, and everyone nearby saw it too. Face's face was no longer Face's face. Face's face sported second-

and third-degree burns from his chin to his hairline. The flames had scorched and partly melted, partly charred his skin some hue you'd find in a mine shaft, near the dirtiest, rustiest rock. The front swath of his great hair had been singed to the scalp, with pieces curling off like huge russet flakes of dandruff.

The dread in me that had been for Bill was now a dread in me for Face, because I knew what this meant. Jacki and Mario knew it too. The only one who couldn't be sure what this meant was Face, since Face couldn't see the damage, though he must have felt how dire this new datum was. In Mario's arms Face was trembling slightly from the singe and shock of it.

Mario then screamed over to me and his goons. "Cover him. Come round. Those phones!" He meant the filming ones on Arlington Street and up the sidewalk. We crouched round Face and Bill, a protective semicircle.

"Hold on," Mario said. "Hold tight now, sir. Help's coming," and he looked frantically about to see where said help might be. "You're gonna be okay, sir," but his voice wasn't at all convinced by this.

Jacki could triple-task: she had one hand on Bill, one on Face, and her cellphone was clamped between her ear and shoulder, into which she barked professional sounds.

The smell of Face and Bill was one you do not want to smell on men. I'd put down my meatballs and macaroni and had one hand on Face's quivering thigh and another hand clasping a hand of his. In my handholding I heard that the sounds coming from him were not gurgling or gagging sounds, but delicate *hmm*ing sounds, almost the cooing sounds of a newborn floored to find himself alive and cooing to shield himself from the stun of such a place as this.

As I looked from Bill to Face, I saw that Bill was breathing, if you could call it that. And as I saw the magnitude of worry in Jacki's and Mario's expressions, I tried to stay my own quivering limbs. But Face's burnt lips were moving now; his Chiclets teeth, perfect behind great lips, were equally perfect behind burnt ones. And Face's burnt lips were moving, it seemed, for *me*. His now eyebrowless eyes too, those once-in-a-millennium eyes, were aimed at me, and something was clear: he wanted me to bend closer because he had something to say.

Between Jacki and Mario I bent, put my ear to Face's mouth, my hand still in his, the backyard-summer-grilling smell not at all appetizing. "Face," I said, "can you hear me?"

"Seger," he said—weakly. How *else* could he say it?

"Yes, *paisan*. It's me. I'm here."

"Ever wanna vanish?"

I'm not sure for how long I looked at him before I said, "Face, hold on. Look, help's here."

But then I thought I knew what he meant by *vanish*. He was referencing our heart-to-heart from the night before, on the deck of his parents' house.

I said, "I won't vanish on you, Face. I'm not leaving you. Help is here."

Though I knew that no help in Boston or anywhere else in America would be capable of wholly undoing what had just been done to his face. What Face himself had done to his face. And on the sidewalk beside us? The blanket of Face's face, right side up and half flat, so that you could see the blackened embroidery, the charred artwork that now grievously matched its inspiration.

■ ■ ■

A SCENE ENSUED: cops, firefighters, EMTs, news crews, the whole of Arlington Street barricaded, plus whole blocks of Commonwealth and a block of Newbury, crowds wadding wherever they could wad, stretching, straining round all the barricading cops and lit-up crimson trucks so that they might glimpse the celebrity and his calamity. One gal scaled a maple to ogle over an ambulance.

By this time all of Face's team had descended from the upper floors to see and assist, to see and sob. Nimble, whom I'd expected to take top prize for fright and maybe frenzy, was the one attempting to soothe all the sobbing others. Her assistant, Boris, that *my-my*er of me, was an animated mess of fret. Shitsy, in one arm, wasn't doing much better: it yipped and snipped at first responders. Jacki Jaworski, supremely cool and in control, was filling in her fellow cops.

As the EMTs loaded Bill into one truck—they'd wrapped him in a clear jellied cocoon of some kind—and then began loading Face into another—Face's face and throat immured in the same jellied wrap—Nimble was right there beside the gurney, clutching Face's hand, getting loaded in along with him. Mario was there too, and he had a look that was half-horror, half-I-told-you-so. When an EMT tried to tell him that only the spouse could come, Mario said, "Step back, fucko. I'm the bodyguard," and in he went.

I looked over at Face's handlers on the sidewalk to see if I could get some signal as to what we were supposed to do now, but all had a phone in one hand and a tissue in the other, and no one was looking at me. When I turned I saw beside me a thirteen-year-old boy who'd granted himself the day off from school. Skateboarded and cell-phoned, epidermally challenged, he'd somehow breached the barriers and was right there beside me filming Face getting loaded into the ambulance, sporting a grin that said: *My friends won't believe this shit!* Inspired by Frank, I snatched that phone from him and flung it over the fence into the Garden. "Scram, you little Beelzebub," and I chased him off.

Jacki, the cops, and firefighters remained there in front of the hotel doing what they do after an occurrence such as this. They yapped to one another; lots of pointing and nodding took place. Someone clicked photos of the burn scene on the sidewalk while someone else with a notebook and pen checked with bystanders. Face's brigade of minders and assistants, interns and bodyguards and techies, assembled first in the hotel lobby—lots of hugging— and then before long up we elevatored to the largest suite to engage in soft, tear-filled jabbering. These handlers then commenced their calling and clicking, their typing and swiping. In my rattled state I'd forgotten about my bounty: I was still holding the meatballs and macaroni.

And then a new crisis whammed us, an outrage even the techies were outraged by. It had been less than an hour and already videos of Bill and Face on fire were everywhere on the web, from one end of social media to the other. Headlines were popping up at news venues and gossip sites. Some of them erroneously and probably intentionally declared that Face was dead. The accumulating comments expressed about an equal amount of grief and glee. The posts kept coming; they seemed to double every minute. And every manic handler in that room was utterly helpless to do anything about this. Some attempted to counter-post; some attempted communication with the sites, ordering them to nix the videos and posts. Some clutched their hair in desperation. But nothing worked.

How do you fight cyberspace? How do you slow it, stop it? You don't.

Another minute of this awfulness was about all I could take. Fifteen wigged-out workers, in an atmosphere only slightly less pressurized than an operating room, is a lot of wigged-out workers. So I found another available suite to wait in until news arrived. But reliable news of Face's face was slow in coming. My appetite had been sacked by the drama and I couldn't rouse the will to feast on Mrs. Detti's macaroni and meatballs. Had anyone contacted Face's parents? Should *I*? By noon, after a text fest with Estelle, and after typing into my phone all the details I needed to remember, I was dampened by an inexplicable sweat and began hunting for water and a bucket of aspirin.

Rather suddenly I got to feeling all-out frayed; my excursions with Val Face were starting to strafe my immune system. All my antibodies seemed displeased; some were clearly on hiatus and hated me. Flu season hadn't officially begun but that didn't mean that the virus wouldn't try to warm up on the vulnerable, get an early workout in. I'd got my flu shot, of course—the Walgreens in Central Square speared you free of charge—but the thing about flu shots is that sometimes they make up their minds not to help you out.

The assistant or intern who dealt me the aspirin was a leaky picture of what happens when makeup meets weeping. I asked her if any news had arrived from Mario or Nimble at Mass General and she said "surgery" before she buckled into a corner to cry some more. So Face's face was now in the handsome hands of surgeons. But from what I had seen of Face's face on the sidewalk, it needed to be in the handsomer hands of God if there was to be any hope of repairing what had been done to it. Or, as I had to keep reminding myself, what Face himself had done to it. That was the most difficult part to digest. Bill hadn't done that to Face and Bill hadn't intended to do that to Face. Face had intended to do that to Face, and he had succeeded.

I believe I zonked out on a couch for a few minutes because when I woke Jacki Jaworski was there in the room with me.

"Any news, detective?"

"He's in surgery."

"And Bill?"

"Same. Worse."

"What happened out there, Jacki?"

"You saw. Maybe you can tell *me* what happened. Why'd he do that?"

"Crazy people do crazy things."

"Not Bill. Face. Why'd he do that?"

"I guess he tried to help him. I don't know, detective. No one was helping."

"I've never seen anything like that. And I've seen things."

"No one was helping."

"Tell me why Face did that."

"To help. I don't know, detective. Plus running into flames runs in his family. His dad was a fireman."

"Something else was going on there. I don't know what."

"We should have got him yesterday in the woods, Jacki."

"We tried." She cracked open a Diet Coke and downed it whole. "I'm meeting Bunny at Mass General. You coming?"

"No. I don't feel so great. Please text me if you find out anything."

When I passed Vip in the hallway en route to the elevator, I asked him too to text me if he had any news, and he nodded his tearful nod, his hand giving my shoulder a goodbye pat. Then I trained back to Central Square, dozing off again as the car did its soothesome rock. I almost missed my stop. My houseless chums were where they always were, clotted beside the Quik Mart.

I said hello to everyone and Felix said, "Why you *look* that way, man?"

"What way?"

"All *sick* like, man. *Green*ish like."

Mrs. Detti's macaroni and meatballs? Felix feasted.

■ ■ ■

FOR TWO AND A HALF DAYS I lay fevered and writhing when I wasn't fevered and sleeping, so doped on generic cold syrup my dreams were sickly, episodic reinventions of what the Mayans used to do in appeasement of their gory gods. On and on unfolded these full-color epics. Freud liked to contemplate the sex/dream connection but he didn't at all seem interested in the flu/dream connection, which I thought too bad. Robust dissertation to be had there.

Estelle had swaddled me in our bed, smashed shut the curtains, cooled my egg with a damp rag, confiscated my phone and laptop, and, with the aid of a funnel, dumped Campbell's and tea into me. For nearly seventy hours, *seventy*, I did not move except to urinate or moan or let Estelle water me. When she left for work or walks in the mornings it was as if I'd been stranded in Nod. The numbers 911 appeared to me frequently.

I could feel all the pathogens having a party in my softer parts, a bacchanal that left them with malignant hangovers, which made them even meaner in me. The muscle aches were more like bone aches across my legs and back, without mercy in their flattened throbbing. I could not chew (my tongue was some prehistoric slug lying there in my mouth), could not swallow (my throat was all lava), could not read (my irises were injured and wet from fever), could hardly sit up, such was the body-wide throe indifferent to ibuprofen or whatever Tylenol/aspirin cocktail I threw at it.

Polluted through the tissues, I was, at one point, positively sobbing with the hurt of it all. The congestion in my head was Mesozoic—Sudafed couldn't touch an ache that cold-blooded. The paradox of high body temperature and chilled shivering presented a problem Confucius himself could not help. Sneezes would soon burst my appendix and, I was sure, my spleen.

Influenza elongates the hours, or else amputates and cauterizes them, leaving you estranged from the reliable workings of time. Einstein defined the relationship between time and motion, sure, but did he consider the relationship between time and influenza? Was there a Nobel Prize for me too if I could puzzle through it? One would need math, I presumed, so others would have to take up the task, though they could certainly consult me if they wanted to know how a clock behaves when your temperature is kissing 104. It's what you might call *twitchy*, doesn't seem to want to be bothered by sequence or chronology, nor does it see any reason to adhere to the number 60. Some minutes had twice that number; some hours had half. That's part of why I was sobbing: sheer confusion. An hour ago kept colliding with an hour from now, deleting the middle part I normally know as the present.

During one particularly hellish spell toward twilight, Estelle floated blurrily in and I mistook her for my mother, which probably irritated her. Some of us get the flu and function; Estelle, for instance. In such a state Einstein still works for her. But others of us? We get the flu and all the laws of physics get the flu too.

Two things I could be thankful for though, as I lay curled in death's domain. One: I was in the process of sweating out five to eight pounds. And two: for those seventy pound-losing hours, I did not have too many waking thoughts of Val Face. He did, however, make a few cameos in my febrile dreams, the ones with all the Mayans. When you emerge from such an infirm, phoneless two-point-five days, you really begin to develop your empathy for Rip Van Winkle. It's a tenuous reentry into the world. For example, I didn't know for certain if Bill had actually made a bonfire of himself, if Face's face was really ruined, or if those had been plot points in one of my Mayan dreams.

But when I was once again properly plugged in, and I saw all the voicemails and text messages from Jasmine, my editor, from Jacki Jaworksi, and from Face's functionaries, and when I saw all the new news about Face and his face, I knew that Bill hadn't been burned by Mayans in my dreams but very much for real. And I knew too that Face's face was irrevocably ruined.

My phone call with Jasmine went like this:

"Do we still have a piece? Will we still have a piece?"

"I just emerged from the dead, boss, I'll have to—"

"You were *there*, right? You were with him when it happened. Can we get this into our piece? What do you think?"

"I have to see how—"

"Because, think about it, it's gold. You were *there*. You can write it as no one else can. You had the ultimate access. Seger, you are right now the envy of every cultural journalist in the land."

"Jasmine, I don't want to be—"

"*You were there.* This is gold."

"Well, he's hurt. It really isn't gold."

"For us, it's gold. Think about *us* for a second here."

"Look, boss, let me see what I can—"

"*It's gold.*"

My hardihood was maybe 50 percent after such a fluing crucible, but I footed it to Central Square to get the Red Line to Face's hotel, where I found a brood of paparazzi camped out on the sidewalk next to a tumult of newspeople and a cavalcade of Face fans. A cop was there to keep company with the put-upon doorman, and once they let me inside I was confronted by bouncer-type heavies and then had to withstand a windstorm of queries about who I was, what I wanted, and why it mattered. Then came fifteen minutes of phone calling and standing there and more phone calling and standing there before these heavies would let me elevator up to Face's suites.

A goon guarding the main suite, who I thought was pretending not to recognize me, didn't recognize me. I forgot to mention that I'd shaved a pound of hair from my face that morning, robbing it of its Tom Selleckian shrubbery. After nearly three days of plague, my natural rosiness not completely restored, cheeks dented, this award-worthy mustachio, I thought, two years in the making, had me looking more Canaanite than I cared to look. Plus Estelle had been grumbling about the tickle. So I razed it. And when my bare face had hit the twenty degrees outside, it felt newly blossomed.

At desks and tables and on sofas, a clutch of Face's melancholy minders blinked at their screens, speaking in whispers, wading through online flotsam. Everyone looked unshowered; no one, I was sure, had flossed. The upturned food cartons, dropped candy wrappers, and wrung water bottles were too many for the cleaning staff to keep up with.

A word about celebrity melodrama, which Face's facial calamity had surely become. We love it—the melodrama. It makes us feel good in two ways: first, the spoiled fuckers surely deserve whatever canker is upon them; and second, it's the old Aristotelian formula at work: the witnessing of tragedy, in its stirring of pity and fear, endorses the catharsis of those emotions. Except that celebrity melodrama isn't tragedy. Not even a little. But in our vulgar, degraded age, it'll have to do. And it does. It does do. For many inept millions, it does just fine. But here's the thing: what was celebrity melodrama to the internet was a calamitous injury to the human being it happened to.

Remembering names and faces now, I whispered to Valerie, "How bad is it?"

She whispered back, "Who are you?"

"Seger? The chosen writer?"

"You don't look like you."

"Oh, the, uhh, the facial fungus. Gone. Plus I was flued."

"You were food?"

"Flued."

She seemed to consider this a beat longer than was good for my self-esteem.

I said it again: "So how bad is it?"

"Pretty bad."

"How is he?"

"Hard to say."

"How is *she*?"

But she couldn't answer. She only shook her head.

I now whispered to Violet, donned in pajamas, staring into a steaming mug of something. I beseeched her in whispers for an update.

"Who are you?"

"Seger. The royal scribe?"

"Oh. You look different."

"Yeah, the facial fungus. It's gone. Plus I was flued."

"Food?"

"No, *flued*. I had the flu."

Dead expression. Meant to convey extreme annoyance. This exchange might sound familiar:

"So how bad is it?"

"Pretty bad."

"How is he?"

"Hard to say."

"How is *she*?"

But she couldn't answer either. She, too, could only shake her head.

When I found Vip at a desk by the windows, this paragon of manly fashion was in the same duds he'd been wearing when I'd last seen him three days ago—a bad sign. After wondering about where my mustachio had fled, and commenting on my pallor, he told me that the surgeries had gone well but that no one was certain how Face's face would look after the healing was done or even how much healing was possible.

"But definitely not the same," I said.

"Definitely not the same."

"You've seen him?"

"Saw him yesterday, yeah."

"It's bad?"

"He's bandaged so you can see only his eyes and mouth."

"What now?"

"Back to L.A. I'm leaving tonight."

"And for Face? What now for him?"

"I can't answer that," but the moistening eyes were answer enough.

■   ■   ■

I trekked through the Garden and cut one corner of the Common and wasn't at all confounded to see that I'd walked the length of Charles Street and was now standing near the T stop, just around the bend from Mass General. It was as if there were a street festival underway, musters of Face fans everywhere, in clumps of three, five, ten. Many I recognized from the performance at the Boston Opera House and from their invigilations outside the hotel. Some wore Face T-shirts beneath padded jackets; some were armed with flowers, teddy bears, boxed chocolate. One warp wielded a large driftwood cross on which he'd scrawled *Christ for Face*. Prayer circles over here, singing circles over there, sobbing circles to the right, humming circles to the left, and the closer I hoofed to Mass General, the denser these clumps became. Silent, handholding vigils were being kept. Reporters gave reports into cameras; some were interviewing fans who had wet mascara paths forming from the eyes. One middle-ager in a Karl Marx beard blasted Elton John's masterwork of bathos, "Candle in the Wind," and when it was finished, the self-appointed DJ had more bathos on deck, this time Bette Midler's "Wind Beneath My Wings." He had a fondness for wind, this guy. I got out of there.

Not being a regular at Mass General and not wanting to be, I didn't know which building I needed, which entrance. It's a splaying complex, Mass General, spread over several blocks. I hung a left, edged sideways between a crowd reciting passages from Face's memoir, and saw chalk artists pasteling Face's face onto a sidewalk. I hung a right and saw monkishly dressed tenors crooning Italian up at windows they thought were Face's. Their aria? I had to ask an older listener who, all smiles, looked as if she knew. Puccini's "Nessun dorma."

I hung a left again and saw paparazzi camped out in clots, long-lensed vulturine yellows angling for that first and pricey pic of the bandaged Face. Later I'd learn that one ambitious dolt got gussied up in scrubs, stethoscope, and false ID to imposter himself past security. And he'd almost succeeded, made it all the way to the burn unit, until Mario detected and damn near concussed him.

On the sidewalk I asked a lunch-carrying seraph in scrubs where I'd find the burn unit and she dished me the route, adding: "But there's no way they'll let you up there." I knew she was right, but I went anyway. Turned out that all I'd needed to do was locate the entrance with the densest, weepiest crowd. They sat, they stood, they hugged, they hummed. Some lookalike picketers toted tall placards with Face mantras. Other placards bobbed with Face's face. At the glass doors, on either side of the two security dudes barring entry, were an Andes of floral arrangements and nonplussed teddy bears bearing get-well notes. It would have taken a tandem dump trunk to cart away all these offerings.

I stood as far apart from the crowd as was possible while still being able to see the doors, although if someone had asked me what I was doing there, I'm not sure I could have provided an answer adequate enough. I knew my time with Face was finished, and I knew there was no hope of being admitted into this building, and yet I couldn't leave.

Then a finger poked me in the middle of the back. I turned, expecting someone in official garb who'd tell me to beat it. But it was Talia. I'd never before been more elated to see a human being.

"Hey, precious," she said.

She carried a cardboard container of lunch and wore a lanyard round her neck. One of Mario's men, escorting her, wore one too. The lanyards were how they got in and out of the building.

"Talia! You recognized me!"

"Of course I did. That mustache was doing nothing for you, bucko. I'm not a fan of facial moss. Good call."

"How is he, Tal? How's your brother?"

"He's burned. But you know that. You saw it. He said you tried to help him."

"He said that? He noticed?"

"Yup. He's the great noticer, my brother. On fire or not. Come in. It's cold."

"I can go with you?"

"With me, people go places, sweetie. Come," she said, and we went, around the quivering crowd, past the scowling security dudes, and into the building. Then up to the burn unit, but I stopped there in the hallway, at the doors. My stomach told me that I didn't want to see him, that I might never be ready to behold what he was now. Talia seemed to understand and told the bodyguard to go.

"But will he be okay, Tal?"

"He'll live."

"Your parents . . ."

"Yeah. They're in with him now. Nimble and Mario too. He's been asleep all day."

"Did the surgeries work?"

"Yeah, I think so. We don't know for sure. He'll need another one, they said. I don't know when."

"How are *you*, Tal?"

"You know what he said to me? He said: *I've missed you, sis.* How about that, buster?"

"I don't doubt it. You're eminently missable, Tal."

"Oh, you angler you. Say *more*."

And I said that I really was sorry about all this, that I should have persuaded Face to use the back entrance at the hotel that day, that Mario had told me to do that, but I didn't.

"Oh stop. No self-pity in my presence, bucko. This is on my brother. Him alone. Didn't you see the videos? Val did this, not you. He's a moth."

"He wanted to help."

"Maybe. And maybe he wanted something else."

"What?"

"*This*," she said, and indicated the hospital, the burn unit—this new reality with a new identity. A new face.

"Will you tell him I stopped by? That I'm thinking about him?"

She took my hand and told me to come with her, but I assured her again that I couldn't.

"It's a family's time," I said. "I just wanted to come pay my respects. How long will he be here?"

"Not sure. A week maybe? Nimble's already arranged rehab in L.A. How do you think I'll do in L.A.?"

"In L.A.?"

"Yup. I'm going to L.A., precious. Who do you think is taking the lead with the rehab? There's nothing I don't know about skin," and she hit a pose, did her best Madonna, framed her poreless face with fingers.

"Tal, that's terrific. You'll be with your brother. And L.A. will never be the same after you. Will you have to sign that contract?"

"No no. No more contracts for my brother. His contract days are done."

"How do you mean?"

"Oh, silly, surely you know. You saw that fire on him. You saw what he did. Val Face died there on that sidewalk, and Valentino Detti came back. My brother came back."

We both stood tearlessly firm. No way Talia was going to let us get maudlin now, though the wet temptation was there.

"He's gonna make a good dad," I said.

"He will after I teach him how. I've got to get in practice for being an aunt. I'm gonna pamper the shit out of that little witch. Make her a real spell-caster," and she squinted to show me that although she was kidding, she was only half kidding. I'd noticed this at the Dettis' home three days earlier: her mischievous squints could unman you in exactly the way you needed unmanning.

"Well. You take care, Tal. I'll be thinking of you."

"Don't worry: I'll tell my brother to get in touch with you as soon as he can."

The embrace she draped me in just then, her pale scent of shampoo and face cream, her white ribbed sweater, her arms on me . . . In a different life, with different DNA, I could have loved her and her alone.

Behind us now, into the empty hallway, appeared a girl. Tall, teenaged, thin and trembling, Irishly complected. She had a faded pink band dyed into yellow hair so long it brushed her belt. Her eyes were worn with crying, and I suspected that I'd seen her before but could not guess where. In her hand not an obnoxious bouquet but a single rose.

She looked lost, and that's what Talia asked her: "Honey, are you lost?"

Looking at us through tears, she said in a voice only slightly more than a whisper, "Do you . . . do you know Val Face?"

"Know him?" Talia said. "When he was nine years old, I punched the jerk in the mouth. How did you get past security, sugar?"

"I'm . . . I'm not sure," she said.

Talia asked if the rose in her hand was for her brother, and the girl said, "Will you give it to him?"

"No," Talia said, "but *you* will. Come, dear," and she held out her arms as if to embrace her.

The girl went to her then, a once lost child now found, dashing to her mother. Talia held her, stayed her tears, then buzzed the buzzer to be let into the unit. I watched them go until the doors shut again and they were gone. And on my way down, in the quiet caul of the elevator, swiping at a lone tear on my chin, I remembered who that teenager was: Ruth, from the night of the Boston performance, the girl who was doing her senior research project on Val Face. She was, just then, thanks to Talia, the luckiest Face fan in the nation.

■   ■   ■

WHEN I HAVE TO THINK, I walk, no matter the clime. I hear Nat Hawthorne did the same.

When I left Mass General that day, I went into Copley Square and, just as Face had done during his vision at eighteen years old, I stopped there midway on Dartmouth between St. James and Boylston. I peered across the squared expanse of wintered grass, between pedestrians and photo takers, and took in the Trinity Church and those still searching for a fortune of soul. Then I looked right at that still mighty mirrored slab, our scraper aimed at the Boston skyline: the Hancock Tower. And if I could float on air outside those windows on this day, I knew I'd see strivers still hived in cubicles, that seemingly endless tableaux of aisles, those clickers and scrollers with a very different idea of fortune.

At my back, across Dartmouth, hulked the Boston Public Library, with its own clickers and scrollers, its readers hunting yet another kind of fortune. And across Boylston, at the corner of Dartmouth, hulked the Old South Church, all 350 years of it, still silently reminding us that wealth of mind and wallet counts for zilch without that goodly wealth of soul Val Face preached of. Then I turned again toward the Trinity to study, there on the sidewalk, that rectangular plaque of bronze on the slanted sarcophagus of stone. Val Face's first inspiration, guru and mystagogue Kahlil Gibran. He died of alcoholism at age forty-eight, after he wrote the epitaph that appears on his tomb: "I am alive, like you. And I now stand beside you. Close your eyes and look around, you will see me in front of you."

And the epitaph for Val Face? Valentino Detti wrote it in flame.

■   ■   ■

IN THE YEAR SINCE ALL THIS HAPPENED, I have not seen or heard from Val Face, and I don't expect to. I never wrote my piece for *Beantown*, despite Jasmine's promises of gold. Estelle and I wed two months ago and we've already eased into the calm passion of a working marriage.

Jacki Jaworski and I are now pals and co-authors. She actually cared about and followed the edits I suggested she make on her novel, *The Falcon*, which, thanks to my interference, sold for more than we could have hoped. Jasmine, who was a pretty big deal after her book on the Boston desegregation busing crisis of 1974–1976 became a bestseller, connected Jacki to her agent in New York. It was Jacki's eureka that she and I collaborate on her follow-up, a spy novel starring her heroine Jacki Falcon. It's my job to concoct the villains. One of them lisps. Another wears an eye patch and, worse, a ponytail.

About Bill More: he lived, if you could call it that. With those injuries, what could living now mean for him? But what did living mean for him before his fire? The internet tried to find out who he is, or was, and couldn't do it. Cyber sleuths camped at a Dorchester address said to be his, where, rumor told, he was bed-bound and tended to by an Episcopalian aunt. But no one could get a handle on the facts of him. He'd disappeared—*poof.* It seemed Bill More wasn't anybody at all. Bill More wasn't even there. His self-fire was the most present, the most *person*, he'd ever been.

About a month after the fire, Boston's December freeze now a mostly forgotten fling for the diary of a meteorologist, the weather had taken another surprising swerve, this time into balminess. T-shirt temps, socklessness, shorts, SPF, sunglasses. Few things are sadder than Christmas decorations in late January, especially in such weather, those forgotten Santas and faded Rudolphs looking forlorn and unneeded on front lawns, the rainbow lights around doors no longer even pretending to be festive, several bulbs gone dark like missing teeth in an unhappy smile.

Bostonians strolled around looking at the weather, then at their phones, and then back at the weather, wondering if it could really be January, their faces giving speeches about the greenhousing of our planet. (When Bostonians have something to say, they make speeches about it.) As I passed through the Common on my way to the office, I saw people lounging on swards of yellowed earth, and pushcart hawkers roasting their wares.

And then, I was sure, I saw Bill More. He was standing there ghoulishly beside an oak, and he was looking at me from behind burn scars the color of rosewater—directly, intently at me. I halted there to look back hard, to be sure my vision wasn't fibbing, but I had to wait for bikers and skateboarders to zip by. And when they did, Bill wasn't there any longer. I went to the oak to see if he was standing on the other side of it, but he wasn't. No one was.

Ghosts: they're everywhere in this city.

I've passed the year penning this tale, trying to make sense of what I saw and what it means, and turning over Talia's words to me, *My brother did this*, and Face's own words to me about the chances of vanishing. I've tried to tease out a parable from Face's fall: *Our neediness will cut us down*. Maybe that's it. Maybe Bill's fire was precisely the opportunity Face had been looking for in order to extinguish his fame, a fame that had switched into a force he did not want and could not sustain. In a way, things got much too easy for him after such fame. His authenticity became compromised when the untainted connections he wanted were no longer possible, when people began responding to the celebrity and not to the charisma, to his intimate skills of knowing. Maybe he'd dried up inside without the mojo he began with, his original talents of communion that so much fame interfered with. He couldn't have had much longer at the top anyway: history says that all charismatics are comets.

For over a decade he had been charmingly adept at maneuvering through the crassness of celebrity, but in the end, the crassness was almighty—the crassness was all. The bacillus of American super-celebrity is such that when it gets you, it really gets you, and when it leaves you, it really does that too. By the zeitgeist is the celebrity made; by the zeitgeist does the celebrity die. And most celebrities are fated to die not once but twice. Their second death is the one we will all undergo, but their first death is the death of their renown. They

must return to the mortals they once were. Val Face, like Sister Fal-
coner before him, was consumed by the flames of his own making.
Which, quite possibly, with a new daughter on the way, was precisely
what he had wanted.

But he wasn't so different from the lot of us, after all. He sired
his own destruction. If he had listened to Mario that morning and
used the hotel's rear entrance, Bill wouldn't have had the opportunity to char himself in Face's presence, which was the whole point
of the charring: Face had to see it in order for it to mean anything.
The famous make most of us into Bills, I'm afraid, though our fires
are figurative.

For many, the truest life is the life they did not choose. But some
of us luck into choosing well. We've got a great past ahead of us all
right, if only we can stay normal.

ACKNOWLEDGMENTS

Heartfelt thanks to:

Bob Weil, editor par excellence and last of a breed, without whom this book would not exist.

Haley Bracken, wise compatriot without whom nothing happens.

David Patterson, steadfast 007.

Steve Attardo, artist without equal.

Steve Almond, who gave this more than I had the right to ask for.

The devoted staff of W. W. Norton/Liveright, the very best in the business.

ABOUT THE AUTHOR

William Giraldi is author of the novels *Busy Monsters* and *Hold the Dark* (now a Netflix film), the memoir *The Hero's Body*, and a collection of literary criticism, *American Audacity* (all published by W. W. Norton/Liveright). He is the recipient of a Guggenheim Fellowship, an Artist Fellowship from the Massachusetts Cultural Council, and is Master Lecturer in the Writing Program at Boston University.